PRAISE

"An ambitious novel students of nineteenth century baseball will love..."

-Leverett T. Smith, Society for American Baseball Research

"One of the most thoroughly researched baseball novels ever!"

-Andy McCue, baseball bibliographer

"Historical fiction, with the emphasis on history."

-Larry Gerlach, author of *Men in Blue*

DEDICATION

To John Ake, Chief Zimmer and every man in between on the alphabetical list of players who appeared in a major league box score in 1884, the most wonderful and exciting season ever.

ACKNOWLEDGMENTS

I owe my deepest gratitude to J. Thomas Hetrick, Carlos Bauer and Bob Hoie for their abiding belief in *Early Dreams* and for providing me with the kind of painstaking editorial assistance that every writer dreams of but precious few find.

I also would especially like to thank Ray Nemec for running to earth the complete professional career data for two of Earl Draves's personae— Elmer Cleveland and Tom Forster—and the late Larry Zuckerman for sharing his vast knowledge of nineteenth century major league parks and their immediate environs.

In addition, I would like to thank the many other baseball historians and friends who were kind enough to help me find the best way to tell Earl Draves's story.

And a special tip of the Outlaw Reds cap to the Yaddo Corporation for awarding me the time, workspace and inspiration at Yaddo to craft an embryonic draft of *Early Dreams*.

AUTHOR'S NOTE

I've tried to remain faithful to the vernacular and the idiosyncratic usage of capital letters in vogue at the time of this tale. Spelling and punctuation have been modernized for the most part, however, to ease the reader's task. As for the visual inserts—the box scores and newspaper items—they are meant to add flavor and dimension to the tale. Special note: In the Cincinnati-Wilmington box score Draves is substituted for his real persona that day, Elmer Cleveland.

The more things change, the more they
remain the same.
> —Anonymous

Hope springs eternal in the human breast;
Man never is, but always to be blest.
> —Pope

Next to "crooked" play was the evil of drunkenness in
the ranks, and this, we regret to state is still in existence,
it being the most conspicuous evil that was connected
with professional ball playing during 1884...It is useless
to point out to players of drinking habits the folly of the
evil course they are pursuing. Treat them with all the
kindly consideration possible by condoning their faults,
they will only return it with more indulgence.
> —*Spalding's Official Base Ball Guide*, 1885

Early Dreams

David Nemec

Pocol Press
Clifton, VA

POCOL PRESS

**Published in the United States of America
by Pocol Press.**

6023 Pocol Drive
Clifton, VA 20124
http://www.pocolpress.com

Publisher's Cataloguing-in-Publication

Nemec, David.

Early dreams / David Nemec. -- Clifton, VA :
Pocol Press, 2004.

p. ; cm.

Reprint. Originally published: San Diego :
Baseball Press Books, 1998.
ISBN 13: 978-1-929763-04-7
ISBN 10: 1-929763-04-2

1. Baseball players--United States--Fiction.
2. Cincinnati (Ohio)--Fiction. 3. Historical
fiction. 4. Baseball stories. I. Title.

PS3564.E4797 E27 2004
813.54--dc22   0404

Cover art © 2004 by Todd Mueller.

"I believe I do remember him," the club secretary said. "Suffered an injury, didn't he, that made him quit the game?"

Young Draves lowered his eyes. "Actually, he lost a leg in a railway mishap."

"Ah...too bad. Given the chance he might've made a name for himself."

While Draves continued to stare at his boots, the secretary, who also worked as a newspaperman, made a note on a pad of yellow paper. He wrote a column called *Diamond Dust* and was always collecting odd bits of information.

"And your father, is he too a former ballist?"

"No, sir. He was a tailor."

"Was? Does that suggest he's no longer with us?"

Draves's eyes dropped again. "Both my parents died in a typhoid outbreak back about twelve years ago."

"Brothers and sisters?" asked the secretary, who liked to know a man thoroughly before committing the club to him.

"I had a sister, but she perished in a fire."

Tragedy everywhere you turned here. "Then how were you raised, Draves?"

"By my uncle, sir, on his farm out near Blue Creek. Leastwise until I completed my schooling. Since then I've been on my own here in Portsmouth."

The secretary paused to make it seem he was thinking. Actually, his mind had been all but decided when Draves had entered his rooms at the hotel smelling of a fresh haircut. Learning that his father had been a tailor clinched it. All else being equal, it behooved the club to take on men who knew how to care for themselves.

"How old are you, my boy?"

"I'll be twenty-two come November, sir."

Ripe enough. And it was a safe bet that a ball player was being truthful about his age when he tried to make himself sound older.

"Excellent. You can act as your own agent then if you're made an offer. How would you like to join the Red Stockings this coming season?"

"There is nothing in this world I desire more, Mr. Caylor."

Nodding and smiling, Caylor took two identical documents out of the hotel desk. Along with his secretarial duties, he had been performing this task for two years now and become masterful at it. Of course it helped that he had legal training and many of the men up against him had never even finished grade school.

"I have here a club contract," he opened, "for the sum of $1000. Please look it over carefully before you sign both copies. Yours to keep will be posted to you after I return to Cincinnati and obtain Mr. Stern's signature of agreement."

Draves sat with the papers in silence for some while, his lips moving. Not a good sign. It meant that he could read.

"Question?" Caylor preempted when he saw Draves frown.

"Yes. It says here I'm only to be paid $700 this season."

"That's in there just in the event you serve on our reserve team. Read on and you'll see you'll get $1000 if you make the regulars. As you surely will if you show the same stuff Charley Jones says he saw you show with the Riversides."

"Thank you, sir."

"It's no more than the truth. You're cast from the same mold as your uncle," said Caylor, glad for the point of comparison with which he had been presented.

He watched Draves start to reach for the carefully inked steel pen he proffered and then hesitate. "Before I sign...I'm obliged to ask what position you're hiring me to play."

"What else but the one Jones says you play so brilliantly? You're a born short stop, and we're stuck for one. Just prove you can do the job and it's yours."

It was a small exaggeration, but Draves could not know that the club was only protecting itself in the event Chick Fulmer made good on his threat to retire and his understudy continued to falter down in New Orleans.

"Fair enough," said Draves. "All I ask for is a chance to make my mark."

Caylor mentally rolled his eyes. It was incredible that men, even out in the hinterlands, still talked such blather. In the hollow of his mind flickered an umbra of guilt. Draves seemed almost painfully earnest, yet he was of age, no babe in the woods, so Caylor strove to feel only his due sense of triumph.

Ever since leaving the railway depot in Portsmouth he'd been trying to write in his diary. But again and again, as he touched pen to paper, the little girl asleep beside him rolled her head against his arm, rocking his hand. He would have changed his seat, but there were no others vacant in the car. Finally he began jabbing the girl with his elbow, hoping to waken her. He quit that, though, when he felt her mother's eyes on him. He'd never seen a woman like her. She had dark, almost dusty-olive skin and jet-black eyes. Her hair was oily and black as her eyes, and her clothes were strange; her dress appeared to be made of buffalo hide, and so did the girl's. He supposed they were Indians, full-blooded Indians—they frightened him, especially the woman. Her eyes made him feel he was staring into two bullet holes whenever he chanced to meet them.

The pair of them had boarded the train at the Sugar Grove junction. For some while now the woman had been looking at him as if she meant to scalp him if he didn't quit trying to waken the girl. Her head felt heavy as a boulder. He wanted to trade seats with the woman, giving her his beside the girl in exchange for hers beside a bearded man who was barricaded behind a newspaper, but he could not make her understand him. Maybe she didn't speak English.

He made one last attempt. "Ho there," he said to the man, intending to ask him to swap seats with the girl. He was even willing to surrender his coveted spot by the window if it brought him peace to write. But the man refused to come out from behind his newspaper.

With a sigh Draves gazed out the window, watching mile upon mile of snow-laden fields roll past and feeling the girl's head grinding like a watermelon against his arm. He had wanted to write so his mind would be occupied, but now he could not escape his thoughts. Good Lord, Cincinnati was a long way. They had already been traveling for over two hours, and they were still barely halfway there. He ought to get up and move to another car, but probably there were no seats there either.

And besides, it was ridiculous to be cowed by a woman, even an Indian.

No, the sensible thing was to wait. Maybe they'd get off soon. They couldn't be going all the way to Cincinnati. What would Indians do there? It was hard enough to imagine himself in Cincinnati and he had a goal awaiting him. He was about to fulfill his lifelong dream— quickly he tore his eyes away from the window, but it was already too late. He had begun thinking, and there would be no stopping his mind now unless he found some way to distract it.

Draves tried shifting in his seat and using his left hand to write. This worked somewhat since he did most other things left-handed, but the girl's head continued to plague him. It bore deeper and deeper into his side, and he was about to waken her regardless of her mother. Somewhere he'd heard that Indians all carried knives. Wouldn't that be hot if he were scalped now? Thirteen years ago Fate had sandbagged his uncle when he was on the verge of launching his base ball career. Wouldn't that be some luck if a similar catastrophe befell him? It could not really be that he was about to embark on his life's mission to become the greatest base ball player in the land. He, Earl Draves...*think*...the new King of Short Stops!

Charley Jones stood in darkness behind the drawn window-blind in his laundry shop. Half of a dozen times that day, for the benefit of his customers, he had changed clothes to live up to his nickname of "The Knight of the Limitless Linen." Now that the shop was closed, however, Jones no longer cared about his appearance. He was brooding again about his swiftly approaching 34th birthday.

He had made an irrevocable mistake. He had lied about his name but revealed his true age. Now everyone knew he had but a few more years to play base ball. Already he felt himself starting to miss it. Frequently this past winter he'd had nightmares. He dreamed he was trying to play again after being told he was too old, and he couldn't hit the ball. Pitchers fed him tosses right over the heart of the plate and he could hardly get his bat off his shoulder. There was another even worse nightmare. He was outside the park (it seemed like South End Grounds) and he couldn't get in. He heard the crowd inside shouting his name, for him to pole a long one, and he couldn't get past the gatekeeper. He heard Soden say, "Where's that Jones, out mashing again?" It was infuriating. He was not drunk. He was cold stone sober, but he couldn't get in.

Born Benjamin Rippay in rural North Carolina, he had gone from there at an early age after his parents died, north, to the great cities, calling himself Jones after the uncle in Indiana who became his guardian. He'd done nothing to learn a trade, caring only about base ball. Every clement day he squandered on the diamond field. Then at night he went to this or that saloon and celebrated the day. Base ball came easy to him. He was that rare slugger who could more than hold his own in the field. Then with all his drinking and rich living he began to put on weight.

In July 1880, Jones ran afoul of Arthur Soden, principal owner of the Boston Red Caps. Although he had led the National League in home runs the previous year and was again carrying the team, Soden claimed his play had been "unsatisfactory to the management and his conduct in Boston aggravating beyond the patience of most people" and refused to pay him his month's wages. When Jones protested he was suspended and fined for insubordination and then expelled from the National League.

Jones would never again play base ball in the city of Boston. He made several appeals to National League officials, but they refused to give him an audience. Although the courts upheld his grievances, he remained blacklisted. He bided himself by operating his laundry shop in Cincinnati and playing semi-pro ball with the Riverside club in Portsmouth. In 1882 he persuaded the Riversides to take on a talented young local named Earl Draves. The following spring Jones joined the

Cincinnati Red Stockings after Cincinnati voted with the rest of
American Association teams not to honor the National League's blacklist
any longer.

In a few days Jones would begin training for his second season
with Cincinnati. The previous year he had clouted 10 home runs, second
in the American Association only to the great Harry Stovey, but during
his salary negotiations for the upcoming season, the first topic was his
batting average. "You hit only .294," said Caylor, "and we expected
something in the neighborhood of .350."

"Where's the credit for my fielding?" Jones said. "I had the most
catches of all our outfielders."

"I doubt that. Sommer I'm sure made more."

"I beat him by one. It says so right in the final season report."

"And we know how unreliable those can be. But in any case,
you were in centre field where you were bound to get more balls than
Sommer or Corkhill."

"I was stationed there for good reason, you know."

"Yes, well, this year we're putting you in left field. At your age
it'll be easier on you."

"Don't let my age—"

"All right, all right," Caylor broke in as if surrendering. "I
appreciate you have to do right by your wife and kiddies, so we'll give
you a $200 raise provided you pledge to keep yourself in A-one
condition next season."

Pledge? He'd had enough of them in Boston. "In writing?" he
asked warily.

"Not when we both know it wouldn't be worth the paper it was
scribbled on."

Caylor said the oral promise was only so he could put in his
newspaper column that Jones was vowing to turn over a new leaf. He
was sure the public also would take it with a grain of salt. Still, it would
create an impression that the club was taking steps to curb Jones's
notorious profligacy.

Jones lifted the window-blind and gazed at the row of saloons
across the road from his shop. He underwent the usual argument with
himself, an argument he knew he was destined to lose. Since his
meeting with Caylor, he had already lost more arguments with himself
than were healthy to count. Nevertheless, Jones would have a banner
year in 1884, leading all Association outfielders in putouts and finishing
second in runs scored. Again given a modest raise, he would have
another strong season in 1885 and then begin to slip. By 1889 he was
out of base ball altogether and living in New York City. For some years
he served there as an inspector of elections, his faultless appearance

continuing to induce his superiors to overlook his indulgences. As Jones aged, his popularity within the base ball world seemed only to grow. He was often recognized and begged for his autograph when he attended local games. Then his star began to wane. He was seen less and less by his friends and finally not at all. There were rumors that he was gravely ill, and they became rampant when reports circulated that a benefit dinner was being planned for him. After that, though, nothing was ever again heard of Charley Jones. It was as if he had fallen off the face of the earth. There is a thread of evidence that he was living in New York as late as 1909, which was no longer a time when death records were kept haphazardly, but to date all efforts to learn Jones's final disposition have been in vain. To some historians his disappearance is base ball's greatest mystery. How could the game's first great slugger drop so completely from view by the end of his life that his final resting place is unknown?

Cincinnati, O., March 20

Dear Sam:

Finally, life begins again! Last night White invited all the recruits to his drug store where he fed us his rules for getting into condition. Then today he assembled the whole squad in the gymnasium to start working off the suet. Being already in top fettle, I scarcely broke a sweat and hence was raring to go along when a bunch of the boys hied down to a hall on Sycamore Street afterward to play hand ball. But Jones cautioned me their game was restricted to regulars and I must become one before I could join it. That will occur any day now, Sam. Peoples is still the only other short stop in camp, and even though he has the edge on me as yet in White's eyes, it's solely because he played with the regular nine this winter down in New Orleans. If I may say so, I should soon prove I'm his master in every department save perhaps throwing.

Yes, unhappily I still have a smidge of my schoolboy wildness. Today in the gymnasium I threw two balls clear over Reilly's head, which takes some doing. Reilly is well above six feet tall, about as big as any first baseman in balldom. He is justly called Long John, and when I overflung him the second time it provoked Caylor to remark: "Well, they must play on stilts out in Portsmouth."

Caylor, I'm learning, has a snake for a tongue. Ever since he inked me to a contract last month his fondest words to me have been if only my play smelled as good as my hair oil, and he is no kinder to the men who have stood the test of time. This afternoon he stared at Jones's alderman and asked if he was looking at the first man in history to be

with child. Knowing Jones from when we were cronies on the
Riversides, I expected him to sass right back at Caylor, who is about one
tenth his size. But instead he kept his trap shut until Caylor went on his
way to flame somebody else. Then he muttered to Snyder: "I swear I'll
brain that cockroach with my bat one of these days."

By the bye, most of the boys still make Snyder their sounding
board even though he's no longer captain. For my jugful, Pop wasn't
stripped of his title because the Red Stockings fell short of the pennant
last year but because he's too much his own man. White, in contrast, is
already being called "Telephone" because every complaint that's aired in
his hearing is guaranteed to find its way into the auditory canals of
Caylor or one of the owners.

Still, Will White isn't a bad fellow, Sam, and Caylor has also
been square with me thus far. Their ways take some getting used to,
that's all. The same applies to a few of the other boys, namely this Phil
Powers and Tom Mansell. Being Easterners, those two are of the
opinion that any man who was born and bred in Ohio can't play base ball
worth a wuss. That will change, wager your bottom dollar, once the
river goes down and we forsake the gymnasium and start training on a
real diamond field where I can show my wares with a bat. From what
I've heard, Peoples didn't hit a lick down in the Crescent City this winter
and toward the end of last season Fulmer presented a sorry sight up at
the dish too. His lame batting most of the boys think is the real reason
Chick hasn't reported this spring. He knows he is near the end of the
trail and it's time for a younger man to take his place.

Sam, I swear to you I will be that man or die in the effort. Base
ball is my life's blood now, and when I step up to the marble on Opening
Day in American Park, it will be the moment to demonstrate my
gratitude to you for setting me on my way. Modesty dictates that I leave
it to your imagination what I mean to do to that pill on my first swing of
the bat.

But I do have to tell you the true story of our new park, which is
contrary to everything the *Enquirer* has reported. Sam, please don't read
that rag anymore. The lies they print in it are near criminal. McLean is
behind them, he and Thorner and the other Union team crooks who
pirated our old park right out from under us. They somehow duped the
Consolidated Street Railway Co. into leasing it to them for less money
than we paid last year. The dirty politics beneath it I and the other boys
aren't privy to, but we all had a rich laugh when Thorner tried to begin
improvements on the park the other day only to be informed he couldn't
bring his workmen onto the grounds until April 1 when our lease
expires. Then to his chagrin Thorner also discovered that we have a site
now for our new park.

It'll be on the corner of Findley and Western Avenues, Sam, and how we acquired the property there will tell you that clever as the Unioneers might think they are, the Red Stockings will always be a step ahead of them.

Thorner and McLean not only rented our old park but snatched up all the other prime locations for a ball ground on the sly. They claimed in the *Enquirer* it was because they planned to put a local team in the Union Association this year, but the real truth is they thought they could browbeat the Red Stockings' directors into surrendering control of the American team to them. Lacking a worthy site for a new park, they figured Caylor and Stern would be forced to give up the ghost. Well, were they ever shocked when we rented the old Hulbert property! Because it had cottages on it with immigrants living in them, Thorner never imagined it could be converted into a ball ground. Only we got Hulbert's lawyers to tear down the cottages and eject the immigrants as part of the bargain. That stuck Thorner with the rent on our old park and obliged him to make good on his threat to bring a Union team to Cincinnati or else lose what little face he has left here in town.

The Union men, Sam, are all curs like Thorner. This millionaire Lucas who is behind the whole plot is especially low. He has some of his St. Louis gang in town right now trying to lure McPhee and Corkhill into breaking their contracts and jumping to teams in his circuit. What teams you might wonder? Lucas avers he has clubs all set to go in St. Louis, Chicago, Philadelphia, Baltimore and here in Cincinnati. But that's still only five teams and a couple of them are known to be just hot air. Who in Philadelphia would be foolish enough to hop aboard Lucas's bandwagon when they already have the champion Athletics there and a League team besides? But to make sure Lucas can't pull off his scheme the Americans are installing clubs in Brooklyn, Toledo, Indianapolis and one other place he might otherwise pilfer. Twelve teams we're going to field this year, Sam, and the League will again have eight to cover the cities on the map that we miss. So the offers Lucas's minions are making to players truly are nothing but empty promises, and the smart ones know they'll be left holding the bag if they enlist with the Union outlaws.

Fat chance Lucas would have with me even if that were not the case. I have waited too long to play for the fabled Red Stockings to throw away my chance because some Mound City pitchman dangles a wad of greenbacks before my eyes. Besides, I've already signed a contract with Cincinnati and my name on the dotted line is my bond.

But the boys who know Fred Dunlap say Lucas really did give him $6,000 to desert the Clevelands and sign with his Maroons. Can you believe it, Sam? A man getting that much money to play base ball!

The new park the Red Stockings are building won't cost a deal more, only about $10,000, and for that sum Cincinnati will have the best ball ground in the land. I've glimpsed the plans, Sam, and yesterday I and two other boys, Reeder and Bowers, took a street car out Western Avenue to see how the builders are faring. If what we saw is any indication, the Queen City will soon be the capital of the base ball world once again. Our park is going to have sliding oak doors between the vestibule and the street, two turnstiles, cushioned seats in the grandstand and a toilet room exclusively for ladies. There will also be a director's room and a special chamber for press members situated under the grandstand behind the backstop.

All told, the park will be large enough to accommodate 6,000 patrons. A far cry, Sam, from Portsmouth where I thought I was the cat's whiskers when I played in front of 200 or 300 people.

Big news, I can't wait till the Championship Season starts. And it's only 42 days away now! I just wish you could be here on Opening Day. The long train trek would be an ordeal for you, I appreciate that, Sam. But if you arrived a day or two in advance you could rest up for the gala occasion. Please give it your utmost consideration. Now I must close in order to get sufficient shuteye to prepare myself for tomorrow's practice.

Your nephew, Earl.

In the lamplight Julie Reeder scraped powder over his teeth with his index finger as he stood before his bedroom mirror in black wool trousers and an overcoat, a pair of rubber galoshes on his feet. Reeder was going hunting that morning with several of his teammates on the Cincinnatis, and he was unaware of the proper attire. He was also unaware of the reason he had been nicknamed "Icicle". It was his belief that his teammates called him that because of his icy demeanor under fire. The truth, though, lay closer to the fact that even though Reeder was around twenty-five years old, no one doubted him when he claimed to be only nineteen. Long John Reilly said, "He acts most of the time like his brain has been frozen solid his whole life."

Except for a spell of wanting to be an outlaw, back when Jesse James was the idol of every midwestern boy, Reeder had never fancied himself as anything but a ball player. It was his ambition to replace Charley Jones someday as the Red Stockings' most feared batsman, and to that end he emulated Jones fanatically. At the plate he used the heaviest bat he could find, and in the field he copied Jones by taking imaginary swipes at the ball while standing idle between pitches. He'd also tried to grow a mustache but with such dreary results that he'd given up trying to look like Jones. When he became a great batsman, that would be time enough to concern himself with how to look and dress the part. In the meantime he could get away with dressing like a "greenie," which was Mansell's word for him as well as for several of the other recruits. He supposed it was just their punishment for being new to the team.

As yet, Reeder had not had any luck in reminding anyone of Jones. That is, no good luck; he'd had considerable bad luck. His drinking, which he'd cultivated only because Jones swore it helped to relax the batting eye, had already drawn Caylor's reproach, and was, furthermore, in danger of becoming an addiction. Reeder couldn't yet actually say he liked the stuff, but he definitely liked the change it wrought in him. Under the influence of spirits, he felt he grew more relaxed and even garrulous. That was another of Mansell's words whose meaning he only dimly grasped. "Icicle, you're becoming downright garrulous," Mansell had said yesterday during the imbibing session that had followed practice. "In fact, you might no longer sedate us with your company if you went hunting with us tomorrow morning." So, while he didn't like the sick headaches with which he awakened now, this newly acquired taste for German tea had its good side. He hoped the invitation to go hunting would lead to other outings with the boys, and in that expectation he had gone to the extreme of buying a rifle yesterday evening. Knowing it would never do for Mansell to discover he didn't know how to operate a gun properly, he had then gone to the house on 6th Street where Draves kept a room and sought instruction. Draves had also been invited on today's hunt, the only other recruit to be so favored by Mansell, after he'd claimed expertise in the sport. "Early Bird, you amaze me with your plethora of talents," Mansell had said. Draves was so called because his first name was Earl and he was always the first to arrive at practice. As he was being shown how to use his rifle, Reeder had heard himself told that Draves would soon have a new nickname. "In Portsmouth I was dubbed Easy Earl because that's how I made playing ball look, and mark my words, it'll happen here too."

On the buggy ride across the Suspension Bridge that linked Cincinnati to Kentucky, Mansell and Powers sang, `I Dream of Jeanie.' Their voices were gruesome, but their Eastern accents made the song sound nonetheless grand to Reeder.

"There's no sleep with them," said Reilly, who was trying to doze in his seat between Reeder and Hick Carpenter. "It's no use. How many you reckon we'll get?"

"How many what?" said Reeder when he realized he was being addressed.

"This morning. How many's your ma expecting you to bring back for her kettle? I'm figuring on at least a dozen myself."

"Well, but a dozen what?"

Reilly turned to Draves and Jamie Woulfe, who were standing behind him. "You boys hear? Icicle doesn't know what we're after. Early Bird, tell your partner."

Partner? Draves whistled in perplexity. "Ducks I gather."

"Ducks? Why would we come all the way down across the river for ducks? Hell, we're after the queen of all birds today."

"Eagles?"

"Jesus, Draves. You ever et an eagle? What's the sense hunting a bird there's no eating? For my taste, give me a couple of sandpackers."

"Sandpackers?" Reeder said. "What're them?"

"Found only in this neck of Kentucky. And rare. So rare, Icicle, that you who've lived in these parts all your life never even heard tell of them, did'ya now?"

They traveled through the town of Covington with only desultory conversation. Then Reilly took charge of directing the driver. "This'll do," he said when they came to a thickly wooded area. Reeder felt himself shiver as he alit from the buggy. Even though dawn had broken, the temperature was still down near freezing.

He watched Reilly, Carpenter and Woulfe walk off into the woods without explanation, saddling him and Draves with Mansell and Powers. Before he could think to protest, Mansell said they were splitting into two groups so as to outsmart their quarry. He and Powers then set off through the woods, leaving the two recruits to follow as best they could. In a while the four arrived at the edge of a dank-smelling marsh. There, Mansell bade Reeder and Draves to give Powers their rifles to hold for safe-keeping. "We don't want to shoot these birds if we can help it," he said, "because they're better eating if they're taken alive." He then produced two burlap sacks from under his coat and gave one to each recruit after saying that he and Powers were off now to hook up with the other boys and start flushing the sandpackers out of their nests in the bushes and running them toward the marsh. When Reeder and Draves saw them coming, all they had to do was open their sacks and snag them just like they would daisy cutters.

"I still wonder how we're supposed to recognize these birds," Draves said.

"You'll know them," Mansell said, "because they always travel in pairs."

"And, boys," Powers cautioned, "whatever you do, don't let one of them trip you or you'll find out right sudden why they're called sandpackers."

To guard against that danger, he told Reeder and Draves to stand back-to-back so nothing could come up behind them and catch them by surprise.

When Powers and Mansell were gone, the two recruits stood there as they'd been instructed to do. They stood and waited for one whole hour by Draves's watch before they figured out that the others meant for them to stand there forever.

"We're a couple of monkeys," Draves said.

"They could just not've remembered where they left us," Reeder said, to save face, he thought.

"You hold that fancy. Me, I know when I've been made a fool of."

"But why'd they do it? Shit, we could catch our death out here of pneumony."

Draves looked at him and sighed. "I should've smelled a rat right away when it was you they abandoned me with."

"Maybe it's mutual." Reeder spat at the ground as he spoke, but he hated himself for spoiling it by blushing.

It took them nearly two hours to find their way back through the woods and hail a buggy to haul them to Covington. By then it was past noon and they still had to cross the bridge and return to their homes for their base ball gear.

They didn't reach the practice field till three o'clock, and the humiliation was not done. White told them they were both fined $5 for being so late. He feigned fury at first as they began telling him their excuse for their tardiness, and then he could no longer contain himself. He burst out laughing and said it served them right for not looking at the calendar when they got up that morning.

Draves's diary entry for that date ended with this:

Since today, being April 1, was All Fool's Day, I ought to have been more wary of treachery. Reeder's a dunce, so he has an excuse, but sandpackers—where could my brain have been to believe there was a bird in these parts I'd never heard of? The punch line to the joke, when the boys finally told it to me, is they travel in pairs so that one of them can trip you while his partner packs sand up your behind.

Now I'll allow today could have been amusing if I didn't forever have to think of myself standing in that marsh with my back to Reeder's. The thing is I ought to have known the boys were up to no good, and maybe I did. Maybe I thought if I went along with them it would somehow benefit me. Maybe then the boys would look upon me as one of them and stop calling me Early Bird. Instead, after today's humiliation, they've begun calling me other things too that I'll spare your pages, dear Diary—and I haven't recorded the worst news yet. Along with being a fool, now I'm not only playing second fiddle here to Peoples. I'm playing third fiddle. Fulmer reported today, and they gave him his old job back without his having to do any more than say, "Well, look who's here again to separate the men from the boys."

Columbus, O., April 5
Dear Sam:

Right you are to advise me to tell myself: "I have just begun to fight." Sure as sugar, this grand country wasn't built by men who took down their sails at the first ill wind. Only the fight here is ended for the moment. Fulmer has the short stop post sewn up tighter than a Shylock's purse, and Peoples has also bested me in White's estimation because he can play behind the bat too in a pinch.

So goes our dream of my becoming the new King of Short Stops. Now it looks as though I won't even be on the Red Stockings this year. I'll be on their reserve team.

We played our first game this afternoon here in the Capital City against the Columbus regulars. When I say "we" now, Sam, I mean the colts, and believe me, it is sour medicine to swallow that I'm one of them. Here was our batting order today so you can gauge for yourself why I feel so disheartened:

> Podgie Weihe, LF
> Icicle Reeder, CF
> George Winkelman, RF
> Earl Draves, SS
> Cooney Bowers, 1B
> George Miller, C
> Ed Pendleton, 3B
> Gus Shallix, P
> Horace McPhee, 2B

Miller is the only veteran of major league play although Winkelman was with the Louisvilles briefly last season. Miller and Bobby Mitchell formed the "Pony Battery" for the Red Stockings back in `77. They were so called because neither of them is much taller than a pony, and if you listen to Miller, they won the pennant for Cincinnati. The truth, Sam, according to Jones, who was also on the team that year, is that Miller was only the change catcher and the Red Stockings finished dead last.

Now Miller is about 30, a deal older than most of the rest of the colts. Because of his age he's been appointed captain, but not even his best friends would say he leads us by example. Miller is helpless with a bat in his hands and too small to take the punishment that catchers must nowadays. Most of them are still playing right up behind the bat with runners on base, Sam, even in the League where pitchers now are allowed to throw overhand! It's a brutal job, catcher, and I must admit Miller has plenty of sand if nothing else. His hands, toughened as they are, looked like raw meat after today's game, and you ought to see Pop Snyder's hands sometime. Snyder does not have one normal-shaped finger left.

McPhee's hands are almost as gnarled, from refusing to play with a glove. It's his brother who's at second base with the colts, and all that makes them brothers is they have the same surname. Horace is a weaker batsman even than Miller, hence his being put last in the order, and he's no great shakes either in the field.

Bid is the total opposite. When you see us play, Sam, (once I rejoin the regulars) you will witness the most phenomenal second baseman in the land. Bid McPhee can catch and throw with either hand, which is the benefit of not being encumbered by a glove. But even gloveless he almost never misses a ball. Some claim Dunlap is the top second baseman today, but that's the League men talking. All the sharps who've seen both of them play agree McPhee is superior.

The Buckeyes beat us only 4-3 this afternoon, but that was because they aren't much of a team and weren't half trying. Schmelz alternated Morris and Dundon, their deaf and dumb wonder, in the box, saving Frank Mountain for when they play against some decent competition. The Dummy gave me no grief. I could see he likes to keep his pitches low, so I called for high ones and whanged the second toss he threw me for a clean single to right field. But Morris is a lot swifter than you'd guess from his size. The first time I faced him he whistled three in a row right by me, Sam, quicker than you can say Rutherford B. Hayes!

Before the game some of the boys who played last year in the Inter-State Association with Morris warned that he was known as "Cannonball" there, so I shouldn't be deceived by his delicate visage. Being left-handed helps him too since many of the good hitsmiths, like me, are also lefty, and his outshoot therefore curves away from us. Still, he can't last. It's already been amply proven, Sam, that no man who throws with his left arm can ever succeed as a pitcher. Lee Richmond, the boys say, was the only southpaw to get away with it for a while, and even he had the sense to quit last year when everybody started getting the hanker of his slants.

But speaking of oddballs, Sam, Dundon and Morris aren't all the Buckeyes own. Schmelz, their manager, sports a beard—bright red, no less! Seeing him strolling about the diamond got me to thinking what it must have been like to play this game in your day. Harry Wright I know you've told me was bewhiskered, and in the picture of the immortal `69 team on Stern's office wall several of the other boys also wore Burnsides. Times definitely have changed but maybe not here in Columbus. I guess when you're a punk team you'll try anything to shift your luck. Schmelz's beard and Dundon's dumbness won't win any games for the Buckeyes this season, but Morris's left arm might. It already helped win one today, if you count beating a colts team. Here they do. In Columbus they'll take every crumb they can get.

The Red Stockings slaughtered this team last year, Sam, and we'll do so again this season. We murdered every club but the New York Metropolitans. All the sharps think we will win the pennant this year hands down if we can fill our one weak spot, and see if you can guess what that is.

Right you are again, Sam. Fulmer is still so atrociously out of shape that it's a pathetic sight to behold. This past winter he was a constable in Philadelphia and meant to quit base ball. But his wife begged him to give up his new profession after he was beaten nearly to death by tenants he tried to serve with writs of ejectment. She must never have seen him play short stop or she'd worry he runs a worse risk of being slain by a ground ball.

Your nephew, Earl.

April 9

Well, dear Diary, the Louisvilles ruined us today. It was bitter cold, but that's no excuse for our contemptible showing as the weather was the same for both teams.

Again I say *our*, although I myself have scant reason to feel abashed. One errant throw that gave them a run, but in my four turns at bat against Hecker I smote three hits. Three safe strokes against the Louisvilles ace! After the last one, a triple, even Browning complimented me while I was waiting in vain on third base to be driven home. For a short stop, he muttered, I wielded a wicked willow.

Coming from Pete Browning, that is precious praise. He is all they say: a daisy at the dish, nigh impossible to retire, and he seems a regular fellow to boot.

But, alas, all the reports maligning his fielding also appear true. He plays third base as if afraid a street car might run him down. Whenever a runner is on second base, he stands at the hot corner like a stork on one leg with the other pointed warily toward the runner. And no matter the situation, he shies away from air balls, letting his teammates call for all but those that would skull him if he didn't throw up his hands to protect himself.

Browning was born and raised in Louisville, and all the cranks here love him. Jimmy Wolf, also a Falls City native, is only slightly less adored; and little Monk Cline and the short stop McLaughlin, two other local products who have naught else to recommend them, likewise have the cranks here blowing them kisses.

Our boys in contrast took the vilest abuse I have ever heard from the mouths of allegedly civilized people. The crowd called us names, dear Diary, that would make your pages catch fire if I wrote them down. Plainly, they loathe us here as much as we loathe them up in the Queen City. Before we boarded the train this morning, Caylor said: "Boys, prepare to journey from the river's navel down into its a—hole." Then he said if we didn't win at least one game against these Rebs, he personally would make us feel like something that emanates from that low orifice.

Well, tomorrow is our last chance to avoid Caylor's wrath although, as I've said, I could feel pretty good now. But Shallix, who pitched for us today, is so deep in the dumps that some of the boys are going to drag him out of his hotel room in a while to wash away his sorrows with a cup or two of "German tea."

I have a hunch, dear Diary, that even my beloved uncle would counsel me to join the boys in this instance and show them I can be one of the gang when the occasion warrants it. Hence I shall, but with my usual moderation, have no worry.

April 11

The Grand Rapids nine came down today to play our regulars, dear Diary, and they must have brought their Michigan clime with them. It was even colder than the weather we endured the previous two days in Louisville. The Cincinnati Unions are slated to begin their championship season next Friday. They're hoping to get the jump on us and the League by starting so early, but with the weather having been so wretched this spring I hear the entire outfield in their park is still under water. More rain to wreck their efforts to ready the field in time for their opening game would be wished on them if it would not likewise hinder our own progress.

As it stands now, tomorrow and Saturday, Mother Nature permitting, we will play the regulars and I'll finally be able to show Caylor and White their mistake in putting me on the colts. I offer that proviso about Mother Nature because I can already see out the window here in my room that it's starting to drizzle.

I'd say a prayer for the sky to clear overnight, but I have to confess that life in this city has begun to infest me with skepticism about there being a Divine Influence. How can there be when the world is laden with so much misery and suffering? Every day at my street-car stop, for one, I have to see the same little red-haired newsboy whose whole face has been eaten away by sores the size of walnuts.

But then there are times when I'm a true believer again. Strange times, like the night before last, when it does seem as if there is Someone watching over me.

Dear Diary, the other night is of course the reason I haven't taken pen to you for two days now. But before I put you in the know about it I first must record the startling effect it had, not only on me, but on all the boys with the colts.

To everyone's amazement, we nearly beat the Louisvilles yesterday. They threw one of their change pitchers, Heinzman, against us, certain we'd be pudding again, but I led off the second inning with a three-bagger and scored on a hit by Shallix. That one tally held till the seventh inning. Then they wore down Ren Deagle for two runs, but prior to that their cranks had little to do but sit in wonder that this could be the Cincinnati same bunch who had looked so ghastly only the day before.

The thing I'm trying to explain is that somehow we were not the same outfit.

Dear Diary, there is no denying that even though a number of the boys got corned the night before our second game with the Louisvilles and I myself got practically no sleep, we all played better for it. Now I know one day isn't forever, but you still have to wonder if Jones doesn't have the right approach. Our Charley argues that base ball is meant to be fun and to assure it will be a man must come to the park every day in the proper spirit. Caylor says he has no quarrel with that, only with the *spirits* Jones employs to elevate his spirit.

What I fear anyone reading this might think is that I went out on the town the other night and am now on the road to becoming a lusher. But such is not at all the case. I'm merely taking a roundabout route to put on record something that is even more inconceivable than the possibility that I could fall prey to Demon Rum.

In plain English, I have met a girl.

Now that in itself is nothing that should chip anyone's paint. But prepare yourself, dear Diary, for the shock that the girl of my new acquaintanceship is engaged in an occupation that would make my poor mother roll over in her grave were she ever to find out.

It's not as if I went looking for her or even any girl that night. I chronicled that I and the boys meant to try and cheer up Shallix, and that was truly all we set out to do. But Winkelman, who played for the Eclipse last year, insisted that we see a little of the Falls City as long as we were out and about anyway.

It isn't much of a town, one-horse compared to Cincinnati, and Winkelman was hard put to find any high spots to show us. We went hither and thither without staying anywhere hardly long enough to draw a breath until we got to a place on Market Street where a group called the Alice Oates Ideal Comic Opera Co. was performing. The comedians were rank and the music was pretty frightful too. We would have left at the intermission if Winkelman had not thought he recognized one of the girls in the chorus and begged to stay until he could ascertain if she really was the beauty he knew back in Philadelphia. It turned out she wasn't, but while guying with her Winkelman got us all roped into buying drinks for some of the other girls.

It was around then that the night turned almighty strange. Everyone knows how little regard I would ordinarily have for a chorus girl. With their flounced skirts they're fine to watch when they kick to display their legs. But never under normal circumstances would I have stooped to talk to one. They're only interested in the contents of your purse, as every man knows, and they seem young and fresh-faced only until you see them up close where all the paint they wear on their lips and around their eyes makes them look like dragons.

But the girl who was seated beside me was not at all like that. Firstly, she wouldn't let me treat her to anything but sarsaparilla. Then she looked at me like I was the one who'd crawled out of the gutter when she learned we were all base ball players.

"And here I thought you were a preacher," she said.

She was only having me off, I reckon, although in my new cassimere suit that I bought with my first pay from the Red Stockings I probably do somewhat resemble a man of the cloth. And it surely strengthened that impression when I addressed her as "ma'am" and otherwise behaved with my customary politeness when I'm in the presence of women, even ones who are not truly ladies.

"What do you have against base ball players?" I inquired after her face had made evident her disapproval.

"They're all so full of puffery," said she. "They think every woman should fall at their feet if they so much as glance at her."

Before I was aware of it, I found myself arguing with her. Only it was not a real dispute which put both parties in a fury. Instead we seemed to have gained a mutual respect for one another after we'd each said our piece.

More than respect, I venture to say we had become comrades. The others at our table were carrying on quite raucously, but we had begun to talk to one another as if they were no longer there. For that to occur with a girl—and a stranger, no less—well, anyone would concede it was extraordinary. But for it also to occur at a place where I was least expecting anything like it, now that truly is the work of a Force I cannot profess to understand.

It was like a stroke of magic, dear Diary, that out of all the colts there at the table she chose to sit beside me.

She told me she is from Hillsboro, Ohio, and left home two years ago to make her way in the music field. She worked in Evansville giving piano lessons until she was discovered by the Alice Oates organization. But her true ambition in life is to sing at Heuck's Opera House here in Cincinnati, and someday she'll achieve it.

She has the sweetest voice a man could ever hope to hear. We sat and talked till eleven o'clock, and then she bade me to walk her to her domicile at the St. Cloud Hotel and on the way she sang a song that would have melted even the heart of Simon Legree. She wrote it herself, the music as well as the lyrics, to demonstrate still more how talented she is. It has no formal name yet, her song, but when I suggested one, she stopped short in the street and said: "Why, that's perfect, Earl. I do believe I will call it `Home in Ohio.'"

I should note here, dear Diary, that we'd been on a first-name basis almost from the outset. It struck me as fast at first, something that must be a custom of stage people, but soon it began to seem perfectly natural.

Her name is Constance—Constance Voss—and she is why I got no sleep that night even though I returned to my hotel at a decent hour. Before midnight, dear Diary, so there's your final proof that I wasn't out lushing till all hours and that relations between Constance and me are wholly honorable. She wouldn't even let me hold her hand during our walk although the boys won't believe that. They're all convinced we left the saloon early to go back to her hotel room and mash.

Their speculations are idle of course, yet I'll admit they are right in believing I left a portion of my heart behind in the Falls City.

The Red Stockings will make two trips to Louisville this season, the first one not till mid-July. That should give me ample time to prove I belong on the regulars so that I'll be invited to accompany the team when it goes on the road.

Well, dear Diary, I'm off now to bed. Tonight, let's pray, to get some sleep so that tomorrow I can set to work afresh on my mission.

Until the beginning of the 1896 season he remained the only one on the diamond field who still eschewed a glove. They remember him for that and for his having played his whole major league career in Cincinnati. They can see he must have been an extraordinary fielder because no one played 18 years, even back then, with a .271 batting average. And it must have been more than stubbornness that made him keep playing barehanded. Something he once said about not wanting to lose the feel of the ball suggests there was an aesthetic consideration. The way he could throw with either arm gave him a practical advantage too. On hot smashes between second and first he had no peer at snagging them with his left hand and flipping the ball to the first baseman in the same motion. He, perhaps more than any other player of his time, made you crave a film clip of the game as it had looked in 1884.

"Sometimes when you're playing," Caylor said, "I see myself out there if I'd been just a little more athletic. Then you'll suddenly do something that I can't believe my eyes saw correctly."

"Maybe you need White to loan you his specs." It was his wont to speak away from the point whenever anyone complimented him.

"Now if you could just learn to hit a trifle better."

"I'm improving."

"Yes, but so is the caliber of the pitching in the Association."

"I reckon I can keep up."

"Enough to ever top the .300 figure?"

He shrugged. It was too hard to keep making claims for himself.

Caylor laughed. "Ah, I'm only egging you on. You're worth your weight in gold even if you can't break .200."

"That isn't what you said two years ago when I nearly didn't."

"Because then you weren't anything spectacular in the field yet. Now you seem to get better every day." He was the lone exception, the only one Caylor would flatter before coming to his subject.

"Thanks," he said to hurry matters along. Even though the game with the Cleveland colts had been over now for twenty minutes, his uniform was still binding him. He could feel his feet—cramped inside the new pair of shoes he was trying to break in during the training season.

"And you'll keep on getting better," Caylor said, but then, "provided you're teamed with a partner at short stop who won't hold you back."

"That would help," he agreed, beginning to unbutton his shoes now that he realized this could take a while.

"Which of our candidates do you favor?" Caylor asked neutrally.

"They each have their good and bad points, I suppose."

"But if you had to choose one?"

At every question from Caylor he felt the ground beneath him less solid.

"Chick is all right, unless we can pick up another hand with experience."

"Neither of the new men strike you as capable?"

"Capable maybe, but not nearly ready."

"So your view is we ought to stick with Chick this season?"

"Yes." He could not be sure now whether he was fencing with Caylor the lawyer or Caylor the newspaperman. "But it was McPhee's idea," he feared they would someday say, yet he overrode the sly wish to add, "Don't quote me, though, on that."

John Alexander McPhee was born in a small town in upper New York near the Canadian border but grew up in Illinois along the Mississippi River. He never played professionally for a team anywhere but in the Midwest. McPhee began with the Iowa Davenports in 1877, dropped out of base ball for a time to work as a commission agent, and then joined the Ohio Akrons in 1880. Two years later he was acquired by the newly reorganized Cincinnati Red Stockings of the American Association and played on his first and only pennant winner in his rookie season. Until 1900 the Queen City club needed no other second basemen. Year after year McPhee stood among the leaders in every important fielding department. Although a relatively small man—his ideal weight was only 152 pounds—he could hit too, though never much for average. Once he led the Association in home runs and on several occasions he ranked high in triples, but not until 1893, when the pitching distance was lengthened by 10 and a half feet, did he crack the .300 barrier for the first time.

A crippled finger convinced McPhee finally to end his disdain for using a glove, and the result was astonishing. His fielding average in 1896 topped the existing record for second basemen by a full ten points and remained the new standard until 1919. By then McPhee had been out of the game for a decade. After scouting for Cincinnati on the West Coast for a number of years, he left base ball completely in 1909 and died in San Diego 34 years later.

Only glimpses of him still linger: photographs in full regalia, his bare hands set to catch a ball. In each he looks dedicated and intent, his mouth a grim line below his flaring mustache. He never had the grace that let Fred Dunlap make playing second base appear so simple. He will be written of long after Dunlap, however, and some distant day he will even have a place in the Hall of Fame despite his one grave failing. McPhee walked away from base ball. He did not utilize the many connections he made in it. He could have remedied that; in his old age there were numerous opportunities for him to return to the fold. But he chose to remain aloof. It was easy for the world to conclude that the game had disappointed him in the end, and that was no doubt the case. A man who turned to a glove only under duress would have found constant reason to be disenchanted as the years wore on.

St. Louis, Mo., April 20

Dear Sam:

So as not to spoil the surprise, I purposely didn't write you that the colts were making this jaunt. The St. Louis trip will be our longest jump this season, and we're slated to come out here again in June. I can't entirely say I'm looking forward to our return visit. If Cincinnati has grown too big for its britches, this burg is in even worse straits. There are simply too many people here for comfort. Still, what they say about it is fact. Because of its mammoth population it must now be considered the true Queen of the West.

Yet it's not altogether without redeeming features. I'll get to them after I've brought you abreast of my progress on the diamond.

On the way out here we stopped off in Indiana to play the Evansvilles twice. Tuesday, in the first contest, we beat Clem, their ace, with Shallix's arm and my bat leading the way. Sam, it would be bragging if I told you the name of the top hitter on the colts, but I can fairly state that the fault for our poor start is hardly mine. To date we've won just one game, that over the Evansvilles who promptly turned the tables on us the next day. Not a championship beginning, is it?

But our record is not quite so bleak as it seems. All but one of our losses have been to regular American nines: Columbus, Louisville and now, today, St. Louis.

We let the Browns know they were in a dogfight today though, before my old nemesis, Jupiter Pluvius, halted proceedings in the seventh inning. The final score was only 3-1, and it would have been tied if I hadn't failed in my last turn at bat to bring home the two men on the bags.

Raw as it rubs me, Sam, I must allow that I met my match today in Jumbo McGinnis. Though only 20 years old, he's already been with the Browns for two seasons and will become their ace now that they've lost Mullane to the Unions. McGinnis's lone weakness is that he's a slipshod fielder and thus can't be stationed at another position on days when his arm needs to recuperate.

Tony Mullane is the exact opposite. His versatility allows him to play anywhere on the diamond, but despite that, the scribes here in St. Louis think the Browns are well rid of him. They claim his braggadocio made him a bad influence on the younger men. For them to single out Mullane for censure he must really flaunt himself something awful. The Browns are rife with players who think they're God's gift to base ball. Charlie Comiskey and Fred Lewis are bad, but the worst is Arlie Latham. He's called Jimmy Fresh, Sam, but I'd call him Johnny Nasty.

In today's game he outright assaulted me. He was on second base, taking his ground, and when I snuck behind him to try to pick him off, instead of sliding back into the hassock when Shallix spun around in the box and threw my way, he leapt on top of me, slicing my blouse sleeve with his spikes and gashing open my arm.

It was uncalled for, as he would have been safe anyway. But that's Latham for you. As we were rising from the ground, he grinned at me in his smirky way and said the lettering on my blouse was red anyway, so a little blood wouldn't show. "Since the lettering on yours is brown," I countered, "I'll knock stuff out of you that won't show either if you ever sic yourself on me again." I was welcome to try right now, he said, and he meant it, Sam. He would have fought me then and there on the diamond field. But when he doubled his fists I let my good sense prevail and walked away to take my post again at short stop.

The boys think that was a mistake, Sam. They say I ought to have challenged him to meet me somewhere after the game, not only for my own satisfaction but for all of Cincinnati's. The Browns, the opinion is, will be our main foe this season. They lost the flag last year by a mere one-game margin and are confident that even without Mullane they're the team to beat in 1884. What better way to rattle their wagon, the boys told me, than for someone to bust Latham in his cocksure mouth.

He and the rest of the Browns need a fat lip, no question of it, Sam. But I truly don't believe a man can prove anything on the diamond with his fists. Base ball is an endeavor demanding skill. You best your adversary with grace and guile, not by knocking him senseless like a hooligan. Aren't I right, Sam?

At any event, the injury is painful and will hamper me some for a while although thankfully it was my right arm Latham butchered so my throwing won't be hindered. Nevertheless, I'll carry a scar now always to remind me of my first visit to the Mound City. Lest you think the trip has left a bitter taste, however, I hasten to record that I'll depart with some flavorsome memories too.

Yesterday was one although it didn't begin so. It rained all morning, canceling what was to have been our first game with the Browns. Still we had to go out to Sportsman's Park in case it miraculously stopped pouring, and while we were huddled for warmth under the grandstand, Von Der Ahe, the Browns owner, happened by. He chatted with us until it grew evident that Mother Nature would triumph once again and then he invited us all to come next door to his Golden Lion Saloon.

Chris Von Der Ahe is the most generous magnate in base ball, Sam, although you'd never guess it to see him. You sure know he is a Kraut. He has a huge red nose the size of a turnip and a tiny clump of whiskers under his lower lip that look like something his razor keeps missing every time he shaves. He's almost as tiny as Nicol, which is probably why he has wee Hugh on his team, so as to seem less of a shrimp himself. He wears loud checkered suits, does Von Der Ahe, and a flattened black derby that he must have sat on since birth to give it its mealy design. And, Sam, if you heard him talk you'd swear he had just got off the boat. With his thick accent, every word Von Der Ahe utters sounds like he has a mouth full of mush.

He had to say it several times before we understood we'd heard him aright when he told us everything we ate and drank at his saloon yesterday was on the house.

There we were, the Red Stockings colts, in our enemy garb— and he was doing everything short of throwing open his cash drawer to us!

Of course, as Winkelman pointed out, it wasn't really a philanthropic gesture. The Golden Lion panders to a sporting crowd, and with us sitting there, eating and drinking and chewing the fat with the patrons at adjoining tables, it was a close second to our entertaining Von Der Ahe's fans in his ballpark.

That's what they call cranks out here—fans. Nobody knows for sure where the word comes from, but some say it was Ted Sullivan, the Browns manager last year, who coined it and it has to do with so many of the team's rooters thinking they know everything there is to know about base ball but really just blowing air every time they open their mouths to talk about the game, much like Von Der Ahe.

Still, Winkelman says that Von Der Ahe is a born showman. Last year when the Browns came to Louisville while Winkelman was there, Von Der Ahe led the team in a parade from the train depot all the way to their hotel as if they were a circus come to town. He also dresses all the waiters in his saloon in Browns caps and blouses, and this year he plans to make every weekday at Sportsman's Park Ladies Day, meaning that all members of the fair sex can attend for free. But there is a small catch to it, Sam, which will tell you this Von Der Ahe is one shrewd operator.

The free seats for women are only in the bleaching boards. Once they've sat out there on hard wood awhile in the roasting sun, Von Der Ahe is banking that most of them will gladly fork over the regular 25¢ admission charge so they can move to a reserved seat in the grandstand.

Von Der Ahe is a regular P.T. Barnum, Sam, along with being likable. Were I not a Red Stocking, I might consider playing for him if it wouldn't mean that I'd have to look upon Latham and the other ruffians they have here as my teammates.

Latham and Comiskey were in the lobby when we got back to our hotel after the game to bathe. They sat innocently reading newspapers, but I now believe Pendleton was right when he whispered that Latham had really come in the hope I'd changed my mind about challenging him to a fight and Comiskey was there as his second.

If so, they were on a futile errand. My bat and my glove will do all my talking for me, right, Sam?

Your nephew, Earl.

Piqua, O.,
April 26

Dear Sam:

Mother Nature has let us be for three days straight now and it appears that she was our real enemy all along. On the trip back to Ohio from St. Louis, rain canceled our scheduled games against the Terre Hautes and the Springfields. But Wednesday when we got to Dayton, Jupiter Pluvius's hex on us was finally broken.

It was sunny, Sam, on both afternoons that we played the Daytons, and the change in climate was just what the doctor ordered. We skunked them twice in a row, 5-0 and 9-0, with yours truly pelting two hits in each game. And then today, here in Piqua, we took the measure of the Border Citys, 14-4.

After the game Miller telephoned Caylor from our hotel to report the result, and it would be a crime if I weren't the main topic of conversation. I collected four hits today, Sam, and if that's still of no moment to Oliver Perry Caylor, it definitely registered on a certain other base ball potentate. All during our game this afternoon a chap sitting near our bench kept eying me up. Then, as I left the field after the last out, he tapped my shoulder and asked if he might speak to me. I would not have consented if I'd known what his game was, but I thought he merely wanted to commend me on my showing against his hometown nine.

Only it soon emerged that he was no local. He was Dan O'Leary, the captain of the Outlaw Reds in the Union Association, up from Cincinnati in search of players. "We're solid everywhere now but at short stop," he said. I pretended not to catch his drift. I said: "Well, I wish you luck in your quest." And O'Leary said: "It may be at an end because, see, you're a man we could fancy."

He then said I was too good to rot away on a colts team and he was set to offer me $850 for the rest of the Union season. When I told him I was committed to Red Stockings, he said: "I hear you, Draves. They have you now for life if they want, but it's a one-way path. With us, no man is our property for longer than this season. Once it's over he's licensed to sell himself for next year wherever he chooses. So, see, by joining a Union club you retain your freedom." That emboldened me to say it sounded as if he called the Americans and the League slave dealers, but he just smiled and said he wasn't there to flame anyone, only to find a short stop who was blue in his present situation.

At that point I informed O'Leary of his misapprehension. No one who wore the uniform of the Cincinnati Red Stockings could ever color himself blue, I said. Playing for them was every man's dream.

He laughed in my face, Sam! And he said: "You mean the old Red Stockings who're only a dim memory now. The game's changed, Draves. Nary a player from that crew could row at the pace needed today." Not so! I challenged. What of George Wright, the greatest short stop ever until his retirement? Wright hadn't retired, O'Leary said. Actually, he'd quit when he faced that the game had passed him by. He then revealed that Wright now owns a piece of the Boston Unions team and had contemplated playing for them until wiser heads had persuaded him not to embarrass himself. "Embarrass himself!" I hooted. "In fact, he would put all the other short stops in your circuit to shame." Years ago maybe, O'Leary said, but no more. If not, I rejoined, it was only because Wright was now nearly 40 years old. No, said O'Leary. It was because Wright could not hit a curve ball. He'd tried to keep the speed for a while after the pitch came into vogue but then had put himself out to pasture.

O'Leary likewise tarred Al Spalding, claiming that Tommy Bond and George Bradley were both superior to Spalding because they had a variety of pitches. Spalding could throw only a straight ball and quit pitching for first base when he could not master a curve, then quit altogether after discovering he couldn't hit one either. Bond and Bradley learned the curveball art, which was why they were still around. In actuality, he said, they were both now with Union Association clubs. If I didn't yet know, the Unions had already corralled many veteran stars and would soon have them all. They would also soon have all the up-and-coming young players who wanted to compete against the best men in their profession. "Players like yourself," he said.

Sam, all O'Leary's flattery got him nowhere. For his every argument I had a counter. Bond and Bradley are has-beens, I said, next to White and Keefe and all the other star pitchers the Americans have. McPhee is a better second baseman than Dunlap, and there are no hitsmiths on any of the Union clubs who would bat within a hundred points of the averages Browning and Jones and Stovey would compile if they were to face the same easy pickings.

I didn't really say all that, Sam. I only thought it. But I did speak my mind when O'Leary finally said: "So, my man, what will your future hold?" I said: "My future is still to bring the Red Stockings the new King of Short Stops."

I expected a hot reply when he saw his pitch had come to naught, but he surprised me. He only said: "Well, you're young yet, Draves, and so is the season."

Sam, he's right on one count only. The season may still be young, but I'm not. Only a newborn baby would fall for O'Leary's game even if he is a man who obviously knows quality when he sees it.

        Your nephew, Earl.

        April 30

It gives me great pleasure, dear Diary, to announce that I'll be a member of the Red Stockings on Opening Day after all!

Just minutes ago Miller received a cable from Caylor ordering him to tell me and Shallix to catch the next train to Cincinnati. It is now clear that Caylor wanted me to stay with the colts for a few weeks just so I'd play every day and gain confidence. When it comes to psychology, the man is a genius. Spurred by Shallix's pitching and my three hits in each game, we slew the Akrons 21-3 yesterday and then 10-2 this afternoon. And when I say *we* now, it's only habit speaking. As of this moment, I'm a colt no longer. I'm a full-fledged Red Stocking!

Tomorrow when we begin our Championship Season against Columbus I'll be on the field for the Opening Day ceremonies alongside Reilly and Carpenter and White and Jones and Snyder and Corkhill and McPhee. In our grand new American Park!

Isn't it the most incredible confluence? One day I'll be able to tell my grandchildren I made my debut with the Red Stockings on the same afternoon the finest park in the land first opened its doors.

Dear Diary, although I can't be absolutely sure I'll be in the starting lineup tomorrow, would Stern, cheapskate that he is, have authorized Caylor to spring for train fare only to have me sit on the bench?

The lone fly in the ointment is I can't get word to my uncle in time for him to attend our opening game. But we play the Buckeyes again Friday and also Saturday. Then on Sunday Indianapolis comes to town for three games. So I'll post Sam a copy of our complete home schedule and let him choose when to make the one trek to Cincinnati that must be his limit this season due to his disability and his fear to spare any more time away from his farm lest the sharecroppers he has working it take advantage while the cat's away. Though I wish him to come as soon as possible, he may rather wait until both the weather and the pennant race are at full heat.

The Browns, he'll note, aren't scheduled to hit town till late July. If he can wait that long to see me in action, he can be sure of seeing me show up "Jimmy Fresh" with my bat and my glove.

I know my beloved uncle's letter affirming they're my proper weapons is awaiting me in Cincinnati, as I know the fulfillment of our mutual dream now also awaits me.

Tomorrow when I go to bat in American Park wearing the colors of the Red Stockings my first swing will bring a base hit. That, dear Diary, is a promise.

The sun was shining and people were everywhere, throngs of people with expectant faces. Never would he tire of the sight. It was like being in a dream, a dream in which something wonderful was about to happen, something inimitably spectacular. Others might say it was just another Opening Day and once you'd seen one you'd seen them all, but for him there would always be a dreamlike quality about it.

He folded his hands at his belt buckle and allowed his eyes to sweep the grandstand, not looking for anyone in particular, looking only to make it seem he had a reason for standing at the center of the pitcher's box and doing nothing more than idly drinking in the crowd. He was about to begin his sixth season in a Cincinnati uniform, his first as captain. He was not yet thirty and had a degree from Brown University. He was married and owned a prosperous drug store in town, and he had already won 176 games in championship play. He had a brother, Jim, seven years older, who was a star third baseman with Buffalo of the National League. All seemed settled and secure. To the crowd he must have looked the epitome of confidence. But Will White was worried. In his dual role as captain and ace pitcher he no longer commanded the same respect from his teammates that he had when he was simply a player. He was aware of that without yet knowing why it had occurred. Moreover, the realization that his underhand style of pitching was now outmoded came sooner to White than he ever indicated. Perhaps the *Enquirer's* comment on his work the other week had already registered on him as true, even considering the source.

"White can give his pitches any fancy new names he likes, but they are still the same old pitches."

In 1884, Will White would still be crafty enough to win 34 games. Age remained on his side and his arm seemed hale. Yet he would lose his stature as the team's number one pitcher the following year and then retire during the 1886 season after appearing in only three games. It was not an easy decision. He still thought he could pitch, but having to endure the additional ribbing about his "old-fashioned" delivery became finally more than he could bear.

They had always been telling stories about him behind his back. He was only five or so years older than most of his teammates, but he seemed like a patriarch. It was not just his hangdog mustache and the wire-rimmed spectacles he wore. Listening to him for the first time, people thought he must be guying them. He was perilously close to sounding like a crackpot. By the mid-1880s no one with his education should still have believed the world was flat. When asked why none ever fell off it if that were true, he would counter: "If the earth is round and constantly spinning, then how does a fly ball perpetually alight where a skilled outfielder predicts and stations himself accordingly?"

After his playing days were over, White studied ophthalmics and then took up residence in Buffalo, where he started the Buffalo Optical Company, still a thriving concern. In his employ for a time as a lens grinder was his brother Jim. The two parted ways in 1910 when Jim moved to Illinois to live with his daughter. Will had meanwhile broadened his horizons, founding the Christ Mission of Buffalo. A year after his brother left for the Midwest, he was teaching two young nieces to swim one August day at his summer home in Port Carling, Ontario. Although unable to swim himself, White tackled the water boldly to set an example for the girls. Suddenly his chest felt like it was about to explode. He recognized the symptoms of a heart attack, but it was too late. Before he could gain the shore, he drowned.

Will White was only 56 when he died. His brother lived to be nearly 92 before expiring of heart failure hastened, according to one obituary, by disappointment at not being among the first group of base ball immortals named to the Hall of Fame in June 1939. As of yet, neither of the White brothers has been granted a plaque in base ball's pantheon at Cooperstown, New York. Yet they are well remembered, Jim as one of the first catchers to use a mask, Will as the first major leaguer to wear glasses, and together as the first brother battery.

Cincinnati, O., May 1
Dear Sam:

Well, it seems I was both right and wrong about Caylor and Stern. Their view of me hasn't changed one whit, but they sure are cheap. They had Shallix and me entrain to Cincinnati last night so we could work at the turnstiles this afternoon and they could thereby avoid hiring extra men to cope with the Opening Day crowd.

Their frugality cost them dearly, however, both on the field and in the cash drawer, as you already know if you read about today's ghastly events prior to receiving this missive.

Sam, in your last letter you again neglected to mention whether you're following my exploits in the newspapers or relying solely on my accounts of them. When you wrote me last month that you'd canceled your subscriptions to the local journals because they were supporting Blaine for the nomination, I reckoned it was only temporary. Now methinks your protest could become permanent since they're still backing him despite all the shady dealings of his that have come to light. So, henceforward, I'll write as if all I'm recounting is fresh news.

But alas, Sam, I will be able to recount only as hearsay events that I myself haven't witnessed.

Here is a sad example. By the time Shallix and I finished our duties behind the turnstiles, all the Opening Day festivities were done and the game had already begun. In truth, I missed seeing not only the first pitch of the Championship Season but the entire home half of the first inning.

The Red Stockings had scored two quick tallies I saw on the bulletin board behind third base as Shallix and I took seats on the bench. But even before Mountjoy could finish telling me how the runs had been manufactured, Tom Brown led off the Buckeyes' half of the first inning with a blow that sent Mansell leather hunting. It rolled all the way to the fence in right field, granting Brownie ample time to circle the bases and slide into home ahead of the relay throw from Reilly.

While Pop Smith, the next batter, was setting himself at the dish, I watched White pace the pitcher's box, agonized over seeing his new curve ball that he calls the "patent-combined-tripartite-quadruplex-quiver" so rudely manhandled. In an effort to regain his aplomb, he removed his glasses and polished them on the sleeve of his blouse. But it was to no avail.

The Buckeyes clubbed him practically senseless, Sam. All told, they made 11 hits today, including another home run, this by Mountain, that traveled clear out of the park. After Mountain's blast, White came undone at the seams. He even stopped giving his pants a Deadeye Dick hitch before each batter as is his wont when he feels in command.

Morris fared little better in the box for Columbus. All his speedballs that had been so lethal in the Capital City against a colts team were pudding today for our boys. Corkhill especially had on his batting clothes, clouting a gigantic home run, and Jones and Reilly also belted balls that landed nearly in the next county.

Actually, so many long ones were smote by both sides that Caylor himself wondered aloud if perhaps the new park was designed too small. "And whose fault is that?" White muttered under his breath. "Who was too miserly to lease enough ground to build a park that would give pitchers a fair shake?"

Not only was it the first time I'd ever heard White bruit anything derogatory about the front office, it was also my first hint that Caylor and Stern may have practiced false economy in building our park.

The crux of it is that while I was on the road with the colts two factions have formed among the regulars. The heavy batsmen like Jones and Reilly adore the new park for its short fences whereas the pitchers all loathe it.

Cincinnatis		AB	R	1B	PO	A	E
Mansell	l.f.	5	1	1	2	0	2
Carpenter	3b	5	1	1	1	0	0
Reilly	1b	5	2	3	3	0	0
Jones	m.f.	4	2	1	3	1	0
Corkhill	r.f	5	1	2	3	0	0
McPhee	2b	5	0	1	7	1	0
Snyder	c	4	1	0	5	3	1
Fulmer	s.s.	4	1	0	0	1	3
White	p	4	0	0	0	0	0
Totals		41	9	9	24	6	6

Columbus		AB	R	1B	PO	A	E
Brown	r.f.	5	2	2	0	0	0
Smith	2b	4	1	1	3	1	3
Kemmler	1b	3	1	0	7	0	0
Richmond	s.s.	5	1	1	0	1	1
Mann	m.f.	5	2	1	0	0	1
Carroll	c	4	1	1	15	2	1
Kuehne	3b	4	1	2	0	1	0
Mountain	l.f.	4	1	1	2	0	0
Morris	p	3	0	2	0	2	3
Totals		37	10	11	27	7	9

Innings	1	2	3	4	5	6	7	8	9
Cincinnatis	2	0	0	4	0	0	0	1	2—9
Columbus	1	1	0	0	0	2	6	0	x—10

Runs earned— Cincinnatis 1, Columbus 7. Two-base hits— McPhee 1, Smith 1, Richmond 2. Three-base hits— Kuehne 1, Carroll 1. Home runs— Brown 1, Mountain 1, Corkhill 1. Total Base on balls— Cincinnatis 13, Columbus 23. Left on bases— Cincinnatis 5, Columbus 7. Struck out— By White 5, Morris 13. Base on balls— By White 4, Morris 1. Bases on balks— By Morris 2. Wild pitches— White 1, Morris 1. Passed balls— Carroll 1. Time of game— Two hours and ten minutes. Umpire— T. C. Carroll, of Philadelphia.

Leastwise that was where matters stood until today. Now every man on the club is unified in the feeling that something rotten is astir in our new abode.

First off, Sam, we lost by a 10-9 count. We staged a two-run rally in the ninth inning that had every man, woman and child in attendance on their feet exhorting us to triumph, but in the end we fell short. We lost our opening game of the Championship Season to a team we had expected to just roll over and play dead.

But cast down as we were by the defeat, it was instantly dispelled by the horrible tragedy that occurred just moments after the last out was made by McPhee, standing frozen with the bat on his shoulder as he watched a third strike.

Exactly how it came to pass is still a mystery. All I know for certain is that I suddenly heard a fearful crack like a clap of thunder as I and the rest of the boys were leaving the field. When we whirled around we saw that a section of the bleaching boards in right field had given way, causing the entire southeast end of the platform to collapse. It was a sight beyond comprehension, Sam, watching row upon row of men and boys topple from the bleaching boards to the earth far below.

Just about every player on both teams rushed to offer aid once we'd recovered our wits. But for the most part we were too late. By the time we reached the disaster site bodies were piled on top of each other, Sam, like on a battlefield. Many of the injured were unconscious or even dead, and others were trying feebly to crawl out from under the carnage of broken and bleeding flesh.

I tugged one man free and was trying to help a young red-haired boy out of the rubble when Jones grabbed my arm and warned this was a job for policemen and physicians. I was about to protest—what man could stand by and refuse to aid the wounded? But then I remembered your own horrendous accident and I realized Jones was right. Many of the victims were so brutally maimed they needed to be moved only by men with medical expertise.

All three of our owners, Stern, Herancourt and Kramer, came into the dressing room while we were bathing to issue details of the catastrophe. There were over 200 injured, Herancourt said, but thus far only one person, a man named Langan, had expired. The second positive note was the park hadn't been damaged so badly that tomorrow's game would have to be postponed. All we'd need to keep closed were the bleaching boards, pending their repair.

"Nevertheless someone should be hung for this," Stern interposed. "Whether it will be Crapsey or Marcus, we'll let the courts decide."

Crapsey is the architect who designed the park, Sam, and Marcus the contractor who built it. Already I hear they're both blaming the Red Stockings for the break down. To their mind they did the best work they could considering they had less than two months to complete the job.

According to Stern, the fault lies wholly with the both of them. Corners were cut he thinks in the materials they used to construct the bleaching boards. Otherwise the platform would not have crumpled like paper when the crowd got to their feet as one man after the game ended and began hurrying from the park to catch the street cars waiting outside.

Stern cautioned us meanwhile to say nothing to the scribes, and especially to no one from the *Enquirer*. We were commanded to refer any reporters to him or some other official representative of the club.

After the owners left the dressing room, Caylor took his turn at addressing us. "Remember you boys are ball players," he said, "and your chief concern is averting disaster on the field. Today's debacle must not be repeated or there'll soon be no danger of the park collapsing again since there'll be no one in it when we play. The Onions will have all our cranks in their basket."

Caylor began calling the Unions "Onions" some weeks ago, Sam, but yesterday was the first time I'd ever heard him express any concern about them.

"They'll crow when they hear about this," he finished. "Our piteous performance today is our own fault, but the park falling apart around us is another matter. I wouldn't doubt the Outlaw Reds somehow engineered its degeneration."

I nearly fell over when I heard that. Thorner and McLean and O'Leary are rotters, no doubt, but could they be so evil as to deliberately cause such mayhem and destruction? Caylor's allegations seemed so monstrous that I nearly lost what little respect I have left for the club after my shabby treatment at its hands.

No man should be made to sit at a turnstile and collect quarters after he dreamt all night of playing in his first major league game.

Your nephew, Earl.

May 11

The bleaching boards have been rebuilt, dear Diary, with extra supporting beams added. To further prevent any repetition of our Opening Day disaster, watchmen have been hired to stand guard in the park at night. There is talk too that the outfield barriers will be moved back some, if only to save the cost of the balls knocked over them and stolen by the urchins who lurk outside the park to watch the game through knotholes in the fences.

The team meanwhile is back on its feed. After dropping two of three games to the Columbuses and narrowly averting an embarrassing loss to the weakling Indianapolises and McKeon, their trickster recruit boxman, we demolished the Toledos on Friday, 9-1, and then flattened them again yesterday by an 11-1 count. White for the first time this season was on the beam while Mullane posed no puzzle for us although in his defense his fielders undressed him naked. Miller, the Blue Stockings short stop, was again the worst miscreant after making three

Cincinnatis		AB	R	1B	PO	A	E
Reilly	1b	5	0	2	10	0	0
Carpenter	3b	5	0	1	2	2	0
Mansell	1.f	4	1	1	3	0	1
Jones	m.f.	3	1	0	2	0	2
McPhee	2b	4	2	1	3	0	0
Corkhill	r.f.	4	3	2	2	1	0
Powers	c	4	1	0	4	3	0
Mountjoy	p	4	1	0	0	0	1
Fulmer	s.s	4	0	0	0	4	0
Totals		37	9	7	27	10	4

Toledos		AB	R	1B	PO	A	E.
Barkley	2b	4	0	1	3	7	2
Poorman	r.f.	3	0	0	7	0	1
Miller	s.s.	4	0	1	0	7	3
Walker	c	4	0	0	3	1	0
Welch	m.f	4	1	1	3	0	0
O'Day	p	4	0	1	0	3	0
Lane	1b	4	0	0	16	3	3
Brown	3b	4	0	3	0	0	0
Tilly	1.f	4	0	0	2	0	0
Totals		35	1	7	27	21	9

Innings	1	2	3	4	5	6	7	8	9	
Cincinnatis	0	4	0	1	0	1	0	3	0—9	
Toledos	0	0	0	0	0	0	1	0	0—1	

Two-base hits— Corkhill 1. Three-base hits— Corkhill 1. Left on bases— Cincinnatis 2. Toledos 5. Double plays— Miller, Lane, and Walker 1, Miller, Barkley, and Lane 1. Struck out— By Mountjoy 5, by O'Day 0. Base on balls— By Mountjoy 1, by O'Day 1. Wild pitches— O'Day 1. Passed balls— Powers 1, Walker 2. Time of game— One hour and thirty-five minutes. Umpire— John Kelly.

errors on Friday and muffing two other balls that would have been charged to his column if the scorer hadn't taken pity on him. It steamed me to see someone of his ilk playing when I sat idle, and Peoples felt likewise. During Saturday's contest, Peoples cozied up to me on the bench and murmured this Joe Miller was really some apples. "But what can you expect," he said then, "from a club so hard up it will even stoop to hiring coons?"

Peoples was flaming Fleet Walker, the Toledos catcher, who made the eyes of our cranks pop out of their heads on Friday when he first took the field as most of them had never before seen a coon play in a game with white men. Yet once the initial furor died down, only a narrow-minded few treated Walker any less cordially than they did the rest of the visitors. I heard names shouted at him that like to have singed all the grass on the field, but on the whole our crowd behaved very hospitably under the circumstances. Actually, much of their reception was fostered by Walker himself. Incredibly, I hear he's got a college education, plus he showed remarkable poise under fire for a colored man. His cocoa face never once lost its stoic cast while all around him his teammates were booting balls. No less than nine errors were made by them on Friday and another batch yesterday, which finally so incensed Mullane that he switched to pitching with his left arm to save his right for a better day.

By the bye, dear Diary, Mullane jumped Lucas's Maroons before the season started and signed with the Toledos. It's about the tenth contract he's broken, and there seems to be no stopping his incessant resolving. From the Browns, one of the elite American nines, Mullane leapt to the Maroons, the cream of the Union Association, and now he's with the Toledos pitching for one of the sorriest outfits ever assembled and to a coon catcher. They call him Count Tony to his face and Count Money to his back as he appears to have a double-dealing brain along with being able to toss with either arm. Caylor claims it's players like him that have enabled the Unions to get their leaky balloon off the ground. Their sole loyalty is to the almighty dollar, and their teammates can go hang the moment somebody makes them a better offer. Mullane all by himself is giving base ball a bad name, Caylor says. Yet in the next breath he will say gleefully: "If we can get just a few more players of Mullane's stripe to defect, it'll bring the Onions to their knees."

Base ball is a maze of contradictions sometimes. For two days the Toledos played as if they didn't belong on the same planet with us, but this afternoon they rose from the ashes and nipped us 3-2 behind Hank O'Day, he who could do naught right on Friday. O'Day's fielders were mainly to thank, the same crew of fumble-fingers that previously gave Mullane and him only grief. Today, though, Miller made two glorious stops, Barkley turned a hot smash into a double play, and then in the seventh inning Curt Welch scampered a country mile to spear Carpenter's liner and kill our last rally. Welch's circus catch was all the harder to stomach because he ought to have been too corned even to see the ball. Before the game Mansell reported he'd found a jug of beer hidden behind a loose board in the centrefield fence. What Welch does is mosey back to it and sneak a nip whenever an argument with the umpire interrupts play and lures away everybody's attention.

It takes all kinds to make up this world and I'm encountering my fair share here in Cincinnati. Where else could I play with men as deft as McPhee and Jones and against such a motley assortment as Walker and Mullane and Welch? I say "play" because I'm finally about to get the splinters out of my behind. Tomorrow we're slated to meet the regulars in an exhibition game. By "we" I again mean the colts since I'm back with them now that the homestand is over and the club will be going on the road for the next month.

It was in my best interest, White said when he gave me the news this afternoon, since I could only grow rusty sitting on the bench.

I yearned to say I wouldn't be rusting away now if he'd let me play in even just one championship match. But I swallowed that and instead begged him to wait until after tomorrow's exhibition game before he finally decided my Fate.

White said only: "We'll see." Yet even so lame a pledge as that heartened me when it was coupled today with a letter from Constance. Frankly, I'd about given up ever hearing from her after penning her twice since our meeting without a reply. The gloom that created explains my silence of late about her in your pages, dear Diary.

But now all the joy of meeting her has been revived. In her letter Constance apologized for not having written sooner, explaining that illness had confined her to bed for the past fortnight. It was a form of scarlet fever but happily a mild strain. Now that she is recovered, she wrote, she can again turn her thoughts to the pleasanter aspects of her life, myself among them. "I sincerely treasured our time together," wrote she, "and shall look ahead to another such event, perhaps, should you and your base ball club ever journey again to Louisville."

Her words, circumspect though they be, are still a boon after all these weeks of wondering if I alone felt the bond between us. They gave me faith again—faith that a brilliantly played game tomorrow will devour these gnawing doubts I sometimes still have of myself.

The reason White broadcast for not pitching the opening game of the series with the Toledos was that he wanted to pit himself against Mullane the following afternoon in the expectation that their matchup would attract a handsome crowd. Some of White's teammates bought his logic even though it forced Mountjoy into the box despite a sore arm, but others thought that White might be exercising his managerial prerogative to hold himself out of a game in which no man with a free choice would want to participate. One of the skeptics voiced this to Charley Jones before Friday's game, believing him an ally since he'd been born in Dixieland. Jones made no reply then, but at the bottom of the first inning, before taking his station in the outfield, he strolled to the pitcher's box. Picking up the ball where it had been rolled by Fleet Walker after the Red Stockings' final out was made, he turned toward Reilly as he began rubbing it over his crotch. He then handed the ball to Mountjoy and said with a wink, "There, that's taken the hex off it." Later he told the man who had sought his commiseration for having to play on the same field with the Toledos' Negro catcher his true motive for massaging his privates with the ball. "Mixing the dinge's scent with my own will make women in the grandstand pant like dogs when the wind is right," he said. "Try it if you doubt me. Your wench will wear your pecker to a frazzle tonight."

Near the end of the 1884 season, after a summer of controversy and not long before the secret pact that assured he would be the last Negro to play in the major leagues until 1947, Fleet Walker was threatened with murder if he took part in a game at Richmond, Virginia. Walker disappointed his followers by allowing Toledo captain Charlie Morton to keep him out of the lineup on the pretext that he had a disabling rib injury. To those in his confidence, Walker made it clear that he would never have buckled under even at the risk of his life if the arena had been more important than base ball, which he regarded as only a way to finance his further education.

Walker laid out his views on racial intolerance in America in *Our Home Colony*, a book he wrote in 1908, and *The Equator*, a newspaper he founded in his adopted home of Steubenville, Ohio, but his private journals have yet to be published. As a result, we have only Tony Mullane's side (possibly invented by sportswriter Hugh Fullerton to make a morality play a quarter of a century later) of how he and Walker interacted while playing for the Toledo Blue Stockings in 1884. Mullane reputedly would later acknowledge that Walker was "the best catcher I ever worked with, but I disliked the Negro and when I had to pitch to him I used to pitch anything I wanted without looking at his signals." Mullane's record in 1884 bears out his words. He threw 63 wild pitches that year, by far the most in the Association.

While Mullane's thoughts, if true, are shocking to us today, they are mild in comparison to what was felt in Chicago. The minutes of the many meetings that were held, supposedly at the instigation of Cap Anson, are still unavailable; the likelihood is that they were never committed to record, as if the participants took care to cover their tracks. About all that is certain is *someone* in Chicago was at the root of the movement to squeeze Walker out of the major leagues. If it was Anson, we might assume it was because he appreciated the weight he carried as the captain and star first baseman of the Chicago White Stockings, the most powerful franchise in base ball.

This Cap Anson was the greatest player of his time, many later came to believe. Others considered him a national disgrace. Their grievance was that base ball was lavishly celebrating a man who should properly be reviled. As their primary evidence, they cited two instances where Anson openly displayed rampant prejudice. In 1883 he allegedly refused to let his Chicago powerhouse take the field for an exhibition game against Fleet Walker's Toledo Northwestern League club and four years later he again supposedly rebelled when the Chicago team was scheduled to play the Newark minor league team that featured a battery of Walker and Negro pitcher George Stovey.

These are the facts:

Adrian Constantine Anson
B. April 17, 1851, Marshalltown, Iowa
D. April 11, 1922, Chicago, Illinois
BR TR 6' 227 lbs.
Manager: Chicago White Stockings, 1879-98
Played: 22 years for Chicago and five years (1871-75) in the
        National Association, a forerunner of the National
        League and regarded by most serious historians to have
        been the first major league
Career Highlights: First player to make 3000 hits
        First player to compile 1000 RBI

First player to score 1000 runs
Led the NL eight times in RBI and twice in batting
Hit .395 in 1894 at age 43
Continued to play as a big league regular until he was 46

Anson might have been any number of things. The country in the years immediately after the Civil War was made for strong-willed opportunists, even ones with little education, and he was all of that. Although he attended prep school for a while at Notre Dame and later, briefly, the University of Iowa, he was sent to both for disciplinary reasons rather than in the expectation that they might make a professional man out of a small-town bad boy. Anson had something in addition that other boys with his assets in life were denied: a father who was all for his son becoming a professional base ball player.

During his early years in the game Anson was known as "Baby" but not just because of his tender age. Other players were already noticing his penchant for whining when events did not go his way. After he was appointed player-captain of the White Stockings, he had to suffer Baby no more. Now he was "Cap" to the boys. By 1884, looking even older than his 33 years, Anson had ceased trying to quiet any who called him "Pop". When he began hearing rumors, though, that the White Stockings, short of pitching help after Larry Corcoran's arm gave way, might hire a promising local Negro tosser, the story is that he went to the office of club president Al Spalding and voiced his horror. Two other players came with him, to support him, and Anson purportedly said that "no African nigger should be permitted into professional base ball until the entire supply of American boys had been given their chance." That fall, when it became evident that many teams were on the brink of financial collapse, and perhaps even entire leagues, others too were in accord that Negro players were only supernumeraries since there soon would probably not be even enough jobs for white men to go around.

Whether it was Anson behind it or not, the Chicago faction eventually held sway because many of its notions were secretly held by most owners, who were already resentful of the exorbitant salaries they were having to pay white players. Even the possibility of a formal ban was given serious consideration until some with legal training pointed out that the courts might not look kindly upon it. Besides, the same result could be accomplished by a "gentlemen's" agreement. The stipulations of that agreement were never put into writing; it was all kept very vague, as if wiser heads already knew that the less the public knew about their business, the better. Walker's banishment came in the form of a pact to pretend he wasn't good enough to play in top company, and so Anson and his fellow National Leaguers finished their days without ever appearing on the same field in a regular League game with a black man.

Another group of historians find it impossible to believe that blunt-spoken, half-educated Cap Anson who knew little more than the ball field could push around his sophisticated boss, White Stockings owner Al Spalding. The man who eventually slickered Anson out of his meager share of the club, the man who built a sporting goods empire that still exists today, seems unlikely to have been told what to do by one of his employees. These same historians contend that Anson—and most other players of his time, for that matter—would never have been opposed to the notion of playing with blacks, as long as the money was right.

What we know for certain is that in the years immediately following his long major league career, Anson formed a team that played in the integrated Chicago City League. He not only owned the park where many of the games were played but took part himself in them on occasion. Thus it was that in 1907, the same year that Sol White wrote in his *History of Colored Base Ball* that "Anson at first absolutely refused to play his nine {in 1883} against Walker, the colored man," Anson and his City League team, Anson's Colts, were on the same field weekend after weekend with the great African American pitcher Rube Foster and his Leland Giants as well as the other leading black teams in Chicago.

Who is to be believed? Those who say that Anson was the Devil Incarnate or his sympathetic biographers who claim he was wrongly identified in a police lineup? More so than any other base ball figure of his time, the man from Marshalltown remains an enigma after the stories of how he thought and acted in his early years are placed beside what the evidence shows he did in his later years. One side swears that black men would have been in the major leagues to stay long before 1947 if not for Anson and his supporters. The other side points to Anson's work in the Chicago City League and the fact that he died nearly penniless and then says, "In life they took away his money, in death his reputation."

Columbus, O., May 13

Dear Sam:

I have both good news and bad news to share and shan't keep you in suspense. The good is I tallied three hits yesterday against the regulars and acquitted myself so ably in the field that even the *Enquirer*, which almost never has anything complimentary to say about the Red Stockings, remarked on my glove work. In spite of my effort, the colts still lost 11-3, but the gloom caused me by the defeat vanished when White told me after the game that there'd been a change of plans and I'd be accompanying the regulars after all on the road trip.

Then this morning, Sam, White gave me even better news. On the train ride to Columbus he bade me to sit beside him and then told me I'd play short stop today since Mountain was due to pitch for the Buckeyes. "We want you in there," he said, "because he's right-handed and you hit lefty. That big curveball of his should be pudding for you." He then glanced toward the rear of the car where Fulmer was playing cards with Reilly and Mansell and said: "What I'm telling you is just between us. When the scribes ask me why Chick isn't playing, I'll say his arm is ailing."

The one bad piece of news, Sam, is our game this afternoon was rained out. However, there is the morrow, and to prepare for it I retired to my room here at the Neil House Hotel right after supper. Peoples, Woulfe and Mountjoy, who are sharing the room with me, tried a while ago to cajole me into going out with them to unearth some of the nocturnal delights the Capital City has to offer, but I declined.

My room looks directly down upon the street, Sam, and the gas lamps have just been lit. In their illumination I can see the row of saloons across the way and my face in reflection in the window-glass looking out at them. It is a face at peace. What I see out there each time I glance up as I sit here writing holds no diversion for me. My lone focus now that our dream is about to be realized is on the picture in my mind of myself standing in tomorrow to face Mountain. Remember, Sam...The very first swing of my bat!

Your nephew, Earl.

May 17

Well, dear Diary, instead of pitching Mountain the Buckeyes crossed us up and used Morris in the first game of the series. Since Morris is a portsider, White opted to stick with Fulmer at shortstop and save me for Mountain on Thursday. But when Morris beat us 8-2, that plan too was scorched. White told me he had to go with an all-veteran lineup until we got a victory under our belts on the road.

Yesterday, after we needed 12 innings to salvage the last game of the series, White told me he was sending me back to Cincinnati to rejoin the colts. They direly needed me, he said. Caylor had cabled him that the Allegheny colts had crushed them 17-5 and to rush help immediately. My heart in my throat, I asked why he didn't send Peoples instead? Because Peoples can also play behind the bat in an emergency, he said, and hence couldn't be spared. Whereupon I said I'd take up catching too—I'd do whatever it took to stay with the regulars!

No, White said adamantly. My rightful position was at short stop. I could best serve the club by giving the colts the benefit of my bat and meanwhile working on improving my throwing so I could be trusted in a championship contest.

But only a few days ago, I reminded him, he'd been ready to trust me.

White's eyes flashed behind his spectacles as if to accuse me of impertinence. And he said: "It's Caylor's and my wish that you return to the colts. That is all I have to say on the matter, Draves."

I quieted my own eyes then, a plan forming. I launched it by requesting permission to stay another night in Columbus since the colts weren't slated to play again till Sunday. I fibbed, saying there was an old school chum I wanted to visit before returning to Cincinnati. White acceded but only after advising that the club would not pay for an extra night's lodging in Columbus.

After the team left for Indianapolis on an evening train, I toted my carpetbag from the Neil House to a hotel that charged only 20¢. Its seedy accommodations were of no moment to me, knowing I would not sleep anyway. All last night I lay awake and wrestled with my decision. On the one hand, I didn't want to betray my dream by quitting the Red Stockings. Yet I felt they had betrayed me by never giving me the chance Caylor promised.

By morning I'd concluded the current Cincinnati Red Stockings are not the same club my uncle had yearned to join prior to his accident and that even he must unite with my desire to play for a nine that is fair to its members. The Louisvilles are just such a club. Unlike the Red Stockings, they aren't burdened with a captain too blind to see who his best short stop is.

And, yes, dear Diary, there was another consideration.

Her name alone seemed to pledge that I'd find in Louisville the clarity of purpose that had eluded me in Cincinnati, and I took it as a further omen when I considered that my reduction to the colts had occurred in Columbus on the very eve of the Louisvilles' first visit of the season to the Capital City.

At first light I leapt out of bed and wrote Constance that she could expect to see me again very soon. Then I rehearsed how I would approach Joe Gerhardt, the Louisvilles field general, that afternoon at Recreation Park.

Come game time I still had no good notion. Gerhardt might say the Louisvilles would like to have me, but then he'd surely claim their hands were tied as long as I was still under contract elsewhere. And what could I reply? That I now felt liberated to break my contract because the Red Stockings had broken their word to me?

In truth, they hadn't altogether done so. They were still paying me my salary. Their only grave crime was in denying me the chance to prove I belonged on the regulars.

I realized all the more how rash my thoughts had been once the game began. Instead of the action on the field, I found my eyes watching the nearest bulletin board. I had chosen a seat behind the Louisvilles bench so I could study Gerhardt while I debated more what I would say to him, but when the boy manning the bulletin board began posting the scores of other American games I moved to a new location.

The Louisvilles and all their guying of Mountain and the other Columbus players were now an intrusion. My lone concern was the game in Indianapolis. I waited with bated breath for the first report on the score there, and when the boy at the bulletin board chalked up two runs for the Red Stockings I burst out in a cheer.

I couldn't help myself. I was on my feet constantly, craning to see the bulletin board until it grew certain the boys would triumph. By then all the cranks in my vicinity were fed up with me. They thought I was cheering the Louisvilles' 7-0 Chicagoing of their Buckeyes. But after a while a toothless coot sitting behind me glimpsed the truth. "Hey, bub," he said, "didn't I see you on the visitors' bench yesterday? Ain't you one of the Cincy substitutes?"

When I admitted I was it only further riled the people around me. They began accusing me of being there as a spy. "You boys couldn't beat us," one wag said, "so you're here to see how it's done." That compelled me to remind him we'd won the last game of the series. "And we'll sweep you clean next time we play you," I added.

Immediately upon hearing myself say we, I felt my mind settle. I knew then, dear Diary, that I'd only narrowly stopped my impatience from betraying not only my uncle's deepest desires but my own. In my heart I am a Red Stocking and I shall be always.

May 21

So, dear Diary, the colts are now the amateur champions of Cincinnati for what it's worth. Not much I'd say since we're all professionals and the club we played on Sunday, the Shamrocks, offered so little challenge that we thrashed them 30-1. Billing the game as one for the amateur championship of the city was Caylor's brainstorm, conceived in the futile hope that the colts would attract a big enough crowd to begin paying their own way. As matters now stand, the club is losing money on us hand over fist, and Sunday's venture was no improvement.

We drew a grand sum of 392 people, most of them there probably for the open air concert the Cincinnati Orchestra gave after the game. Then yesterday we didn't lure even 200 when we played the St. Louis colts in the opening game of the reserve championship season. By losing 7-1 we assured that just about nobody would come out to watch us this afternoon, and so it was. Only a handful of diehards saw us wreak revenge on Hungler and Struve, the battery that a lot of sharps think will be with the Browns regulars before too long.

But the sparse turnout wasn't totally our own fault. We'd surely be pulling larger crowds now, as would the regulars, save for the unfair practices of the Onions. In the *Enquirer*, McLean keeps saying the Red Stockings are a pox on the city and, if his printed insults weren't vile enough, he and Thorner sank a step lower this afternoon.

Before our game with St. Louis, Reeder and I and Bowers were accosted outside the gate of American Park by a gang of thugs who commanded us to go to Onion Park where the Outlaw Reds were playing the Philadelphia Keystones if we wanted to see a real base ball game today. When we identified ourselves and tried to pass through the gate, they flung us to the ground and began kicking us like mules. There were so many of them, at minimum eight or nine, that they likely would have made mincemeat out of us if a policeman inside the park hadn't heard the uproar. Cowards that they are, they fled like scared rabbits when he rushed to our rescue but not before they'd left their marks. Reeder suffered a fractured tooth and I still can't breathe without feeling where their boots battered my ribs.

"It's those Onion rats again," Stern said when we were led to his office in the park and had given him the reason for our disheveled state. "That crew of ruffians was in their hire or my name isn't Aaron." He then puffed up his fat cheeks and said the club unfortunately was not accountable for the damage to us or our clothing since it had not been done inside the park. In the future, though, we should retaliate. "Defend yourselves, boys," he egged. "Next time let's see the street run red with the blood of your assailants."

Anyone who still thinks my bat and my glove are the only weapons I need to hold my own in this game may need to think again, dear Diary.

Cincinnati, O., May 25

Dear Sam:

After reading this letter you might no longer say I was right not to seek a place on the Louisvilles. Yesterday the Milwaukee colts failed to show up for the first game of our series with them, and late in the day we got word they'd stood us up because they were disbanding. Miller said it was his duty as captain to tell us there were rumors that other colt teams too were about to fold their tents owing to poor attendance. Pendleton asked him man-to-man if that included our own outfit and Miller said not to his knowledge. But the way he said it, Sam, the hedging we all heard in his voice warned us he wasn't telling all the truth he knew.

Today, in place of the Milwaukees, we played the Muldoons, a local team nearly as feeble as the Shamrocks. But our hearts weren't in it, knowing we might soon find ourselves jobless, and we barely escaped with our status as the local amateur champions, winning only 8-6. The crowd derided us cruelly throughout the game for our indifferent play, all except a scattering of men who had been foolish enough to take the long odds and bet on the Muldoons.

One of them I had the ill luck to meet just before the game. He called me over to his buggy on the sideline while we were having our warm-up and asked me who would occupy the box for us. When I said Shallix he commenced petting the dog at his side as he inquired whether I would give Gus a gift from him. Made wary by his evasive manner, I asked him why he didn't give it to Shallix himself. "Because," he said, still massaging his animal, "I want to give you something too." Then, looking keenly at me, he said: "It will bring you $50, Draves, and Gus $100 if the two of you see to it that the Muldoons come out on the long end today."

Of course I turned on my heel and left him flat. But can you believe his crust, Sam! When I told Miller about him and pointed him out, Miller donned a sour face and said: "Oh, that's only Tierney. He's always betting on something and then looking for ways to hedge his bet."

Tierney has tried his game numerous times, Miller said, but no one treats him seriously. If any player were to take him up on one of his nefarious offers, he'd probably faint from surprise. Ever since the Louisville scandal in '77, Miller said, most gamblers no longer even try to bribe players. They know no professional would jeopardize his livelihood, let alone his teammates' trust, for all the tea in China.

But I'm not so sure, Sam. While I myself never have seen a game that smelled raw, I've heard tell of an American team that's notorious for giving its rooters the dumps. As I don't wish to tar anyone unjustly, the team shall go nameless until I witness its hippodroming for myself. But I may never have that chance owing to that awful rumor I cited earlier. There are hourly mutterings now that the Red Stockings will release their entire colts team anon. I can only cross my fingers that

the next sound I hear will not be the wolf at my door.
Your nephew, Earl.

May 29

Marvel of marvels, dear Diary! Phil Powers of all people did
me a good turn although it was none of his choosing. In Monday's game
with Baltimore, the first on our Eastern trip, he was struck in the hand by
a foul tip, disabling him temporarily, and White wired Caylor to send a
replacement. Whether White requested me specifically I will never
know as all Caylor told me was the club wanted a man in the East who
at least didn't dress like a bumpkin. From Caylor that's probably as close
to a compliment as I'll ever receive, but so be it. The truth is I will
endure just about any slings and arrows now if it means a chance to stay
with the regulars. For the alternative is to be cast adrift, as it is almost a
near certainty tonight that the colts will disband before the week is out.

I feel like I'm hanging on by a mere thread now, and not only to
my spot on the Red Stockings. Baltimore is a grim locale, dear Diary,
even more bung-full than St. Louis. The houses are all crammed in like
sardines, and every place you enter actually reeks with the stench of that
critter and just about every other form of sea life mingled with the stink
of too many people living and working too close together.

This city has a malodorous team too even if the Orioles won two
of their three games with us, including today's 2-0 blanking. Outside of
their incredible luck in catching us in the throes of a batting slump and
their tony uniforms of candy-striped shirts and caps, the only boon they
have is their manager, Billy Barnie. He sits on the bench in a black
derby to conceal that his skull is as bereft of hair as his team is of talent.
With a decent bunch he would win the pennant. Here he has to use
mirrors just to win a single game. Half his lineup is composed of men
the Red Stockings have released as useless, and they are the stronger
half.

One of the Red Stockings rejects is Jimmy Macullar, who is not
much bigger than a flea. With the Red Stockings he played in the
pasture on the rare occasions when he played at all, but Barnie employs
him at short stop. Macullar can't cut the mustard there either—he's too
small to cover enough ground or do much at the dish besides hit sacrifice
dribblers although today he somehow got enough stick on the ball to
whang a home run off White. Still, installing him at short stop is further
testimony to Barnie's brilliance. Bald Billy alone appears to realize the
position is tailor-made for a southpaw. It is far easier for a lefty like
Macullar or myself to scoot behind second base, snare a roller
barehanded and fling it to his first sacker. On a daisy cutter to his right,

a left-hander has the edge again because he doesn't have to stretch his gloved hand across his body to flag it down.

Well, dear Diary, I'm not leading up to announcing that I approached Barnie and put my hat in the ring against the day he quits on Macullar. The truth is he approached me! During our warm-up before today's game I had to ask him to lift his legs so I could retrieve an errant peg from Woulfe that had rolled under the Orioles bench. As he complied, he said: "I like your flash, kiddo. Stay with this game and I predict you'll leave your stamp on it."

If that isn't an outright offer of a future position with the Baltimores, it's as frankly as he can speak while I'm under contract elsewhere. Still, there is no way on earth I could play for a team in this town after the reception I've been given here. As but one of a million examples of its rude and mistrustful citizenry, today the desk clerk at our hotel made me turn in my soiled towel before he'd give me a fresh one.

Washington, D.C., June 2

Dear Sam:

Either the people here believe a man should forgive and forget or else they reckon it's futile to stay hopped up over a team that is just about the world's worst. Anyway, we went to the Washingtons park this afternoon fearing the crowd would slay the umpire and maybe us too after the riot here Saturday. But instead the game passed so serenely that all the extra policemen hired for protection had naught to do but twirl their billies and watch us beat the locals 3-0, thereby sweeping the series. Hollingshead, the Washingtons captain, moaned that we couldn't help win since we had ten men on the field in every game to his nine, and in fairness I have to admit he wasn't altogether singing the tune of a sore loser, leastwise not on Saturday. Umpire Connell truly did make several raw calls against the home side although none so bad that it justified Hollingshead yanking his team off the field in the sixth inning and forcing Connell to declare the game forfeit. No sooner had Connell spoken the word than the crowd surged out of the stands to have at him. Several policemen swiftly formed a cordon around Connell, and White lent a hand too. He had the driver secrete our carriage behind a gate in the outfield fence. At a prearranged signal the gate was opened and the policemen rushed Connell through it and into the carriage. With the crowd in hot pursuit and the driver frantically whipping the horses, he fled down the street in a cloud of dust.

Luckily tempers had 48 hours to cool off since there was no game yesterday, it being Sunday. None of the Eastern cities permit playing base ball on the Sabbath, and there remains strong sentiment against it too in many of the Western burgs. Just two Mondays ago all the boys on the Red Stockings who had participated in the game versus Indianapolis the previous day were arrested for violating an Indiana law prohibiting a man from following his avocation on the Sabbath. The following day the Hoosiers were arrested on the same charge. The cases were all eventually dismissed, but the issue is still up in the air. Cincinnati and St. Louis are about the only burgs that have no quarrel with the Americans' philosophy that base ball and the Sabbath ought to be like two peas in a pod since the Sabbath is the lone day of the week when most working men are at liberty to attend games.

Well, we're off to New York in a few minutes, Sam, for our first series of the season with last year's Jonahs, the Metropolitans, followed by three games with the Brooklyns, another new outfit that is nearly as putrid as the Washingtons. The fact is all the teams that have come on board this season are dead weight. Only the League seems to have no weak sisters unless it's the Detroits. The Onions, in contrast, have seven also-rans and only one decent nine, Lucas's Maroons. The Maroons launched the season by winning 20 straight games before Tommy Bond of the Bostons handed them their first loss last week. Already they are so far ahead of all the other Onion outfits that one team has given up the chase. The other night the Altoona Mountain Citys disbanded and then the following morning re-signed most of their players as an independent team.

In our own loop only four or five teams have any realistic chance: us, the Browns, Louisville, the Metropolitans, the Athletics and maybe the Buckeyes if you can believe their fast start is not a mirage. Most of the sharps are convinced it is. They're betting Columbus will begin falling back into the pack any day now and then go the way of the Altoonas by the end of the season. If that happens still more players will be thrown out on the street.

So saying, I'm brought to the first of two sad items of news, Sam. On the same day the Mountain Citys quit the Onions, our colts team was disbanded following a 21-2 loss to the Alleghenys in front of only 73 spectators. Shallix, Miller and Weihe were ordered to join the regulars when we return to Cincinnati and the rest of the boys were released outright. There but for Powers' injury could now go I too, Sam, but even at that I'm not yet out of the woods. The second unhappy item is that I still haven't gotten to play a single inning for the Red Stockings and after today I have to think I never may.

Carpenter was down with boils this afternoon, Sam, and I held my breath upon learning he would miss the game. But whom did White put at third base in his stead? Peoples! "You're a lefty," White said, reading my disappointment. "It's an unnatural position for a southpaw." As if that held water! Carpenter is also left-handed, as I was obliged to mention. "But Hick's played there all his life," said White, springing another leak in his own argument. "And Peoples has never played third base in his," I parried.

To which White didn't even give me the courtesy of a reply. He spun around as if something elsewhere had got his eye. Then he said: "You're out of line, Draves. From now on when your feathers are ruffled I recommend you keep it to yourself."

It's a hard thing, Sam, but I hereby pledge to follow your counsel to keep my lip buttoned. Soon my new nickname will be Dummy. They can call me anything they please just so they don't ever stop calling me a Red Stocking.

Your nephew, Earl.

He was among the first to realize his skills were deserting him, his confidence was ebbing. Yet he couldn't understand how or when it had happened. Only a year ago he had felt great. Now he dreaded his turn at bat and prayed balls would not be hit to him. He knew it was nearly over and the years seemed so short since 1870 and his first organized team, the Forest Citys of Cleveland. Always a quick dresser, he now found himself wanting to linger in the dressing room after a home game knowing that there were few afternoons left to him, and in hotel rooms before road games he could not seem to stir himself to start changing into his uniform until the last possible minute.

So much of it came down to the question of when a ball player should be judged a has-been. But in attempting to answer that, Chick Fulmer's critics must first be able to say whether the trouble was his advancing age or a slowness to adapt to the new type of pitching that prevailed in the Association now that hurlers were allowed to deliver their tosses from any point below their necklines. There was one Cincinnati owner, who once said without a trace of jest, that if the true birth dates of every base ball player were revealed, he, at 34, might be no more than the average age. Certainly Fulmer was not so old even for a short stop. Dickey Pearce and Davy Force had shown a man deep into his thirties could still do the job. Yet it was undeniable that Chick was not the same fielder he had been but a year earlier. Perhaps it was merely a temporary drop in confidence.

Why not give him a thorough chance to work himself out of his funk? The alternative was Peoples, a sure-handed fielder but slow afoot, or it could be Corkhill, which would mean weakening the outer perimeter, an area that was already thin. Then there was Draves, the recruit who could play with the best one day and look absolutely green the next. Fulmer was the safe choice, at least for the moment. Peoples was the logical successor if Fulmer did not pan out. Corkhill was a last resort, and Draves—Draves was at once promising and exasperating. It did not help his cause either that he was left-handed. Southpaws were notoriously erratic, both in performance and behavior, and Draves was hardly an exception. Caylor sometimes debated whether to convert him to first base where his brashness would have less opportunity to damage the team. But then what was to be done with Reilly who could play nowhere else either without causing complete havoc?

In the absence of a resolution that strongly recommended itself, Caylor left the decision to White, offering only his advice that he personally would go with the veteran hand for the moment.

June 3

Well, dear Diary, here I am in the nation's den of iniquity. We're staying at the St. Nicholas Hotel in a neighborhood they call "The Devil's doorstep," but from what I've seen this entire city has fallen into the hands of Satan. For each church there must be a hundred saloons, and it is a rare face that has not been ravaged by the pox or some other disease. Most of the denizens act as if their brains too are afflicted. All along our carriage ride this afternoon to the Metropolitans park hooligans pelted us from rooftops with rotten fruit and other unmentionable offal, and the mob that awaited us when we got to the Polo Grounds was even more barbaric. Of all the names they screeched the only one that could be put in a family publication is "Porkapolitans," slung at us because they remember when Cincinnati was the meat capital of the country before Chicago robbed it of the distinction.

But they got their comeuppance. We dunked their boys 10-6 to the shock of everyone, most of all the poolsellers who figured the Mets were a shoo-in today with Tim Keefe in the box. All Keefe had to do last year to subdue us was toss his glove on the field, but that's now ancient history. The Red Stockings are riding a four-game winning streak at the moment, our longest yet this season. It's a wonderful feeling, being part of our great surge and seeing the fear and loathing we've sparked in the entire base ball populace in this huge metropolis.

Near the end of the game, when the crowd glumly recognized we were going to prevail, they shifted their wrath from us to their own boys. Reipschlager, after making a bushel of errors behind the plate, became their primary butt. The more savagely the crowd ragged him, the worse he played. It finally got so he looked like he wished the ground would open up and swallow him. Seeing his misery, some of our boys joined in the frolic. Powers, never averse to kicking a man when he's down, waved his poulticed hand and heckled: "Charlie, even with this sick paw and my good one tied behind my back, I could outshine you!"

When we returned to our hotel this evening after supper, a parcel of men in top hats and cutaway coats were gathered in the lobby. One of them peeled off from the cluster and boarded the lift with Jones, Peoples, Reilly and myself. As we were ascending, he said: "Can you figure the poolsellers making the Porkapolitans the favorites tomorrow?" "As they should," I said. "Now that we have taken care of Keefe we will murder Lynch." "Oh, are you boys affiliated with the Porkers?" said the intruder, lofting his eyebrows in surprise. "You bet your boots we are," said Peoples, and I would have seconded it if Jones had not trod on my foot.

"Get your heads out of your buckets," he said to Peoples and me after we'd got off the lift. "That was a flushing gambler who only pretended not to know who we are, hoping to dupe us into providing him with a tidbit of inside information."

I've edited Jones's words, dear Diary, and I'll also not besmirch your pages with details of the byways he and the other boys no doubt are now exploring. Only my own thoughts remain uncensored so I can fairly record the mixture of elation and chagrin besieging me tonight. Should I be alone here now in my room like the mooncalf Jones makes me feel, or out savoring our lustrous victory with the boys?

WILL WHITE'S SCOUTING REPORT ON THE METROPOLITANS

1: Candy Nelson, short stop, has slipped in the field but is still a fair leadoff hitter as he will use his smallish stature to wait for his pitch. I do not like this man being on base either and will hit him in the leg if his base on balls is imminent anyway. Let's see him run then—if he can.

2: Steve Brady, right field, a man you must get out as he is their weakest hitter at the top of the batting order. I have only moderate respect too for him in the field. He is too old now to be of championship caliber and may never have been that.

3: Dude Esterbrook, third base, I thought not much of last year, but he is allegedly better now. He has no real flair, though, and is one who may be older than he lets on. I would fear him more than Brady though not a lot.

4: Chief Roseman, centre field, is too rotund to represent much danger on the bases. Nor is he anything extraordinary in the pasture. I would not be at all afraid of him in the pinch even despite what he did to us at times last year. Too, he has a hot temper and can be baited into losing it.

5: Dave Orr, first base, reputedly is the hardest hitter in the land now, if you listen to their scribes. But I still am unconvinced he is so much better than last year when he could not even make their club. He is too big to be taken lightly, I will concede that. However, he will surely scoff his way out of base ball before long.

6: Dasher Troy, second base, is hardly more harmful with the willow than a schoolgirl and no great shakes in the field. If he is the best they could find to replace Gracie Pierce, we will look for them in the cellar.

7: Charlie Reipschlager, catcher, is more reputable at the marble than Holbert though that is still no reason to play him. Holbert is the man I would much rather have handle me, but that is just another of this team's mysteries. I truly cannot see how they win as much as they do.

8: Ed Kennedy, left field, is pitiful. He hit nearly nothing last year and has grown even more defective. Even our colts like Reeder and Weihe are better.

9: It tells everything that Mutrie will bat his pitcher last, whether it be Keefe or Lynch, in preference to Kennedy. I fear Keefe far more than Kennedy, but then I would fear Keefe's mother even more.

For a long time, earlier that evening, Draves had stared out the window of his hotel room at the Manhattan street far below. Finally, cradling his left hand against his chest, he picked up his pen and wrote: "Dear Sam: It used to chafe me when our school marm put a mitten on my left paw and forced me to write with my right one, but now I'm grateful. If I had not learned to write right-handed, I wouldn't be able to pen this to you tonight..."

He paused then, his left hand throbbing, to look out the window again. Through a miasma of pain—as yet the injury was too fresh for him to feel depression too—he watched the Manhattan sky slowly begin to darken. He was perpetually cold, as if he sat there naked on a cake of ice. The coldness had started some two hours ago when Snyder had begged permission from Jim Mutrie, the Metropolitans manager, for a substitute after being struck in the throat by a foul tip in the eighth inning. Instantly he seemed to know that White's bespectacled eyes would look down the bench, pass over Peoples, and then come to dwell on him. Even in the late-afternoon New York heat the chill had crept through his pores with each word White uttered.

"All right, Draves, you claim you can catch if the club is strapped. So get in there and show what you're made of."

Dear God, he could not confess now that he'd never gone behind the bat in his life. And besides, it was a chance at last to prove himself even if the cause was hopeless. So he sprang to his feet, borrowed Snyder's mask and chest protector, and sought Umpire Kelly to announce himself into the game. After getting the signals set with Deagle, he then went behind the plate and crouched down with a pounding heart. The hot sun shining through the wire mask made the blood thrum in his head. He closed his eyes for a moment and then opened them. The tips White had given Deagle before the game on how to pitch to each of the Mets drifted into his memory as he looked up at the man who stood at the plate. He saw a sallow mustached face that returned his gaze as if trying to probe the recesses of his mind.

Esterbrook, the third baseman and among the Association's leading hitters. He glanced away nervously. From the diamond field he heard a few polite words of encouragement to him from McPhee. Then he was suddenly aware of Kelly behind him calling for play to resume. He repressed a shiver. The isolation of command was like a cloak of ice on his shoulders. Deagle would not deliver the ball up to Esterbrook until he gave the signal.

A traitorous wave of emotion took him unexpectedly, turning the muscles in his knees to water and

Cincinnatis		R	1B	PO	A	E
Mansell	l.f.	0	0	2	0	0
Jones	c.f.	1	1	3	3	0
Reilly	1b	1	0	10	0	0
McPhee	2b	0	1	1	4	5
Corkhill	r.f.	0	1	3	0	0
Snyder	c	0	0	3	1	0
Woulfe	3b	0	0	1	3	1
Fulmer	s.s.	0	0	1	1	6
Deagle	p	0	0	0	2	5
Totals		2	3	24	13	17

Mets		R	1B	PO	A	E
Nelson	s.s.	2	2	2	6	0
Brady	r.f.	1	4	0	0	0
Esterbrook	3b	2	1	1	1	2
Roseman	c.f.	1	0	0	0	0
Orr	1b	2	3	13	0	0
Troy	2b	4	3	2	2	2
Reiff	c	2	3	3	3	2
Holbert	c	0	0	2	0	0
Kennedy	l.f.	3	0	3	0	0
Lynch	p	2	2	1	1	1
Totals		19	18	27	14	7

Innings	1	2	3	4	5	6	7	8	9
Cincinnati	2	0	0	0	0	0	0	0	0—2
Metropolitan	0	2	0	4	3	2	1	7	x—19

Runs earned— Cincinnatis 0, Metropolitans 4. First base on errors— Cincinnatis 4, Metropolitans 9. First base on balls— Cincinnatis 1, Metropolitans 5. Struck out— Cincinnatis 4, Metropolitans 0. Two-base hits— Troy 2, Lynch, Orr, Esterbrook. Passed balls— Reiff 2, Snyder 2. Wild pitches— Lynch 1, Deagle 4. Time of game— Two hours and twenty-five minutes. Umpire— Kelly.

causing him to rise out of his crouch.

It was several moments before he was able to stoop behind Esterbrook again.

Why could he not calm himself? Surely he had no good reason for being so wrought up. With the Mets already ahead by 15 runs, the game was decided.

Still, a foreboding of catastrophe filled him like a dark cloud.

The first pitch to Esterbrook was a wide, but on the next Dude hit a foul tip that might have skulled him if he hadn't ducked his head just in the nick of time.

Immediately, Mutrie jumped up from the Mets bench and bellowed, "Hey, look at the ducker! Who's the new ducker you have out there, White? Hey, hey, Ducker!"

The crowd took up Mutrie's cry at once. Voices chanting "Hey, hey, Ducker" seemed to boom from everywhere in the park. To add injury to insult, Deagle crossed him up on the next pitch, throwing a curve in the dirt when he'd ordered up a fast one, and he had to stick out his bare hand to stop the ball from bouncing past him.

It smashed into his forefinger, making the whole member instantaneously begin to swell and ache. As he stood shaking it and fighting back tears, someone in the throng behind the backstop hollered, "Lookie, Ducker got a stinger on his finger! Ducker got a stinger! Ducker got a stinger!"

He felt the words like a slap in the face. Turning in spite of himself, he looked through the wire mask into the mire of faces in the grandstand and saw none. He was about to pull his head back around when his eye caught—or seemed to catch—a glimpse of a red-haired boy grinning at him. A sudden pang of apprehension came and went. He gave his finger another shake and heard again: "Ducker got a stinger!"

His face tightening under the bitter memory, he resumed his letter, determined to finish it this time. *Ducker got a stinger*

"Over and over I heard that refrain, Sam, until everyone in the park seemed to be singing it. Somehow I barricaded my ears and lasted the inning although by the end of it I had to toss the ball back to Deagle underhanded since I no longer could use my forefinger. It had ballooned up by then to twice its normal size.

"It was both my good luck and my bad luck that I didn't come to bat in our last turn. If I had, Sam, I could not possibly have held the stick firmly enough to make a hit and fulfill my pledge to you. But because I played only in the field, my name will never appear in the box score. Hence in a few weeks, when everyone else has forgotten how I came by this dreadful new nickname, it will have become only our secret that I played today.

Your nephew, Earl.

June 7

The crowning blow! White finally awoke today to the folly of using Fulmer and sent Corkhill out to play short stop against the Brooklyns. The move bolstered us there. How could it not, dear Diary? But it weakened us in right field where Woulfe, Corkhill's replacement, can't begin to carry his glove. Hence we wound up losing 3-2 on Woulfe's error in the 10th inning to an outfit that only yesterday was trounced by the Shetzline-Myers amateur team from Trenton, New Jersey.

On the carriage ride across the Brooklyn Bridge and back to our hotel after the game, White chewed out everybody aboard. He even jumped on me, complaining I'd hindered him in his warm-up before the game because I used only one hand to catch his pitches and so had to waste time chasing the balls I missed. When I reminded him that I was hampered by a bum finger, he said: "Well, if you can't help out even in warm-ups, why are we paying your keep? Maybe we should send you home, Ducker, until your finger is again as nimble as your tongue." Some of the other boys laughed at his feeble slice of wit, but as for myself, when he said "Ducker" my whole face froze. To think I could once have loathed being called Early!

I would gladly tolerate Early for the rest of my life if I could just make all those who witnessed my Waterloo the other day erase their memories of it. Must I forever be punished because I didn't stand dead still like a wooden Indian and let Esterbrook's foul tip smite me in the head? Jones, the lone man who's been at all consoling, told me it was just my hard luck that the foul I ducked followed so closely on the heels of the one that felled Snyder. In the crowd's glee at the way the home nine was piling up the score, the second incident fed upon the first.

What a wicked chain of events. Even if I one day live down this abominable sobriquet, how can I stop feeling I brought it on myself and lost what could have been my golden opportunity? If I had not volunteered to go behind the bat in my hunger to play in a championship game, White would never have called on me to substitute when Snyder was injured. And if I were not bunged-up now myself, undoubtedly I would have been in there at short stop this afternoon.

But such is life, dear Diary.

And so I sit here alone now every night in my hotel room alternating between soaking my finger and telling you my thoughts. But lest anyone think that I can't find humor in my predicament, I just held my hurt finger up to the mirror over the washbasin and laughed at the sight. It's the size and color of a leech that has just finished gorging itself on a cow. Fortunately I can still practice diversions like this to keep from getting too low. Let it never be said that I am one to stoop to feeling sorry for myself.

June 10

This evening White sent a message to my hotel room, dear Diary, bidding me to report to his. No sooner had I obeyed than he said he'd just gotten a telephone call from Stern instructing him to release me and furnish me with return train fare to Cincinnati. After my finger is healed, Stern had further said, there'll be a job awaiting me with the club as an assistant grounds keeper. In between my duties at American Park I can play for one of the local amateur teams on the chance the Red Stockings might need me later in the season. Although I shouldn't count on that, White hastened to add. He said: "For the rest of the campaign we're going with Peoples at short stop, beginning Thursday when we open our series with the Alleghenys. I know how this makes you feel, but think what Fulmer is feeling, relegated to the bench after so many years in the limelight. You at least have the majority of your career ahead of you, provided you work the rawness out of your throwing."

Actually, I'd been prepared for the worst ever since the mishap last night that aggravated my injured finger. While the boys sharing my hotel room were out pressing brick, I was in bed asleep. Suddenly a sound woke me. Sitting up I heard no more, but I observed the door to the room was enough ajar to let in a bar of light from the hallway. I listened to my own tense breathing while my eyes combed the room. At the foot of the bed where Mountjoy and Peoples sleep I saw a crouched figure. Instantly I leapt to my feet and raced out the door and then held it fast so the intruder could not escape. I felt something push against the other side of the door but without the strength to overcome mine. Soon the pushing ceased and I heard a faint whimpering and then a sound of a body falling to the floor. When I opened the door and peered into the room, I saw a figure lying on the carpet. Momentarily I realized it was a woman. Even as I identified her sex she emitted a groan. "Where am I?" said she, rising out of her swoon on one elbow. "You're in my room," I said. "Oh, Lordie!" she cried and gave another groan. "I done it again." She then sat up all the way, allowing me to glimpse her face. She was young and not at all bad-looking. When she extended a hand to me, I aided her to her feet.

Once upright she staggered over to my bed and fell across it. To my consternation she began weeping. "What's to become of me?" she said through her sobs. "I've tried everything, but I can't control myself

once sleep comes over me. See, I suffer from what doctors call
somnambulism. Know what that is?" When I allowed I didn't, she said:
"The lay word for it is sleep-walking. I must've risen from my own bed
and then roved the hotel unconscious till I wandered into your room.
You are right to treat me as a thief by barring the door so I couldn't get
out. But you also did me the favor of jolting me awake. Now if you'll
kindly accept my embarrassed apology for disrupting your sleep, sir, I'll
return to my room and barricade the door to prevent another lapse
tonight."

      With that she sprang up from my bed. As she made for the door
I noted she was garbed not for sleep but in diurnal attire, and something
else struck me. Grabbing the sleeve of her dress, I said: "One moment,
miss. How could you have entered my room accidentally when the door
was locked?" "Leave go of me," said she and commenced to struggle.
"I'll scream if you don't," she hissed. And I said: "Please do. I'll
welcome the audience it will bring." Hearing that, she gave a violent
wrench that left a piece of her dress in my hand and made my maimed
finger feel as if it had been torn out of its socket. I saw stars, dear Diary,
and by the time my vision cleared she was out the door and down the
hallway.

      Before I came fully to my senses, she had gotten a good start on
me. I chased after her, but by then she was too far away. She sped
down the fire stairway with me too far behind to do more than shout for
someone below to stop her. No one did, but our din drew a hotel
detective. When he'd heard me out and certified that nothing was
missing from my room, he said the presumption still must be that I'd
been the prey of a hotel thief. I wanted only to retire and soak my
finger, but he insisted the police be summoned. Two officers came in a
patrol wagon, took my story and then bade me to accompany them to the
station. There I was closeted with an Inspector Byrnes, who had me
examine a packet of photographs until I lit upon one that resembled my
transgressor. "Ah, Little Annie Reilly," said he. "You're lucky, friend,
she didn't pick you clean." He then told me Reilly had a record of hotel
thefts as long as my arm, at which he glanced in speaking. "What's
wrong with your hand?" he said upon seeing I was cradling it in the
other. When I explained my encounter with Reilly had re-injured the
finger I'd hurt in a base ball game the other day, a look of dawning
crossed his beefy features and he said: "I was there! I was at that game!
Oh, saints preserve us, you're the Ducker!"

      It caught me like a shove from the rear. My left hand doubled
reflexively into a fist inside its protective cocoon, but I relaxed it when I
remembered Byrnes's official position. I was actually able to talk civilly
with him a while about base ball once my shock wore away and might

have remained there longer had my finger not begun throbbing a blue streak.

By the time I got back to the hotel it was swollen the size of a banana. Woulfe, who had returned in my absence, begged me to show it to White when he had taken a horrified gander at it. Our captain came to the door of his room in his nightshirt. Beyond him I could see McPhee splashing water on his face and Snyder putting his teeth in a glass. Their beds had not been turned down yet, however, though it was past midnight. Sensing my curiosity, White said: "We're up burning the night oil over the deepest puzzle in the universe. Why, if the earth

ANNIE REILLY
alias
LITTLE ANNIE

alias Katie Cooley
alias Kate Connelly
alias Kate Manning

DISHONEST
SERVANT

DESCRIPTION.

Forty-two years old in 1886 ; looks younger. Born in Ireland. Married. Medium build. Servant and child's nurse. Height, 5 feet 1 inch. Weight, 113 pounds. Brown hair, gray eyes, fair complexion. Round, full face. Speaks two or three languages.

RECORD.

"Little Annie Reilly" is considered the cleverest woman in her line in America. She generally engages herself as a child's nurse, makes a great fuss over the children, and gains the good-will of the lady of the house. She seldom remains in one place more than one or two days before she robs it, generally taking jewelry, amounting at times to four and five thousand dollars. She is well known in all the principal Eastern cities, especially in New York, Brooklyn, and Philadelphia, Pa.

Annie was arrested in New York City, for grand larceny, on complaint of Mrs. A. G. Dunn, No. 149 East Eighty-fourth Street, and others, and committed for trial, in default of $6,500 bail, by Judge Ledwith. She was convicted, and sentenced to four years and six months in State prison, by Judge Sutherland, in the Court of General Sessions in New York, on April 23, 1873, under the name of Kate Connelly.

She was arrested again in New York City, on August 3, 1880, for robbing the house of Mrs. Evangeline Swartz, on Second Avenue, New York. She was convicted of this robbery, and sentenced to three years in the penitentiary on Blackwell's Island, on September 8, 1880, by Judge Gildersleeve, under the name of Kate Cooley. After her release, in January, 1883, she did considerable work in and around New York. She robbed the guests of the New York Hotel of $3,500 worth of jewelry, etc., while employed there as a servant.

This woman is well worth knowing. She has stolen more property the last fifteen years than any other four women in America.

is round, do some not fall off it every day? What's your theory, Ducker?" I said, ignoring the name-calling, that I had sustained a further injury to my finger. "What the devil," said White, donning his spectacles to inspect it. "It looks broken now." I said that it well may be, but the fracture had not occurred tonight. White ardently disagreed. Upon hearing my story of the fracas with the Reilly woman, he said it was a shame coming on top of my other damage, but the club could not be held culpable for the lax security in this hotel. He then said he would contact Caylor in the morning to learn what course the club wished to pursue and ordered me to return to my room and remain there the next day rather than travel to Brooklyn with the team. "With the harm your finger seems magnetically to attract," he said, "we won't want to situate you anywhere you might experience yet another injury."

By that point, dear Diary, I'd already seen the handwriting on the wall, but White's news this evening was still a hard blow. I remain undaunted, still having my youth and most of my health. Wither, however, will I go from here? Certainly I cannot become a assistant grounds keeper at the very park where I once dreamt of carving my name in the earth at short stop.

Portsmouth, O., June 15
Dear Sam:

I meant to write you Thursday as soon as I got here so you'd know where to reach me now. But then I decided to wait and gather all the pieces of my crumbled dreams into one letter before I begged your help in putting them back together.

Have you penned me lately, Sam? If so, nobody in the Red Stockings' organization forwarded your epistle to me, which is no more than I expect now that the club has washed its hands of me forever. The boys on the colts at least got a promise from Stern that he'd try to place them with other clubs while I have been cast out of the fold like a leper and all because I stood up on my hind legs and told him I thought it criminal to release a man when he's disabled. He accused me of gross exaggeration. My injury was only a minor inconvenience, he said. In a few weeks my finger would be as good as new and I'd then be free to auction my services wherever I chose. Meanwhile the Red Stockings could ill afford to keep paying a man who was unable to work. Surely I must see, he said, that in that respect base ball, even if a sport, must operate like a business.

All I saw, I said, was I had never once received a chance to show my skill at short stop in a championship game, and those were my parting words to Stern, Sam. In my mind though, I added: "Someday you will be sorry for what you've done."

To be wholly fair, however, I must note that the club did arrange for me to visit a Dr. Loft in Cincinnati at its expense when I got back from New York. Loft confirmed my fear that the finger was broken and said that since it had already begun to heal on its own without being properly set, it might never regain its normal alignment. I should recover the use of it in short order though, he placated. The only unpleasantry was it might always be a tad crooked. To combat the pain I'd have for the next few days, Loft gave me some pills, one of which I took in his office while he straightened my finger as best he could and put a proper splint on it.

All in all, the finger doesn't feel too bad at the moment, Sam. Meanwhile I've put out feelers to the Riversides and Mr. Hampshire at the store, and both are ready to welcome me back should I choose to pick up where I left off here in Portsmouth. To them I've said the only stumbling block is my finger, which will keep me from swinging a bat or doing any physical labor at the store for a while yet. To you, however, I will reveal there's another reason why I've been wavering ever since my homecoming—and, the fact is, I think I just hit upon the problem myself.

Sam, when I wrote homecoming just now it seemed the most natural thing in the world to say until I found myself at a loss what my next words would be. Then I read what I'd just written aloud to myself and I realized what was impeding my pen. The other evening didn't feel at all like a homecoming, Sam, and nothing since has either. What the past few days have felt like I can't quite say, except that I feel nearly as strange here as I did all those nights in New York. Cincinnati felt more like home to me, or anyway it did until I saw Stern and the doctor and then paid my last board bill and cleared my belongings from my room. After that Cincinnati felt like a place I never wanted to see again.

I'm going all around the mulberry bush. What I'm mustering myself to say is it feels like there's something spoiled in me now after my sojourn with the Red Stockings. Or, if not spoiled, then it's something I've been cheated out of.

I don't know what it is, Sam, but I do know what it is not. It is definitely not my dream of playing short stop for the Cincinnati Red Stockings. I would never play for that bunch again if they were the last team on earth.

If that grieves you irreparably, so be it. I hope, however, that even as you read this you are expressing your accord with my desire to dissolve all bonds to the Red Stockings after the way they treated me and will soon favor me with a letter saying so now that you know where to reach me.

Or if you're thinking it's high time I trekked to Blue Creek so we could talk man to man, I may soon surprise you, perhaps even this weekend.

Your nephew, Earl.

Louisville, Ky., June 21

Dear Sam:

I beg your forgiveness for not visiting you as pledged, but your reply to my letter of the 15th arrived just as I was about to depart for Blue Creek. Once I read it I felt too heart-sore to see you just now.

Sam, you are right to be outraged over my failure to win the Red Stockings' short stop post, but how can you tell me to swallow my pride and accept Stern's offer of a job as an assistant grounds keeper? Doing that would not be a matter of swallowing my pride. It would mean murdering it.

Knowing we would disagree and wound each other still more, I deemed it best not to see you before I left Portsmouth. I dared not even write for fear that in my mind I would see your anguished face as I framed the words informing you of my decision to come to Louisville.

Sam, you mustn't feel I've deserted you. I pray you'll write to tell me you don't and meanwhile I'll keep writing to you as if all is still the same between us even though I fear it is not. Although I will always be bonded to you as my guardian and only living relative, I can never again feel allied with you in your dream.

From now on I must pursue my own dream, which is to win a place on the Louisvilles so I can be in their lineup when the Red Stockings visit the Falls City next month. There can be no sweeter revenge than to play against the Red Stockings in the uniform of their archrival. I have already spoken to Gerhardt and he's agreed to give me a test at short stop as soon as my finger mends. Everyone here, he confided, is growing disenchanted with McLaughlin's light stick work.

For the time being I'm residing at 1427 West Jefferson Street. When you write to me here, please put "In care of Browning" on the envelope.

If the name rings a bell, Sam, well it should. I'm dwelling with Pete Browning and his mother and sister Fannie. He was taking batting practice when I went to Eclipse Park yesterday seeking Gerhardt, and to my pleasure he remembered me from the two games I played here with the Red Stockings colts. He even recalled my last name although he thought my first name was Early because that was what the boys on the colts were calling me then. I let the misnomer stand. Browning and everyone else here can call me whatever they wish just so it isn't Ducker.

Happily, nobody in Louisville knows about the Ducker incident and I aim to keep it that way. When Gerhardt asked why my finger was in a splint I said I caught it in a door. By then we had moved from the field to a chamber under the grandstand where several kegs of beer were stored. Gerhardt himself owns the park's suds concession and sprang the tap on one of the kegs. Then he filled mugs for both Browning and me and left us for business he had elsewhere.

Being alone with Pete Browning made me uneasy at first, Sam, as conversation with him is awkward because he misses most of what you say. Last night I learned the reason for this is he had ear surgery recently and still isn't healed. But at first his aloofness made me think I'd put him off. Imagine my astonishment when he suddenly invited me to sup that evening at his home! I accepted with some reservation, but it vanished once I met his mother. She is such a friendly, forthright woman that I took an instant shine to her, and the feeling evidently was mutual. Upon learning I was staying in a hotel, she said there was a vacant room in her house now that her eldest son had married. Would I care to rent it? I thought would I ever! But I managed to allow a full second to elapse before I said yes.

I'm paying Mrs. Browning $6 per week, Sam, which is 50¢ more than my room in Cincinnati cost. But here I'm also getting full board and an opportunity to observe the greatest hitter in the game intimately. The boys on the Red Stockings think Browning isn't altogether there. His odd conversational lapses are part of the reason, but they're the smallest part. Even not overly self-effacing men like Jones think it's the ultimate in puffery the way Browning records his batting average on his shirt cuff, recalculating it after each game. And everybody thinks it's plain loco that he has half a hundred bats and assigns Biblical names to his favorites. Then there are his shaggy eyebrows that he refuses to trim, claiming the Lord designed them that way to protect his lamps. That's his word for eyes, Sam, and he stands for several minutes each morning staring directly into the sun to replenish his lamps with its strength. Myself, I don't find Browning crazy so much as eccentric. He's far and away the most superstitious man I've ever met. Before setting himself in the batter's box, he never fails to touch all four points on home plate with his bat. Asked why he does it, he'll only say he must. But most of his superstitions concern his lamps. Along with making sure they get plenty of sunlight, he feels jinxed whenever he sees someone with eye trouble. Knowing this, Caylor hired a man with a patch over an eye to follow Browning into a saloon on Vine Street one night last year and sit beside him. Caylor hoped the encounter would cause Browning to go hitless the next day, and it did. When Caylor tried the same ploy down in Louisville, however, Browning escaped the hex by blindfolding himself.

To me, though, Browning's strangest feature of all is his habit of always referring to himself in the third person. Last night, as his mother and sister were clearing away the supper dishes, he said: "Well, he and Early are going out for a breath of air." When we'd gained the street he said: "Old Pete's tonsils sure could do with a drop of oil." And after we were seated in his favorite neighborhood haunt: "Now that we're free of the women folk, you and Old Pete can talk shop."

With that, Sam, Browning held forth for two solid hours last night about the art of hitting a base ball, and the whole time it was as if I were no longer there. He was his own audience, interrogating himself on the nuances of batting and then answering with comments like: "A really shrewd batsman will deliberately make out sometimes on a ball he could ordinarily powder to kingdom come just to fool a pitcher into believing he's found a weakness," or: "Old Pete still has to learn to get his hips out of the way faster when he swings on them inside pitches."

Naturally the longer he talked the more oil his tonsils required, until he began to lose his train of thought. Sensing this, he pulled on his mustache and muttered: "Old Pete's got to remember there's a game to play tomorrow."

He then ordered another libation. He was on his ninth, Sam, when I left. Watching the Association's most lionized hitter sink into his cups was a blue ending to what previously had been a red-letter day, and I worried what his mother would think of me for accompanying him on his toot even if mainly as spectator. This morning when I went to the Browning house with my carpetbag, sure enough, she met me at the door with a stern face and then steered me to the front room, where she said she hoped her intuition about me was correct and I didn't suffer from the same malady as her son. When I averred that it was and apologized for my role in last night's dissipation, she said: "Well, I must remember that you're still new to Louis's ways. I reckon you couldn't have known that he can't stop once he starts."

Louis is Browning's true first name, Sam, but only his family calls him that. Her eyes misting a little, Mrs. Browning said: "The wonder is that he won't touch a drop of spirits all winter. He conditions himself by ice skating and chopping wood and retiring early each night, but come base ball season all his resolve flees." Then, dropping her voice, she said: "Louis is still dead to the world, but my daughter's in the kitchen making breakfast. Should she hear me say this she'd be very upset. She's against your living here, you see, because she thinks base ball is the root of Louis's trouble. I believe otherwise, Mr. Draves. I believe it's the best thing in his life, and from what you said last night about why you came to Louisville, I'd say it has the same magical hold on you. Your presence here, then, may actually have a healthy effect on

Louis. In any event, I'd still like you to stay, although I'll forewarn you that my daughter won't make you feel welcome."

Hers was an understatement. At breakfast Fannie looked daggers at me the whole meal. But Pete was still too bleary to notice. This afternoon, on the trolley ride to the ball park, he said: "Well, what do you think of Old Pete's sister? Ain't she a hummer?" The truth is she's rather plain, but I said tactfully that she was indeed a hummer and then, to nip in the bud any ideas Browning harbored when I saw him grinning at me, I said: "But I've learned base ball and girls are like oil and water, inclining me to have nothing to do with them for now."

I meant it too, Sam, lest you think my desire to play for the Louisvilles is at all linked to that chorus girl I met here back in April. So much water has since gone over the dam that I hardly recall her name—and that's the gospel truth.

Browning and I got to Eclipse Park at two thirty, an hour and a half before the game was slated to start and ample time for me to nab a seat high up in the stands behind first base. I sat there so as to be as far as possible from the visitors' bench, which is on the third base side of the field here. What caused my wariness was the Mets being in town now and the fear that if they saw me again so soon some of them might be reminded of the Ducker incident. Next time the New Yorkers come to town, I'll be wearing a Louisville uniform and chances are they'll no longer recognize me. But even if they do I'll have a new nickname by then: Easy Earl, with any luck.

The game almost didn't come off today because Valentine missed his train to Louisville and it was too late to round up another qualified umpire. A rumor buzzed through the stands that the two clubs would play an exhibition contest, but the cranks weren't about to sit still for that. They howled that they'd paid their good money to see a championship match. Finally Mutrie hit upon a solution. He made it known his Mets were ready to play a game that would count in the standings, but only if he could choose the umpire. When Gerhardt consented, Mutrie then designated Keefe to officiate since Tim had the day off anyway because Lynch was due to pitch.

Gerhardt realized right away that he'd stepped into one, as did the crowd. By the end of the first inning they were already calling Keefe a robber and all the other usual insults, most of them prefaced by that F word. From my perch, though, it didn't look like Keefe was doing anything too reprehensible. I'll allow he wasn't much good at the job, but leastwise he doled out his horrendous calls so evenly that the game was tied 2-all at the end of regulation length.

The Mets nicked Hecker for two runs in the eleventh frame, but Louisville awoke in the bottom half, filling the bases with two out. Then

Brady broke our hearts, nabbing Dan Sullivan's foul fly to deep right field on the first bounce to retire him on a ball that would have plated the tying runs if it had landed fair.

In my next letter, Sam, I'll enclose the report of the game from tomorrow's *Courier-Journal*, plus its reports of Louisville's other two games with the Mets. They will prove to you that the Falls City is just as gone on base ball as Cincinnati. The entire town is on Cloud Nine at the moment. Even despite today's loss all the cranks here remain supremely confident that their boys will win the pennant. That kind of civic pride gives me a warm glow inside, knowing I'll be part of it once my finger heals. And it would be grand too if I could also feel by then that I'm here with your blessing.

Your nephew, Earl.

June 25

I just checked downstairs again in vain. The Brownings get two mail deliveries a day, so maybe there'll be something for me this afternoon or else tomorrow. But failing that, dear Diary, Sam will surely write once he reads my latest letter—if only to say he could have told me so!

Yes, it looks like I counted my chickens before they were hatched. The Louisvilles trounced the Mets 10-2 on Monday and 6-1 yesterday to take over first place, and now Gerhardt is hedging on his promise to test me when my finger is healed. Not only is he loath to break up a winning lineup, he says, but McLaughlin is suddenly doing a capable job at short stop. In Tuesday's paper McLaughlin was actually lauded for his outstanding fielding the previous day although I didn't see anything to praise. And besides, the game was so one-sided there was no pressure on him. Lynch, after being virtually unhittable on Sunday, had no steam at all on the ball. Afterward Jack told the scribes he'd been dosed by gamblers the night before and woke up on Monday morning with his nerves so unstrung that he was hardly able to shave his beak, let alone pitch. But he had to work as Keefe had a sore arm.

Yesterday Keefe's wing must still have been ailing because even McLaughlin hit a couple of loud fouls off him. In God's truth, the way the Mets are playing a grandmother would look like a world-beater against them. The New Yorkers hold second place now just a few percentage points behind the Louisvilles, but by the time they end their western swing they'll be down about sixth. It couldn't happen to a nicer bunch if they finished in the cellar behind even the Washingtons. The Mutriemen seem to think just because they represent the nation's largest city they should be universally beloved. In their greed for affection yesterday they resorted to the old "Bouquet" racket. Before the game

Esterbrook was given a gift-wrapped gold watch, and the local cranks cheered him, thinking he'd received the timepiece from the cranks in New York as a token of their admiration and all the Mets must be immensely popular. But Hecker recognized the watch as the one Keefe wore the day he umpired! What the Mets likely will do is wait a few days and then present Keefe's watch to another of their boys in St. Louis or Toledo.

At any event, they've become my nemesis, pinning the Ducker tail on me along with a broken finger and now allowing McLaughlin to save his job. There is more news too that will make Sam crow. When the Red Stockings played the Alleghenys on Monday in Cincinnati, who was back at short stop for them but Fulmer—and less than a fortnight after White said Peoples had the job for the rest of the season! The sharps here are saying the Red Stockings are already so down on Peoples they're dickering to buy a veteran short stop from one of the other American clubs. Yesterday at Eclipse Park I approached John Haldeman and asked him what he knew of this rumor. Haldeman is the sports-editor of the *Courier-Journal* and the Louisvilles' official scorer, but I couldn't have made a poorer choice. Firstly, he had no information to shed, said he, about the doings in the Red Stockings' camp. Then several of the Louisvilles glowered at me when they saw me talking to him, and Whiting actually spat on my boots. This afternoon Cline told me to be thankful Whiting hadn't pissed on them. He said none of the boys here will give Haldeman the time of day because he was the one who opened the can of worms that launched the infamous "Louisville Scandal" back in '77. Suspicious that some of the boys were in cahoots with gamblers to dump games, he kept putting a bug in the ear of Chase, then the owner, until Chase was finally persuaded to look into the matter. Chase's probe revealed that Hall, Devlin, Craver and Nichols had been bribed to swing the pennant to Boston. Furthermore, it got all four players barred for life and Louisville booted out of the National League. Cline said the boys will never forgive Haldeman. They feel he should have kept his trap shut and let the League weed the bad apples out of the barrel on the q.t. rather than forcing it to rebuke them publicly and penalize all of Louisville. "If not for Haldeman," Cline said, "we'd still be in the League, and no matter what the boys say, Draves, that's where every man with sense wants to play. Their parks are bigger, their crowds are bigger and then you don't see their clubs resorting to taking on jigaboos."

Now you know, dear Diary, the boys on the Red Stockings don't feel that way about the League. They're all happy as not it ejected the Red Stockings four years ago and forced them to start a whole new federation so they could legally sell beer in their park and play on

Sundays. And they don't give a hoot what color a man's skin is if he can help the team although all other things being equal they'd prefer it was white. But the Louisvilles are a horse of a different breed. The only ones who don't think they're still fighting the Civil War down here are Browning and Maskrey and maybe Hecker. Browning says he can't feature playing in a park that won't sell a man the proper beverage to wet his whistle while he's watching a game. Maskrey thinks there'll soon come a day when there are coons on every team and Dagos and Hunkies and Sheenys too. If base ball wants to keep calling itself the National Pastime, he maintains, it will eventually have to open its doors to every man-jack in the country. Leech Maskrey in his way is as strange a duck as Browning. He spends his winters concocting oil paintings, and when the club is on the road he remains in his hotel room every night absorbing the Classics. Yet he is not above reading dime novels too. The other afternoon, seeing a Deadeye Dick in my hand while he and I and Browning were waiting outside the park for a trolley, he offered to swap me a Nick Carter for it when I was done. And during our ride out Magazine Street, having perceived our common interest in the written word, he led me to talk about myself at a depth no base ball personage has ever done. With my aptitude I ought to consider attending a university, he said. A high school education is no longer sufficient to get ahead now that the world is changing so swiftly. It will soon require every waking hour in the day, he forecasts, just to keep abreast of all the new-fangled developments.

Maskrey, even more than Browning, is the man I most wish to befriend on the Louisvilles as Hecker is the man I would most want on my side. Guy Hecker is the complete base ball player. His arm must be iron, the way he was able to pitch all three games versus the Mets, plus he is second on the club in hitting only to Browning. In the late `70s he had numerous offers from League teams but stayed an amateur until the Association formed. His wife was against his turning professional, he says, while offering no explanation for her change of heart. She's back in Pennsylvania training for a domino tournament and will remain there for the rest of the season, he says, while providing no comment either on their estrangement.

Hecker is something of a mystery to all the boys here, but at least he acknowledges their existence. Me he won't even give the time of day. The other afternoon he said to Browning: "Who's this kid that keeps following you around stage-dooring?" I could have taken the wind out of Hecker's sails by telling him that this kid he failed to recognize had smacked three hits off him in a practice game barely two months ago. But I held my water, thinking I'd soon enough get the chance to let my bat and glove do all the talking necessary to reacquaint us.

Now that it appears I won't I do feel like I'm stage-dooring. Maskrey speaks to me because I can reply in words of more than one syllable, but all the rest of the boys treat me like dust under their feet. It serves you right, Sam would say now, because you don't belong down there, Earl.

Well, that may be, but I'm still sticking by everything I put in words to him. I've made my bed here, for better or worse, and now I'm going to have to lie in it.

Like many men of his day who had the privilege of a college education, Samuel Leech Maskrey planned to become a teacher. He was careful never to own up to this ambition when he first began playing base ball for money; he feared ridicule. Not until he was in his late twenties and had established himself as a regular with the Louisvilles did he gradually permit his secret self to emerge. None of this altered how as a youth in Illinois he had wanted only to be left alone to paint watercolors of the landscape around his family home. Not even his younger brother Harry was ever taken completely into his confidence. It was not just that Maskrey sensed he was different from other men. It was more that he feared he would grow ashamed of his difference if he ever tried to explain it to anyone. Maskrey assumed his life would be spent mostly in seclusion even while he taught, as he would need to in order to support his artistic bent.

But one day on a base ball field he realized how akin he was to other boys in one vital respect. He still had no thought of making a profession of the game, even temporarily, but as this flirtation with base ball went on—Maskrey hardly knew how—he grew more and more apprehensive that he would sooner or later inevitably reveal his distance from his teammates. Only on the playing field it seemed could he hide his true self. Among men united each day in the same common purpose—winning—he would find sanctuary. Who could know too but what the experience might enable him to develop another side to himself? Maskrey, in part because of the anxiety that constantly besieged him, never became the player he might have been. But he did grow enough in confidence to spend his winters openly earning commissions from his watercolors, and in the meantime he swallowed the icicle of terror that rose in his throat each time a teammate called him by the nickname that had first been saddled on him when he was ten or twelve…*Mask.*

June 28

It now looks as if my perseverance will pay off after all. The Louisvilles played abominably today against the Washingtons, making 11 errors behind Driscoll to blow a game they should have stuffed into their hip pockets. Save for Hecker, who had the day off, the whole team had to share in the ignominy of losing to the circuit's tailender, but McLaughlin bore the brunt of it. He kicked away so many rollers that eventually I stopped counting and just sat back and relished the massacre. My seat was near enough to the field that I could read Gerhardt's lips each time he had to race over from his second-base post and retrieve a ball McLaughlin had booted. The first couple of times he said things like "Buck up, Tommy." But by the end of the afternoon he was calling McLaughlin that F word that begins with mother.

The reason I had such a prized seat is because Bud Hillerich, a friend of Browning's, had an extra ticket and invited me to sit with him after Pete introduced us. Hillerich and his father own a wood shop here in town where they make butter churns, wagon tongues and whatnot. A few weeks ago Bud agreed to make a bat for Browning, designed to Pete's specifications, and now he has a contract to make all of Pete's bats. He offered to carve one for me too, a replica of Lazerus, the stick Pete summons whenever he gets in a slump, after he learned I was idled at the moment by an injury. Hillerich laughingly said he'd make the bat for free if I promised to get a hit the first time I used it and then tell the world who'd manufactured it.

In all, dear Diary, it was a grand afternoon and the evening was no slouch either. After the game Hillerich treated Browning and me to supper at a place on Market Street where we ran into several of the other boys out putting on the feedbag. About eight o'clock Hillerich asked Browning to go to his shop so he could show Pete a new species of bat he'd lathed just this morning. They invited me to go along, but by then I'd struck up a conversation with Sullivan and Juice Latham and they were telling me I ought to brown up to John and Phil Reccius if I really wanted to catch on with the Louisvilles. The Recciuses weren't much as players, but their older brother Bill, who owns a piece of the club, carries a lot of weight with the other owners. More than that, he wasn't too enamored of McLaughlin—or Gerhardt either, for that matter. Now that pitchers had begun throwing sidearm they both looked pretty anemic at the dish. Latham admitted to having his troubles too. "If the Americans ever do like the League and allow twirlers to dish `em up overhand, we'll all be skewered," he said. "This Sweeney of the Providences that struck out 19 men the other day would kill you if his fastball ever hit you in the bean. And in the League an umpire still won't even give you your base if you're skulled."

It was tempting to go off with Hillerich and Browning, knowing that Sully and Juice mightn't be so friendly toward me after they left. But I had to take the risk since it felt like I'd been riding a winning horse the entire day. The lone disappointment I'd had was the two occasions when the postman came.

Sam's silence may persist once I write him about the turn events took tonight, but that's a further risk I must take. I can't restrict my reports to him solely to my diamond doings now that there is suddenly another side to my life again.

While I was still at the restaurant with Sullivan and Latham, Whiting and Jimmy Wolf joined us and then we all went around the corner to a saloon called the Kentuckian that had a band and, since it was Saturday night, a special stage show. There were two tenors on the bill, neither of them worth a rap, but then, after a brief intermission, a dark-haired woman in a red velvet dress came out of the wings and began singing with only a piano for accompaniment. Her handle, according to the program, was Zena Withers, but the instant I heard her voice I knew it was Constance. She'd changed her name for some reason and was wearing her hair differently, cascading down over her shoulders. But her voice could not be disguised. It had the same sweet lilt that was like no other I'd ever heard. She sang "I'll Take You Home Again, Kathleen" and "Believe Me All Those Endearing Young Charms," and then for her finale she sang "Home in Ohio" after telling the crowd she'd authored it herself and was performing it tonight for the first time ever in public.

I was sitting with the boys at a table about 40 feet from her. With spotlights shining down on the stage and no lights shining outward from it, there was no way she could have seen me. Yet I felt she knew I was there and had waited to debut "Home in Ohio" until I could be present to hear it.

Beside me Whiting was imitating her singing in a falsetto voice, but I ignored him. My attention was all on her as she exited the stage like a show pony, head high, eyes shining. Never have I heard such an ovation for a singer! Almost every man there was on his feet, stamping them on the floor and pounding his hands together like cymbals. The applause swelled until at last she came back out on the stage and sang "Bring Back My Bonnie to Me" for an encore.

She disappeared into the wings after that, not to return despite more vociferous applause. I was still on my feet hoping for another glimpse of her. "She's a new number here and a winner," said Whiting as he clubbed me on the back, and Sullivan said: "Too bad she ain't Irish or I'd believe God gave her that voice to ruin my vow never to be mashed until I'm too old to have fun."

They both laughed at me when I asked who could give me paper so I could write Constance a note. "What will you tell her, sport?" Whiting said. "That you can't sit down now because there's a pole in your britches?"

It was Wolf who found a scrap of paper in the same pocket with his kerchief.

"I'll just say I'm here," I said as I wrote my note.

"That should really dampen her knickers," Sullivan said. But he peered at me with a changed expression after I gave the note to a waiter. "Say, Draves, is that a bill of goods you're selling or do you really know this wench?"

"You'll see," said I, basking in the new look he and the others were giving me and at the same time fearful Constance wouldn't respond to my note. What if she'd shucked her memory of our meeting as she'd shucked her name?

I sat tensely for some while. Then a door beside the stage opened and she emerged. I rose and held up a hand to signal my location. As she started my way I left the table, feeling four pairs of eyes on my back.

"Hello, Constance," I greeted her. Seeing her eyes waver, I said, less confidently: "Or should I say Zena?"

"I'm still Constance to my friends," she said. "If you're one."

"Absolutely. I only said what I did in my last letter because—"

"No," she said sharply. "We've both been through rough water since April, and there's no need to talk of it."

"But you're doing what you want now. You're singing as a solo. So things must be looking up for you—and they've certainly begun to now for me."

She smiled then and her eyes steadied. "It must be Fate," she said, "that I chose to sing "Home in Ohio" tonight. It's as if a voice whispered to me that it would be heard by the first person who made me feel it might be good."

She had echoed almost my exact thoughts, and it bound me to say that same voice had brought me here.

"Then you must come back and hear me sing it again." She turned away. "I have to go now and so do you. The men at your table are getting up to leave."

"No they aren't. They're coming over here to be introduced to you."

"Are they base ball players too?"

"Yes. They're with the Louisvilles."

"Then I won't meet them. Thank you just the same."

She glided away. But before she could gain the door beside the stage I caught up to her. "Does your aversion to base ball players now include even this one?"

"Oh, it's not you." She shrugged. "I just have to be on my way."

"Well, will you let me see you home later?"

She hesitated, her eyes darting to my right. Turning that way, I saw the boys standing in wait to be introduced. "All right," she murmured. "But meet me outside. Wait at the side entrance on Market Street."

"Ain't we spiffy enough to meet your betrothed?" Sullivan guyed me when we were all back at the table. "Or are you scared one of us might steal her from you?"

The conversation went on like that a while and then the boys desisted when they saw they couldn't get a rise out of me. By and by two harlots sashayed past our table and Wolf invited them to sit down. Once they did the banter they invoked became my cloak to slip unnoticed from the place. I walked down to the river and stood for many minutes watching the water move darkly below me. I leant over the pilings to find my reflection in it but could not. Unable to see my face, I was made to guess my thoughts. Did I really want to try to pick up with Constance again? Wasn't she too something that should be finished and behind me?

I tore my eyes away from the river and started back up the hill toward the lights of town. The true source of my uncertainty, I now perceived, was Constance's behavior. She seemed as confused as I, and the more I thought about our reunion tonight the more confused she seemed and I felt. One moment she'd acted glad to see me again, the next she'd tried to rush off, and yet she'd agreed to meet me later. I debated not waiting for her, fearing her contradictory actions meant she wouldn't keep our date, but the disappointment I'd face if she didn't was more than outweighed by the promise of the time we might have if she did. I realized then that I wanted to talk with her again above all else. As much as her radiance, I missed the stimulation our conversation two months ago had provided me.

I stood in a darkened doorway cater-cornered from the Kentuckian, passing the time while I waited watching other men, solitary as myself, drift up and down Market Street. Periodically one of the saloonists came out of the side entrance and added an empty beer keg to the stack in the alley, but otherwise the door was unused. A beggar asked me for a penny, and I gave him two. One for a bowl of soup and one for luck, mine as well as his. Midnight came and I vowed

I'd wait ten more minutes for Constance and not one second longer. But at 12:30 I was still there.

Fog had begun floating up from the river, befitting my mood. I surrendered and left the doorway. After a few steps I turned and gave one final look behind me. A man and a woman were standing now in conversation outside the Kentuckian's side entrance. In a few moments they bade each other good-night and parted, he going down toward the river while the woman headed my way.

When she passed beneath the streetlamp I saw it was Constance. She was wearing a wide-brimmed hat that concealed her lush hair and had changed to a simple blue dress, but her face and especially her eyes, even in the fog, were unmistakable.

"I was afraid you'd given me up by now," she said.

"I was about to."

"That fellow was the new pianist I'll be working with starting tomorrow. I needed to stay after the show and rehearse with him a while."

"What happened to the pianist you had tonight? I thought he was good."

"He was, but that's how it is in my line. Nothing is ever the same for long."

"What about your name? Who will you be next?"

"Who knows?" She smiled. "Have you any idea how many names songstresses often must try out before they're finally established?"

"Well, are you at least still living in the same place?" I asked as we set off up Market Street.

"Yes, but I've had two new roommates since I last saw you and suspect I'll have another soon." Noticing my splint, she said: "What's wrong with your finger?"

"I bunged it up in a ball game," I said and then told her about the injury and its aftermath, omitting only the Ducker part. When I was done she said it sounded like not much ever stayed the same for long in my profession either. I couldn't argue that although I did say it might if I could hook on with the Louisvilles.

"Is that why you've come here?" she asked.

"Yes, but it's only part of the reason."

As I spoke I knew the truth. I wasn't in Louisville only to avenge myself. The Browns and the Buckeyes are archrivals of the Red Stockings too, but I hadn't gone to St. Louis or Columbus. I had come here. I glanced at Constance and tried to read her thoughts. Was she remembering the last time we'd walked this same route, when she serenaded me? Or the moment when, with glistening eyes, she'd confided her dream to sing at Heuck's Opera House? Or her quiet nod of understanding when I'd revealed mine to make my uncle proud of me?

She's the only one I've ever told about Sam's and my mutual dream and now she's the only one who knows of the rift between us. I hadn't intended to tell her about it, but all at once I found myself pouring out the whole story, how Sam had longed in his own youth to play for the Red Stockings and the pact we'd made after he became my guardian that I'd fulfill the destiny that Fate had denied him when he lost his leg and how he'd stopped writing to me after I turned down a job as an assistant grounds keeper and struck out on my own instead. "You did right," Constance said when I finished. "You did what any man worth his salt would do. You let them bow you, but you wouldn't let them break you. Your uncle ought to understand that."

I said I was sure he would once he got over the hurt he felt I'd done him. Am I right, dear Diary? Will he ever understand?

We were standing outside her hotel by then. She held out her hand and I took it and bowed to kiss it, thinking she meant to bid me good-night. But then I realized she'd only made the gesture to gather a thought. "You've talked a lot about your uncle's dream for you," she said, "but what is your own dream, Earl?"

I released her hand and stared away at an empty buggy in front of the hotel. While I waited for a reply to form, I felt her take my arm. When I turned back to her, she said: "Pray, don't tell me if it's too difficult."

"I want to," I said. "But the words aren't there."

"No, how can they be here on the street?" she said, misunderstanding. Then, after a pause, she murmured: "Well, if it were not so late, I might ask you in."

Feeling her hand let go of my arm, I said in a rush: "Will you see me again tomorrow? It's Sunday—we can go on an outing—a picnic."

"I can't, Earl. I have another engagement." She bit her lower lip when she saw my disappointment. "But the Kentuckian doesn't have a stage show on Mondays. I'm free that evening if you'd perhaps care to escort me to supper."

"Of course I would!"

We set an hour to meet at her hotel on Monday and then she extended her hand again. "Good-night, Constance," I said, kissing it. "Good-night," she echoed. But then we both went on standing there, unable to part. We each said good-night again and finally I swallowed and said: "May I somehow kiss you more personally?"

Dear Diary, I won't embarrass you or myself any further. Suffice it to say that it is now four a.m. and rekindling the manner in which Constance and I finally parted has left me no closer to sleep than I was when I started this entry.

Louisville, Ky., July 2

Dear Sam:

There was no game today due to wet grounds, but the postponement was only a momentary lull in the war brewing all along the Ohio River. The combat has now begun in earnest between the Falls City and the Queen City. All the sharps down here are claiming the pennant for the locals after they beat Stovey and his defending champion Athletics twice this week while up in Cincinnati they're bruiting the Red Stockings' three straight slaughters of the Washingtons, following their sweep of the series with the Mets, as proof of the Porkers' superiority. There is no denying half of the upriver argument: the Louisvilles truly did drop a game to the lowly Statesmen. But the loss to the Mets the day Keefe officiated has been expunged by Mutrie's greed. When the Louisvilles protested the game, claiming Keefe wasn't a fit umpire, Mutrie said he'd happily take the half of the gate receipts the Mets were entitled if the contest was declared an exhibition game even at the sacrifice of a win that counted toward the pennant.

Hence the Louisvilles are that much more firmly in first place and Gerhardt is no longer keen to test me at short stop when my finger mends. Knock on wood, Sam, that ought to be soon. The splint came off accidentally on Monday evening (during an activity I prefer not to disclose) and I left it off when I felt no more pain, only a stiffness that should go away with exercise. Yesterday morning I even tossed a ball a while with Browning in his back yard. It felt strange, almost as if I had to learn to throw all over again, and one of my tosses went so awry that it bounced in front of Browning and cracked him on the kneecap. "Damn your hide, Early," he groaned, falling to the ground as if shot. "You've crippled Old Pete."

He was limping so badly when we got to the ballpark that I worried my errant toss might keep him from playing and put me still deeper in dutch with Gerhardt. But instead, bruised knee and all, Browning had his best day thus far this season, banging five hits off Atkinson and Cub Stricker.

By the bye, Sam, I'm not in dutch now with Gerhardt because I spoke out of turn again to a manager. To the contrary, I've been walking on eggs around him, not about to repeat the same mistake you think I made with White. But as Fate would have it, Gerhardt and Juice Latham were dining at the same restaurant where I took Constance on Monday evening. Spotting us, and especially her, Gerhardt suggested we all four share a table. Upon learning his station during the introductions,

Constance whispered to me that she didn't wish to sit for a discussion on base ball while she dined and then said to Gerhardt: "Thank you, but Earl and I have something we need to talk about alone."

I thought she handled the situation with utter politeness, but later, while Gerhardt and I were in the gents room emptying our hoses, he said out of the side of his mouth: "Sullivan is right. That is one smarmy twat you've got there, Draves."

I said nothing, Sam. I just thought to myself: How little you know, Joe. For Constance is not at all snobbish. It is just that she genuinely dislikes base ball players—and with good reason. The other evening, walking back to her hotel, she confided that she'd had a very demoralizing experience with one back in Evansville. That the man was a ballist she knew wasn't grounds to despise the entire profession, but the hurt she'd suffered was still too fresh for her to help herself. After this confession we strolled in silence while I searched for a reply. Then she suddenly gave me a sidelong look and said: "Earl, am I wrong in thinking you like me a bit?"

"Much more than a bit," I owned.

"Would you still if I were to confess the most awful thing a woman can?"

I said yes although I'll admit the word did not quite spring from my mouth.

"Even knowing that I'm fallen?" she asked, putting a name to that which I would have preferred to leave unspoken.

"Yes," I repeated. "We all make mistakes."

To which she only nodded at first, but in a while she said: "You're a good man, Earl. Too good for me I'd say, but that's for you to decide."

Well, Sam, now you have it all. Think what you will of Constance, but know that I still think she's the grandest girl a man could hope to find. I'm writing these words at the Kentuckian even as I sit in wait for her to perform tonight. In a few short minutes I will cap my pen. The likelihood is that all my letters for some while will contain almost no mention of base ball.

Who would not write about the half of his life that is nearly perfect when the other half is a horror? Last week the Red Stockings released Ren Deagle, mostly due to his foul outing in New York, but unlike his last batterymate that day he's landed on his feet. Yesterday, when I entered the Eclipse dressing room before the game to show Gerhardt that my finger was ready for action again, who but Deagle was hanging his trousers on a hook? "Ducker," he said. "What the H— are you doing here?"

I might have asked him the same if I hadn't known the Louisvilles were shopping for a change pitcher to replace Denny Driscoll. Feeling my face begin to freeze, I heard Cline say: "Ducker you called him? Why so?"

Deagle did me the favor of not contradicting Sullivan when he opined that it was because I was an ace at ducking out the door before a drink bill was presented. Sullivan is still miffed that I stole off from the Kentuckian the other night when the harlots joined the boys, and now I'm glad for it. But it's only a matter of time probably before Deagle bares the true origin of my nickname.

Enough of that sour note though as Constance is about to sing and inject a sweet sound into my life again. She ends all her performances now with "Home in Ohio," and I never tire of hearing it and doubt I ever will even if the feeling it rouses in me is not quite as soft and blissful as before.

Your nephew, Earl.

Louisville, Ky., July 3

Dear Sam:

I'm following so close upon the heels of my last letter because I fear I wrongly maligned Gerhardt, and also to bid you not to write to me for the moment because I may soon have a new address.

The Louisvilles lost 6-2 to the Athletics today behind Deagle, putting him in the doghouse in his very first game with the club. In fairness to him though, he pitched decently, and it wasn't his fault that Cline and Wolf and Maskrey were made to look like monkeys by little Bobby Mathews, who's so old his fast ball can scarcely break a cobweb. The rest of the Athletics are playing like a shadow of last year's champions. Tomorrow they journey to Cincinnati for a Fourth of July doubleheader they'll surely lose to just about end their last hope of claiming the pennant again. The A's still have Stovey, currently the leading batsman in the Association, but the other A's are struggling to hit their weight and you can judge for yourself how woeful their pitching staff is when I tell you Mathews is their ace and George Bradley, who's even more hoary, would have been their change boxman if he hadn't jumped to the Onions.

After the game, I went to the Louisvilles' dressing room to console the boys and Gerhardt summoned me over to his bench. As he disrobed he asked after my finger. When I informed him that it was nearly right again, he said he had a proposition for me. The Louisvilles were angling to purchase Dave Foutz, the Bay Citys pitching ace, but needed to provide the Michigan club with a replacement. If I'd agree to take Foutz's spot, Gerhardt would promise me first crack next spring at any open infield job on the Louisvilles.

It was not the greatest offer, but leastwise it was something concrete from Gerhardt's mouth after all his vague promises. So I said I'd mull it over, meanwhile telling myself I won't answer him until I'd consulted you. The Bay Citys are respectable, and playing for them I'd receive around $75 a month, nothing to be sneezed at considering that I'm down to my last $20 at the moment. Bud Hillerich, sensing my financial plight, offered me a loan the other evening, but of course I could never accept a dime from him, almost a stranger, any more than from you, Sam. The only avuncular aid I seek is word as to whether you endorse Gerhardt's offer to me.

Please reply as soon as possible to the West Jefferson Street address as I'm only paid there through the 5th of the month. After that I may be on the street if Browning has his way. This afternoon Gerhardt made reference again to Constance while he and I were talking and Browning happened to overhear. "Yeah, who's this chanteuse?" he blurted. "Old Pete thought you wanted no truck with women." And on the trolley ride home he said some Judas I'd turned out to be, spurning a man's sister while all the time I've been mashing with another girl. Horrified, I said: "What are you talking about, Pete? Your sister can't abide me." She only acted as she did, he said, to hide that she was wearing her heart on her sleeve. "She's been mashed on you ever since she set her lamps on you," he said. "Pete knows—he knows his sister. He knows too now why they call you Ducker. You got a string of hearts you've broken and then taken a powder on!"

The absurdity of his jibe would have made me laugh, Sam, if I hadn't feared there might be an awful grain of truth to it. In an attempt to make amends, should that be the case, I aim to ask Browning's sister to go for a stroll this evening and perhaps even to accompany me to the fireworks display tomorrow night in Central Park. I reckon she'll tell me to go fly a kite if I'm any judge of the female of the species; but regardless, I won't be caught between two fires because Constance and I, unbeknownst to Browning and everyone else, are no longer an item.

She told me something else about herself last night, Sam, that I cannot possibly tolerate. She confessed she is a Catholic.

Your nephew, Earl.

There is no telling when or why Harry Duffield Stowe decided to make a profession of base ball against his mother's wishes nor what led him to adopt the pseudonym of Stovey so she would not see his name in box scores. Sometime in his early twenties probably covers the moment itself. As for the motivation, there were many who pursued the game because they had no other skills that could earn them anywhere near as much money, and Stowe's life after he left base ball suggests he may have been one of that body. Men who had seen him play would come upon him sometimes in the streets of New Bedford, Massachusetts, without recognizing him. He would be strolling along, swinging his billyclub, and they would wonder, Do I know this Stowe from somewhere? Then he would notice them looking. A slow smile would come over his face and they began to feel that he too found them familiar. Ah, they said to themselves, so we have met before. But while they were still trying to place him, Stowe would make his face a blank again and move on. It is unclear whether he deliberately sought anonymity when he dropped the heralded name of Stovey and again became the undistinguished Stowe upon the finish of his base ball career. In any case, so little stands out in his many years as a New Bedford policeman that we can suppose his highpoint was 1884. The evidence is that he went to his grave in 1937 believing he had led the American Association in hitting that year with a colossal .404 batting average. It's too hard to accept, though, that he wasn't aware his true mark was nearly 80 points lower. Browning was not the only one who kept scrupulous track of his average.

But if Stowe knew he had been the beneficiary of an egregious error, why did he say nothing? Was there a plot in 1884 to make him the Association bat king? He was the loop's most prized player at the time and surely Association magnates wanted to avoid a repetition of the awkward incident the previous year when Ed Swartwood of the seventh-place Alleghenys had perforce been crowned the leading hitter after the snickers that greeted an attempt to bestow the honor on Tom Mansell, then of the Browns, who had boasted a .402 batting average, the highest in the game, but in only 112 at bats.

In any case, Stowe's career batting average has since been reduced 13 points from the .301 figure given him when he retired in 1893. That places him well below .300, which would tarnish his stature considerably if he were noted only for his hitting. But Stowe was valued equally for his fielding and base running. Credited with being the first to wear sliding pads, he twice was a league leader in stolen bases and averaged better than one run scored for every game he played.

During the 1884 season Stovey—as he was then called—was courted more avidly by Henry Lucas than any other Association player. "We both concede you're bound at the moment to the Athletics," said Lucas. He always opened negotiations on a conspiratorial note.

"Unfortunately," Stovey advised him. He had already determined to lead his wooer on a little.

"Why do you say that, Harry?" Oh yes, this could be providential.

"Have you noticed how weak we are since your Onions robbed us of Bradley?"

"Well, things can't be too bad when there is still the great Stovey. My God, what is your batting average now? Somewhere above .400, isn't it?"

Stovey answered reluctantly. "Give or take a few points."

"Just so it stays as high as Dunlap's, right?" It was a random shot and Lucas saw with surprise that it had struck home. Stovey, about to speak, was silenced.

"Far be it for the Onions to produce a batsman who tops everything the Association has to offer." It was suave.

"It's still only July. Who believes Dunlap will be hitting his .400 when the season ends?"

Lucas said, with deep sarcasm, "But what of those who believe you aren't hitting anywhere near .400 now?"

Stovey's resentment boiled over into anger. "Your implication is ridiculous. For Christ's sake, my average is down on paper in black and white."

"Yes, but who computed it and on whose totals was it based?"

The silence was long and heavy. The floor creaked as Stovey pushed his chair away from the table when a waiter approached. "This man is paying." He then rose and addressed Lucas. "We have no more to discuss."

Lucas got to his feet too. The air when he had come into the saloon had a sweet fresh promise. Now it was sour with acrimony. There was no one but himself to blame. Once again he had allowed his fervor to decry the work of a competitor to get in the way of business that might have been done. He waited until Stovey had gone out through the swinging doors into the Louisville night and then he turned and gave a single negative shake of his head toward two men from the Chicago Unions club who stood along the bar rail at a discreet distance.

So Stovey remained with the Athletics. He would have been content to finish his career in Philadelphia. He had been born there, after all, and he knew that nowhere else could he receive as much adulation. The City of Brotherly Love even in 1884 had a peculiar love-hate relationship with its sports heroes. Every man who played there understood his popularity was in direct proportion to the level of wrath each mistake made by him incurred. Stovey was hissed more than the villain of any stage play in his day, but he could handle it. He knew what it meant.

Why then would he never make the Hall of Fame? Did he have an unforgivable vice? He played most of his career in the American Association, of course, and the AA will probably always be viewed with suspicion. Even disdain. Every year it survived made the task of National League moguls that much tougher. Their profits were reduced still more, or so they thought until the AA surrendered its autonomy to them in the winter of 1891 and their profits continued to shrink. There was an economic recession during the 1890s, followed by a depression, it's true, and National League officials were quick to attribute falling attendance to this. Perhaps that was all it was, but we'll never be sure. We are morally certain, though, that the man buried in New Bedford under a headstone that reads Stowe is alive still under his base ball name. More than one panel of authorities on the game has voted Stovey the pre-1900 player most deserving of Hall of Fame recognition who has yet to receive it.

July 5

It looks like I was wrong in thinking Sam would get my last letter in time to cable me today. But I was dead right, dear Diary, in my assessment of Browning's sister Fannie. She did consent to stroll with me night before last, but we scarcely were underway when she said she was glad of my invitation because it gave her a chance to clear the air between us. She was aware, she said, that her brother had some silly notion of acting as a matchmaker for her and hoped that wasn't why he'd brought me into their abode. The fact was, if I didn't mind her speaking plainly, she felt somewhat put out by me although it wasn't really anything personal. "It's just that I don't care for any of the chaps Louis associates with," she said. "My mom thinks it's because you're all ball players, but the truth be, I cotton even less to this Hillerich chap." When I inquired, out of polite curiosity, what type of man she could fancy, Fannie said she didn't suppose I'd been reading "The Lady of Ashmere" in the Sunday *Courier-Journal*. "There are actually two chaps in Mrs. Montgomery's novel I could condone," said she, "and it rankles me to no end that the heroine can't feature either of them." Upon my saying I had a hunch she'd change her tune along about the last installment of the serial, Fannie cried: "Now see—there's a perfect illustration of what I mean! Today's men are all so cynical. Need we walk any further, Mr. Draves?"

We did stroll longer but mostly in silence. On the homeward leg though, Fannie was good enough to pledge she'd be more cordial toward me as long as I lodged in her house if only because her brother and her mother, for whatever reason, both liked me.

So I still have a place to live, leastwise till my money gives out. On that score too there is a welcome development. Yesterday noon, between games of the Independence Day doubleheader with the Brooklyns, Hillerich took me to his father's shop to show me the expanded premises now that they've also become bat manufacturers. On the journey back to the ballpark he detoured his buggy to an embankment overlooking the river at its widest juncture. There, while we were both drinking in the view, he said he'd perhaps misworded his offer of a loan the other day and I'd been right to reject it. What my refusal had done though was inspire him to see a better business arrangement. Hopefully I'd soon be playing for the Louisvilles. On that assumption, he was prepared to advance me $25 against the time when I could join Browning and several other local luminaries in using Hillerich-made bats and touting their superiority.

I said what any sane man would have. I said I'd be flattered to accept his terms, and upon our handshake had several crisp new bills in my notecase.

That was only the beginning of what was to become the most gala Independence Day I've ever celebrated. In the afternoon the Louisvilles completed their sweep of the twinbill with the Brooklyns, Iron-Man Hecker working both games, while the bulletin boards heightened the crowd's ecstasy by posting the stunning news that the Athletics had taken a pair from the Red Stockings. When Hillerich and I fought our way into the thronged dressing room afterward, the mood we found was festive beyond description. Hecker cavorted stark naked with wee Cline perched like a jockey on his shoulders. Browning and Gerhardt were dispensing filled mugs from a beer keg in the center of the floor. Elsewhere Mayor Jacobs stood with his arm around Juice Latham's gigantic midriff and cried over and over: "Who's the best? D——- it, we are!" Around the club flag that graced the wall two teenage boys were pasting tiny felt replicas of the nation's flag to form a halo. Even Haldeman for once had the ears of the players as he asked them his questions rather than their backsides.

Oh, I thought, to be a participant in this and not a mere spectator. What I also thought was that I would accept Gerhardt's offer to replace Foutz on the Bay Citys. Playing in Michigan will distance me that much farther from Sam, and not just in miles. But how can I continue to take into consideration the feelings of someone who no longer seems to care to make me aware of what he feels?

That said, dear Diary, I must record that I took another step on Independence Day toward independence, impelled by my sense that I'm now wholly on my own. What is so wrong anyway with people of the Catholic faith? Much as I believe that a man must find his own way in this world, how am I renouncing that merely by keeping company with someone who believes in being led through life by a ring in her nose?

And besides, my spirits were so elevated that I naturally wanted to share them with the one person whose very smile can make every day feel to me like a holiday.

I got to the St. Cloud Hotel about 6:30, hoping to catch Constance before she left for the Kentuckian, but there was no answer when the clerk telephoned her room. I was about to depart, thinking she'd already gone, when she emerged from the lift. Upon seeing me, she looked for an instant as if she meant to dive back inside it. Then she dropped onto a divan in the lobby instead and cast her eyes down at the carpet. Reckoning she was still disturbed by our quarrel of two nights earlier, I put on a contrite face as I sat beside her and began my planned apology.

"Constance, I can't tell you how sorry I am for what happened."

"Oh," she said woodenly. "Then you've already heard...?"

"Heard what?"

"I'm like you now, Earl. I lost my job last night. I suppose because too many found it objectionable that I made "Home in Ohio" my theme song when I was being paid in the coin of Kentucky."

"Oh, that can't be. Surely they wouldn't fire you for that!"

"I've been fired for a lot less and suspect I shall be again."

"Constance, how can you be so philosophical about this? I'd be furious."

Her eyes rose slowly from the carpet and found mine. They glistened as she said: "I've been all through that. Now I no longer let myself get angry."

"Except at me?" I ventured.

"Oh, I can't be mad at you after showing you so flighty a nature. One day I tell you of my wanton past, the next that I still think of entering a nunnery."

This was not at all the exchange I had anticipated, but I kept to my plan.

"Can I lighten your heart by inviting you to top off what for me has been an unparalleled day by accompanying me to the fireworks display in the park?"

She hesitated. "Are you sure I wouldn't spoil your mood?"

"Not a chance," I said.

"Then allow me a moment to return to my room and repair my face. I promise when you see it next it will be gay and carefree."

But it never quite was that. We didn't get to Central Park till past eight o'clock, by which time the concert had ended and the crowd was so dense that we were a long while in wending our way through the ticket line and finding a vacant patch of grass where I could spread my coat. No sooner were we seated than three huge electric signs that said "Pain's English Fireworks" were lit. After a minute they dimmed and the show commenced.

It was well worth a quarter apiece, but not the dollar it would have set me back to purchase two reserved chairs at the forefront of the display. There were some new wrinkles I'd never seen before, whirling skyrockets for one, but until the very last stage of the "Historical Finale" none of them bowled me over. Then after the usual fare of cannons and shooting stars, a giant American flag suddenly lit up the entire sky. It hung in thin air for what must have been a full minute, just about the most glorious sight imaginable before its blue stars and red and white stripes began to melt and drip away into the darkness.

When I glanced at Constance she was crying. I'm sure there were tears in my eyes too at that moment. But when I squeezed her hand it felt limp rather than shot with excitement like mine, and she murmured: "It's just so sad...how nothing really beautiful in this world can ever last."

Yet to come was the drawing for a $100 gold watch and a suit of clothes, and I had expected we would stay even beyond that and join the crowd around us in songfests and merry-making. But Constance was almost frantic to leave. I thought at first the loss of her job had finally sunk into her, but it was more than that. By the time we were back on the western side of the river she had stopped speaking altogether. My efforts to draw her out were useless, until at last I had a bright idea.

I said: "After all the hours of listening pleasure you've given me, it's my turn tonight to treat your ears." With that I began to sing "Home in Ohio."

If I'd thought that would cheer her, I was wrong. Hearing my dreadful voice didn't bring so much as a smile. But she did wilt into me a little when I put my arm around her as I croaked the last stanzas. "Earl, would you think me too terrible a paradox," she said, "if we went somewhere now for something to still your vocal cords and I didn't order sarsaparilla?"

Here, dear Diary, I'll remark only that every man (and woman too) can be forgiven one fall off the wagon on an occasion so auspicious. Still, it wasn't as if either of us drank ourselves under the table, although she fared notably worse than I, not having even my limited training with any substance stronger than malt juice.

Hence I was obliged to assist her into the lift when we got back to her hotel and then with the key to the lock on her door and finally in lighting the gas lamp in her room. I had been there only once before and then just for a minute because her roommate was due home shortly. But last night it didn't seem improper for me to sit a while in the chair beside Constance's bed and minister to her as she lay fully clad and beseeched her head to stop spinning. I would leave, I thought, as soon as her roommate came home and relieved me of the duty to see that Constance would not expire as she was lamenting that she was surely about to do. But I must have dozed off, for when I next consulted my watch it was past two. I bolted to my feet, startled not only by the time but also by the observation that her roommate had not yet returned. Constance too was awake and recuperated enough to watch my eyes take in the empty bed on the opposite wall. "It's all right," she said. "Ruth won't compromise us, if that's your fear." After a long pause she said: "She's spending the night with her beau."

My heart, I'll admit, winced a bit. But then I realized her candor was in keeping with everything else I had noted about her. It helped me over my mortification too when she sensed it and said: "I'm telling you this, Earl, just so you'll know that if you don't want to journey home at this ungodly hour, there's nothing to oppose your staying here. You could even borrow Ruth's bed if you like."

I could not impose myself to that extent. I stayed the night in the chair, but I did fall asleep in time. When I awakened again the lamp was out and I could see nothing of Constance but her dim shape still lying atop the covers on her bed. She was making what I thought were sleep sounds, until I heard what was unmistakably a sob. I put out a hand to comfort her. It touched her face and I let it stay there, stroking her damp cheek. For a long while she seemed unconscious of my hand, but then she asked if I thought I could ever still care for her after the tawdry streak I'd now seen? I said I already did a lot more than just care for her. Then everything was not hopeless? Beginning tomorrow, I said, I was going to do my uttermost to show her it was the opposite. "You've already begun," she said, "just by being here. You can't know how glad I am my behavior didn't drive you away tonight."

She fell silent then, and so did I although I continued to stroke her cheek. When next either of us spoke it was nearly dawn and in the gray light from the window I could now see her face. She bit her lower lip as she said: "At moments like now I'm thinking life could be so rich if only I hadn't spoiled myself for you." And I said: "You haven't."

And I meant my every word.

After yesterday, dear Diary, there is no longer even a shred of doubt in my mind that the Louisvilles are now my team and Constance is now my girl.

"We will take good care of him," Bill Reccius assured Pete Browning's mother in 1877. She had accompanied her 16-year-old son to his first meeting with the organizer of the Eclipse club to speak for him. It was not that Pete was shy to the point of seeming at times to be a mute. It was rather that he didn't always hear everything that was said to him. "He drifts off like smoke even in the midst of the most vicious discussions," said Guy Hecker once in the Louisville dressing room after a bitter defeat. "It's as if he can't follow what's going on," suggested Haldeman, who had been in the background until then. Browning, whose failure to heed Hecker's cry to let Tom McLaughlin manage a pop fly had caused a collision that contributed mightily to the defeat, stood behind them like a tourist in a strange land. He knew they were talking about him, but with their backs turned he could only catch snatches of their conversation. Anyway, it was easier all the way around if everyone thought he was an imbecile.

Browning supposedly once said, "I can't hit the ball until I hit the bottle." After his death in 1905 an obituary in the *Louisville Times* reported that his drinking problem began innocently enough in his late teens during a sandlot game when it was decreed that any man reaching third base would get a free stein of beer on the spot. Browning then hit so many triples and home runs there was scarcely any beer left for the other players. Haldeman may have been the source of this story since he was responsible for many of the tales that eventually went into the Browning legend. To Haldeman, it was horrifying how much Browning misused his talent; he preferred a player like Monk Cline. He said one spring, comparing the two, "They keep telling Browning to shorten his swing and chop down at the ball. He's got the strength to hit it to the fence just by jabbing at it. He keeps being told to stop trying to pole every ball, but he never listens. That's the difference. You tell Cline something, and he goes out and does it. You tell that Browning anything and he acts like you've told the wall." That year Browning hit .362 to lead the Association and Cline was handed his release by Louisville after playing just two games. Yet most of the base ball community continued to listen to Haldeman on the subject of Browning.

His mother's domicile on West Jefferson Street was the only home Browning ever knew and Louisville was the only city he cared to know. It was like no other city in its heyday—temperate in the winter and yet cold enough oftentimes to ice skate on the river, dull to the point of being boring by day, wildly glamorous at night. Browning lived only for the day but could not resist the romance of the night, or so it seemed, along with countless other paradoxes. The youngest of eight children, he was just turned 13 when his father died of injuries sustained in a cyclone. Being fatherless freed him to play hooky from school without risking a whipping, and he began hiding his classroom books under a neighbor's stoop each morning and spending the day at his passion:

shooting marbles. Eventually he became so formidable a marbler that he had to travel by street car to East Louisville, where he was unknown, to find new victims who would contribute to his trunkful of treasured agates.

Browning loved water too, but he refused all his life to swim. In this instance it was not a paradox; swimming hurt his left ear too much. The mastoiditis surgery he had in the spring of 1884 to stem the infection was only partially successful. Browning still had considerable pain and some think he took to drink in an effort to deaden it. If so, the medicine failed. Browning went mad when he was in his early forties— whether because the infection had spread to his brain or he had syphilis will always be a topic for debate at this late juncture—and was locked away in Lakeland, also known as the Fourth Kentucky Insane Asylum. After 12 days there he showed enough improvement to be released, but little more than a month later he underwent surgery for ear trouble and a breast tumor. In early September a new tumor appeared on his neck. Even before it could be removed, he died in Louisville's Old City Hospital with his mother, one brother and two sisters, Florence and Fannie, at his bedside. "Called out" blared the headline of Haldeman's old paper, the *Courier-Journal*, while the evening *Times* ran Browning's obit under the headline: "Pete Browning Out of Life's Game."

The metaphors are apt, for base ball was his raison d`etre. Yet he was never one to relive his days in the game. Rarely in fact was he heard to bear a tale about base ball. When he told stories they most commonly involved dogs, horrible tragic stories of beasts he had seen killed or cruelly maimed. The odd thing was that Browning was never known to keep a dog or even to be particularly fond of dogs. If anything, he ought to have despised them. There was a one-eyed dog that taunted him for some years—although maybe not the same dog—by appearing out of nowhere time and again, on the street as he sauntered along or when he came out of a saloon, making him instantly weak with dread. It was believed that Browning feared the dog was his dead father reincarnated. People who knew of this phobia wondered if his father had lost an eye to the cyclone, but that could never be more than conjecture.

The supernatural powers that Browning ascribed to dogs also had an everyday application at times. One afternoon, seeing Draves's new lady friend waiting for him outside Eclipse Park, Browning crossed the street as if in a hurry somewhere and then paused at the corner and stood watching her from that distance. It was the first time he had seen Constance, but he needed only a few seconds to complete his assessment. Actually, he had only to witness an incident between her and the little black and gray mongrel that made its home in a deserted shed behind the ball park. By that time Constance had observed Browning scrutinizing her. Nothing could have been more devastating for both of them than what they recognized in each other.

Much later, when Draves was in his room at the hotel to which he had recently moved, Browning paid him an unannounced visit. Browning knew that Draves had left his family abode so that he wouldn't have to account to anyone for the nights he didn't come home, but he pretended to accept Draves's explanation that he needed to be by himself while he planned his next move. Gerhardt had informed him just that afternoon, he said, that the arrangement with the Bay Citys had fallen through because the Browns had made the Michigan club a higher offer for Dave Foutz.

"Would you still have wanted to go up there otherwise?"

"I'll go anywhere for the chance to play again."

"Ain't you getting in enough playing right here?"

Draves's mood dropped. "What do you mean?"

"Pete saw your new flame today."

"So?"

"She's quite a lampful."

"You really think so?"

"To hear what Old Pete really thinks, you know what you have to do."

So they went downstairs to the bar in the hotel, and Browning was immediately beset by a tableful of cranks that insisted he and Draves sit down with them and have a drink. Draves went along with it; it held off the anxiety. Soon it was nearly time for him to meet Constance at the St. Cloud, and they still had hardly mentioned her. When he got up from the table though, Browning rose too and excused himself to his hosts while he went to see a man about a horse.

He then accompanied Draves to the gents' room and stood combing his hair in the mirror while he spoke.

"Is that woman your chosen?"

"She may well become that."

"Pete wants to say then that you'd best be on your toes."

"You don't like her, do you?"

"Pete likes her fine—she's a beauty—but there's no better judge of a woman than a dog, and they don't like her."

"On what are you basing that?"

"Pete was watching Tigger this afternoon. You know old Tigger?"

"I know, I know who he is."

"Well, he steered clear of her. He picked up some scent about her that maybe you and Old Pete can't."

"Like what?" Draves said resentfully.

"All Old Pete knows is any hand a dog won't lick he wouldn't want whittling on his joy rod."

"That's the big news you came here tonight to tell me?"

"That's it in a nutshell, Early boy."

"You crazy tadpole. You and your dogs." They laughed and it was over.

That was the only time in Louisville that Draves spoke to anyone about Constance. He couldn't even write frankly to his uncle about her anymore. The whole burden of sex was something he could not possibly confide to another man, and of course women were an even poorer audience. One time he tried to speak to Constance of a delicate matter and was desperately afraid that she might misunderstand his part in the incident. But she smiled at him like a kind of accomplice.

"It's only normal when men are drinking for them to lose sight sometimes of who the other body is with them."

He did not tell her that the man with whom the disconcerting interaction had occurred was a teetotaler.

"Besides, the only men like that are in monasteries and such."

And how little more, he realized, she knew than he. But there was one area where he thanked his lucky stars that he was with someone who understood what was happening to him. It was like a bottomless well. It felt like an eternal spring whose depth could never be known, a fountain that could gush eternally. He could not imagine there was anything else like it in the universe, and each renewal of it only increased his amazement at himself. How could he have thought for so long that anything so marvelous was sinful merely because a lot of fuddy-duddies said it could be right in God's eyes under only one condition? What of all the religions that believed in a man having many wives or none at all? What of all the savages in the jungle who had never heard of God?

Yet he did wish at times that Constance had come to him as pure as he had to her. Not that she was so much more experienced in lovemaking than he. In some ways she was actually painfully naive. He would never betray her confidence in him by disclosing any instances of her ignorance to another person. But he didn't think it broke any covenants when he admitted to himself that it did still prey on him fiercely sometimes that to coax them both over the final hurdle she'd said there could be no use locking the barn door after the horse had been stolen.

Louisville, Ky., July 14

Dear Sam:

If you've been chomping at the bit this past fortnight to dish out a gram of your sage advice, I swear I'll embrace it now with open arms. Hence I'm enclosing the telephone number of the hotel where I'm presently situated. I haven't forgotten your vow that your chickens would have to lay square eggs before you'd entrust your thoughts to any such contraption, but it may behoove you to put aside your aversion as I'm not apt to be here much longer or perhaps even of this earth.

No, it's not what you're thinking. Constance hasn't decided she wants no more to do with me. Instead she's taken to her bed with a recurrence of the illness she had back in the spring. Only now she says it isn't scarlet fever but a female disorder. "Time and Lydia Pinkham are all that can help," she said the other night on the telephone when I begged her to let me attend her, especially now that she has nowhere else to turn since Ruth is gone, having run off to Nashville with her beau.

Still, I don't quite know what to make of her illness, Sam, except that she won't consult a physician and now she can't even bear to talk to me on the telephone. "Pray, stop this concern," she said when I called up to her room this evening from the hotel desk. "I'll either recover or I won't. Now just leave me be."

Constance's craving for solitude has left me feeling like a ship without a rudder. Until her withdrawal I hadn't realized how much I'd come to rely on her. I miss the joy we've found together, but what I miss just as much are our conversations. Sam, I'm now willing to concede that in some respects Constance might not be the ideal companion for a man, but at least, when hale, she is both an avid listener and a steady supplier of food for thought. There is no subject we've left unexplored in the short time we've been beaux, from the vagaries of the dry goods business to the nature of the universe. With all the other people here, Browning and the boys included, I've been given to feel I'm merely shooting the breeze.

Need I name my ailment? Yes, it's loneliness, and mixed with homesickness. For Ohio, I reckon, and even maybe for Portsmouth, but definitely for your letters, Sam, and the wisdom they delivered me even while I couldn't always agree with it.

In my low mood I stooped last night to seek out Jamie Woulfe for no other reason than to wallow with him in the past. He too was released last month by Stern and has since joined the Alleghenys, who are in town now. He's nearly as miserable as I am, it emerged, even despite playing yesterday and scoring the winning run in the 12th inning to give Deagle his third straight loss with the Louisvilles. The Pittsburgers are nonetheless so hapless that McKnight, their owner, has already fired three managers this year including himself. Woulfe began our outing by toasting McKnight facetiously and then we both toasted Deagle with like irony and moved on to the Red Stockings in general and finally to the club members we agreed merited special citation. Caylor and Stern and White got two calls each and eventually not even Corkhill and McPhee, two who'd never shown either of us anything but amity, were spared. After that we turned to our personal banes. Woulfe, being from New Orleans, had no patience with my nostalgia for Ohio, but he did commiserate vociferously when I allowed that in retrospect my Red Stocking days hadn't been wholly a bed of thorns. "F—ing aye," he said. Then he seized his empty schooner and banged it down on the table. "Know the truth, Ducker? F—ing truth is I'd rather be back on their colts team than with this f—ing Smoke City bunch!"

As you see, Sam, my mental state is such that I no longer feel obliged to edit either my own thoughts or another's remarks. The same brutal candor from you is now in order, given the monumental grief I appear to have brought on myself. You can even call me Ducker if it pleases you. Why ever not? Everyone else is now, save Constance who prior to her retreat into solitary confinement called me something not even the threat of death could make me reveal.

Your nephew, Earl.

July 17

Well, dear Diary, either Sam still hasn't overcome his abhorrence of the telephone or else he reckoned my spirits were not so low that I'd heave myself into the river before he had time to draft a letter advising me properly on all the matters that have gone without his comment since I left the Red Stockings. Should the latter be the case he can save himself a few pieces of foolscap if he's thinking what I suspect he is with regard to Constance's recent illness.

It didn't occur to me, I'll confess, till I lay sleepless the other night that she might only have feigned illness to throw dust in my eyes while she took up with another beau. It pained me to imagine this, but, happily, Constance turns out to have been as honest with me as the day is long. I saw her last evening, and there is no more question she's been under the weather. She looked peaked as a ghost and like she'd lost substantial weight. About ten pounds to my eye, and from a frame that had little to spare in the first place. But she is still as beautiful as ever— and as brave! Although she's not fully recovered, she had to get back on her feet prematurely because she was running low on funds, and her pluck was immediately rewarded. She landed a new job just minutes before she trysted with me at her hotel. Beginning Saturday next, she'll be singing at a place on Magazine Street that's only a stone's throw from Eclipse Park. The one drawback is she won't be a solo act. Instead she'll form a duet with another girl who's a redhead now but will dye her hair dark so that the two of them can then be billed as sisters. "The Singing Simpsons," Constance said, and smiled when I rolled my eyes as if to say is there no end to the masquerading in her business?

Louisvilles		AB	R	1B	PO	A	E
Cline	c.f.	4	0	2	2	1	1
Wolf	r.f.	4	1	1	0	0	0
Browning	3b	4	1	1	0	2	1
Sullivan	c	4	0	1	7	0	2
Maskrey	l.f.	4	0	1	3	0	0
Latham	1b	4	0	2	11	1	0
Hecker	p	4	0	2	0	6	1
Gerhardt	2b	3	0	0	3	3	2
McLaughlin	s.s.	3	0	1	1	4	1
Totals		34	2	11	27	17	8

Cincinnatis		AB	R	1B	PO	A	E
Jones	m.f.	4	0	0	1	1	0
Reilly	1b	4	1	0	5	0	0
Carpenter	3b	4	0	0	0	1	0
McPhee	2b	4	0	1	2	3	1
Corkhill	r.f.	4	0	1	3	0	0
Snyder	c	3	0	0	8	0	0
Mansell	c.f.	3	0	0	1	0	0
Peoples	s.s.	3	0	1	3	0	1
White	p	3	0	0	1	1	0
Totals		32	1	3	24	6	2

Innings	1	2	3	4	5	6	7	8	9
Louisvilles	1	0	0	0	0	0	0	1	x—2
Cincinnati	0	0	0	0	0	0	0	0	1—1

Runs earned— Lousiville 2. Two-base hits— Wolf 1. Left on bases— Louisville 1, Cincinnati 4. Double plays— Gerhardt and Latham 1, Browning, Gerhardt and Latham 1. Struck out— Hecker 6, White 2. Passed balls— Sullivan 2. Time of game— One hour and thirty minutes. Umpire— John Dyler.

Of course the best feature of her new job is we'll be working right down the street from each other after I'm with the Louisvilles. When I made this observation, Constance said then it was definite now they were going to hire me? Not yet, I had to admit. But with a smile of my own I then told her it was only a matter of time, which it is. Now that she's on the mend, dear Diary, I too am back to my old self, once again supremely confident a brilliant future awaits me in Louisville.

This afternoon I went out to Eclipse Park higher than a kite. The day I'd been looking forward to ever since I came here was finally nigh, and even though I'd hoped to be with the Louisvilles by now, my disappointment was swallowed by the moment. I arrived at ten minutes past three, plenty early ordinarily to nab a seat behind the home bench, but this was no ordinary day. The grandstand was already filled to bursting and I was hard put even to find a vacancy in the bleaching boards. I watched both teams perform their warm-ups and then I watched Umpire Dyler flip a coin to decide which side would win the choice whether to bat first or last. Once White made the right call and chose lasts, Dyler yelled, "Play!" And hardly a minute later I was on my feet for the first pitch of the game, scarcely able to distinguish my own voice from the animal roar that engulfed the entire park.

The next hour and a half were an answered prayer. Over 3,500 people, the largest weekday crowd in Louisville history, narrowly missed witnessing Gerhardt's fair-haired boy McLaughlin hand the Red Stockings the first game of the series everyone upriver and down had been awaiting for weeks. But instead it was White's boy Peoples whose critical error gave the Louisvilles a gift-wrapped 2-1 decision. I ought to have found it a dream come true watching that pair of short stops take turns playing butterfingers. And while the game did have a dreamy quality for me, it was overall an unsettling occasion, dear Diary. For the first time in my life I felt I was at a base ball game as neither a player nor a spectator. Instead I seemed to grow almost paralyzed even before the first inning ended, unable to root for either team. It wasn't that I didn't know whom I wanted to win. I wanted the Louisvilles to win—but not for their own sake. I wanted them to win so they would remain in first place ahead of the Mets. Yet there were also moments when I seemed to want the Red Stockings to win, if only so the Louisvilles wouldn't. It was a test of my loyalties, I guess, and maybe of some other things too. In the end I reckon I failed it because I seemed to feel nothing when the Louisvilles won other than baffled that I felt so little. It's strange. Maybe it means I can no longer root for anything, only against something.

Then again, the strange paralysis I felt this afternoon may have a different meaning. Whatever it is, I'm beginning to feel it again, just knowing I'll be seeing Constance in a few minutes. I'd almost say I feel a sense of impending doom if I hadn't felt so different when I sat down with you, Dear Diary.

Louisville, Ky., July 19

Dear Sam:

Surely this letter will flush you out of cover! Nine errors the Louisvilles committed yesterday in losing 6-5 to the Red Stockings. It was murder what Hecker's mates did to him—and right after the cranks here had given him a floral anchor as a token of their esteem! He received another tribute after the game from an O&M Railroad official—fittingly, (some might say, in view of the defeat hung on him) a floral wreath. To add to your exhilaration over the Red Stockings' triumph, Sam, I'll let you in on two secrets.

The first is that between the wretched support the Louisvilles gave Hecker and the cartoon in yesterday's *Courier-Journal*, I burst out of my paralysis and rooted for the Red Stockings. It helped too that Mountjoy was in the box rather than White, for whom I could never cheer. But the cartoon of Snyder was the straw that broke the camel's back. In it Pop was portrayed as a bawling baby for having kicked to Dyler the previous day that Hecker was jumping out of the box illegally on many of his pitches. The fact is Snyder had a legitimate beef. Hecker really is often times outside the box when he releases the ball. But Dyler ignored the fouling because he's from Louisville and even skippered the Eclipse a while two years ago. Is that cricket, Sam, employing an umpire who reeks of favoritism? And then poking fun at a man who's only trying to see the game is played fairly? But the final rub for me came after Caylor took his seat behind the Red Stockings' bench before yesterday's game and Ed Whiting cried loud enough for every ear in the park to hear: "Hey, look, a pimple on a stick just sat down." Now, granted, Caylor is not the most robust specimen, but still, to publicly humiliate a man like that!

Actually this whole town is rife with bigots and scalawags and ingrates, and their most insufferable trait is their smug conviction that the Louisvilles are destiny's darlings this year. The way the sharps here have already conceded their boys the pennant is all-fired nauseating. Judge for yourself from the standings today of the top clubs in the Association how ridiculous they're being:

	W	L	PCT
Louisville	37	16	.698
St. Louis	35	16	.686
Columbus	36	17	.679
New York	38	18	.679
Cincinnati	35	18	.660

True, the Louisvilles are 12 points ahead, but the Mets have more wins and all five clubs are so tightly bunched that only two games separate them. What's more, the Louisvilles for the past month have played at home where their rowdy partisans and servile umpires have given them all the advantage. When they take to the road, beginning this Sunday in St. Louis, you can bet their lead will swiftly melt.

It grieves me, Sam, the time I've wasted imagining this city could become my home and its nine could replace the Red Stockings in my heart. You and I both know the true reason I'm still here is because I didn't follow my own proverb that base ball and the female of the species mix about as smoothly as honey and vinegar.

Well, now the cat's out of the bag as to my other secret. Constance told me the night before last that she thinks we should part ways. At first her reason was that she'd had a severe bout with her conscience while she was ill and feared her latest moral collapse portended that she was bound for the gutter unless she reformed. But when I started to say I would gladly legitimize our union, she cut in to accuse me of only trying to keep her on the string a bit longer. I was just lonely and homesick, she maintained, and she'd happened along to fill the breech. Well, that wasn't true, I said. And besides, what rule was there that a man couldn't feel lonely and homesick and still be mashed on someone enough to wed her?

She nodded as if she saw my logic, but then she said: "You know I'm very fond of you too, but I daren't let my heart sweep me away, Earl. You must see why." I had no idea what she was driving at, Sam, until she said how could she let herself fall in love with a man who had no prospects at the moment? The world was harsh enough without adding poverty to the burden. And I protested fairly that I was hardly headed for the poorhouse. Why, I'd made $25 the other day just for agreeing to use Hillerich's new-fangled ashwood bats, and that was but a drop in the bucket compared to what I'd earn once I joined the Louisvilles. And when exactly would that be? she asked. Any day now, I said firmly.

At that she dropped her head and began gnawing her lower lip. When she looked up again there were tears in her eyes but her words were no less hard. "I don't think so, Earl. My heart tells me you're a rolling stone that will gather no moss for some time yet. And there's nothing wrong with that, understand, except that I'm on a similar course. We're too much of a pair. What kind of life could we build together when neither of us may ever be a reliable provider?"

There was a lot I might have said to that. I might have said there was still a bright future awaiting me in the dry goods trade if base ball didn't pan out. But all that leapt to mind right then was how some ball players were making as much as $6,000 per annum nowadays! Was she aware of that? She said what of it? Etelka Gerster and Christina Nilsson probably made ten times that sum, but they were only two of the many wondrously gifted singers in the world, most of whom would never earn a sou.

Sam, I ventured several more arguments until I saw Constance's mind was set against me. I did get her to make one concession, though, before we parted. I made her pledge not to write me off permanently as I might yet surprise her. I had nothing definite in mind when I said that, but I've since realized I really do have an ace up my sleeve—and for the moment it's the one secret I won't share even with you. All I'll say is there's no use writing to me now in Louisville. In fact, by the time you receive this I'll probably be long gone from here.

Your nephew, Earl.

Cincinnati, O., July 21

Dear Sam:

Now that your eyes have absorbed the postmark on the envelope, sit down in your rocker and prepare for an even bigger shock. Not only am I back in the Queen City but there is every chance that I'll soon rejoin the Red Stockings, possibly even in time to be in their lineup when the Louisvilles come to American Park this weekend. Imagine Gerhardt's face when he walks on the field and sees who's out there at short stop!

Saturday, after I wrote to you, I went to the Louisville Hotel where the Red Stockings were staying and sought out Charley Jones. He'd just come back from Eclipse Park and was in the dumps, the boys having lost the series finale to the Louisvilles. But he brightened some when I offered to stand treat at the hotel bar until the team left for the depot to catch their train to Indianapolis. Once there, I sounded him out as to the reception he thought I'd get if I went to Stern and said I was now ready to become an assistant grounds keeper if it would put me back in good stead with the club. Jones replied it depended on whether I wanted to wag my tail or have it wag me. He then said that since my real aim was to return to the Red Stockings as a player, the shrewder way to do it was to join one of the local amateur teams in town and prove I was back in form. A couple of good games, and Caylor would persuade Stern to take me back. Just between me and him and his empty glass, Jones said, even Caylor now realized that Fulmer was completely washed up and the club would go to Hell in a hand-basket with Peoples. When I'd boughten another round he went on to say there was definitely truth to the rumor that the Red Stockings were in the market for an established short stop. But they'd about given up that ticket because the only men available were worse than what they had.

Carpenter stuck his puss into the bar then to tell Jones the carriage to deliver the boys to the depot was waiting outside and, upon seeing me, he said: "How're they hanging, Ducker?" And a couple of the other boys also hailed me as I left the bar with Jones. Even White gave me what for him was almost a cordial nod.

But I'm no longer wet behind the ears, Sam. I realize I could languish on an amateur nine for some time before the Red Stockings rehire me. Hence I've taken a job, starting Monday, as a clerk at Mabley & Carew to earn my keep in the interim. This morning, while at the store to interview for the position, I saw something on a haberdashery counter that my eye couldn't pass up. The item will come your way in a few days from their shipping department. Consider it a peace offering and wear it in the spirit in which it was given.

Well, I'll close here so I can get out to the Onions park where the Muldoons are playing a nine from Covington this afternoon. The Muldoons captain greeted me practically like a long lost friend when I ran into him yesterday after I got back in town. He said they've been seeking a short stop for over a month now, and we both know what I've been seeking all that time in the wrong place.

Your nephew, Earl.

P.S. If the return address on the envelope seems familiar, it's because the place where I'm lodging is only a block from my old habitat. So even if you should slip and post your envelope to my former address when you write me, it'll get to me alright. Everyone in the neighborhood remembers me, Sam, down to the Negro bootblack at the street-car stop. It's sure good to be home.

Cincinnati, O., July 22

Dear Sam:

Well, I did it—I fulfilled my pledge to you on the very first pitch I faced in a major league game!

It was a fastball up near my collar, and I lined it smartly back through the box nearly decapitating Boyle. That's Pudge Boyle, Sam, of the St. Louis Maroons, the finest team in balldom. They've already won almost 50 games this year while losing but eight, and in my next letter I'll include a detailed account of their amazing record as well as a box score of today's game. But tonight I just want to share the joyous events of the past 24 hours while they're still vivid in my mind.

Yesterday I made three hits for the Muldoons in my first game back in harness after my injury, and Jones was right, Sam. My performance drew immediate notice. Dan O'Leary was at the game, and he cornered me the instant it was over. I'll allow I didn't remember him at first, but he sure remembered me. He even called me Ducker and he was also aware that my finger had been broken. I still seemed to be favoring it some, he said, judging from a couple of throws I'd made in which the ball had appeared to sail. After I admitted as much, although still only making chit-chat, O'Leary asked me without any more ado how I'd like to play for him, beginning tomorrow when the Cincinnati Unions opened a four-game series with the greatest team in the land. A series that was certain to attract international attention and that his club stood to win if my fearsome bat and magnetic glove were added to their lineup card.

Sam, I want you to know I didn't jump willy-nilly at O'Leary's offer, not even when he sweetened it by saying the Outlaw Reds would throw in a $20 bonus if I signed by dusk so a statement about my capture could be drafted in time to appear in tomorrow's *Enquirer*. I wrestled with my warring desires for a good hour, eager to be back in the major leagues and yet remorseful that it would not enable us to revive our mutual dream. Should I wait on the prayer that the Red Stockings would also make me an offer? And what if they didn't?

With that fear in mind, I signed with the Outlaw Reds last evening. I won't brag about how much money I'm being paid beyond saying it's a lot more than I would have made at Mabley & Carew and will tide me well until November unless I'm disabled again or the club folds. The latter is improbable now that the public has seen the Union Association is the McCoy, but injury is always a risk and there is of course nothing that I or any other player can do except to pray against it happening.

What's more, O'Leary has confided that I'll be at short stop soon in place of Ry Jones, the hand there at the moment. But O'Leary said to keep it our secret for now because Jones thinks I'll remain at third base, where I played today.

O'Leary also clued me that other historic changes are in the works now that Thorner and McLean realize the Red Stockings' miserly tactics have left them vulnerable to a competing franchise in Cincinnati. Union officials everywhere are likewise girding themselves for a massive assault on the League and the Americans. There's already a story going around town that the Maroons are at this very instant about to sheer one of the League teams of its best pitcher. The rumor is he'll arrive in Cincinnati tomorrow to replace Bollicky Billy Taylor, who jumped to the Athletics the other day. Lucas is just serving notice that turnabout is fair play. If our enemies steal one of our boys, we'll swipe one of theirs.

Moreover, the pitcher's box is the lone sector where the Maroons are deficient. With Taylor absconded and Hodnett on the shelf with an ulcerated foot, they're down to Boyle, who's tolerable but no more than that, and Perry Werden, who's just a kid. Give them a first-rate boxman, Sam, and they'd be the equal of every American team and superior to all the outfits in the League, which has become a laughingstock by allowing its pitchers to throw overhand and then trying to make it appear its hitters haven't been overmatched by counting every fair ball hit out of Chicago's hatbox park worth four bases. One of the White Stockings, their third baseman Williamson, already has 16 home runs this season— 16, Sam! There isn't another team in the country that has that many, let alone a single player.

We journey to Chicago to play their Unions after our series with the Maroons, so I'll get to see for myself the quality of ball the League offers since the White Stockings will also be in town while we're there. But I seriously doubt I'll see a man anywhere who's a match for Fred Dunlap. Sam, forget everything I said a while back about Bid McPhee. Dunlap is the best second baseman in base ball now and the sturdiest batsman as well, worth every penny Lucas is paying him. And to follow Dunlap in their batting order the Maroons have Orator Shaffer, Jack Gleason and Dave Rowe. It's a murderous lineup and we did well today holding them to a mere 6-4 conquest that would have fallen to us but for Devinney, the umpire. In the seventh inning he ruled Tom Ryder safe on his roller to me, claiming my throw pulled Martin Powell off the bag. Then two minutes later he made an even more rotten call when Ryder came sliding into third base after Whitehead's sacrifice bunt and I tagged him squarely in the pan. Only Devinney said I'd missed Ryder even though his mouth was just about bleeding, thereby opening the gates for him to score what turned out to be the winning run before we could get the side out.

O'Leary was apoplectic after Ryder was called safe, storming in from his post in centre field and kicking dirt all over Devinney's trousers. Powell and I and Sam Crane, our second baseman, had to drag him away and muzzle him before his cursing got him booted out of the game. O'Leary has about a five-word vocabulary when he flips his lid and a voice that can be heard clear across the river in Kentucky. A minute later, though, his temper has cooled and he's his rollicking self again. As we were all jogging toward our bench after the Maroons were retired, he crept up behind little Dick Burns, our pitcher today, and goosed him brown right in front of the crowd. "Just to remind people," he cackled when Burns jumped a foot into the air. "Even if we don't always win, we're always fun to watch."

Boston, June 7, 1884							
Providences		AB	R	BH	TB	PO	A	E
Hines	c.f.	4	0	1	1	1	0	0
Farrell	2b	4	1	1	1	0	0	1
Radbourn	1b	4	0	1	1	5	0	1
Sweeney	p	4	0	1	1	1	19	1
Irwin	s.s.	3	1	1	1	0	1	0
Denny	3b	3	0	1	1	0	1	0
Carroll	l.f.	3	0	0	0	1	0	1
Nava	c	3	0	0	0	19	3	0
Radford	r.f	3	0	0	0	0	0	0
Totals		31	2	6	6	27	24	4
Bostons		AB	R	BH	TB	PO	A	E
Hornung	l.f.	4	0	0	0	2	0	0
Sutton	3b	4	0	1	2	1	2	0
Burdock	2b	4	0	0	0	2	1	0
Whitney	p	3	1	1	1	0	11	0
Morrill	1b	4	0	1	1	11	1	0
Manning	c.f.	4	0	0	0	1	1	1
Crowley	r.f.	4	0	1	2	2	0	0
Hines	c	3	0	0	0	7	6	2
Wise	s.s.	3	0	0	0	1	1	1
Totals		33	1	4	6	27	23	2

Innings	1	2	3	4	5	6	7	8	9
Providences	0	0	0	0	1	1	0	0	0—2
Bostons	0	0	0	0	0	0	1	0	0—1

Two-base hits— Sutton. Crowley. Base on balls— Bostons 1. First base on errors— Bostons 3. Providences 2. Struck out— Farrell, Radbourn, Sweeney, Irwin, Denny, Carroll, Nava (2), Radford (2), Hornung (3), Burdock (4), Whitney, Morrill (2), Manning (2), Crowley (2), Hines (2), Wise (3). Triple plays— Manning, Morrill and Sutton. Passed balls— Hines 1. Fumbles— Wise, Farrell, Radbourn, Carroll. Muffed fly— Manning. Wild throw— Hines. Attendance— 7387. Time— 1 hour and 35 minutes. Umpire— Burns.

That we definitely were this afternoon, Sam, although it being a weekday only about 750 people saw us. My sole regret, apart from having lost, is that you weren't here to watch me debut, as promised, with a base hit. You'll notice I lauded the Maroons without saying much about our own club, and that's because I'd rather you judged for yourself whether the brand of ball we play is on a par with what you'd have seen if Fate hadn't decreed that I fulfill my pledge in an Outlaw Reds uniform. But I should note that my new livery nonetheless has "Cincinnati" emblazoned across the front of the blouse and that its red and white colors are identical to those worn by the Red Stockings. And it's also fair to remark that Union Park, where I performed today, is the same site the Red Stockings occupied last year and that we both thought, until a few months ago, you'd visit the first time you saw me play as a major leaguer. So much of our dream is still as we pictured it, Sam, that why would anyone quibble over the one small difference?

Your nephew, Earl.

I laid it on pretty thick in my last letter to my uncle, but no doubt he surmised the reason. Yes, dear Diary, I signed with the Outlaw Reds so I could write one loved one I now had definite prospects even at the risk of again painting myself into a corner with my other loved one. But all the claims I made about the Maroons and the Union Association may turn out not to be so outlandish after all.

Dunlap genuinely is a daisy of a player, maybe even the best, and now Lucas really has netted one of the biggest fish in the ocean. Yesterday all the papers, even the ones in the League bastions, acknowledged that he'd inked Charlie Sweeney, the strikeout king the Providences suspended the other day for insubordination. Lucas's audacity leaves the Grays with Radbourn their only proven pitcher and demolishes their hopes of winning the League pennant, as Radbourn hasn't drawn a sober breath since he vacated the cradle. At the same time it probably spells doom for our own flag race. We lost three of our four games with the Maroons, beating only Whitehead, their short stop, when he was pressed into service in the box on Wednesday. By dropping the series we put ourselves 20 games behind the Maroons with the season half gone. Now that they have Sweeney, our cause seems utterly lost unless we too can nab someone of his caliber. And even then, I have to grant, we still won't be a great team. Ry Jones is at most an average short stop, some of our outfielders aren't even that, and Powell, for all his height, can't handle any throws to first base unless they're right in his breadbasket. The other day he just waved at a peg from me that Reilly would have snared with ease. And naturally I got stuck with the error, being the newest man on the team. But I may not wear the greenie's horns much longer if Kick Kelly doesn't pick up his work behind the plate. Even Bradley lost his perpetual grin today when Kelly handed the Maroons four of their seven runs on a silver platter. Then in the dressing room after the game Kelly had the gall to single me out when all the boys began flaming him for his butchery. "If you think you can do better, Ducker," he bleated, "why don't you try hiding your ugly mug behind the mask sometime?"

Kelly doesn't know that I once did just that and it's why everyone now calls me Ducker. None of the Outlaw Reds seem to know—or care—how I came by my nickname, but I'm not so secure about the men on the management end. From certain remarks he's dropped, I fear Thorner may have heard about my ruination in the Mets game, and then this afternoon Lucas uncaged something that let me know he has a finger in just about every pie. "Your throws didn't have that curve to them before your injury," he said. "Is it my imagination or is it natural now?"

He was standing behind third base watching our infield drills before the game, and until he spoke I hadn't even realized he was there. Lucas is very stealthy, insinuating himself in places where he has no business just so he can unearth the odd fact like the one about my throwing. He's right, you know. Some of my throws do seem to have a natural curve now, but I'd hoped to iron it out before anyone else noticed. I wondered how he'd spotted that and what else he might know about me. Henry Lucas is not a fellow I'd care to leave you around, dear Diary. He looks unprepossessing, baby-faced and about half bald, but the boys on his team know that beneath his mild mien lurks a tiger. Even though the Maroons have been leading our circuit all season, he ruthlessly fired Ted Sullivan in order to take the manager's reins himself and has repeatedly shown that no player in the land is untouchable if the Maroons covet him. Yet Mound City denizens have only esteem for Lucas and most sharps are now of the opinion that he's not the gadfly the League and the Americans have painted him to be. Actually, he is destined to become the most revolutionary force the game has yet known unless his rivals hasten to make peace with him.

Many say Sweeney is only the first stroke in a homicidal raid on all the established clubs that will not cease until the Maroons have the best players money can buy at every position. If so, dear Diary, why would Lucas have been analyzing my wares so intently this afternoon unless I figured in his master scheme? Whitehead, his present short stop, is probably the lone man alive who can make even Fulmer look like George Wright. Lucas surely must consider him just a stopgap until the right man comes along, and who's to say I'm not he? I got five hits in my four games versus the Maroons—five hits in just 12 at bats, a feat that I'm sure didn't elude Lucas. And if he's detected that my throws now curve somewhat, he's probably also hit upon a solution to remedy the problem. One he's not about to impart to me while I'm still a member of an enemy team, but come October 31 when my contract with the Outlaw Reds expires...Well, a man's entitled to dream. It all follows when you think about it. Since 1869 St. Louis has replaced Cincinnati as the gateway to the West, so I'd still be playing in the queen of cities. And I'd still wear the colors too because the Maroons play in red on white.

But if Sam thinks I'm building castles in the air, let him only say so. At any event, I mean to hold off writing him again until we get to Chicago and I can enclose the full itinerary for our road trip. It's still somewhat up in the air because of all the kinks the Altoonas created in the schedule when they folded. But the rest of our clubs are solid as granite, dear Diary, and I have to say I'm looking forward to seeing a little of this great country of ours now that I'm in a situation where I'm not just along for the ride.

    In the 1880s base ball was still so rudimentary an enterprise that one might come upon a man without outstanding business acumen who was nevertheless considered a daring and resourceful pioneer if only because he never hesitated to indulge his imagination. Dan O'Leary was just an average player of the game and no master strategist, yet he kept everyone wondering. Is the man ahead of his time or merely a huckster? But while one was deciding O'Leary would introduce some new twist that would have to be taken into account. Oh, he'd get behind the most bizarre schemes, like playing base ball on roller skates in indoor arenas during the winter months, but then he would upset all opinions of him by doing something quite shrewd. If there was one criticism of him that universally held true, it was that he was open to a fault to suggestions from players he supervised. At the same time, he was deft at assessing talent and swift to discard those he found lacking.

    Of all the players the Outlaw Reds jettisoned during O'Leary's tenure at the club's helm, none ever played again in the major leagues with any impact. But even more extraordinary was his assessment of which players should be signed as replacements. O'Leary had spotted Draves way back in the early spring at one of the Red Stockings' first outdoor workouts, which he had attended looking like a railway laborer. The kid might never make a short stop, but his batting alone demanded that a place be found for him somewhere. O'Leary could do nothing for a while after the Red Stockings released Draves because Thorner would not hear of hiring a player who was not fit right away for duty. But he bided his time and it bore fruit when Draves came back to town from Louisville with his finger mended.

    O'Leary was not really among the more memorable figures of his time, even in Cincinnati. But he worked hard at becoming one, living at the Gibson Hotel in a room with a private bath and seeing to it that he always had a fresh carnation in his coat lapel. The carnation was his trademark. As was his intention, base ball writers in every city where the Outlaw Reds played observed that he was never without one and made mention of the fetish in their papers. Only the men who played with O'Leary in Cincinnati knew that he was not so fastidious in his home life, for unbeknownst to the hotel management he harbored a dog in his room.

    It was not an appealing dog either. The natural reason to have a dog is for companionship, but O'Leary's animal did not even offer much of that. It had a nasty disposition, its hair looked like soot, and it drooled constantly. Any guess as to what mixture of breeds it was

would have been as good as another. O'Leary saw it running recklessly
around Bank Street outside Union Park one afternoon before a game and
tethered it to a gate post so it wouldn't be run over by a buggy. When no
one claimed the dog by the time the game ended, he lodged it in the
team dressing room. The dog might have resided there indefinitely as a
kind of maudlin team mascot if it had not picked a fight with Thorner's
bull terrier, Redleg. Thorner, whose dog was a purebred, properly had a
fit when Redleg was set upon by a mongrel, and O'Leary took the stray
away forthwith. No one could have imagined he would not drown it.
Sam Crane was the first to learn O'Leary had ensconced it in his hotel
room, when he was summoned there for a consultation on how to
improve the team. If it had been any other man but Crane, his report
might have been doubted. The dog had a red and white brocade pillow
for a bed and wore a carnation pinned to its collar. O'Leary confided
that he smuggled it in and out of his room in a leather bat bag whenever
it had to do its business.

Several other team members saw the dog when they visited
O'Leary's room over the next two weeks, but none ever saw it with
O'Leary anywhere else. The dog did not appear in public again until
O'Leary was fired by Thorner. There were many diverse stories about
why this occurred, but O'Leary's dog was not prominent in any of them.
Perhaps it ought to have been. Certainly Thorner had not forgotten the
molesting given Redleg when he learned of the brush O'Leary had with
Henry Lucas.

"If you want a new first baseman, don't look for him in my
stall," Lucas had said to start it.

"What makes you think we're not content with Powell?" said
O'Leary.

"Then why were you stoking Werden today?" It was always
tiring talking to O'Leary.

"We're chums."

"Dan, listen. You're a smooth operator and Werden's still green
as grass. If you tell him you'll make him your first baseman and let him
pitch now and then too if he wins his release from us, he'll be eating out
of your hand. But all you'll do is add to his frustration because we're not
about to let him go."

"Why not? Now that you've nabbed Sweeney the kid is excess
baggage."

"Not necessarily. We might eventually use him at first base
ourselves."

"And do what with Quinn? For that matter, why are you
stockpiling these players like Ryder you know damn well you don't
need?"

"Haven't you forked that one out yet?"

"Maybe you'd better fork it out for me. And don't try to sling any of your shit. As one shit-slinger to another, I know when I'm being fed it."

So they got into it and O'Leary was fired. When he entered the Outlaw Reds dressing room to bid farewell to the team, his dog trailed him. Everyone strove to ignore it. They kept their eyes fixed on O'Leary, they shook his hand, and their imaginations ran riot that the dog was down there drooling on their boots or worse.

O'Leary snapped his fingers when he was ready to go. "Come, Lucas," he said as he made for the door, and the dog loyally followed him. Now that his back was turned, the constraint on the faces of his former teammates was apparent. Until that moment none of them had known the dog had a name. It gave the creature an unwanted status. Now they could not but remember Lucas whenever they remembered O'Leary, and their memory of him was already tainted by the frightening suddenness with which he had been discharged. Still, it was faintly consoling that he had named the dog after his antagonist.

Chicago, Ill., July 29

Dear Sam:

We'll be in Chicago at the Continental Hotel on Wabash and Madison Streets till August 3 when we journey to St. Louis. So there's still time to write me here and I can also assure you that if your letter arrives after we're gone it'll be forwarded to me in the Mound City or else in Kansas City, our next stop. After that we'll return home on the 18th to play the Chicagos a rematch and then be off again to St. Louis and Cow Town. Then it's back to Cincinnati for another series with the Kansas Citys, followed by our last Eastern road swing of the season.

Now you know my itinerary for the entire next month, so there can't be any more excuses on your end or any more surprises on mine. I'm only kidding, Sam. I know you have a good reason for not having written and, Lord knows, I'll probably have provided you with a rash of new surprises between now and then. There are already some in this letter, one being that I'm still playing third base and not about to bug O'Leary at the moment over his promise to switch me to short stop, if only because my batting eye has suddenly dimmed to the extent that I've worn the collar in our last three games. The first was on Friday versus Werden of the Maroons, then here on Sunday versus Daily and finally today versus Atkinson, who recently jumped to the Unions from the Athletics. I've had company, though, because most of the other boys haven't exactly been knocking the leather off the ball lately either.

Nevertheless, we eked out a win over Atkinson this afternoon, but Daily was another kettle of fish. Sam, did you ever dream that in spite of your grim disability you might still have made a name for yourself on the diamond? Hugh Daily is doing just that with only one arm after losing half of the other in an explosion while a boy. And to boot, he struck out 19 batters in a game the other week to tie Sweeney's World's Record, even though he got credit for only 18 because his catcher missed a third strike allowing the batter to reach base. Against Daily's inshoots I went down on strikes twice myself, and I also made another wild throw. But Ry Jones flung one away too and Crane outstank us both by committing three miscues. So O'Leary had plenty of choices if he wanted to name a scapegoat for our loss. But he didn't because he's one, as I've said, who doesn't cry over spilt milk. Actually, about all he said when Daily demolished us was that anyway we'd pulled a nice crowd, somewheres around 3,000, and we'd get them tomorrow.

We didn't lure even half that number today, Sam, but that's really the Chicagos' fault. They wear the dreariest uniforms ever, black blouses and gray pants with striped caps. They look more like a gang of convicts than a ball team, and then they play at the 39th Street Grounds, way south along the lake in a neighborhood where you take your life in your hands just to venture. Actually this whole city is one enormous dung-heap, but at the same time sections of it are amazing. I've never seen buildings anywhere near as tall as here, not even in New York. Even as I'm writing this, I can see one going up right next to my hotel. Actually, I've spent more time than I care to admit alone here in my room just so I can watch members of the construction crew amble high in the air like tightrope walkers on bare steel beams without even any nets below them. Sam, all over town there are other buildings just like my neighbor springing up quicker than fleabites on a sleeping dog's fanny. The buttons here at the hotel tells me that most of them are not going on prairies—that's what they call vacant lots here—but on land with buildings less than 10 years old that were erected just since the Great Fire of '71. Here at the drop of a hat they tear down perfectly good buildings just to build bigger ones. They say Chicago has more than twice the population Cincinnati has now, but it definitely has about ten times as many thieves and beggars. And the smell of it! Every afternoon going out to the ballpark we have to pass near the stockyards on our street-car ride. I like to have gagged from the stench, which can even reach all the way to our hotel in the "Loop" when the wind is wrong. The Loop is the downtown area, so called because the street-car lines run in an enormous loop that circles it, mostly following the river.

Since yesterday was a holiday for us, Hawes and Ry Jones and I went to see a League game at Lake Park. It was nice having to walk only about a block to the park from our hotel, and when we first got inside it I believed I must be in the wrong place. The White Stockings' home ground is like no other ballpark in the land. The grandstand has private boxes in it, just like in a theater, with upholstered chairs, each with its own personal spittoon. The base paths must be at least eight feet wide and are made of crushed stone and cinders. And the infield grass is immaculately kept, all green and freshly trimmed. But then your eyes travel to the outfield and suddenly the park is no longer such an architectural gem. The fences there, just like I'd heard tell, are so short it looks like you're playing in somebody's back yard, the one in right field especially, where first base is almost in the shadow of it by late afternoon. Then too, as the game wore on, the trains constantly pulling into and out of the Illinois Central yards bordering the park made it nearly impossible to hear yourself think. Confidentially, Sam, I found Lake Park a splendid place in some respects but a poor stage for a base ball game. Plus the League brand of ball, judging from the sample I saw yesterday, truly is a farce.

After all these years of reading about the fabled Chicago White Stockings, I was all set to see nine Greek gods trot out on the field. But what I saw instead was a crew who put their trousers on one leg at a time like everybody else—if they can find a pair to fit, that is! This Cap Anson is so big he can't help making a fair target at first base, but he moves about as fast as a lamppost. In the game he hit a home run, a lazy air ball that just did clear the short barrier in left field and allow him to trot around the bases, which was extremely lucky for him because if he ever had to leg out a four-bagger he'd perish from the exertion. But Anson at least reputedly harbors a decent physique underneath his uniform whereas Ned Williamson, another air-ball specialist in this hatbox park, looks like there is one head but two bodies underneath his. Williamson has a bay window that makes any roller he has to bend for an adventure in gravitational pull. The only genuinely worthy players the White Stockings have are Gore and maybe Dalrymple and of course the one and only King Kelly (when he's not stewed to the gills) and then their keystone pair of Pfeffer and Tommy Burns. Flint and Corcoran, for all their reputation as a battery, had their hands full yesterday against the Detroits, and if there's a lamer nine than those Wolverines it can only be a grammar school team. A Rhinelander named Meinke pitched for Detroit and came in for a steady dose of guying because his home is here in Chicago. But it was mild compared to what Buker, the Wolves short fielder, heard every time he came to bat. If Buker were ever to get a hit, they'd have to stop the game and revive everybody in the park. He stands up there at the dish as if he's terrified the ball's going to bite him, and Weidman and a couple of the other Wolves are only a notch less timid.

Still, the Detroits got three runs off Corcoran, and the White Stockings were only able to nick Meinke for five. The entire game was an exercise in mediocrity, neither team showing any flair, and I'm certainly not liable to squander 50¢ again when I'm guaranteed a better game for two bits at any of the American parks and can participate in one every day for free with the Outlaw Reds.

But don't take my word for it, Sam. Circle August 19 on your calendar. That's the day we open our next homestand against the Chicagos, and I've already reserved a seat for you behind our bench. I'm telling you now so you'll have three full weeks to plan the trip to Cincinnati. But please wear that item I had shipped to you. So much time has passed since we last saw each other that otherwise I may not recognize you—haha, Sam, only kidding again, as you know.

Your nephew, Earl.

He would be "King" forever. Though he lay dying of pneumonia at 36, ravaged by two decades of drinking and revelry, gazing up at the shadows and stains of time on the ceiling of his hospital room, he did not fear his passing. Something of him would survive. The King could never die. There was a power of legend that could outlast him and every one of his actual deeds.

Near death, shriveled and sweating, Michael Joseph "King" Kelly feverishly remembered the final day of the 1884 season when word came to him in the White Stockings' dressing room that he had won his first National League batting title. Already ten years ago. How quickly the time had fled. He could still feel the thrill that had been all his own the first time he came to bat in a League game. As he had stood there at the plate, fresh from the ranks of the International Association, he had been almost dizzy at the lack of fear and his own confidence. The memory was as sharp and full and satisfying as his vision now was blurred. He could barely hold his eyes open any longer. He could scarcely see at all. He could little know that he was only moments away from being the first of a sacred breed to die—the first great base ball player who would one day be named to the Hall of Fame.

August 4

Even though I headed this entry "August 4," it may actually still be August 3. I'd check my watch for the exact time but, alas, some galoot in the crowd picked it out of my pocket as we boarded the train this evening in Chicago. Luckily, he didn't get my notecase, which I've been carrying in my boot ever since three of our boys—Hawes,

Sylvester and Powell—had theirs pilfered while they were celebrating the other night in one of the local hotspots.

I'd be apt to celebrate some myself now but for the theft of my timepiece and the bulletin I saw in one of the Chicago papers just before getting on the train. The blow it dealt me must have made me too numb to feel the criminal hand that penetrated my watch pocket. Before then I'd been euphoric, having played short stop today for the first time in a major league game. Granted, it was only an exhibition contest; but our opponents were the Chicagos, the same nine we'd battled four times this past week, so all that impedes me from considering the game my official debut at my rightful position is that it won't count in the standings.

But then I saw in tonight's paper that the Red Stockings had released Fulmer and were going to sign Frank Fennelly of the now defunct Washington Americans club as his replacement. Ha, I hear Sam saying, there you go, Earl—you lost out again. Well, maybe so. But then I'm a regular tonight on the Outlaw Reds and where are Fulmer and Peoples? One's out in the snow and the other's back on the bench. So it could have turned out a lot worse, right, dear Diary?

And what's more, we split our four games with the Chicagos and rate to move up in the standings if we can take two of three from the Maroons and then sweep the weakling Kansas Citys. By the time we come home, we could be in third place or even second. Most of the boys privately think the second rung is the highest to which we can reasonably aspire, but that's not to say we've completely despaired of catching the Maroons. Just the other day, in fact, Thorner and McLean fulfilled my prophecy to Sam by getting rid of Kick Kelly and taking on a new backstopper.

His name is Joe Crotty and you're likely to hear more of him, dear Diary, as he's a rough item. He sports a mustache twirled at the ends like a stage-play villain and he's a deadly card shark, so skilled with a deck of 52 that many of the boys have already ceased sitting down across the table from him. But he does know his trade behind the bat. On Tuesday, in his very first game with us, he caught Bradley so masterfully that the Grinner whitewashed One Arm Daily, 3-0.

That same night, while three of the boys were out making a gift of their notecases to some of Chicago's lowlifes, Crotty conducted me and Bill Harbidge to one of the local faro parlors. Harbidge lost everything but the shirt off his back and, strain as I would to hold to a conservative style of play, I still lost $8.40. But Crotty won over $30 and then went back the next night for more despite knowing the sharps would be laying for him. Harbidge chose not to accompany him this time and I went only as a spectator, having learned my lesson. I expected to witness Crotty being savagely fleeced, but instead we both became spectators when he saw one of the men who would be pitted against him was none other than Dick Higham. "Thanks but no thanks," he said when he was offered a seat at the table, and to me he whispered: "That there just may be the crookedest man on the entire earth."

I would not have known Higham from the Man in the Moon, but Crotty met up with him two years ago while playing with the Browns. Von Der Ahe's men were stranded in Cleveland one night when their train had a mishap, and Higham was in town at the same time to umpire the Blues game with the Detroits. Even though he was already suspected of betting on the games he officiated, he had no qualms about being seen in Cleveland with a boodle of gamblers. Crotty said Higham was suspected of crooked work as far back as nine or 10 years ago when he was playing for a Chicago team in the old National Association and the mystery is that anyone could think he would reform if he were appointed an umpire. It should have come as no shock to anyone that he slanted his calls to favor whichever team had his bet for the day, and it was certainly no great surprise when he was permanently cast out of base ball. Yet Higham appears little the worse for his banishment. Now he's one of the most prominent bookmakers in Chicago as well as a first-rate card shark. Crotty claimed he would not even play Ring-Around-the-Rosy with Higham without fear of it being rigged.

By the bye, dear Diary, Crotty is one of my roommates while we're on the road. There were only four of us to a room on the Red Stockings, but the Outlaw Reds, being a fledgling enterprise, must be more frugal and hence I had to bunk with five other boys in Chicago. Fortunately Crotty isn't the one with whom I have to share a bed as he has the breath of a dead dog. My mate at the moment is Dick Burns, who is so small and slenderly built that—

Well, I hope no one strains his eyes trying to read the words I just crossed out. Suffice it to say that it's lonely out here at night over 300 miles away from Ohio and even farther than that from a certain other locale. (And especially now that Sam isn't the only person to whom I'm writing without ever getting a reply.)

August 7

Not having received any pleasant surprises here, I'm now hoping there'll be one awaiting me in Kansas City. Exactly when we'll be going there is indefinite though, as things are in disarray owing to some pending changes in the schedule and the heavy casualties the Maroons inflicted on us. Bad enough that we lost all three games of the series, but today we also lost Bradley, possibly for the rest of the season. In the seventh inning his wrist was fractured when he covered the plate to keep Dunlap from scoring from third base on a passed ball, and Dunlap barreled into him, knocking him backside over elbows. It was a clean blow, dear Diary, don't get me wrong. Dunlap and the other Maroons simply play the game for keeps, which is why they're the top nine in the country, although the personnel they have has something to do with it too. Sweeney pitched two of their victories over us, today's and Tuesday's, and if there is a more awesome pitcher on earth, I prefer not to see him. I managed just one scratch hit off Prince Charlie in two contests and at that fared better than most of our boys. On Tuesday Sweeney nearly tossed a no-hit game against us, ceding only a single to right field by Sylvester, who came within a whisker of being retired when Shaffer grabbed his stroke on one hop and fired the ball to Quinn at first base just as little Lou crossed the bag.

Today's defeat left us with 34 wins and 30 losses and killed our last dream of winning the pennant. We'll be hard put now just to finish above .500, but at least we can't land in the cellar. The Kansas Citys have the basement all locked up, owning only five wins and over 30 losses since joining our circuit. They're in peril of collapsing, we hear, which may be why it's unsettled at the moment where we go next from St. Louis. We also learned this evening that the Philadelphia Keystones folded after their game today in Boston and that Lucas has begun casting the waters for a team to replace them.

It begins to look as if Lucas is keeping our loop afloat just about all by himself. He has unlimited capital apparently, having inherited a pile from his father, who was a railroad baron; but he is nevertheless turning out to be the first humane owner I've encountered since I met Von Der Ahe on my last trip to St. Louis. (And can it be only coincidence that both of them are operating here in the Mound City?) But whereas Von Der Ahe has been accused of venturing into base ball mainly to increase the sales of his beer, Lucas is in the game for the love of it. He's a player himself, though you'd never think it to look at him. Last year he sponsored a team here called Lucas's Amateurs and served as his own third baseman. So he knew his oats when he analyzed my throwing the other day, and last evening he made another keen observation about me. He said that since my finger was now permanently crooked I'd probably always impart a natural curve to my throws and hence should consider becoming a pitcher.

The circumstances under which this discussion occurred bear explaining lest it seem that Lucas and I are now bosom pals. We are far from it, much as we might mutually respect one another. The actual truth is it was entirely Crotty's doing that I found myself in Lucas's company last night.

Yesterday confirmed that Crotty is a man you can trust no farther than you can throw him. At supper he claimed he suddenly remembered he'd left his catcher's mask behind in the Maroons park and asked me to go back with him and help look for it as he feared it would be stolen if it were left out on the field overnight. When we got to the park and found all the gates locked, he suggested we seek out a key. Lucas's private estate adjoins the park, so it seemed a rational errand. Actually, I suspected nothing until Crotty led me up Cass Street to a beer garden, saying he wanted a quaff to muster his nerve before he approached the guard-booth that defends the estate, and who did we see seated at an outdoor table but Lucas, who immediately invited us to joined him.

Naturally I knew at once that this meeting had been prearranged. But I'm still unsure why I was included. At any event, no sooner were the amenities done than Crotty came right out and told Lucas he'd seen enough after just two days in St. Louis to know he wanted to play for the Maroons and he was ready right now to pledge himself for next season if they could agree on terms. Lucas seemed amused at first by the proposition. He asked what made Crotty think his services were desired? Because, Crotty said, of the two catchers the Maroons now had, Baker couldn't hit and Brennan couldn't throw, and he'd already shown he could do both. "Yet two years ago," said Lucas, "you hit and caught next to nothing while you were with the Browns."

And Crotty said: "But that was two years ago." Putting in a smile, he then said: "In base ball a man must be judged on what he does today." Lucas manufactured a smile of his own and then asked Crotty how old he was? Twenty-two, said Crotty. Still smiling, Lucas said: "If that's really your true age as opposed to your base ball age, from your look, friend, you've had a hard life." "Could be," said Crotty, abbreviating his smile. "But then we all aren't born with silver spoons in our mouths, Saint Henry."

I expected Lucas to take umbrage at that brash retort, but he just sat a moment in silence, and then he said, grudgingly fascinated: "Pray, tell me your terms, Crotty." Said Crotty: "The same sum you're paying Baker or Brennan, whichever you decide to dump. Plus a written assurance I'll get a piece of the price if you sell me to another club." When Lucas's expression hardened and he said such an assurance was out of the question, Crotty said: "Wasn't it in *Sporting Life* the other week that you said: `I cannot see how a body of men has the right to dictate what another man shall do.'" True, admitted Lucas, but that had been in reference to the Reserve Clause binding a player to a team against his will. Well, inquired Crotty, didn't selling a player to another team without his consent amount to the same thing? Either way, it was an attempt to rule a man's life. Lucas hemmed and hawed a while and then finally acknowledged that Crotty might have a point. But even so, he said, he was in no position now to make any commitments for next season, particularly not to a player on a rival team in his own circuit. Why, the very fact that he was meeting with Crotty like this could be construed as tampering with another man's employee.

"Yet he agreed to meet me," Crotty said later as we rode back to our hotel. "So why did he, Ducker?" The real question at the moment, at least to me, I said, was why I'd been invited along. "Feed me your guess," said Crotty. I reckoned that it was as a witness in case Lucas said something Crotty worried he'd later deny having said. Crotty didn't admit I was right, but he did say: "Well, and I thought you were a greenie. Now why do you think Lucas didn't tell me to take a long walk off a short pier when I asked to meet with him?"

When I had no good answer to that, Crotty laughed. "See, Ducker, it's this way. His aim tonight was the same as mine. We're both just trying to cover our backsides." He then said it was already plain to him after a barely a week in the Union Association that he'd boarded a sinking ship. In that event, I said, angry at his cynicism, why didn't he get out while the getting was still good? Because beggars couldn't be choosers, he said. I wanted to ask how he meant that, but something about his face suggested I wouldn't like his answer. And I was right. For a few minutes later, after we'd got off the street car and stopped for something to slake our thirst, he said I was in the same boat as he. Most of the boys in our loop were, for that matter. Take away Dunlap and Sweeney and one or two other big-name stars, and what was left? You had a crew of misfits and has-beens and hand-me-downs. You had old George Bradley and Sam Crane, who'd been released last year by the Mets, and O'Leary, a fine man with whom to be stranded on a deserted island. Then you had Harbidge and Hawes and Powell, League rejects all, and Sylvester and Burns, two bantams who could stand on each other's shoulders and still not see over the top of a bar stool. Yet we'd won over half our games, making Crotty wonder about the clubs he still hadn't seen. How awful must the Kansas Citys be if they couldn't win even one game in seven? No worse than some of the League and American outfits, I said without quite understanding why I was arguing against a view that I secretly held myself. But there's something infuriating about Crotty. He's the kind of man you desperately hope to prove wrong even when your heart tells you he's right.

At the same time, I found myself warming to him. Even if most of what he said last night was bull, of all the boys on the team he picked me to accompany him for his confab with Lucas. Actually, he seems to look upon me as a crony now. Today he even saved a seat for me beside him on the carriage we took to the Maroons park. Now that may not be much, but it's more than anyone else has done for me lately.

Cincinnati, O., August 10

Dear Sam:

Before you leap to the conclusion that I'm back in Cincinnati because I was released again or else our club folded after the disastrous series in St. Louis, let me swiftly put your mind to rest. Before journeying to Kansas City we detoured here to play an exhibition game against the Maroons and then a makeup championship game today. Ridiculous, you say—a total waste of train fare in these hard times to come all the way back here for only two games, one of which won't even count!

Well, Sam, the truth is Thorner and McLean had a very shrewd motive for staging these games now. What's more, the train fare they expended is a pittance compared to the money they shelled out on Friday to sign three players who have made us, in one fell swoop, the equal of the Maroons.

We beat the immortal Sweeney this afternoon 7-4 and would have crushed him in yesterday's exhibition too if our new trio hadn't taken a day longer to report than anticipated, thus disappointing the mammoth crowd that came out to welcome them to Union Park. The turnout today was only about half as big, probably because some people feared being stood up again. But those who came are sure to return and meanwhile to tell their friends the Outlaw Reds are now the go. The club still isn't done cleaning house either. Ry Jones has already been ordered to pack his valise and Powell is near certain to be next. I'd be worried for my own fair skin if I were not the team's third-leading batsman at the moment.

Oh, incidentally, Sam, our new men are Jim McCormick, Jack Glasscock and Fatty Briody.

It has now come out that we weren't left dangling in St. Louis the other day because of some problem with the Kansas City team. Instead it was because Thorner and McLean had a coup in the works that has made even Lucas's theft of Sweeney look pallid in comparison.

On Friday, Frank Wright, our club secretary, took his check-book to Grand Rapids, where the Clevelands were playing an exhibition game that day, and filched Glasscock, Briody and McCormick right out from under the Blues' noses. The first two reportedly each got $1,500 to join us for the rest of the season while McCormick got $2,000. But Briody has confided those figures are less than the true amount. He swears that Wright gave them each several hundred dollars more under the table.

The Clevelands are up in arms over our daring raid and threaten to take us to court, not that it will do them any good. Mark my words, Sam, Friday will go down in history as the turning point. Now that we have allied with Lucas in wreaking havoc on the League, there will soon be no sacred cows. Already there's a rumor afoot that Buck Ewing will desert the Gothams any day now and sign with us so he can play in his hometown. And if the peerless Ewing jumps ship, can King Kelly, Anson, Brouthers and the rest of the League's stars be far behind? By the time we get to Kansas City we may not be just the equal of the Maroons—we may be the most powerful nine ever assembled.

But as every cloud has a silver lining, so it must have a speck of gray. With Glasscock's coming, so goes my last chance this season of playing short stop. Still, there is even a sunny side to this development. Glasscock ranks among the best short fielders alive now, rivaled only by Bill Gleason and Tommy Burns. So by playing beside him at third base I'll be able to study at the feet of a master.

Already I've learned plenty from him, Sam. Today I was taught that a short fielder should handle most pop flies hit into foul ground behind third base. His angle of pursuit is better than a third sacker's, Glasscock says. To illustrate, he drew a diagram in the dirt with his finger. It looked so obvious when he made his case, yet none of the other diamond fielders I've seen play this year seem aware of it. On the Red Stockings, Fulmer always let Carpenter take charge of foul flies, and the only reason the Louisvilles don't expect the same from Browning is because he never goes after air balls of any kind unless they'll otherwise hit him on the head.

And while I'm on the subject of those two teams, the Louisvilles were here in late July while we were in Chicago, and the series, from what I've heard, was a joke. Ross, the umpire, robbed the Louisvilles of the first game at everything but gunpoint. And then the next day he ruled that one of Hecker's pitches grazed Mountjoy's blouse and awarded Billy his base to force home the tying run in the ninth inning. After the game Mountjoy gleefully confessed the ball had never touched him!

Before the series, White laid a row of smooth stones in front of the box at American Park so that Hecker would slip on them if he finished his delivery outside it like he had down in Louisville. Dirty pool, right, Sam? But the Louisvilles were no paragons of virtue either. When Cincinnati went to Eclipse Park for the return series earlier this week, Gerhardt piled stones on the right side of the box where White always stands to start his delivery. White hollered a blue streak, but Gerhardt just told him tough sugar, there was no rule in the book forbidding it.

So you see the level to which the game has descended in the American Association. And the League version is speedily becoming our own now that we're in the process of purloining most of their leading lights.

I'm not done strutting, Sam. In the past few days there have been three other glorious occurrences. One is that Gerhardt has been stripped of his captaincy in favor of Walsh, his former assistant. It would be grand to report that Will White had suffered a like Fate, but I can't as yet although many of the Queen City sharps believe it's just a matter of time now before he too is asked to step down.

I can relate, though, that Briody's arrival has knocked some wind out of Crotty's sails. From thinking he was a superman among men of straw, he now is no better than second-string on the Outlaw Reds, rated to catch only on days McCormick doesn't pitch. Which means about once a week since Scotch Jim was the League's top heaver last year and doesn't appear to have slipped at all contrary to the stories out of Cleveland that he was no great loss because his arm was about cooked anyway.

And last but far from least, Sam, today on my way home from Union Park I stopped at a drug store to buy some ointment for heat rash, and while I was at the counter paying for it there was commotion behind me, causing me to turn from the clerk. Whereupon I saw four young boys gawking at me. They immediately clamed up and shyly looked away, but when I went to leave the drug store they started up again. "It is, I'm sure it's him!" I heard one of them say. "That's Ducker Draves!" And, Sam, the awe and worship I heard in his voice was worth a million dollars.

Your nephew, Earl.

P.S. We'll return here from Kansas City on the 19th to play the Chicagos. Seats for that series are going like hot-cakes, but I still have one reserved in your name behind our bench for all three games. Just a single word letting me know what day you're coming and I'll be at the train depot with bells on.

Kansas City, Mo., August 17

Dear Sam:

When you're hot you're hot! And I'm not referring to the weather although every day here the temperature's been over 90. One day, Sam, the air on the field was so torrid that I burned my finger when I accidentally brushed it against my belt buckle. I exaggerate not. The skin was scorched so bad that between innings I had to rub some of the ointment on it that I've been using for this infernal heat rash I've contracted. Then I went back to soaking my feet in buckets of cold water with the rest of the boys just so we could endure the next inning in the field.

Yesterday, when a thunderstorm washed out the game and cooled things off a tad, I actually said a prayer of gratitude. Feature that, Sam—my being thankful for rain after all the grief Mother Nature caused me back in the spring!

It's strange how the worm has turned. We swept the series here with ludicrous ease although we did toss the Cowboys a bone in Friday's exhibition game, putting Sylvester in the box so they could look good for once in front of their cranks. It paid off too as nearly 7,000 people came out today to investigate whether the Cowboys' exhibition win had been more than a fluke. But all they got for their money was the sight of McCormick setting down their boys without even a whisper of a run.

McCormick is stupendous. Grin Bradley hasn't a Chinaman's chance of regaining his status as our ace twirler when his wrist heals. And despite his heft Briody is amazingly agile back of the plate. He can stroke too, never mind the terrible .169 batting average he brought with him from Cleveland. The reason it was so low, Briody avers, is because scorers in the League refused to believe a man of his bulk could beat out all the infield hits he did and kept calling them errors.

But Glasscock is the real prize we got in the package from the Blues. Every game I play beside him is an education. He moves like a wraith, gobbling up grounders so effortlessly that I would surrender my dream of being called Easy Earl and present the nickname to him if he didn't already have one that fit him like a glove. Because of his penchant for ridding the earth around short stop of even the most miniscule pebbles to prevent bad hops, he's known as Pebbly Jack.

Owing to his unfortunate surname, he also has another sobriquet. But anybody who utters it in his presence risks losing a mouthful of teeth although he will tolerate being called Moneybags. McCormick, however, will not. For a man who's carved a sizable notch in the world, McCormick has skin the thickness of a schoolgirl's. During the first game he pitched here the Cowboys had him near tears just by shouting that he'd run out on the League because he couldn't raise his arm high enough anymore to throw overhand. At last, to show them wrong, he flung a pitch from above his shoulder and then when the umpire warned him for employing an illegal delivery, he bellowed: "Don't you see I had to do it? How much must a man take?"

About the only criticism he's not too tender to endure is that he's got what amounts to a private suite here in our hotel. He has only two roommates, his fellow Blues, and because the three of them are being treated like royalty by the club, the rest of us are being put up like sheep. There are eight of us in my room here, Sam, to occupy two double beds and four cots that are crammed so close together all of them have to be removed each time Hawes, the man nearest the wall, has to get up to use the toilet. Too, the room is right over a boiler, which pounds all night. Between that and the snoring and the three million mosquitoes that feasted on me since it was too hot to hide under the sheets, I didn't get a wink of sleep our first night here. The next two nights I spent in a chair down in the lobby, and then last night, when my back wouldn't take any more torture, Crotty and I and Harbidge walked the streets till the wee hours of the morning, something I would never do alone in the lawless atmosphere that prevails in this town.

I can't claim to have seen any gun fights here yet, Sam, but no one is at all bashful about using his fists. Last night I saw two men beat each other to a pulp in a dispute over which of them had the faster horse. You'd think they would have let their steeds settle it civilly by racing, but the fact that one of the men was an Indian no doubt helps to explain how the barbaric outburst came about. In this burg, Sam, there are Indians nearly everywhere and not only fighting with white men but drinking and eating right alongside them often as not!

As for Western women, I have no comment save to note that there were two junctures on my nocturnal amble when I had to stand in wait with only myself for company. All discussion of where Harbidge and Crotty were during those intervals ought to be omitted, but I'm obliged to open your eyes to another Cow Town custom that my own orbs still can't believe they witnessed. Out here, Sam, people don't always even bother to go behind closed doors when a fleshly urge overcomes them.

But enough of my doings, what of yours? How is the corn looking back there this summer? Here it's already as high as my spirits at the moment.

Will there be a letter from you at my boarding house when I return to Cincinnati tomorrow, telling me which of our games with the Chicagos you plan to attend? Once again, Sam, the dates are the 19th, 20th and 21st. Of course I'll be at the train depot all three days, but have no worry that I'll just sit there twiddling my thumbs on the prayer you'll come because I aim to bring ample reading matter to occupy me while I wait. I have a lot of catching up to do, Sam, now that I've stopped spending all my nights alone with a good book.

Your nephew, Earl.

P.S. Hawes has been playing first base for us since Powell left, but O'Leary says we'll have a new gateway guardian soon and it'll be a man even bigger than Powell. Long John Reilly? Cap Anson? Big Dan Brouthers? Who else can it be since they're the only first basemen in balldom even close to Powell's size?

Jim McCormick was born in Glasgow sometime in 1856; the exact date may never be unearthed. Most of his early life remains a question mark too—we don't even know when he came from Scotland to America or with whom. In all, less is known about McCormick than any other great player. Those who would doubt his credentials for stardom have only to look at the particulars of his career. In his prime he was the best pitcher in the game, buried on a mediocre team. "Don't you ever wish you were free to play elsewhere?" asked Fred Dunlap the last year the two were teammates, once Cleveland had fallen out of the 1883 National League race. "No, son," said McCormick, "not when it would mean starting all over somewhere new." "You'd do it if the money was right," challenged Dunlap. "If I was in this for the money, it would take at least four grand to turn my head," McCormick contended.

No one ever knew for sure—the beauty of the Outlaw Reds' coup was that no one ever discovered just how much—but about half the booty went to McCormick, maybe a third to Glasscock, and Briody got the leavings. Each, in any case, received a packet more than the Blues would have paid him if he remained in Cleveland.

Around $10,000, and it was for less than half a season. There were teams then that didn't squander that much on their entire payroll. The Chicago White Stockings were not one of those miserly teams, but the following year, when McCormick joined them, he had to take a large salary cut because the Ansons and the Kellys had to be given theirs first. What was worse, he learned that despite winning 40 games in 1884 he would not even be the club's ace pitcher, the honor falling to John Clarkson, the previous season's rookie phenom. McCormick's decline came swiftly after that, although there was nothing wrong with his arm. He simply lost heart, for while he had a world of ability he had only a thimbleful of confidence. He needed constant praise, and Anson and Chicago owner Al Spalding were not about to offer it.

At the close of the 1884 season the sharps who kept count of such things in those days were wagering that he would be the first hurler to win 300 games in his career. He was only 28 and he already had 199 victories under lock and key. Certainly, he seemed good for another 100 or so. But McCormick quit in 1887 still 35 wins short of 300. Later he opened a saloon in Paterson, New Jersey, his adopted home, and died there in 1918. Cap Anson, although his actions bespoke otherwise while he had McCormick on his team, remembered the Scot as one of the best pitchers "that ever sent a ball whizzing across the plate. He was a great big fellow with a florid complexion and blue eyes, and was utterly devoid of fear, nothing that came in his direction being too hot for him to handle."

August 21

I'm penning these lines at the train depot where I've been now to no avail for the past three mornings. It's raining cats and dogs at the moment, meaning our game this afternoon will likely be postponed and made up tomorrow, but I won't be here waiting for my uncle then or ever again.

Tomorrow I think I'll just sleep in and then have a leisurely dinner and sit around reading the paper till it's time to go to the park. Understand, dear Diary, I'm not blaming my lackluster play since we returned home on Sam. There have been some other contributing factors too, the main one being all the things I've had to do to take my mind off the disappointment his absence has caused.

Still, I'll continue to stick faithfully to my half of our bargain although he'll have to excuse the brevity of my next letter to him. Frankly, my heart isn't in writing at all just now. The shame is there are a host of new developments I'm recording only in passing. We split our first two games with the Chicagos (which on Tuesday became the Pittsburgs) and now have a new first baseman and also a new manager. For details on why the Chicago franchise was transferred to the Smoke City, Sam will have to begin reading the papers again. Likewise, if he's curious about the identities of our new first baseman and manager, he can consult one of the local journals. *The Enquirer* would be my choice. It's by far the best of the lot.

But I suppose I'll have to tell him the true reason O'Leary was fired when we got back from Kansas City since it's contrary to what McLean said in *The Enquirer*. The problem wasn't that too many of the boys disliked O'Leary. No, he was axed because he got into a brawl with Lucas one night in Cincinnati. During the melee he and Lucas inadvertently wound up with each other's coats, and in O'Leary's were the train tickets for our upcoming trip to Kansas City. Lucas returned the tickets to Thorner, but O'Leary didn't learn that until after he'd already gone to Thorner with the tale that he'd lost them when his pocket was picked.

It's too bad Sam never got to meet O'Leary. Well, he'll have a chance to meet his replacement when we return to Cincinnati late next week to play Kansas City. After that we go back on the road till near the end of September, but I hope he's not contemplating waiting that long to see me play because there's little guarantee I'll still be with the Outlaw Reds by then. The truth be, dear Diary, the quality of my play has deteriorated markedly in the last few days...along with some other things.

Cincinnati, O., August 22

Dear Sam:

If you'd seen today's game, you'd readily know why I feel as if all I've done since you quit writing to me is go in circles like a dog chasing its tail.

The Pittsburgs hopped all over McCormick and led 3-2 after five innings. But then we started to chip away at Daily. McQuery was on third base in the top of the sixth and Crane held second with only one out and yours truly about to step into the batter's box. I had my hand out level with my chin to signal I wanted high pitches from the one armer— and then all of a sudden the heavens parted!

Now why, Sam, does Jupiter Pluvius always arrive just when I'm due to bat?

I could see Daily breathe a huge sigh of relief when Umpire Hengle waved his arms to halt play and then ran for cover. It was the first time all day Hengle had moved faster than a snail. To protect their thin lead the Pittsburgs began stalling as soon as the sky darkened, and instead of making them desist Hengle abetted them. Once he stood dead still for practically a full minute before signaling a ball foul that landed a good foot outside the third base line. Even though it consumed more precious time, Crane exploded into an argument with Hengle that he shouldn't be officiating the game in the first place because he'd been captaining the Stogies until just a few days ago when they ceased being the Chicagos. The way it looked, Crane screamed, Hengle was still secretly a member of our opposition.

Crane is our captain now, Sam, as you know if you heeded my advice to resume reading the papers, and Mox McQuery is our new first baseman. Neither of them is much of an improvement on the men they replaced. And no matter what McLean says in the *Enquirer*, the team isn't a deal better either since the Clevelands dumped McCormick and his two cohorts on us. The fact is today's defeat just about cinches that we'll finish fourth or fifth and even lower if Bradley's wrist doesn't heal in a hurry so we can put a man in the pitcher's box who won't snivel every time one of his teammates shouts at him to bear down and get the flushing ball over the plate.

It's gotten so rank around here that Crane went to all the boys before today's game and begged us not to say anything to McCormick unless it was complimentary. Crotty and Harbidge then spent all afternoon lauding McCormick on his mustache and pleading with him to reveal how he maintains his face at such a rich red color.

None of this you'll find in the paper, so I'm not reneging on my word to stop being your only source of information. But I can't refrain from gloating a moment in print over Will White's expiration. If you believe the tale in the *Commercial-Gazette* that he gave up the Red Stockings' captaincy this week because worry over outside affairs kept him from giving the job his full attention, you're the lone man in the state of Ohio who does. The rest of us all know Caylor fired him and reinstated Snyder in the hope that Pop can save the club's bacon this year. But forget winning the pennant—Pop will need a Herculean effort just to bring the Red Stockings home ahead of St. Louis and Louisville. Here are the current standings of the top American clubs in case your paper didn't have them today:

	W	L	PCT
New York	55	21	.724
Columbus	55	23	.705
Louisville	49	25	.662
St. Louis	49	27	.645
Cincinnati	47	29	.618

It appears the Mets have the American flag secured since the sharps are still convinced the Buckeyes can't hold the pace. Personally, I want to see Columbus win so the flag in at least one major circuit this season will flutter over our fair state, but the Mets are my second choice. Much as I still hate them for ruining my finger, I'll now allow they did me a favor when they christened me Ducker.

In all, my nickname may turn out to be my fondest memory of this season.

Have you guessed my present mood yet, Sam? The lone remission from it was yesterday's visit to Dr. Loft. At first I wasn't sure he knew his business when he gave me the same pills for my heat rash I got to kill the pain when he set my broken finger. But he said: "Trust me, Draves. They'll work fine." So I did and it seems Loft knows his stuff after all. When I woke up this morning, the area around my privates was still a mite sore but the inflammation had begun to subside. Loft explained too why it had never itched. It wasn't actual heat rash but probably something I'd picked up in one of those hotels we inhabited on the road. The conditions in them aren't terribly savory, as I've already hinted without going into graphic detail.

The ailment is better now anyway although I risk a recurrence since we'll be going back to the same locales, St. Louis tomorrow for a makeup game and then Cow Town. The thought of living eight men to a room again!

Your nephew, Earl.

"I was, I guess, lucky I ever got the chance to pitch ball at all," Hugh Daily told a writer from the *Cleveland Leader* in one of his rare communicative moments a few days before the Blues released him in 1887. "See, until the age of about 22 my prospects were as bleak as a blind man's. But since then I've had my day in the sun and I can truthfully say I'll feel no regrets when it's over. After all, there's no other man on earth who's ever done what I have. Still, I could've done a whole lot more if I'd had the full use of my left arm, and they wouldn't be so quick now to think me washed up, would they?" As commonly happened whenever the surly pitcher deigned to speak, the writer took what he was given and was grateful for it. So we can only wish now that he had inquired into Daily's early life beyond the day at the Front Theatre in Baltimore in 1872 when a musket discharged in a container of explosives in the prop room where 15-year-old Hugh worked and forever disfigured him. His base ball ambitions seemingly terminated, he labored on at the theatre a while with the one sound hand and arm left to him after he healed. Then early in 1880 he learned that he could still pitch if he wore a thick pad on the stump of his amputated arm to block balls hit his way.

Daily did a stint with St. Paul of the Northwestern League after Cleveland dismissed him in 1887 and then wandered through the Eastern semipro leagues and even turned to umpiring for a time. Then one summer, his absence from the game was noticed, and when notes were compared observers of the scene realized that it had been several years, actually, since the one-armed hurler had offered himself for hire anywhere in baseball. Where Daily had gone and what he was now doing were anyone's guess—perhaps he was back at work in his adolescent business as a scene shifter at some one of Baltimore's theaters— but no one thought enough about it to seek him out. Many years later, when details of Daily's life became highly prized, there was no place to start the search for them, no clues to his final way station on this earth.

August 23

Sam will never know how close I came to not accompanying the team to the Mound City. After posting my letter to him yesterday, I was within an ace of following it to Blue Creek so we could thrash out in person the terrible grudge he must still hold against me. But just as I was about to leave my boarding house to go to the train depot, in came McQuery to ask if he could store his belongings at my abode while we were on the road so he could give up his hotel room here in town. He'd even pay me $2 for the privilege, he said, pointing out it would still represent a sizable savings to him and at the same time be found money for me. Since our new first baseman is still an unknown quantity to me, I could not confide that I felt too low at the moment to go on the Western swing with the club, let alone the nature of my grief. I would only seem a bleeding heart to him for letting a family spat come in the way of professional obligations.

And besides, wouldn't it be the final rub, dear Diary, if I visited Sam and then had the Outlaw Reds fire me even while I was pleading my case in person for having joined them?

Hence I went west with the boys rather than east to Blue Creek, and now I have McQuery to thank for the way it worked out and Sam to convince I did the right thing. That should be easy as taking candy from a baby. We beat the Maroons 2-1 this afternoon in a game so brilliantly played it was a tragedy one side had to lose. If any man pitched more valiantly than Sweeney did for them today, it can only be McCormick for us. He showed himself to be cheap at the price we paid him, and Sweeney must have made Lucas feel he too got a bargain. We touched Prince Charlie for five hits in all, but four of them were bleeders. The lone cleanly struck blow was a single to centre field by yours truly, and two innings later I would have had another safe stroke if Dunlap hadn't robbed me with a barehanded stop behind second base. It was only poetic justice though, as I'd already burglarized him twice on balls he smashed down the third base line. The first theft he accepted silently, but when I victimized him again he shouted: "Graves, you're one lucky son of a b——!" Even though he doesn't quite know my name, I couldn't have felt more gratified.

Better yet, there were over 8,000 in attendance, the biggest crowd ever to see me play. But even at that the grounds weren't full as Lucas's park can hold more than 10,000 if ropes are run around the field to contain the overflow. Lucas also had the foresight to build stands that can be expanded if necessary, as it will be now that we've proved the Maroons are not the only top-drawer Unioneer attraction.

It's just a shame we won't play here again tomorrow instead of going to Kansas City. It being a Sunday, we'd surely fill Palace Park to the brim.

But the best news of all is the gossip now that Thorner and Lucas are plotting to shift their respective franchises to the League next year. *Sporting Life* has been printing vicious lies like that about the Maroons all summer, but this is the first time they've alluded to another Union team being strong enough to be coveted by one of our rival circuits.

Of course there isn't a gram of truth to that kind of dirt, Dear Diary. Lucas would never forsake the Union cause, and Thorner is just as loyal.

Kansas City, Mo., August 27

Dear Sam:

It's only about six a.m. here, and I'm writing so early because I want to grab some shuteye before our game this afternoon, not having been to bed yet, and also to ensure this letter will reach Blue Creek in time to remind you we'll be back in Cincinnati the day after tomorrow for a series with the Kansas Citys, our last homestand till late September.

As for whether I'll be at the train depot in Cincinnati on the 29th, 30th and 31st, who knows, Sam? But if you don't spot me, every hack driver at the depot can tell you which street car to take to Union Park or else haul you out there himself if you think it's worth the fare to see your only living relative play.

I'm just feeling ornery because I haven't been to bed yet. You know I'd never leave you in the lurch, Sam, after you've journeyed all that way.

And you needn't fret either that I was out all night doing what I did on my last visit here. One experience like that was enough, plus the weather here hasn't been nearly as sultry this trip. There was even a cold rain yesterday evening, and I'd have been content to remain in my hotel room, assured of having it to myself because my bunkmates were all out feting Burns. But two of the Cowboys, Bob Black and Kid Baldwin, invited me to sup with them after the game, and before we knew it we'd wound up talking till all hours on the front porch of their boarding house and might still be going strong if a neighbor lady hadn't summoned the police to make us stop disturbing the peace. It was a colossal exaggeration, Sam, although I guess the three of us did get carried away at one point. I can't think how else I could suddenly have started singing "Home in Ohio" at the top of my lungs or why Blackie and Baldwin would have begged me to teach them the words to it and then begun singing along with me.

Blackie hails from the Queen City and Baldwin lives there now too after being born right across the river in Newport. They've been batterymates ever since grammar school, Blackie pitching and Baldwin catching, and they signed last season with the Illinois Quincys on the promise they'd be sold as a unit to a major league team near their home once they proved themselves. But instead they were boughten a couple of weeks ago by Ted Sullivan, the Kansas Citys manager, and shanghaied all the way out here. They feel, rightfully, that they got a rooking. Cow Town is the farthest city from Cincinnati on the big league map and has the worst team. Sullivan ships players in and out like cattle, the turnover so rapid that Black and Baldwin are both fearful they'll be sent packing any day now and even more fearful they might be stuck out here all season. They'd give the world to be in my shoes, they said. Here they were dying to play in their hometown and I'd had the luck to play for both the Red Stockings and the Outlaw Reds!

As you can guess, they'd given me the glad hand partially in the hope I'd put in a good word for them with Thorner. I said I would, not wanting to destroy their illusion of me by confessing they'd overestimated my influence on that front. But the truth came out anyway after it began to rain. Sprawled on the front lawn of their boarding house and gazing up at the open sky, I'd felt nearly as mighty as they thought me. But once we were all huddled together on a glider under the protection of the porch roof, I no longer felt any great shakes. They're both only 19 years old, Sam, and sandwiched in between them I could see cobwebs of peach fuzz under Black's jaw and that Baldwin didn't have much beard to speak of yet either.

Somehow I started feeling as if I too was a long way from home. I think it was the bone-chilling rain that caused my mood to shift although the bottle of hops we were passing among us probably contributed some too. Anyway, I began to regret I'd allowed the insufferable time I'd had two nights earlier to persuade me that I was better off with these two than with the boys.

Harbidge had started it by saying they ought to call this hick pitcher Veach who'd beaten us that afternoon "Peek-a-Boo" because of the way he turns his back to the plate as he makes his delivery. And Hawes said that was the best nickname he'd heard since O'Leary had dubbed Ry Jones "Angel Sleeves" for wearing a uniform blouse so big on him the arms billowed whenever a breeze caught them. Then all the boys began talking about nicknames and how they were born. Hawes wondered why McQuery was called "Mox." But the question died since McQuery wasn't there to defend himself, so Hawes turned to me and asked: "Hey, Ducker, how'd you get your handle?"

I should have made up some fairy tale, Sam, but instead I just sat there like the cat had got my tongue. My silence led the boys to take turns speculating on the reason for my nickname, their guesses ranging from Sylvester's notion that someone must have thought my snoring had a quack-quack sound to Briody's near to fighting words that the only serious mashing I'd ever done had been with a duck.

A stronger man would have told them about the Ducker incident and let them make of it what they would, but once again my whole face froze until Glasscock took pity on me and switched to guying Briody, saying there was no mystery anyway why he was called Fatty. But I knew I wouldn't be let off the hook so easily again if a similar occasion arose, and last evening seemed likely to become one.

Actually, every man on the club was feeling his oats once we got back to our hotel and changed out of our uniforms. I felt like celebrating some myself. It's not every day, after all, that your pitcher doesn't permit a single enemy base hit even if the opposition is as feeble as the Cowboys. Burns being my bunkmate put a further onus on me to join the revelry last night, but I just couldn't do it, Sam, not when I was still writhing under the memory of the time the boys had given me over my nickname. Then too, I'd already pledged to spend the evening with Black and Baldwin and didn't want to go back on my word to them.

And besides, Burns's no-hitter didn't really rate that much acclaim. Along with being achieved against a weakling crew, it came on a day so dark that even Browning's eyes would have been hard put to see the ball. Black, who pitched for the Cowboys, I thought was just as stalwart as Burns but lacked his luck. All of our blows that the Cowboys fumbled yesterday the scorer called hits whereas everything they smote either landed right in somebody's hands or else was ruled an error.

In the very first inning Stooping Jack Gorman drilled a shot that probably would have torn a hole in the left-field fence and still be rolling across the prairie outside the park if I hadn't hurled myself in front of it lightning quick and taken it in the chest. But because I was down on my knees with the breath knocked out of me and couldn't make a throw, the scorer charged me with an error and deemed the run unearned that scored on the play. All the Cowboys were furious. They cried bloody murder Gorman's ball was a base hit if there ever was one, and most of our boys privately agreed. Glasscock even told me I'd done well on the play to save the family jewels. But everybody's tune changed when the game was over. It was just too bad, Crane said, that Burns's gem had been marred by that one run. He and some of the other boys looked to me as if for an apology. So I said I still hadn't fully adapted to the Union type of ball. It like to have fractured a rib it was so much harder than the pill used in the Association.

I was just echoing something lots of boys who've played in more than one circuit this season have said. Compared to the Spalding ball the League uses and the Reach ball used by the Americans, our Wright & Ditson ball has too much rubber in it and is like a bullet to stop when it's hit on the button. The sharps say the Unions were foolish to let George Wright hornswoggle them into adopting his ball. In trying to increase hitting in our loop we've also made for more injuries as the bruise on my breast after today's game should have testified. But instead some of the boys took my explanation for being handcuffed by Gorman's blow as an alibi.

McCormick, for one, remarked snidely that it wasn't the hardness of the ball but the softness of the man that caused my miscue.

There were some more remarks like that too that affirmed I would only have let myself in for more abuse if I'd accompanied the boys. So I went off last night with Black and Baldwin instead and had a lot better time although I would probably have stayed home alone in my hotel room if I had it to do over again.

Your nephew, Earl

Cincinnati, O., September 1

Dear Sam:

They not only know me now at the train depot but at plenty of other haunts in this burg as well, although anyone seeing my long face each time a westbound train finished emptying all its passengers for the Queen City would never have recognized it as belonging to the same man who'd been seen on Vine Street only a few hours earlier. If you're reading the papers again, you know why I now wear two very opposite faces. In case you're not, I'll just announce I made seven hits in our series here against the Cowboys and we'll be taking a six-game winning streak with us when we leave soon on the overnight train to Delaware, where we'll open our last Eastern road swing of the season tomorrow versus the Wilmingtons.

Should you be curious when Wilmington joined our loop, please refer to last week's edition of *Sporting Life* for the particulars of how Lucas persuaded the pride of Delaware that its future lay with us rather than with the Eastern League. Likewise, any reliable journal will have the box scores of all our games this past weekend with the Cowboys if you crave details of them. But I do owe it to myself (if to no other) to mention that everything between McCormick and me is hunky-dory again after my spectacular hitting display on Friday in his behalf.

Another reason my expression is sunnier now is because just a few minutes ago I reduced my living expenses significantly. McQuery has proven to me that two can live as cheaply as one. Hence on the first of the month, which is today, we leased the large front room here at my boarding house. It has a small dressing room in addition and a semi-private bathroom that we share with just two other men and an old maid schoolteacher. McQuery and I pay $9 per week for the room, which comes to $4.50 a man or a dollar less than I paid to live alone—hardly chicken feed, especially in view of some of the other expenses I've recently begun to incur.

McQuery is a man who believes money is to be spent, but he's no wastrel. Actually, he shares my conviction that base ball players must dress well and otherwise act like gentlemen if only to decry the public notion that they're oafs. Consequently he has allowed my discriminating eye to help him select his wardrobe. Our garments as a result are so similar that we could each wear the other's if he were not so much taller than I. We differ some too in regard to table manners although McQuery has improved on that front as well. He's definitely not about to repeat the error he made in Schlicking's restaurant on his first night with the team when he thought the finger bowl was a cup of clear soup. And best of all, he's a man after my own heart when it comes to knowing how to take his fun. The two of us and Harbidge, and usually Hawes and Crotty too, went every evening this week to Kentucky Frank's shooting gallery on Vine Street for target practice. Kentucky Frank charges only a nickel for 50 shots up till eight p.m. when it rises to a dime, but the money we save by patronizing his place before dark is just part of its attraction. The girl he has setting up targets, a half-breed named Little Fawn, has us all mashed on her although only McQuery dares to let it show. Coming from the backwoods of Kentucky, McQuery allows that he might be fractionally an Indian himself, making her allure permissible.

Crotty, on the other hand, is oddly smitten by Johanna McNamara, a buxom wench he met the night before last when she barged into Mecklenburg's Garden where we were all eating potato pancakes and sauerbraten and immediately asked who in the house was a gambling man? She'd wager she could drink the special there quicker than he could—the loser to pay for both their orders!

The special at Mecklenburg's is 21 beers for a dollar, Sam, an entire evening's worth of imbibing for two men under normal circumstances. But Crotty could not resist McNamara's challenge. Bidding her to deposit her vast carcass between me and McQuery, he soon discovered himself no match for either her ability to quaff suds or her vile vocabulary. Such language from a woman would have curled the hair of the average man, and even Hawes, who has a pretty rancid tongue himself, finally begged her to mind what she said because he had his mother's photograph in his pocket. But Crotty just seemed to find her ever more entertaining. He nearly fell off his chair laughing when she pointed to a painting of a naked woman over the bar and told Hawes that she wasn't shy about swearing even in the presence of her own dear mother's picture. "This woman has more life in her little finger than most women have in their whole bodies," said Crotty, and laughed all the louder at her observation that her little finger was about the size of the average woman's body nowadays.

The woman does have a fair sense of humor, I'll give her that. Yet she is not so hilarious that Crotty should have invited her to sit down with us and then boughten her drinks for the rest of the night. What makes it all the more preposterous is he can have no conceivable designs on McNamara beyond the dubious pleasure of her company, yet it may simply be part of Crotty's natural benevolence toward creatures less fortunate than himself. He never passes a blind man, for instance, without dropping a coin in his cup, and most beggars and cripples also come away wealthier for having solicited him. But the strongest evidence that he harbors a good-hearted streak is the way he will stick up unexpectedly for a man who's down.

Last Thursday, on the train ride home from Kansas City, some of the boys got on me again about my nickname. Seeing I was in torment, Crotty rallied cleverly to my defense, saying that since I was too modest to toot my own horn someone else had to do it. He then conjectured that I'd earned the Ducker tag for the terrible ducking my bat could give even the best pitchers. Most of the boys all but sneered since I'd hardly hit a ball solid in almost a week. But their expressions altered this weekend, Sam, and I owe it all to Crotty. Since you won't find it in the box scores, I'm free to tell you I knocked home eight runs in our latest series with the Cowboys. That's more than any two of our other boys accounted for.

Browning has the secret to hitting alright, Sam. It's a matter of relaxing and having confidence. And now, between no longer spending my nights alone in my room and having to live up to my new nickname, I've got both.

Your nephew, Earl.

He was Michael to his family and Mox to fellow ball players, a man of dual identities, part Indian but so tall that it seemed he must spring from a race of giants. It was said of McQuery that he could have been a great hitter if he had been six inches shorter. His height made him vulnerable, prey for low pitches once the rule was abolished that had allowed a batter to call only for tosses above his beltline.

McQuery was born in Garrard County, Kentucky, the son of a man and a woman who were both aware they had a tinge of Indian blood in their veins, but neither knowingly possessed the genes that gave their progeny his extraordinary size. In an era when the average ball player was 5'8" McQuery stood two thirds of a foot more. His uniform blouse was usually too short to stay tucked inside his belt, he could not wear a teammate's extra pair of shoes if his own got soaked in a rainstorm, and in team photographs he always took his place automatically in the middle of the back row.

McQuery grew up awkward and strange. He was often the butt of jokes about his height, yet it put him in demand. All he had to do to win the first base job on any team was prove that he could catch the ball. By 1884 he was learning to hit fairly well too. But then pitchers began to throw overhand and three years later batters lost the right to choose the height at which they wanted the ball to cross the plate. McQuery was far from alone in feeling he had been cheated of a skill he had worked so hard to master, and he was not even one of the more pitiable victims. He played four more seasons in the major leagues after 1884. With the lone exception of Jack Glasscock, none of his teammates on the Outlaw Reds would spend as much time in the majors once the Union Association folded. But after only two or three days as a member of the Outlaw Reds, McQuery already knew how complicated his life had become, and before the week was out he began trying to attach himself to Draves. On a team of men who for the most part went their own way, he sensed he had found the only one who craved a companion as much as he.

That settled the relationship; they got along well without ever having to discuss what it was that bound them together. The night before they went on the road to the Union Association's four Eastern cities they fell into this conversation.

"Mox, you asleep?"

"Huh?"

"You really like Little Fawn, don't you?"

"Yeah, I reckon."

"I envy you. I wish I could get mashed on someone again, but I can't."

"Hmmm."

"I mean I know it's useless, but I'm still in love with this girl I met while I was down in Louisville."

"What happened to her?"

"Nothing. Or anyway, I don't know. Everything seemed to be going along great guns and then all of a sudden she told me we had to stop seeing each other."

"Hmmm."

"The thing is I ought to have seen it coming. Do you believe in omens?" Draves asked suddenly in a tone that warned McQuery he was around a farther corner now.

"Omens? Like what?"

"Browning has a terror of seeing a man or an animal with only one eye. He'll do anything to avoid it. Me, I seem to always see a red-haired boy whenever something is about to go wrong."

McQuery first felt the pangs of a kind of dread in that moment. There was a wing shuttered off in Draves's mind that he did not want to have opened to him. He regretted now that he had not pretended to be asleep.

"I saw one sitting behind our bench in St. Louis the day Bradley got his wrist mangled. Then the day we played the Stogies, I saw one wave at me from the stands just before I stepped up to bat—and a second later, no more, it started raining."

"Hell, Ducker, there's a shitload of redheaded boys in this world. We'd never win a game if we let ourselves be squirreled every time one was around."

"I know, but there are only certain times when I notice them. On most days, even if they're there I'm just not conscious of it."

"Then the trick is to stop looking for them. If you don't see them, it's as good as if they ain't there."

"But I can't always do that, Mox. There are moments when I just know I'm going to see a red-haired boy—and bang, I look and there he is."

"Keep your eyes closed then, Ducker, when you feel one of these moments coming on. That's all."

"It won't work. You can't go forever with your eyes closed. And besides, just the feeling that I'm about to see a red-haired boy is all it takes now. Mox, don't you ever have a similar feeling, that you're doomed no matter what you do?"

McQuery muttered something about not wanting to think about such things in the middle of the night. There were times when Draves could be so painfully honest that the truth he made you stare at turned into a gorgon.

The very next day they went on the road where there were eight of them to a room, which brought temporary protection from Draves's nocturnal dialogues. It was exchanging distress for mere discomfort. Everyone was doomed, and McQuery never imagined for a moment that he might be exempted. About two weeks shy of his 39th birthday, while working as a special policeman outside a Covington, Kentucky, poolroom, he was shot and killed by a thug just a few miles from his place of birth. Some three weeks after his death, a benefit game for his family was played with Boston and Cincinnati players contributing funds to the gate receipts.

Wilmington, Del., September 5

Dear Sam:

Knowing how headstrong you can be, I wager you haven't resumed reading the papers yet and will refrain until Blaine loses the election. So I reckon I'll have to start reporting my diamond exploits again or else you'll never find out about all the strange doings here. But first, may I ask what you plan to do for the rest of your life for news other than about base ball if (perish the thought) Blaine thwarts you and all the other Mugwumps and wins?

Well, you'll cross that bridge when you come to it, right? For now it suffices that we're back on speaking terms again (although I

Cincinnatis		T	R	B	P	A	E
Glasscock	ss	4	2	3	1	5	1
Hawes	cf	4	2	2	1	0	0
McCormick	p	4	0	1	0	5	0
Harbridge	rf	4	0	0	3	0	0
Briody	c	4	1	1	7	1	0
McQuery	1b	4	0	0	10	0	0
Draves	3b	4	1	2	3	1	0
Sylvester	lf	4	0	2	1	0	0
Crane	2b	4	0	0	1	4	1
Totals		36	6	11	27	16	2

Wilmington		T	R	B	P	A	E
Lynch	c	4	0	1	5	2	0
Myers	2b	4	1	1	6	6	0
Say	3b	4	0	0	2	2	0
Bastian	ss	4	0	0	2	5	1
McCloskey	lf	4	0	1	0	0	1
Fisher	cf,rf	4	0	0	1	0	1
Munce	rf,cf	3	0	1	0	0	2
Snyder	1b	3	0	1	10	0	0
Bakely	p	3	0	0	0	5	0
Totals		33	1	5	26*	20	5

*McQuery out for interfering with batted ball.

Cincinnatis	2	0	0	0	0	2	1	0	1—6
Wilmingtons	0	0	0	0	0	0	0	0	1—1

Runs earned— Cincinnati 2. Three-base hits— Briody, Draves, Sylvester. Left on bases— Cincinnati 3, Wilmington 4. Double plays— Bastian, Myers and Snyder 3. Struck out— On McCormick 5, on Blakely 4. Passed balls— Briody 1, Lynch 1. Wild pitches— Bakely 1. Time— 1:50. Umpire— Seward.

might like to receive confirmation of that from your end). Hence I'm enclosing a list of the hotels we'll occupy for the rest of our Eastern swing. About our first two games with the Wilmingtons I'll just comment that we were taken by surprise in Tuesday's defeat, McCormick the most so. After hearing that the pride of Delaware had no batsmen strong enough to break a pane of glass, he thought he could save his best stuff. But before he knew it, Bastian, their second baseman, had cracked a double, triple and home run off him, and meanwhile we couldn't do a thing with Nolan.

I'd better say The Only Nolan before he finds out I haven't referred to him by his full title and has kittens. He's not half as wondrous as he thinks he is, but he's a sight better than any of the other pitchers I've faced in this circuit apart from Sweeney and Daily, and this whole Wilmington team isn't the pudding we were given to expect either. They were leading the Eastern League with a 50-12 record when Lucas soldered them into believing they were too good for a minor circuit and ought to test their mettle in ours, and all the sharps are saying they got in over their heads on the basis of their poor start against the Washingtons and the Baltimores. But from what I've seen their problem isn't that they lack for players. It's this town of theirs, Sam. I doubt it's even as big as Portsmouth. You can walk the entire burg from border to border in about an hour, and once the sun has set you might as well just go back to your hotel because all the streets have been rolled up for the night. And it's not as if people venture out much in the day time either, anyhow not to the ballpark. You could take all the people we had at our first three games here and still not fill your barn, Sam, and the only thing that enticed a few more cranks through the turnstile this afternoon was morbid curiosity. They were no doubt hoping the blood would still be on the field from yesterday's near fatality, and they got their wish and then some when several more pints were freshly spilled.

Sam, if I've learned nothing else this season, it's that I can thank heaven I wasn't maimed for life that day I went behind the bat in New York. I've learned too that I'm never going to do like many of the boys once their playing days are over and become an umpire. It's no job for a white man. Catchers at least go behind the plate wearing protective masks and now some of them even use inflated chest protectors, but umpires have to stand back there next to naked, relying only on their own reflexes to dodge foul tips. Yesterday in the fourth inning this new man in our circuit, Pat Dutton, went down like he was shot when a ball Glasscock nicked smote him in the pan. He lay so still everybody thought he was dead after Glasscock and Cusick, the Wilmingtons catcher, bent over to revive him and then rose up with a simultaneous cry that he wasn't breathing. But luckily, among the handful of people in the stands, there was a doctor. He rushed out on the field and diagnosed that Dutton had ceased breathing because a broken bone in his jaw was pressing on his windpipe. Expertly the doctor manipulated the bone back into place, allowing air to get through again, but it was still almost half an hour before the color returned to Dutton's face and he regained consciousness. Since we were leading 5-3 but the game lacked one more inning to become official, Crane wanted to continue play with a local ballist named Wash Williams, who happened to be in attendance, serving as umpire. Eventually he relented when the Wilmingtons insisted on calling it no contest out of a sense of decency toward Dutton, but last night he wired a protest to Union headquarters claiming victory. After what happened today though, Crane ought to just be grateful he'll get out of here without a manslaughter charge hanging over him.

To replace Dutton we were sent George Seward, who was disbarred last month by the Americans for umpiring a game while intoxicated, and to the crowd's glee he suffered the same Fate as his predecessor. They cackled like hyenas when Crane skulled him with a foul ball that split open his scalp like a melon and dropped him to his knees. The crowd loved it. They shouted for Seward to quit faking he was hurt. And when he finally took a kerchief from his pocket and started to wrap it around his bleeding cranium, a boy jumped out of the stands, snatched the kerchief from Seward and ran around the field waving it like a captured enemy flag until a policeman chased him back to his seat.

After the game Seward staggered over to our bench and collapsed on it. When he removed his cap we could see the wound on his dome was still oozing blood, but he refused medical attention until the crowd had left the park. Then he allowed himself to be helped onto a table under the grandstand where he lay moaning and begging us not to let the scribes see him like he was. In his delirium he was afraid they'd write he'd been drunk on duty again.

Well, Sam, the lesson here is if any man's sins will come back to haunt him, it's an umpire. But in any case, we've seen the last of the tiny metropolis of Wilmington. For the rest of the road trip we play the cream of the Eastern half of our circuit beginning tomorrow in Baltimore. The Marylanders are in second place at the moment with Boston right on their tails, but Crane is vowing he won't spare any horses in an effort to overtake them both. That's hardly front-page news though. Managers are always acting the lion, and this Crane is no different. The only difference I've seen as yet between him and O'Leary is he's a slightly better player. But then O'Leary was a deal closer to his men.

Crane scarcely seems to know who I am sometimes. Today before our game he had me stand behind McCormick and observe him throw his warm up tosses to Briody. "Just watch and learn," he said. He didn't realize he had me confused with Burns or one of our other change pitchers until we started infield drills and there was no one at third base. Then he hollered for me to hightail it over there. Still, I'm willing to forgive the man his occasional mental lapses, Sam. Anybody's mind can wander some at times when you're on the road.

Your nephew, Earl.

September 8

Well, dear Diary, I woefully misjudged Crane. He's not missing any marbles. On the contrary, he has one of the keenest minds in balldom.

He had me watch McCormick warm up the other day so I could pick up some pointers, and I guess I did. Dear Diary, prepare yourself: Yesterday we played an exhibition game versus the Portsmouths of Virginia, and yours truly pitched for our side! I'd send Sam the box score, but the morning paper here for some reason omitted it from its roster of all the important games played yesterday. So I'll have to tell the world myself that I beat Stewart, the Portsmouths ace, 11-3, and probably would have hurled a shutout if I hadn't been nervous a bit. Dear Diary, I calculated that it's been five years since I last occupied the box, and the game has changed a lot in that time. There's a ton of difference between pitching 50 feet distant from the plate as opposed to only 45 feet, and it's not the same either facing nine full-grown men who're all striving to take the bread out of your mouth.

But then I'm a man now too, and after the butterflies in my stomach quieted, it amazed me how artful I could be. As a schoolboy I always had a blue-ribbon fastball, but my only thought was to blaze away, and all my heaves were straight as a string. Now I couldn't throw straight if my life depended on it, and by varying my grip on the ball I can get a hellacious curve that's made all the more wicked in that no two in a row ever break alike. That wasn't a huge revelation to me naturally. After Lucas and I had that chat in St. Louis, I'd fooled around some while playing catch and discovered that I really could make a ball bend without half trying. But I never dreamt it would lead to anything, let alone that Crane had made the same observation as Lucas about my throwing. Yesterday morning on the train down to Portsmouth, he tapped my shoulder while I was playing cards and asked to see me alone for a minute. My heart fell. I thought he was fixing to tell me he was fining me for breaking curfew the night before or something. But instead he said: "Ducker, does your arm feel heroic enough today to deal something besides aces off the bottom of the deck?" I would have fainted when I heard what Crane had in mind if I hadn't already seen so many demonstrations of his diabolical genius. Last night he said he might even use me in a championship game one day soon if Bradley's wrist didn't heal. I don't wish the Grinner any more ill luck, but he's about finished anyway. McCormick and Burns probably wish me some more ill luck though, for fear I'll break up their monopoly. Ever since Burns threw that no-hitter to elevate him in Crane's esteem they've been taking turns handling our pitching chores to the exclusion of everybody else; and though both congratulated me after my performance yesterday, I've had more heartfelt handshakes in my time. McCormick didn't look any too chipper either at breakfast today when I said topping in reply to his query about how my arm felt. His own is probably about ready to drop off from exhaustion from having to pitch sidearm all this past month although it can't be anywhere near as weary as Sweeney's.

This is another Sweeney (Bill of the Baltimore Unions) and if Sam's getting fuddled with trying to keep all the Irishers straight that I've mentioned in my letters, so am I. Everybody and his brother in this game seems to be named Sweeney or Sullivan or Kelly, and some of them actually are brothers. But the Sweeneys, Bill and Prince Charlie, are not even though they're both pitchers. And to add to the confusion the Baltimores also have a catcher named Sweeney. On some days then their battery is Sweeney and Sweeney although most often it's Sweeney and Fusselbach. Too often, Bill has begun to lament. He pitched against us on Saturday in the series opener and looked sickly what with the way his face screwed up each time he delivered the ball. Most of the boys made light of Sweeney's agony, yelling out that it looked like he had piles. But Crotty just shook his head and muttered: "This bird is about extinct. If he continues to let them work him like a mule, they'll spit out the bones once the season's over and throw them to the dogs."

Yesterday Crotty tried to dampen my fun too, warning me that I shouldn't get enamored of pitching unless I wanted a very short life in this game. But he got off his high horse some when I told him that was like the pot calling the kettle black, a catcher saying another position could be hazardous to a man's health. And besides, how can you work any ball player to death? All the boys know that compared to every other occupation except maybe politics they're on holiday. They won't any of them publicly admit that of course because it would be playing right into the hands of scribes like Richter who are always bemoaning how soft ball players have it. And what's a sore arm anyway? It's not like a broken hand or an amputated leg. Some liniment rubbed on it, a few days rest and a man's as good as new again. Then there are those who don't even require rest. Ever since Sweeney (Charlie) jumped the Providences, Radbourn has been pitching every game for them. What's more, he avers he'll keep to that pace till the League season's over even if it takes him an hour every morning just to limber his arm enough to comb his locks. Radbourn's a living testament, the owners are saying, that all the complaints of overwork that pitchers are voicing now are nothing but a racket to create more jobs for their brethren. Crotty's reply to that is Radbourn is aptly called "Hoss" because he's a horse's ass. In his mania to occupy the points every day he's set the cause of pitchers back half a century because it'll be years now before anybody gives credence again to Corcoran and Johnny Ward and their tragic tales of how ruthless moguls shackled them to the box day after day until their arms were quivering slabs of jelly.

To be impartial as long as I'm serving as Sam's only reporter on the diamond scene, I mean to give him both sides of the pitching debate. But I can't hide where I myself stand on it. My arm is a mite stiff this morning, but I know I could pitch again today if Crane decides the Baltimores merit the same nasty surprise the Portsmouths got. I have to admit now that I've had a taste of the box it's the one position that could persuade me to forsake my dream of making my name at short stop. You're alone out there, just you versus the batter. True, there are seven men behind you and a catcher awaiting your toss, but until you deliver it they have no parts to play at all. They're like marionettes needing someone to pull their strings. It's only the pitcher who can do it, and then he brings them all instantly to a standstill again when the ball's back in his hands.

What power being a pitcher brings! What prestige!

But one swallow doesn't make a spring, so I'm not pixilated just because I starred in my first turn in the box. Still, it's a crazy world when a man becomes invincible at one end of the points owing to an injury he suffered while playing on the opposite end.

Baltimore, Md., September 11

Dear Sam:

This will just inform you that we're now in second place after polishing off the Baltimores four straight. Their captain, Levis, practically got down on his knees this afternoon and begged Sweeney to pitch so they wouldn't have to use Tom Lee again, but for once Sweeney stuck to his guns that his arm couldn't take any more abuse. Not that it would have made any difference if he'd toiled, but the score might have been less lopsided than the 11-2 scalping we gave Lee and the two recruits who followed him in the box. By sweeping the series we hear we've cost Levis his job, but it matters not because whoever runs the Baltimores for the rest of the season will never see anything of us again but our dust. Take a gander, Sam, at how the top clubs in our loop stand tonight if you think I'm exaggerating:

	W	L	PCT
St. Louis	72	12	.857
Cincinnati	51	34	.600
Baltimore	49	34	.590
Boston	49	34	.590

Remember when we were at 34-30, barely above .500? If only Thorner and McLean had plundered McCormick, Glasscock and Briody from the Clevelands sooner!

Well, this letter will have to be even shorter than I intended. McQuery just stuck his beak in the door of our hotel room to tell me I'm needed down in the lobby to help time Harbidge in his attempt to break his own Changing Record. Last month in St. Louis, Harbidge sped from the rotunda in the Lindell Hotel up to his room on the third floor and returned dressed in his full uniform in 3:52, shattering Fulmer's record for being base ball's "Lightning Dresser" by four seconds. Another interesting turn of events, wouldn't you say, that I began the season stuck on the bench behind the world's fastest dresser and am now a regular on the team that sports the new record holder?

Your nephew, Earl.

P.S. If you count our two recent exhibition triumphs over the Portsmouths and disregard that day when the Wilmingtons caught us while we were fagged from our long train ride, we've now won 15 straight games, including the one we had in the bag before what's-his-name got hit in the jaw and had to quit umpiring.

Boston, Mass., September 15

Dear Sam:

    My sole disappointment here is I haven't met George Wright yet, but we'll be in Beantown three more days so I'm still hopeful I will although if his club doesn't start playing a sight better than it did today he may decide to stay in hiding. That's where we hear he is tonight after we licked his boys, 13-4. The scribes wrote that he skipped today's game so he could scour the country for a pitcher to replace Tommy Bond, who recently jumped to the Americans because he wasn't being treated here with the devotion befitting a star of his ilk. But the ballpark policeman told us on the q.t. that Wright was there until about the fourth inning when his stomach couldn't take any more and he left in disgust. If that's true, nobody can fault him. Burke was a disgrace today. He didn't get much help from his teammates, I'll grant. Crane in particular sabotaged him by allowing a hoard of passed balls. (That's Ed Crane of the Bostons, not our Crane.) But still Burke had no call to start laying his pitches over the heart of the plate. It looked like he'd thrown in the towel or even was deliberately trying to lose the game—which is definitely within the realm of possibility from what I've seen in this town.

    This morning, Sam, while we were all at breakfast, two men skulked into the hotel dining room and sat down at McCormick's table. Their conversation was too hushed for the rest of us to catch its drift until we all suddenly heard McCormick cry out that he'd listen to no more of this s—t. He then rose angrily from the table and stomped out of the dining room. Later we learned he had told Crane (our Crane) that the two interlopers had invited him to sell out today's game. On the ride to the park this afternoon Crane counseled us all to be careful with whom we consorted here as there were rumors abroad that local gamblers had a bundle wagered on our series, most of it laid against the Bostons because we've been winning so often lately. Ergo there might be a rival faction looking to find a bad apple in our barrel so they could take advantage of the favorable odds on Wright's men.

    Now wouldn't that be hot if one crew of gamblers had the Bostons in their pockets and another crew bagged a couple of our boys? Imagine a game in which players on both sides were trying to lose! It could only happen here in Beantown where everything is two-faced anyway. To show you but one example, on Saturday the opening game of our series was postponed when the Bostons claimed their Dartmouth Grounds field was too wet from a recent rainstorm. But it must have been one strange storm because the South End Grounds where the Boston League team plays was dry enough for them to host the Clevelands that same afternoon.

Sam, the real reason Wright's men postponed our game was to give their pitchers two more days of rest before they started their series with us, Saturday for one and then yesterday, the Sabbath. Also, they probably hoped we'd lose our edge if we had nothing to do but sit around all weekend and pet the dog. But Crane saw through that one and arranged a practice session yesterday that we had to undertake on the sly at a ball field down behind a glue factory along the Charles River where nobody was likely to see us. The reason for all the cloak-and-dagger, Sam, is that the Blue Laws here are so strict that every man (and woman or child, for that matter) is prohibited from engaging in any sort of recreation on the Sabbath, and it would have meant a stiff fine if anyone had spotted us throwing the ball around yesterday afternoon. But no one did—or could risk admitting they did anyway—because it would have meant they'd be admitting too that they were out boating on the river or something in order to see us, putting them up for a fine themselves.

The exact words for what I'm trying to say are failing me somewhat right now since it's almost two a.m. and also because I left off in the midst of writing this letter to go back up to my room where a bunch of the boys are still awake playing cards. Now I'm down here in the lobby again where it's quiet or would be if my ears didn't seem to be ringing so. But anyway, Sam, I think I've made my point now about this town although what it is eludes me at the moment owing to my brain being in a jumble with the late hour and the spoiled milk or something I drank a few minutes ago. Sam, I wouldn't send this letter for fear of the impression it's liable to create, only I haven't written you in a while now and there's no assurance I'll have time to write tomorrow or even the next night.

I don't know where the hours go. It's funny how on road trips I used to find myself at night with nothing on my hands but time and now it just seems to fly by me in a blur. Well, that's what happens, I guess, when a man runs out of good books and there's never anything else to read sent his way.

Your nephew, Earl.

He was born in what is now East Harlem when it was one of the most fashionable sections of New York. His father had been a noted cricket player in England before immigrating to America in 1836; his older brother Harry organized the first professional base ball team in 1869; and a younger brother, Sam, may have been the best athlete of all in the family. It was an almost overwhelmingly rich sports heritage, but George Wright would have wanted life no other way. It made him ready for the spotlight at an improbably early age. By the time he was 19 he was already acclaimed the "King of Short Stops." His burgeoning reputation brought him an offer from the Washington Nationals for the 1867 season.

It is doubtful that George would have left his Morrisania Union team in the Bronx to go as far away as Washington unless he received some monetary inducement, but the Nationals averred that all their players were strictly amateurs who had regular occupations. George was listed as a clerk for a business that had as its address a public park. But he felt no guilt over the deception, believing that the time would soon come when all players of his caliber were paid aboveboard by their teams. And two years later his brother Harry helped form the Cincinnati Red Stockings for the expressed purpose of being the first all-salaried team. In 1869 the Red Stockings compiled a perfect 57-0 record, defeating all comers in the process. The following year the streak reached 81 straight wins before the Atlantic club of Brooklyn upset the Red Stockings on June 14 in extra innings. The loss so stunned the Red Stockings that they soon disbanded, and George accompanied his brother Harry to Boston to assemble an entry in the newly formed National Association, the first openly professional league. Over the next five seasons, facing almost exclusively straight-ball pitchers, George batted .412, .337, .388, .329 and .333. There are men who would sooner abandon the spotlight than risk being jeered while they struggle to keep up with changing styles. Perhaps George weighed the stress and effort of learning to hit curveballs, and gave up base ball for business. But a man like that, a man who for seven years had been the best-paid and most famous player in the land, could harbor a grudge against the game that never left him.

George Wright was 37 years old when Henry Lucas came to him in the hope of enlisting him in the Union Association's cause to become a third major league. Lucas asked for an endorsement but would have settled for a covert financial contribution. Instead he walked away with not only Wright's money and support but a commitment to back a Union franchise in Boston. It seems obvious now, the kind of thing that a man who felt betrayed by the established base ball order would do. But in 1884 Wright was painted by the press as only a smart businessman who seized a chance to unload a ton of his inferior Wright & Ditson base balls.

George Wright lived to be 90. Long a trusted consultant on the game, he served on the committee that helped lay the groundwork for the National Baseball Hall of Fame. In 1937, two years before the Hall of Fame officially opened, he was elected to it but not as a player. Perhaps to avoid a battle with men whose memories were long enough to recall Wright's swift decline when curveball pitching came into prominence, friends of his on the Hall of Fame committee deemed him a base ball pioneer and made him the first of that designation to be selected for enshrinement.

He died in Boston on August 31, 1937, some 53 years after his Boston Reds were swept in four straight games at their home park by the Cincinnati Outlaw Reds. The meeting that occurred outside the Boston club's dressing room, while Wright was talking to a group of local writers after the fourth successive defeat, was perhaps just unfortunately timed. "Mr. Wright...?"

"Yes? What is it?"

"Ah...I'm Draves, the third baseman who played against your team today."

"And played well. Congratulations. You boys had a fine series."

"Thank you, Mr. Wright. This is really...well...a momentous occasion for me."

"I'm sure, but will you excuse me? These men are my audience at the moment."

"But this is my chance to shake your hand, the hand of the greatest short stop the world has ever known."

"All right, now you've done it."

"Thank you. And can I just say—"

That night, when he reached this juncture in his diary, Draves wrote:

But he cut me off almost rudely, turning on his heel and leaving me standing with a mouthful of words I'd yet to utter. Then he became instantly cordial again to the scribes who were demanding to know why Murnane had used a recruit like McCarthy in the box today. He stood amid them for a good ten minutes defending his captain's choice of McCarthy and patiently fielding their other queries. And all that time he must have sensed me behind him waiting for no more than a chance to tell him how I'd read almost every word ever written about him, plus all the stories of his heroism I'd been told by my uncle and others who'd had the luck to see him play while I myself had been denied that supreme pleasure because he'd left Cincinnati and gone to Boston while I was still in knee-pants. But when he finished talking to the scribes, he ducked into the dressing room without giving me so much as another glance. It crushed me. Harbidge, who knows him from the days when both played in the League, say he's like that with most people, curt as a hedgehog toward any he regards as inferiors and a dog up on its hind legs when he's in the company of personages he needs to curry. It's just part of his inherent makeup, Harbidge opines, being a Brit by breeding even though he was born in America.

That may be so, but it doesn't make me feel any better. Today's encounter with him left me so dispirited that I see, reading over the last few paragraphs I've written, that I've not once mentioned him by name. I reckon the reason for that is because my brain refuses to believe I met the real King of Short Stops today. I met an imposter or else I just caught him at a bad moment.

Well, maybe I'll get another chance to pay my homage to him when the Bostons come to Cincinnati next month. But that assumes that he'll accompany his team on its final road trip of the season, and I've had it up to here with existing on assumptions. I don't even know for sure that Sam is still reading my letters.

One night in Baltimore I dreamt he died some time ago and all the mail of his that had accumulated since then sat unopened on the big oaken table beside his bedstead. It was a horrible dream, and it wakened me with a pounding heart because they say people get a premonition when someone close to them passes. If that's what my dream signified, I'll never forgive myself for what I did in my last letter. Sam of course immediately realized (I hope) that I was only pretending to be corned the other night when I wrote him in yet another effort to provoke an end to his silence. Maybe my mistake has been in faithfully keeping to my half of our bargain. What if I had told Sam in my last letter that he would never receive another missive from me until I had gotten one from him?

Then he'd definitely have to start reading the papers again to find out the length our winning streak has now reached. As of tonight, our record is 55-34 and the Red Stockings stand at 57-35. So the two Queen City clubs are nearly dead even now, and by the time we return home from Washington, the last leg of our road swing, I predict we'll have the best mark of any major league team in Ohio—better even than the Columbuses, who are 62-33 at the moment. Then only the Louisvilles, who yesterday finally squeezed past the Buckeyes into second place in the Association, will stand between us and the title of the top nine on the Ohio River.

How sweet it would be if the Eclipse finish second and we cop the runner-up rung in our loop and then play them for the Championship of the great waterway! Since it looks like I can't count on Sam to attend that gala event if it's held in the Queen City, maybe I'll wish for Louisville to host it so that a certain other party can watch a man she thought had no prospects make hay of a team who thought him no more than a mascot.

Washington, D.C., September 23

Dear Sam:

Even though I alleged I'd never write you again until I got something from your neck of the woods, somebody has to tell you the true story of why we had to start a new winning streak this afternoon and it surely won't be McLean or his *Enquirer*, which has made out that the railways were to blame for us not reaching Washington on Saturday in time for our series opener and being made to forfeit the game and helplessly watch our old streak go down the drain.

This once an iron horse was innocent, Sam. While it's true that our train arrived an hour behind schedule, even if it had gotten here right on the dot we'd still have been too late to get out to the Nationals park in time for the game. The fact is we didn't leave Boston till that morning rather than the previous evening as planned. Actually, we were all packed to leave the previous morning until Crane raced around the hotel, hollering for us to get out to Dartmouth Grounds on the double because Thorner had just notified him that he and George Wright had arranged a last-minute exhibition game to give the Beantowners one more chance to see if their boys could salvage a sliver of pride by beating us at least once. Everyone grumbled since we had looked forward to a leisurely journey to the Nation's Capital and then a holiday to relax and take in the sights there before we put our winning streak on the line against Scanlon's men. But I stopped my grumbling when Crotty pointed out that I'd likely be Crane's choice to pitch the exhibition clash so as to save wear and tear on our regular heavers. To prepare, he recommended we put our heads together on the ride to the park and work up a new set of signals to confound any Bostons who might have picked up our tricks after playing against us all week.

But it turned out to be in vain because Crane handed Bradley the ball when we got to the park. I was naturally upset , but Crotty was downright livid. He swore a blue streak, Sam, and accused Crane of wasting Grin in a game that meant nothing and also of undermining my confidence by not pitting me against major league batsmen after I'd so handily mowed down the Portsmouths. Crane heard him out and then he said: "Speak for yourself, John." When Crotty reminded him his name was Joe, Crane smiled tartly and said he knew that but what he didn't know was whether Crotty was browned off because I wouldn't be pitching or because he'd have to catch for another man.

Crotty demanded that Crane explain how he meant that, but he would not. He'd remark only that he sensed something fishy behind Crotty's sudden concern over my progress as a pitcher when just a few days ago he'd heard him tell me I was a dunce if I let my arm be used up in the box. Crotty then reminded Crane his point was two-edged. Why, he repeated, was Bradley being expended in an exhibition game—and against a team we'd already beaten four straight times? To which Crane stonily retorted: "Because I want someone in the box who is set on making it five straight."

Sam, I know Crane was trying to tell Crotty more than met the eye and that it was inspired by the odor of chicanery that marred all our games with the Bostons. To put it bluntly, I don't think all their boys gave it their level best and I can even name names with James Burke's topping the list. None of the Bostons looked like world-beaters frankly, but their excuse is that morale here is low ever since Bond defected when he wasn't paid what Wright promised him. Be that as it may, we had no excuse for the way we played in the exhibition scuffle , as morale in our camp has never been higher. Yet we won by a bare 8-7 margin over Mullin, one of their scrubs who was pitching for the first time all year. Why Murnane chose him is a mystery if the Bostons were playing to save face. Dupee Shaw would surely have won for them handed a seven-run cushion. But Murnane probably figured it was a lost cause when he saw Bradley would toss for us, little knowing Grin was in for a bad day.

Whatever the story, their rooters began snarling like rabid dogs upon seeing their boys beaten again. As we were getting into our carriage after the game, a huge pack of them surrounded it foaming at the mouth and smashed out the windows to have at us inside. Eventually we escaped with the only casualties being Bradley and Crotty, both of whom had their uniform blouses torn off their backs. But when we rounded the corner and headed for the train depot, we met up with a new mob wielding brickbats and truncheons. Whereupon our driver had the horses do an about-face, but the street was too narrow for it and we ended up trapped between the raving cranks behind us and the onrushing thugs up ahead. The horses began rearing hysterically, which further panicked the driver. With a terrified yelp he leapt down from his perch and bolted off, giving us no choice but to run for it too or else be sitting ducks.

Well, Sam, we made it alive into the sanctuary of a nearby Catholic church but only after we'd sustained a few lumps and abandoned our carriage with our baggage still inside it. In their wrath, the mob kidnapped the vehicle, horses and all, and we were trapped in the church for several hours before the police were able to recover our conveyance and tame the crowd sufficiently for us to complete our journey to the depot. By the time we got there, however, our train to Washington was long gone and we had to lay up overnight at an inn to await another.

Crane wired the Washingtons of our detention and begged that our Series opener be delayed till we could arrive. But Scanlon saw his golden chance to halt our winning streak. From what we hear, he had his team on the field in uniform and promptly at four p.m. demanded the umpire declare the game a forfeit. He was legally within his rights, but it was still a low way to beat a nine his club could never defeat fair and square. Today, in our true series opener, we proved that, piling up 15 runs against Daily before the umpires took pity on the one-armer and called the game due to darkness although it was still plenty light. Daily is the Washingtons' lone able pitcher, having gone to them last week when the Pittsburgs folded, so the rest of the series should be a mere formality. That means we'll return home on the 27th with a three-game winning streak that rightfully should be over 20 games long now since Saturday's defeat didn't occur on the field of play, the only true place to settle accounts, and moreover, we oughtn't to have been held culpable for the Bostons' inability to control their lunatic fringe.

Sam, it just crossed my mind that George Wright may have abetted that mob uprising. Is it not possible he feared our winning streak might rival that of his own immortal Red Stockings unless he took a hand to halt it? Certainly we can expect to go unblemished for the rest of the season. Upon returning home we play St. Paul, which replaced the Wilmingtons who folded soon after we massacred them all but one game, and then finish up with the Washingtons, the Bostons and the Baltimores, each of whom has already gotten a bellyful of our gunpowder.

With any luck we would have ended the season with 35 or 40 straight victories. That would be the second longest skein in all of history and superior to the Red Stockings' streak in that many of their wins were over puddings whereas ours would have all come against bona fide major league competition with the exception of a few exhibition games against crack local nines. That's not to take anything away from the Red Stockings' feat but only to give us what ought to have been our just desserts if Wright hadn't played upon Thorner's greed to pocket a couple of extra greenbacks and staged that exhibition game that spelled our doom.

By the bye, Sam, if you still think our loop is not of major league caliber, you should read what the scribes here in the East have begun saying about us. They've seen all the evidence they need now to know the Union Association is the real article, and some have even begun opining that the World's Series rumored to be in the works next month between the League and the American champions should properly be a three-way affair if it's to be a true World's Series.

But what are the local papers saying these days? How speaks the *Commercial-Gazette* now that we're spanking all our challengers and about to come home and fill the Red Stockings' old park every game for the rest of the season after Caylor was certain we'd forfeit our lease by Independence Day?

Your nephew, Earl.

Washington, D.C., September 24

Dear Sam:

I wasn't going to write again till we returned home, but I fear the boisterous note upon which I ended my last latter may have driven you to resume reading the *Commercial-Gazette*, in which case you've swallowed a fallacious account of our defeat yesterday that I'm morally obliged to purge.

Purely and simply, we were robbed blind, first by Scanlon, who began to stall when we trimmed the Washingtons' lead to a scant one run, and then by the umpire's ruling that it was too dark to play past the seventh inning even though it was barely dusk. Had the game gone the full nine, our side would have surely prevailed. We had Wise treed, pasting him at will after managing but one tally off him yesterday and that costing us Glasscock, who strained a leg muscle while carrying it home. With Glasscock idled, Crane put Bradley at short stop today and then handed Burns the post when Bradley rescued Burnsie in the box after the Nationals had cuffed him for seven runs. Burns and Bradley both played credibly, so I can't quarrel with Crane's decision to use them at short stop rather than myself, the logical candidate although it would have meant weakening us then at third base. But Crane did license me to object when he didn't employ me in the box instead of Burns. Sam, I won't claim I would have whitewashed the Nationals like McCormick did yesterday, but I wouldn't have given them any seven runs. Against my curves there is only one player on their club capable of the kind of field day all their boys enjoyed at Burns's expense, and that's Henry Moore, their leftfielder. Actually, Moore is so strong a batsman that the Washingtons would be a worthy foe for anyone if they had eight more like him. But they do not. They have naught but Moore—and still they emerged from our series with an even split for the four games. So it will appear anyway in the guidebooks. No mention will be made therein that one of their victories came by forfeit and the second is the result of Crane's having put the wrong man in the box today compounded by spineless umpiring.

Anyhow, Sam, I just want to set the record straight in case the *Commercial-Gazette* is saying we'll sneak into town tomorrow with our tails between our legs. We lost this afternoon on the field, that's true, but in our hearts we still haven't been beaten now for nearly a month aside from that day in Wilmington when we were too exhausted from the long train trek to see straight.

All of us are united too in that belief. This past month we've become like bugs in a rug while all the other teams in our loop have split apart at the seams ever since the Maroons clinched the flag. The Washingtons are the worst, snapping at each other's heels every time one of them makes an error or strikes out and then ostracizing their best player, Moore, because of a report he's a mulatto. I don't know who started that tale, but Crotty and I and McQuery were sitting face to face with him the other night at a place here in town, and I can personally vouch that there is no basis for it. Moore is as white a man as you, Sam, and his one mistake appears to have been sticking up for Fleet Walker a few weeks back when local officials forbade the Toledos to play their nigger catcher during their series here with the Statesmen. All Moore did was remark that he thought this was a free country, but it was enough to get him reprimanded for being a nigger-lover and from there it was only one short step to being called a dinge himself. I know the law considers a man black if he has even one drop of darky blood in his veins, but in Moore's case it's all just a vulgar rumor, and even if there were any substance to it I'd still be apt to take his side. Crotty told it true the other night when he said we all have the same blood in us if it's traced the whole way back to our original ancestors, now thought in some scientific circles to have been monkeys. And besides, as Crotty also pointed out, if Walker and the other darkies are drummed out of base ball because of their color, who knows that moguls won't next ban men with lesser physical afflictions? Men, for instance, like Daily who have only one arm or one eye or, in my case, because they're left-handed!

Even though Crotty was only funning me, his comment is still well taken. We're all brothers under the skin, the sick, the halt and the darkly hued as well as the strong and the fit. And what better show place than base ball that our country has become a true melting pot? If a man proves himself, he should win a niche on the team regardless of who his ancestors were. After all, that's what we fought the Civil War to establish, and it would be a sad turn of the screw if we were to forget its lesson a mere 20 years after so many boys sacrificed their lives.

The upshot is that Crotty means to fraternize blatantly with Moore when the Washingtons visit Cincinnati next month and urges others of us to do likewise as a show of hands that there is none of the prejudice in the Queen City that sullies the Nation's Capital. I will probably join Crotty in his crusade as Moore's plight seems inoffensive even if the worst is true because his affliction is invisible to the naked eye. But I might have to refuse Crotty if I'm busy entertaining someone else while the Washingtons are in town. The exact dates of their forthcoming visit escape me at the moment, but I suppose I could jot them down in my next letter if I thought anyone was still interested in knowing them.

Your nephew, Earl.

P.S. The enclosed photograph is of me, Crotty and McQuery standing in front of the "White House" where the President resides. McQuery is the tall drink of water and Crotty the galoot on the right, with yours truly in the middle, should you need a complete identification of the principals in the picture.

Everyone who followed the Union Association game in 1884 knew him. Sometimes people failed to notice a certain player on a team like the Maroons or the Outlaw Reds, even if he was good, because there were so many other outstanding players on the field with him. But it was Henry Moore who got everyone's eye when the Washington Nationals came to town. They all knew Moore even though none of the players wore numbers on their uniforms then, let alone their names. It was Moore who spearheaded the Washington attack almost all by himself, who made the most hits and had the highest batting average of any player in the Union Association except those privileged to play for the Maroons. He anchored the Nationals outfield, and he could also play a decent short stop. He was the team. Without him the Nationals would have been as pitiful as the Kansas Citys. He even deliberately made himself vulnerable to rumor, chuckling inscrutably if someone asked whether he was really part Negro. Far more than most players of his time, Moore seemed aware that bad publicity is better than none at all.

But no one was sure if his first name was Henry or Harry, or whether he was an Easterner, or from somewhere on the West Coast. For what teams had he played prior to 1884? Was he young or old? Married or single? His date and place of birth were as elusive as his ancestry, and his biographical data conflicted, like someone who might have been an escaped convict. He disappeared completely around 1895 or so. No one knew where he went, but who knew from where he had come?

Ever afterward people wondered. Had Moore perhaps really been a Negro and understood that he would inevitably be found out if he continued to play at the major league level? Or was he on the run from something, afraid of someone? There was an item in a San Francisco paper in the late 1880s that Harry Moore, the ball player, had wed a prominent Bay Area woman, but why then to this day is nothing known of the disposition of Moore's marriage? In any case, the assumption now is that he chose to make his home on the West Coast and play base ball out there with Charlie Geggus, a teammate of his on the Nationals, among others. It is a comforting surmise; the West Coast was still like another country in the 1880s, sparsely settled and hard to reach. Couldn't a man disappear out there without there being anything strange or ominous behind it? But that hasn't stopped the base ball world from speculating and worrying. This Harry or Henry Moore was a one and only—no other player ever left a track like a comet on the game for a whole season without some explanation for why there was no more of him. He might have been the model Malamud used for Roy Hobbs in *The Natural*, if we can imagine that Malamud even knew of him. That is all now that can be expected. No one will ever know anything about Moore, only of him. He is the one in the base ball encyclopedias who persuades readers to say, "This guy can't have been for real." It is Moore who is at once disturbing and reassuring. He brings doubt of how much we can ever really know about the past and acceptance that we will never know it all.

October 1

When it rains, dear Diary, it pours! Upon my arrival home from Washington there was a letter awaiting me at my boarding house like a bolt from the blue. Then after it rained literally for two straight days, forcing the postponement of the second game of our series with the St. Pauls, another letter descended on me this morning from the heavens.

The first surprise was provided by Constance, who heightened it when she wrote how thrilled she is by my recent success in balldom. She herself has fallen upon difficult times again, losing her position as one of the Singing Simpsons when she had another bout of scarlet fever, but she wished me the best of luck in my diamond endeavors all the same and said it's no more than I deserve. In reply to all the allusions in my letters to the possibility of our becoming beaux again, she remarked only that no one ever knows for sure what Fate has in store for her but she had to doubt that I would want her any more.

She is dead wrong of course, but I will let her cool her heels a bit before responding. My uncle's letter in contrast demands an immediate reply much as I'd rather wait until its contents and the shock of receiving it have been more fully digested. But since he seems convinced I've done naught these past several months but act rashly, I won't do anything at this late date to despoil his image of me.

Seriously, dear Diary, his letter was a godsend, and half of me wants to respond this instant out of the sheer joy of knowing my only living relative still cares about me even if his affection is couched mostly in anger. I'll allow that my reply to Constance is being held in check because I felt no great affection in her letter, only a sense that she may be keeping one foot in the water against the time when she's seen more evidence of whether I'll make a lasting mark in base ball or am just flash in the pan. Perhaps I'm judging her too harshly, but balancing that is a fear I may have been too lenient in my appraisal of Sam's letter.

Does he still care about me? It's no easy task to believe some of the things he said were meant only in the spirit of avuncular advice that he's withheld for so long as a test of how I'd fare if made to stand entirely on my own two feet. A test that I've failed miserably! How can he think that when I've clawed my way to a regular post with the best nine in Ohio at the moment?

And as for his allegations about Crotty and Bradley, they're so absurd that I hardly need dispute them. We were not set upon in Boston by that pack of thugs because Crotty and Bradley reneged on their pledge to a cabal of gamblers that they'd fix it for us to lose the exhibition game. Had they been out to do less than their best, we wouldn't have won given the closeness of the score and the numerous opportunities they both had on the points to sway the final verdict. Crotty in particular is as white as the day is long, and I mean that in both senses of the word. Sam's notion that he allied himself with Henry Moore because he too harbors a secret smudge of tar would not even merit rebuttal if I myself had not deliberately provoked his worst suspicions on that score as well as on several others.

Just between us, dear Diary, many of the incidents I've recounted in my recent letters to my uncle were distorted slightly in the prayer that they would finally stir a response from him. If anyone wishes to call me a liar for that, I accept it. But I am not a lusher or a degenerate although it may be that I've been guilty at times of acts that suggest I'm as fallible as the next man when visited by insurmountable temptations. And neither am I a fair-weather nephew nor an ungrateful one. Sam's arrows pierced deeply, and especially because I feel I bent over backwards in my effort to achieve our mutual dream until I understood that it simply could not be and made what I believed was a necessary and reasonable compromise. That Sam remains unconvinced the Outlaw Reds can be a worthy surrogate for the Red Stockings I fear is his own bed of thorns. For he's become a minority of one in still believing our team is no better than "a band of apostates dancing to the strains of a perfidious fiddler." I assume by that he means Thorner although it could be taken to mean Lucas too and indeed just about every owner in the game.

It could even embrace George Wright since he's an owner now himself. But I note that only in your pages, dear Diary, so as not to rub any more salt into what I reckon is the deepest wound my letters opened in Sam. In an effort to smoke the peace pipe, I will even confess to him that my encounter with Wright was one of the episodes I tailored some to get his dander up although Wright truly is a cold fish.

But Sam need not take my word for this. Now that our lines of communication have been restored, wouldn't it be grand if he at long last came to one of our games so he could form his own first-hand judgment of Wright and all the other notables about whom I've written? The Bostons will be here for a four-game series, beginning the 9th of this month, and surely Wright will accompany his club on its last swing of the season through his old stamping grounds.

That still gives Sam plenty of time to arrange to be away from his farm overnight. He could even bunk at my boarding house, having the bedroom all to himself while I throw together a cot in the dressing room and McQuery, who often does so anyway, finds other accommodations for the night.

We'd have a splendid time together in any case, so I'm going to make one last plea for him to come. I'll aver too that I look forward to hearing more from him soon and to his next letter kindly addressing other matters now that he's gotten all the advice he's been hoarding off his chest. Such as whether he ever got that "flag" tie from Mabley & Carew or has resumed reading the papers?

If he hasn't, I can write that we're off and running on our final homestand of the season with two easy romps over the St. Pauls and this afternoon will make a third. McLean and Thorner have meanwhile issued a formal challenge to the Red Stockings and the Columbuses, offering to play either or both of them a three-game series for the Championship of Ohio, but thus far there are no takers.

If we were really no better than renegade upstarts, Dear Diary, can anyone imagine the Red Stockings and Buckeyes wouldn't jump at our offer? There's only one reason both are ignoring it: They know we'd thrash them silly!

Well, if I sound cocky at the moment, it's because I feel so joyous now that I've heard from Sam again, even if what he said stung a tad. But I'll allow that I deserve a swift kick now and then and know that in his next letter he'll focus on an area where an uncle can be of help to a nephew who's perhaps still wet behind the ears in some matters. Am I right about Constance's motive in finally writing to me? Or is she too still carrying the torch?

St. Louis, Mo., October 7

Dear Sam:

Lucas took exception to McLean's public boast last week that we're now the best team in our circuit if not the entire land. So we hopped a train out here yesterday after concluding our series with the Nationals and will play the Maroons a challenge match this afternoon and again tomorrow. If one side wins both games, it will settle for all eternity which of us is the Union Champion this year. But in the event we split the two contests there'll be a rubber game for the prize later this month in Cincinnati.

Naturally, I hope we take both games here, but if we win just one my consolation will be that a certain relative of mine can then be on hand for the decisive clash.

No, Sam, I will not abandon my dream of having you watch me play this season even after your curt note of October 4 that Hell will have to freeze over before you'll deign to see me in outlaw livery. May I just mention that if I'm an outlaw so is George Wright for putting up his good money to back a team in our circuit. Now please be honest, isn't knowing that he too is no longer affiliated with the Red Stockings what really riles your blood? The time was when they meant all to Wright, but that time is now gone for him and should be for you as well. The Outlaw Reds are replacing the Red Stockings in the hearts of everyone in southern Ohio, and that's as it must be. For the Outlaw Reds are now the people's team, and I'm proud to be a member of them and of the lone major league that is run in a true Democratic fashion.

In all honesty, Sam, who cannot laud a man like Henry Lucas for granting us a second chance to claim the Union Championship even after his Maroons have the pennant clinched? Isn't that the very pinnacle of fair play? Lucas could have turned a deaf ear to our challenge and maintained that our brilliant surge in recent weeks came too late, but instead his Maroons are putting their well-deserved flag on the line. For if we beat them in the Championship Series we'll become at worst the co-owners of this season's Union crown.

Well, I've said my piece on the matter save to note that I now have met the man who is as pledged to the notion of giving everyone in the country as square a deal as Lucas is in balldom. The other evening I and McQuery and Crotty went to the Atlantic Garden for supper and found ourselves among a mammoth party given to honor one George Cox. If the name is unfamiliar to you, Sam, then you haven't begun reading the papers again, because this Cox is the chairman of the Republican organization in Cincinnati and has been chosen to head the national Blaine Committee for Election to the Presidency.

I expected to take an instant dislike to him and also to his two chieftains, Garry Herrmann, the Boss of the 11th Ward, and a police clerk named Red Hynicka. But do you know, Sam, they were not really so despicable although Hynicka is a terrible boot-licker what with the way he hies to perform every menial service for Cox, even biting the tails off his cigars. Cox himself can be just one of the boys when the occasion warrants. He invited us all to sit at his table upon learning we were Outlaw Reds, and Herrmann actually recognized our names when we introduced ourselves. They'd been out to our game with the Nationals only the day before, they confided, along with several officials from the Washington faction of the Blaine Committee, and the Washingtoners now owed them a steak supper since we'd won. "You ought to've gone 'em double or nothing," piped up McQuery. "Cuz we won again today." And we were good for another tomorrow, I said, catching the spirit.

"Well, you boys don't lack confidence," said Herrmann, whereupon Crotty said: "Neither can Blaine if all his henchmen are as keen as you to mix with the rabble."

Herrmann looked as if he wasn't sure how to take that, but his face eased when Crotty explained that it was a fine country when common laborers could bend an elbow with the ruling class. "You sell yourself vastly short, Mr. Crotty," said Cox. "I rank ballists among our greatest artisans. With the long balls your bats whang and the marvelous circus catches you make, you lads paint spellbinding pictures that will be everlastingly imprinted on the minds of your rooters." With a laugh Crotty said: "On that speech alone your man could almost capture my vote." "Pray, why are you still hesitant?" inquired Cox, and Crotty laughed again and said before he could continue this discussion his tonsils needed more lubrication. "Right," said Hynicka, and then snapped his fingers to summon our waiter.

Sam, don't let anybody tell you that Blaine's backers don't know what makes the common man tick. Cox has the proverbial hollow leg, and Herrmann and Hynicka don't lack in capacity either. For men who Cleveland's camp would have you believe wear white gloves and twirl gilt-tipped canes, they could not have been more human.

Of course that doesn't guarantee that Blaine himself has the common touch, but it does give wonder if he's really as corrupt as the Mulligan letters have painted him to be. In any case, it surely behooves me to hold an open mind a while longer with respect to the forthcoming Election—especially since it'll be the first in which I'm eligible to cast my ballot for the Presidency.

I won't beat a dead horse by suggesting you do likewise, but I will try once more to persuade you to attend one of our games by enclosing a list of the dates George Wright's men will be in Cincinnati, along with the dates we'll play the Baltimores to close out the regular season. I need not repeat that our homestand will be your last chance to see the greatest team in the country at the moment—unless we should gain only a split in our two challenge games with the Maroons, in which event you'll receive one final chance. But I wouldn't count on that occurring, Sam. The Maroons simply are no longer in our class.

Your nephew, Earl.

P.S. We won the last game of our series with the Nationals, 6-5, when yours truly singled in the eighth inning and Crotty then tripled me home with the winning run. That means that discounting the two games that were stolen from us in Washington and the day the Wilmingtons caught us when we were too fatigued to care, we have now been victorious in every contest for well over a month.

Has there ever been a stronger nine than ours?

October 9

Close but no cigar! We trimmed the Maroons 2-1 in the first game of our Challenge Series, scoring the winning run in our last turn at bat. McCormick was in peak form. He ceded Dunlap a leadoff triple in the first inning, but after Shaffer's sacrifice fly plated Sure Shot it was Katie bar the door the rest of the way. Sweeney was only a shade less invincible for the Maroons, and the truth be, I had to pinch myself over and over to make sure it wasn't just a dream that I was playing in such a game. It must go on record among the great pitching duels of the age, and who could have imagined the following day would see almost its exact replica? The lone difference, dear Diary, was that the 2-1 verdict was reversed thanks to Crane's bone-headed idea to use Bradley in the box instead of McCormick and to a raw piece of umpiring by Seward, who obviously was waiting in ambush to avenge himself for the day Crane's foul-tipper skulled him in Wilmington.

All of us begged for McCormick once we saw Sweeney would toil again for the Maroons. But Crane insisted Bradley's arm was fresher and that to win all we needed to do was field for him as air-tight as we'd done for McCormick. Only he neglected to tell Bradley he had to do his part too! Twice in the first inning alone Grin had men picked off first base and instead threw wild, allowing them to advance. As each man ultimately scored, both the Maroons' runs were unearned.

I'll admit the first one would have been unearned anyway because I fumbled Dunlap's leadoff dribbler. But by rights my miscue ought to have been nullified when Dunlap was caught napping too far off the cushion. All Bradley had to do was feed McQuery the ball. Instead he flung it away in his haste and Dunlap scurried to second base, from where he trotted home on Shaffer's two-cushion hit.

Then, with Rowe at bat, Shaffer strayed off the keystone sack and got caught in a pickle. But Bradley let him off the hook too, heaving the ball over Glasscock's head into centre field. From third base Shaffer came home to roost a few moments later on Rowe's single off

Bradley's leg, which a younger man would probably have snared and had Big Dave out at first.

So there were three instances, actually, in the very first frame when Bradley harmed his own cause, for the Maroons never again came close to denting the marble and we could achieve it only once. Officially, that is. In reality we scored two runs, the second in the ninth inning when Glasscock slid across the plate with the marker that everybody in Palace Park but Seward was certain had tied the game at 2-all. Even Lucas confessed later that he feared Glasscock had eluded Baker's tag until he saw Seward signal out—and then very belatedly. Seward vacillated a good ten seconds before he stuck his right arm up. Now that alone should attest that he was weighing the outraged reaction his rank decision would elicit from our bench versus the satisfaction of depriving us of the Championship.

Of course, the Maroons got only a momentary reprieve because we will unequivocally skunk them when they come to Cincinnati later this month for the rubber game of the Challenge Series. But still we should have polished them off when we had their backs to the wall if only so we could turn all our attention to McLean's newest challenge. McLean has proclaimed now in the *Enquirer* that the Union Champion must be deemed the Champion of all balldom unless the winner of the World's Series between the Mets and Providence will agree to play our winner a match for the title.

Wouldn't even Sam find that an astounding turnabout if I found myself playing for the World's Championship after the Red Stockings pigeonholed me to serve out the season as an assistant grounds keeper?

However, he was right in one respect. It wouldn't have paid him to attend any of our games with the Bostons. Our company now is much too fast for them. Today we slew Murnane's charges 10-6 and would have trebled the margin if we hadn't been given the dumps by Tuesday's putrid loss to the Maroons. What's more, George Wright isn't traveling with the club, preferring to remain in Boston and mind his sporting goods empire, which has some future prospects whereas his team has none. To show how little Murnane still cares what happens, he's agreed to postpone our scheduled game tomorrow with his club so we can play a challenge game against the Nashvilles, who have guaranteed us 60% of the gate receipts if we play them down in Tennessee. The money is only part of the reason, though, for the venture. Of more significance is that the Nashvilles are the top team now in all of Dixie and hence will present us with a fit challenge.

But none of this is candy in Murnane's mouth. He bowed to the request for a postponement because he no longer believes his boys can wrest second place away from us even though they still have a mathematical chance.

It must feel dreadful to be with a team that is just playing out the string. All of the Red Stockings I would hazard are downcast these days, and the Louisvilles too. Even the Browns, so cocksure back in the spring that they'd win the American flag, can do no better now than third place. How the mighty have fallen I could say if I were one to gloat. But I'm bigger than that although I did permit myself to strut for a step or two when I happened upon Stern the other evening. He was getting out of a buggy on Western Avenue while I was strolling with McQuery. I said howdy-do and he echoed it, and that was the extent of our interchange, but I could feel his eyes on my back all the same when I sauntered onwards.

What do you suppose he was thinking, dear Diary?

For close to a decade men who had just seen him play for the first time were continually telling Fred Dunlap, "You're the best player I've ever seen, bar none."

They were speaking their truth, but they were discomfited because they knew they were only repeating what others had said to them about Dunlap. So they worried they might not be expressing their own real sentiments, and often they went away thinking he had tricked them into it somehow, maybe just by being flashy. But still they remembered him above all the other players they had seen perform. They felt something special—it might have been the indifference with which he manned his position as if he didn't believe anything could possibly get past him, or his way of seeming always to be at the center of every critical juncture in a game.

In base ball it is a given that the ball will inevitably find its way to the weakest fielder when the moment of decision is at hand, but there are some players who transcend that. Dunlap was one, as inescapable as death; with the bases loaded, everyone in the park knew to whom the ball would next be hit.

And he was nearly as omnipotent, at least during his peak years, when the shoe was on the other foot. If the winning run was perched at third base, there was no one you wanted up to bat more.

"I wish there were two of you," Lucas soldered him.

"You're having trouble enough paying one."

"Okay, we're behind on your latest check, but you know it's coming."

"I know that some others have already gotten theirs."

"Because they're getting so much less than you they shouldn't have to wait."

"And why should I?"

"Don't, if you think you no longer trust me."

"Are you offering me my release from our contract?"

"Why not?"

"One of these days, you know, I might just take you up on it."

"No, you never will. Now a Maroon, always a Maroon."

"You overrate loyalty."

"It's not loyalty, Fred. It's wanting to be on a winner and be paid as one."

When the Maroons were absorbed by the National League in 1885, Dunlap played for Lucas that year and part of the next. He was then sold to the Detroit Wolverines, who were assembling a powerhouse. In 1887 the Wolves won the National League pennant, but a collision with outfielder Sam Thompson while chasing a pop fly resulted in a broken leg that held Dunlap to just 65 games. He soon found himself in Pittsburgh where his reputation for always making the clutch hit or the big play came to a swift end because the team was so bad the game was seldom on the line.

By 1890 he was about through. Although just 31 years old, he had the legs of a man in his fifties. The performer who more than any other had almost ditched the reserve clause in 1884 could last but one game six years later in the Players League when it surfaced as the next great threat to the established order.

Today, Dunlap's been dead for over a century. A cigarette card of him can still bring a nifty sum, though, and the price will probably climb. The collectors are aware that some authorities rate him the top player of the mid-1880s. They assume there must have been more to him than meets the eye since his batting record, save for the 1884 season, is nothing extraordinary. So they rave about his fielding, what soft hands he had and his great range and especially his terrific arm. What else could explain his having been nicknamed Sure Shot?

Cincinnati, O., October 13

Dear Sam:

The past few days have been such a whirlwind of events I'm itching to share with someone that I won't have time to do more than mention in passing how hard I'm still praying you'll attend our deciding Championship clash with the Maroons on the 21st, a week from tomorrow.

But no sooner did I pick up my pen than McQuery emerged from our bedroom and ruined my train of thought by smoking one of his vile cigars. I begged him to step outside, but he just turned a deaf ear although he did have the meager grace to open the window here in the dressing room. Now I can at least see what I'm writing even if I still don't dare to breathe.

McQuery's sitting here oblivious to the havoc he's causing my lungs (and my eyes too with their having to see his Cat-That-Ate-the-Canary grin every time they glance up from my writing). I'd regret I undertook this living arrangement with him if tonight weren't the first time he's requested the private use of our bedroom and I can't believe there'll be another—leastwise not to host the same party! Chivalry forbids me to identify her by name, but I suppose I'm free to furnish a hint that it's someone you'll find mention of in one of my earlier letters. And I'll add that it isn't any half-breed. The woman is a full-blooded American at any rate and not altogether repellent if you can forgive her sprinkling of gray hairs. I might find her almost attractive myself in a weak moment if I didn't still feel nearly betrothed to—but that's a whole other subject and I would never have brought it up if McQuery hadn't distracted me from my pledge to keep matters sprightly.

Now that he's drained his cigar and retreated to the bedroom I can resume my report until such time as I'm finally able to hit the hay. Truth be told, I didn't get much sleep last night or the one before either. On Friday our game with the Nashvilles ran longer than expected, compelling us to catch a later train that didn't return us to Cincinnati in time for Saturday's fray with Boston. So instead we had a holiday when the Bostons agreed to switch Saturday's game to Monday even though it meant they would have to lay over here in town an extra day. To cajole them into it, Thorner staged a "Field Day" competition prior to Sunday's game with a $25 cash prize to the winner of each event, the funds coming from the larger gate receipts certain to accrue when the special attraction was advertised in the morning papers.

I'd been too keyed up to sleep on the train ride home from Nashville—not that the boys would have let me anyway after the merry mood my performance raised in them. I excelled once again in the box, Sam, as you already know if you saw any of the Saturday papers. But since evidently none of them could obtain a box score to print along with their account of the game, it'll be news to you that I belted a home run and a single on top of holding the Nashvilles to a mere three tallies. That's no small feat against a heavy-hitting brigade like the Tennesseers and especially in Athletic Park, their home ground. Because of its location in a dell next to a sulphur spring, the architect had to erect a right-field fence nearly as short as the partition in Lake Park, where the White Stockings have shamelessly broken every home run record in captivity this season. I and every other lefty batsman naturally drew a bead on the short porch every time we stepped to the plate. But apart from myself none could surmount the barrier although plenty of boys on both sides, in the attempt, did knock a legion of foul flies into the bleaching boards in right field. The reason the game ran overtime, actually, was because it had to be delayed so often while policemen fought with spectators to retrieve balls poked into the stands. Down in Nashville they don't have the manners to voluntarily return foul hits— they play Finders-Keepers with them! And there are some other Dixie customs too that were a revelation.

In all, Tennessee would have been no great loss if it had been permitted to secede unmolested from the Union. Before the game we stopped for dinner at a restaurant that had items on its bill of fare no civilized man should consider eating. In the deeper parts of the South I hear tell they even feast on dogs. And for all their boasting about their "Southern hospitality" I didn't see much sign of it. True, they call every white man "Sir," but that's only to your face. The second your back is turned you hear yourself referred to as "Yankee trash" and some other things that could be grounds all by themselves to start up the Civil War afresh.

But again, Sam, that's neither here nor there, and I'm having enough trouble following my tack as it is now that McQuery's back to devour another cigar. (It's actually his third since this proceeding began although I know it isn't polite to count.)

Then I didn't get much shuteye last night either owing to the festivities I and some of the other boys bemused ourselves with on our holiday, followed by the hours I tossed about in pipe dreams of winning the Distance-Throwing event in the Field Day competition and, with luck, the Fungo-Hitting and the 100-Yard Sprint to boot. But I felt certain of the ribbon for the longest heave since I have by far the strongest wing on our team and I couldn't imagine the Bostons had anybody either in my class.

Well, Sam, nobody warned me about Ed Crane of the Beantowners. Granted, anyone could see that he's big, but a lot of behemoths don't have brawn to go with their size. This Crane is a monster, though. Not only did he win the Fungo-Hitting hands down, propelling a sphere over 392 feet, but he bested me in the Distance Throw. One of his tosses went 406 feet and a fraction of an inch, Sam, breaking the old World's Record set way back in `72 by some gaffer named Hatfield. They measured it four times to make sure they had it right, but for all that Crane still might not be reckoned the new Record-Holder because the modern ball is lighter than the one Hatfield hurled.

But in any case, Crane walked off with a handsome packet of cash, winning two events, and Crotty came in for a slice of pie too. He triumphed in the Accuracy Throw to second base, hitting the cloth target stationed there with seven of his ten throws from behind home plate.

McCormick meanwhile won the Pitching Accuracy event. He put all five of his tosses through the 1-foot by 3-foot target when it was stretched across home plate in the low strike zone and five more without a miss when it was elevated to the high zone.

As for myself, I earned only a disappointing third place in the Distance Throw, losing out both to Crane and Glasscock when I could produce only 346 feet, probably because my arm was still somewhat weary from having pitched a whole game just two days earlier. But I did nab a second place in the Sprint, finishing a full stride ahead of Sylvester and a mere nose behind Tommy McCarthy of the Bostons. McCarthy is fleet afoot alright, but if we raced again I'd beat him by a mile, for he nipped me yesterday solely because he jumped the gun at the start and would have been disqualified if anybody but Kid Butler, his own teammate, had refereed the getaway.

Still, there's no excuse for my sorry showing in the Field Day competition save for the fact that I would surely have done better if I hadn't been handicapped by having had almost no sleep for two nights running. Of course, in fairness, I should remark that Crotty probably had no more sleep than I. But it helped him considerably that he only entered one event and also that Briody is still laid up with a disabled finger in addition to his mother's illness which has made him serve most of his time lately at her bedside. And it didn't harm Crotty either that the Bostons have no catchers except Crane who can even throw the ball as far as second base and Crane, while a demon for distance, has no eye when accuracy is required. His arm, for all its prowess, is so unreliable in a game that the Bostons cannot find a position where he can be trusted. The plan is to make him a pitcher if ever he learns to harness some of his velocity, but meanwhile he's without a regular home on the diamond and stuck besides on a team going nowhere.

So I don't begrudge him his glory yesterday. The $25 I'd have won if McCarthy had been made to run an honest race would have been nice, but I'd probably have had to do like Crotty and McCormick with my prize money and stand treat last evening for all the boys who chose to gather at Schlicking's after the game.

McQuery, for one, was plainly under the weather by the time we got back to our boarding house, so it didn't surprise me when he wanted to sit on the front porch a while and gulp in the fresh air. But I was taken aback when he wasn't diverted from his intention by the person who was already there. Instead he plopped down right beside her on the glider and commenced palavering. It sure was nice, he observed, that the evening still had more of summer in it than autumn. Indeed, murmured she in reply. Then she said on her own accord that a quiet swing on the porch was her favorite way to end a Sabbath, and I took that to mean she wished to be left alone. But McQuery said it was one of his favorite pastimes too and then, after she said fancy that, he looked pointedly at me and there was no mistaking his meaning.

So I went into the house, leaving him to his devices. I reckoned he would bestow on her a few more minutes of his dubious charm and that would be that. But no sooner was I asleep than he aroused me to beg the private use of our bedroom. They could not go to her room, he explained, because it's above the landlord's chamber and any untoward noises would be fatal to her tenancy. The words he chose weren't quite so elegant, Sam, but anyway that was the gist of the situation.

Naturally, in my exhaustion I couldn't be expected to prowl the streets while he disported. So I adjourned to the dressing room, but that was already four hours ago when I figured to be here at most about five minutes.

What breed of animal can McQuery be? The woman is well preserved for someone her age, but she is still no spring chicken and, moreover, she has to teach school in a few hours. Now, what condition can she be in to tutor her pupils when there are already five cigar butts in the ashtray on the dressing table?

Well, maybe it's just the Indian blood in McQuery. At any event, I'm the farthest thing from envious although I do somewhat regret my nearly betrothed state.

Sam, you know I don't tell tales outside of school, but in this instance I must have your advice. With Constance it never seemed necessary or even possible to mash all night. Yet I felt I loved her mightily, and I know McQuery thinks of the woman with him now as no more than a free dinner.

Either those cigar butts don't imply what I think they do or—well, what's your thought, Sam? Perhaps you feel it's too delicate to express in a letter, especially since I now feel this whole letter has become so delicate that I must either not send it or else revise it radically. Actually, I'm thinking we really need to discuss the issues raised herein man-to-man assuming there's a date when that could occur in the near future that catches your fancy.

Your nephew, Earl

October 16

Ah well, dear Diary, Sam's message arrived a few minutes ago and it's now a gray morning here when it ought to have been a glorious one. Probably he wrote before he received my revised missive of the previous day, but I still have no reason to believe he would have modified his announcement even if he'd had the benefit of its contents. Hence I must begin marshaling my plans as though he will not rescind his vow never to see me play in outlaw livery.

So be it. I come away with a clear conscience that I've done everything in my power to convince him otherwise. Nor is the fault mine that the collapse of the entire nation that he sees harbingered in my own moral disintegration has made him aver to continue to abstain from reading a newspaper till after the Election and perhaps forever if events come to pass as per his dire forecast.

I need not remind you, dear Diary, that I never said I was going to vote for Blaine. I only suggested that I might keep an open mind since Blaine cannot possibly be so bad a rapscallion as Sam thinks him. After all, they both stand hard against the very same evils—Rum, Romanism and Rebellion!

Yet I must give Sam's opinion of the Union Association its due. While we're not outlaws, we do have a disreputable element. I'm already on record with my suspicions of the Bostons' honesty, but they're mere suspicions—and besides, both the League and the Americans also have clubs that play under a cloud on occasion. Only we, however, have so utter a disgrace to the game as the Baltimore Unions.

We topped them yesterday to end the regular season with a perfect record in our last homestand. The final score was only 5-4, mostly because Crane put Bradley in the box to grant him what will likely be his last bow since he plans to retire after the season. But the Baltimores had a fair role too in the closeness of the score. They played their all, right down to the last man out.

So it isn't their boys that deserve a flaming—it's their thieving owners! After the game all the Baltimores were notified by Henderson, their new manager, that they were released as of that instant and would have to pay their own way back to Maryland. None of them, it came out, has been paid for over a month now. Hence our boys had to chip in and loan them money just so they could get out of town.

That we'll ever get ours back is doubtful. Not only will the Baltimores all scatter to the winds for the winter, but many of them will probably never be seen hide nor hair of again. Leastwise not in major league garb as it's already a foregone conclusion that Lobstertown will not field an entry next year in our circuit. The Bostons and the Washingtons won't be back either, I hear, which will reduce us to just five teams—ourselves, the Maroons, St. Paul, Milwaukee and Kansas City.

Good riddance to bad rubbish I'd say ordinarily, but who will replace the three fallen by the wayside? We and the League and the Americans have already captured all the metropolises from the eastern seaboard to Kansas City large enough to support a major league team, and out beyond Cow Town civilization ends except for California, which is nigh impossible to reach and still overrun with wild Indians en route.

Still, what skin is this off my back? I've won a place on a crack nine that is in no peril of folding and has banded with the Maroons to establish our loop as a permanent fixture on the national scene. But some of the boys don't share my confidence in Lucas and Thorner. Last night Crotty said that since the regular season was now over, tomorrow would be the dawn of more than a new day. In plain English, it was time for a man to begin looking out for Number One even though we're still under contract till the end of the month. Crotty professed that he'd give the Outlaw Reds his all against the Louisvilles and again in our Championship game with the Maroons, but meanwhile he'll be keeping his lantern lit in search of a new manger. The Baltimore fiasco alone, he said, ought to be fair warning to every ball player not to put all his apples in one barrel for next season.

Crotty's Cassandra cries I normally shrug off, but when Harbidge and Hawes echoed this one I began to wonder. Would I be wise to enter into matrimony while still lacking the firm commitment of a job for next season? And moreover, to enter it with a woman who has already voiced her opposition to hitching her wagon to a man whose prospects weren't rock-solid?

Well, I still have two more days to decide, and if experience is any mentor, tomorrow morning will not look nearly as gloomy as this one. I'm off now to Union Park where we're meeting to rehearse for our first contest with the Louisvilles. Since a certain other team we'd rather play disdained our challenge and thereby eliminated itself from contention, our two games with the Louisvilles will determine which of our clubs is the Champion of the Ohio River.

In only three days time now, dear Diary, I plan to be wearing that crown and expect I'll have something as well around my neck.

Cincinnati, O., October 20

Dear Sam:

Your letter of the 15th influenced my innards about as bad as a gallon of castor oil. Leastwise it arrived before we journeyed to Louisville on Saturday and gave me heart that you didn't mean for me to wrestle alone with the impending milestone I'm facing. But it swiftly dashed my spirit against the rocks again when I read your last paragraph.

Sam, all I can do is repeat: So be it. I will play against the Maroons tomorrow as if you are nonetheless present. The alternative is too awful. I simply cannot bear to think that I've gone through my entire recruit season in the major leagues without ever once having a loved one see me play.

To allay your anxiety in the event that last declaration has not yet done so, your letter did provide valued counsel on one front. As a result, I sit here this evening with nothing about my neck although I'll confess that if Fate had not once again lifted her finger against me I could now be both united in matrimony and a member of the undisputed Champions of the Ohio River.

But your unsolicited warning on the other front could not have been farther from the mark. Sam, whatever possessed you to say that Crotty's words the other day were a slip of the tongue signaling that he is about to become a dog in the manger? No man who is contemplating treachery could play as Crotty has the past fortnight. With Briody idled by his wounded finger and ailing mother, our Joe has been a veritable yeoman behind the bat.

However, he is still not as foxy a hand with McCormick as Briody. Saturday afternoon in Louisville, McCormick typically came unglued when we made a few errors behind him in the early going, and before the flood could be stemmed the Eclipse had tallied five runs and seemed bound for an easy victory. But then their boys began undressing Hecker likewise to the tune of five bobbles.

We had three runs on the board, Sam, and were threatening more when Browning of all people saved Hecker's bacon, careening backwards at full tilt in centre field to make a spectacular tumbling catch of McCormick's bid for a long hit. It could be that in the pasture Old Pete has at last found a home, as he also robbed me once on a low liner that looked certain to fall safely. Then again, he may just have been lucky. But in either event we trudged off the field knowing we had tossed away our chance to be the Champions of the Ohio River and could now hope for no better than a half share of the crown.

Given that heartbreaking blow, a lesser team would have only gone through the motions yesterday at Union Park; but that is not our style even though our powder was further dampened when we saw the paucity of the home crowd. No doubt it was diminished some by news of Saturday's defeat, but we still ought to have gotten a rousing welcome. Instead there were scarcely 700 people in the stands—and on a Sunday!

We gave them full value for their two-bit piece though, and the Louisvilles a hiding in the process that they are never likely to forget. McCormick coated his thin skin with armor and was as magnificent as a pitcher can be, relinquishing just one marker. Meanwhile we plundered Hecker for eight tallies, thereby terminating the Louisvilles' chance to reign as the undisputed Champions of the Ohio River along with the *Commercial-Gazette's* chortling that even the alleged best team the Union Association has to offer can be no match for the Americans' third-place team.

There was talk of a rubber game later this month to resolve the stalemate between us and the Louisvilles, but I prophesy it will never happen because the Kentuckians are feeling too mutilated now to risk their portion of the crown. The real tragedy, however, is that so long as we have only a draw with them to show, the winner of the World's Series between the Mets and the Providences now has an excuse not to play us a World's Championship Series after we beat the Maroons. It would prove nothing, their winner will argue, to face a club that has yet to beat even an also-ran in any circuit but its own.

Well, Sam, there can be no alibis for our having muffed our golden opportunity. We lost Saturday's game 5-3, no two ways about it, although the result surely would have been different if McCormick weren't prone to collapse at the smallest setback or if Browning hadn't had about a dozen horseshoes in his pockets when he staggered backwards to commit that brazen catch.

It didn't aid our cause either that my mind on Saturday strayed at times from the task at hand. I made two hits and was robbed of another by Browning, so I can't be accused of playing with my heart in my boots. But I'll allow it did sink a notch prior to the game when my eyes vainly combed the stands in Eclipse Park for Alma.

That's Constance's true first name, Sam. But before I get to that, first I'll fess up that I wrote her of my coming to Louisville on Saturday and asked her to lend me moral support by attending the game and then to convene with me afterward so we could unburden our hearts once and for all. I'll also confess that I spoke to Thorner before the game, receiving his permission to stay overnight in the Falls City and attend to some business I had there. I did not tell him my true business, however, because he would undoubtedly have refused my request had he known its nature. Much like you, Sam, Thorner believes there are vast areas of life from which women must be excluded if they are not to bring ruin to them.

Your dim view of the female of the species notwithstanding, the counsel your letter proffered was not totally idle. In preparing for my rendezvous with Constance on Saturday evening, I gave full weight, actually, to your caveat that she could never be a trustworthy mate, having adopted a mysterious demeanor to cloak from me the hard truth that she is a woman who has fallen at minimum twice over.

When I got to the St. Cloud Hotel, it was only to discover that she was no longer residing there and the desk clerk would not tell me where she had moved. But overhearing my quest, a buttons sidled up to me and said possibly he could be of assistance. Naturally I first had to oil his palm. It cost me 15¢, Sam, to learn that Constance was now dwelling at a hotel on the other side of the river under her newest name,

Suzanne Wheeler. But it was a cheap price compared to what I had to fork over in pride when I unearthed her in her new abode.

It's one of the fanciest hotels in all of Louisville, Sam—and this for a woman who had written me lamenting that she could no longer earn her own keep!

She was in her room when I arrived. But upon learning of my presence, instead of inviting me up she met me in the lobby and at that could grant me only a few minutes, she said, because she had a supper engagement.

But what of my last letter, I said, and all I'd asked of her in it?

I feared she would claim never to have received it, but she readily acknowledged it had been forwarded to her after her move, and closely read. I should understand, she said, that she would always treasure its heartfelt sentiments. I also must understand, though, that she hadn't replied to it or to any of my other recent letters in the hope of sparing me this painful meeting.

"Please believe me, Earl," she said, "when I tell you that if love could still be a consideration, you would be my absolute first choice." To which I said, dreading the answer, did that mean she now had another beau? Yes, she murmured through bitten lips. Whom she meant to marry? I asked, determined to have it all even if it slew me.

"I hope so," said she, "though at the moment there's an obstacle."

"Meaning his prospects aren't quite up to snuff yet?" I offered coolly.

"No, Earl," she said, looking at me frankly, if despondently. "His prospects are brilliant. There are few men more well-off in Louisville."

"So then," I demanded, "what's this obstacle?"

She dropped her eyes like boulders and gnawed on her lips for a long while before she finally said: "Well, mainly that he's already married."

And then, after another terrible silence, she murmured: "But he's vowed he'll leave his wife if I'll pledge to wait until he does."

"And what if he doesn't?"

It was meant to be piercing, but I was the one stabbed. "It doesn't really matter any more," she said. "As long as he continues to be good to me."

With that, she lured my eyes to her dress, which looked so glossy it had to be silk, and then to her wrist, where she wore a gold bracelet adorned with rubies. We had gravitated, while speaking, to a dimly lit corner of the lobby, and now she bade me to sit down beside her on a green velvet divan.

My knees gone to water, I could only have done so anyway, especially after she said: "I've misrepresented myself somewhat to you, I'm afraid, Earl. I'm not as young as I've led you to think, and I'm considerably more trammeled. For that I apologize. But I don't feel at all sorry about the wonderful times I gave you. They were wonderful, weren't they?"

Upon seeing she had begun to cry, I said: "They were exquisite."

We sat there for a long time without either of us speaking. At last she rose and announced she must go, she was already late for her engagement.

But when I made no move to rise with her, being still unable, she sat down again and said she supposed since she was already late a few more minutes wouldn't matter, assuming I could still bear her company after all the pain she'd given me.

She'd also given me in many ways the most happiness I'd ever known, I heard myself say. Then, to temporize while I fought off tears of my own, I said: "How have you been so badly trammeled, Constance?"

To begin with, she said, her true name wasn't Constance or Zena or Suzanne or any of the other names she'd donned over the past few years. It was Alma, Alma Traum, and even that had not been her name at birth. "You see, Earl," she told me then, "the thing is I never knew my parents."

Sam, I can't go on in this painstaking fashion. Constance's story is too heartrending to relate any way but as swiftly as possible. She spent the first six years of her life in an orphanage and then was adopted by a couple named Traum when she was old enough, they judged, to be of help to them on their farm. It was not in Hamilton, the hometown she'd previously claimed, but clear over on the opposite side of the state, near Steubenville. She lived with the Traums for eight years, glad at first to escape the orphanage but then distraught when it grew plain their motive in adopting her was not solely to have another hand around the place. At age 14 she finally took it upon herself to run away but not before Traum had his way with her and impregnated her. She fled to Cleveland, where she undertook to bear her child in a home for the unwed. But then she fell ill with pneumonia and had to be delivered of it by abortion instead, the surgery done in a crude way that rendered her unable ever again to conceive an infant.

Upon recovering, she worked for several years in Cleveland as a seamstress in a clothing manufactory. When she had some money saved, she went to Indiana to get a fresh start and pursue her dream of becoming a singer and more than a speck of dust that would be buffeted hither and yon for the rest of her time on this earth.

In Evansville she altered her name to Constance Voss and her age from 20 to 16 so she would seem both more glamorous and still in the bloom of youth. She is now past 24, Sam, and far too old, she said, to retain any hope that her dream of becoming someone will ever be answered. A few weeks ago she met a wealthy horse breeder when he came into the saloon where she was performing as one of the Singing Simpsons. She averred that she spurned his advances at first upon learning he was married. But then she took sick again and lost her job. When he redoubled his pursuit of her, sensing her increased susceptibility, she finally relented and became for want of a better word his mistress. "Now, Earl," she said in closing her tale, "think of me what you must, but know that I still think the world of you and am showing it by cutting off our association before you're done serious damage by me."

In my despair, I had to say that I was already irreparably damaged.

"No," she said. "You've been disillusioned, but you will rebound alright and go on to make some much more deserving woman a fine husband one day."

With that she rose again, this time not to be dissuaded from leaving to keep her appointment with—as she then confessed—her new beau. In parting she did let me bestow on her a final kiss and a lingering one although never long enough.

The truth, Sam, is that her story, for all its sordid chapters, rather than end my feeling for her may actually have made me care for her all the more deeply.

In any case, I was bereft when I left her, and still am although perhaps not as blue now that I no longer have to shoulder the double burden of losing on one and the same day Constance and the eminence of being on the best team in balldom.

At least I still have a measure of the latter, knowing that we're at poorest the half Champions of the Ohio River. And we still have the chance for better. All we have to do is whip the Maroons tomorrow, Tuesday, the 21st, and we're liable to be off to New York soon or else to Providence.

Personally, I'm rooting for New York to win their World's Series so I can then avenge myself in the Gotham for the ignominy done me my last visit there. But right now that seems long ago and there's been a lot of water over the dam since.

You win some and you lose some in this world, right, Sam? No man ever has all of his dreams answered. At best he gets an even shake of the dice, and I'll settle now for that. If I've lost the woman of my dreams, then perhaps it means I'll get to play for the Championship of all of balldom after first having had a beloved uncle see me play in the game that will decide whether I'm to gain that chance.

Sam, actually I wrote most of this letter last night but held off posting it till this morning so I could get a current railway schedule at the train depot to enclose with it. You'll note there is only one morning train out of Portsmouth now that summer is over: the 10:32, which reaches the Blue Creek junction at 11:28 or thereabouts. Anyway, you should get this letter before you embark for the depot, but in the bare event you do not you will intuit my plan to meet the 10:32 tomorrow as I intuit yours to be aboard it. Stubborn as we both can be at times, blood is always thicker than water when the chips are down.

Your nephew, Earl.

P.S. Enclosed also is a box score from the early edition of today's paper. The Maroons must be frothing at the mouth now after journeying to the very last day of the regular season before having their Record for never being whitewashed spoiled.

Boston Unions		AB	R	BH	TB	PO	A	E
Crane	r.f.	4	0	1	..	0	0	0
McCarthy	l.f.	3	1	1	..	1	1	1
O'Brien	2b	4	0	0	..	4	7	0
Murnan	1b	4	1	0	..	9	0	0
Hackett	s.s.	3	1	1	..	2	2	1
Slattery	c.f.	3	1	1	..	0	0	0
Shaw	p	3	1	1	..	1	7	0
Brown	c	3	0	1	..	8	2	0
Irwin	3b	3	0	0	..	2	1	1
Totals		30	5	6	..	27	20	3

St. Louis Unions		AB	R	BH	TB	PO	A	E
Dunlap	2b	4	0	1	..	2	3	1
Rowe	s.s.	4	0	1	..	0	2	0
Boyle	l.f.	4	0	0	..	1	0	1
Sweeney	p	4	0	2	..	0	9	0
Quinn	1b	4	0	0	..	8	1	1
Dolan	3b.	4	0	0	..	1	2	2
Baker	c	4	0	0	..	7	5	3
Lewis	c.f.	4	0	0	..	1	0	0
Shaffer	r.f.	3	0	0	..	4	0	0
Totals		33	0	4	..	24	22	8

Innings	1	2	3	4	5	6	7	8	9
Bostons	0	0	0	4	0	0	0	0	x—5
St. Louis	0	0	0	0	0	0	0	0	0—0

Earned runs— Bostons 2. Two-base hits—Sweeney, 1; Shaw, 1. Total bases on hits— St. Louis, 5; Bostons 7. Left on bases— St. Louis, 6; Bostons, 2. Struck out— By Sweeney, 6; by Shaw, 6. Double plays— Baker to Quinn. O'Brien to Hackett to Murnan. Bases on called balls— Off Sweeney, 1; Shaw, 1. Passed balls— Baker, 3. Time— 2 hours. Umpire— Seward.

By the late 1980s, when Chicago finally agreed to build the White Sox a new stadium, there was never any doubt that it would keep the name of its predecessor, Comiskey Park. It solaced those who still revered "The Old Roman." They regarded him as one of base ball's great nobles, who had a long career of prosperity and rectitude, except for one regrettable event in 1919 when eight of his chattels betrayed him and the trust of millions by selling out the World Series.

Strange to think now of Charlie Comiskey as a noble: He began life as the son of a Chicago ward heeler and left school at a tender age to become a plumber's apprentice. Harder still to call him a Roman: It was never a secret that his father was an Irish immigrant and he added to the legacy by marrying one Nan Kelly. In reality, Charlie Comiskey could have stepped right out of a Horatio Alger novel; this "Raggedy Dick" went from lowly semi-pro player to owner of one of the leading franchises, building the greatest base ball stadium of its time in his own name. He began his career as a pitcher-third baseman with an independent team in Milwaukee, moving on west for four years with the Dubuque Rabbits before making it to the big time in St. Louis. In the Mound City, after he was appointed player-manager of the Browns, he was thought of as clever, as innovative. But perhaps that's all that was implied by his nickname. There was something patrician about Comiskey, nothing actually regal or lofty, but an eye for how to act the leader. It was evidenced in his readiness to take credit for being the first to station himself several yards off first base when all he really did was play a step or two farther away from the bag than Joe Start and other veteran first basemen after whom he patterned himself. It was evidenced in the artful way he invited base ball writers to compare him as a fielder to Dave Orr, Long John Reilly and Dan Brouthers, all of them big awkward types, while judiciously avoiding any mention of John Kerins. Kerins was dangerous to Comiskey's self-promotion campaign, light-handed and versatile, like Comiskey a weak hitter early in his career but showing signs by 1885 of blossoming into the best all-around first baseman in the American Association. Fortunately for Comiskey, Kerins was unsure of himself, more awed than inspired when he began hearing his name mentioned in the same breath with Stovey, Browning and the other star players in the Association. A sensation in 1886, Kerins was out of the big leagues two years later when Comiskey led the Browns to their fourth straight pennant.

He would never be on another winner either as a player or a manager, but how much could it have mattered to him? Winning was nice, but control was what brought real pleasure; control was what drove the captains of industry in those years, and Comiskey's industry was base ball. In 1900, Comiskey achieved his ultimate goal when he became founder, president and sole owner of the Chicago franchise in the American League, the first and still the only player ever to rise through the ranks to such prominence. As an owner, he had an edge at first on his confederates in that he knew base ball through and through and could draw on his experience under Browns owner Chris Von Der

Ahe, for whom he had often negotiated salaries with fellow players and decided which to sell or trade. Comiskey knew how to build a team, everyone gave him that. He knew that you started with pitching, speed and defense. For as long as possible, Comiskey maintained absolute control and did everything himself, from owner to manager, but by the turn of the century running an entire club from top to bottom had become much more complex. In 1901 he was forced to find someone who could run his club on road trips since his duties as owner no longer permitted him time to travel with it. For his titular manager the first year that the American League declared itself a major league, he robbed the Chicago National League entry of Clark Griffith, a wily pitcher who was later dubbed "The Old Fox," and was rewarded with an immediate pennant.

Five years later Comiskey's White Sox became the only team ever to win a World Championship despite finishing last in batting. It was the worst thing that could have happened to him. It convinced him all the more that he knew base ball as no one else did. The argument has always been that Comiskey loathed and distrusted players who were good hitters because he was a poor one, but it only partially captures the psychology of the man. As much as players who had the skills he lacked, Comiskey hated any who demanded he pay them more than he thought those skills were worth. Yet it was not that he was cheap. Oh no, he would spring for an Eddie Collins or minor league stars like Ping Bodie and Willie Kamm—in Kamm's case a dizzying hundred grand, then a record sum for an unproven player. But Collins was smart, a college man, and the money for minor leaguers went into the coffers of fellow owners, men who were his peers. To have to dig into his pocket for a Joe Jackson, an *illiterate* who could barely even sign for his money, was beyond him once he had put his days on the Browns among roughnecks like Curt Welch and Yank Robinson behind him. Comiskey was not a snob or a tightwad so much as an eternal parvenu. People never realized that his exemplar was not Al Spalding, the star pitcher who grew into a part owner of the Chicago White Stockings, but somebody like John Kerins. For all he achieved in base ball, Comiskey never felt he had it made. His teams won pennants and world titles, but the memory of Kerins still haunted him. Like so many self-made men of his epoch, Comiskey knew that if you didn't believe in yourself and show it by acting like one of the chosen, who would?

In 1884, Comiskey reached base on an average only once every four at bats, terrible for a first baseman, but he was nonetheless rewarded by Von Der Ahe. Near the end of the season, after his team had failed all summer to mount a serious pennant bid, the Browns owner replaced manager Jimmy Williams with Comiskey, who had held the job briefly the previous year without distinguishing himself to anyone but Von Der Ahe, a lover of ambition as long as it furthered his own to regain his status as the base ball kingpin in St. Louis. "You think you can light a firecracker under my boys?" asked Von Der Ahe. "Count on it," Comiskey said straightaway, never one to be given pause by another's egotism. The Browns were really his team, of course, and had been ever since he realized that Von Der Ahe knew base ball about as well as he knew how to make beer.

And he was ready again, after the regular season ended, when Von Der Ahe telephoned him at his hotel one morning.

"You see in the paper the Maroons got no runs yesterday? They're not so great if those Bostons can do that when who are they?"

"Right."

"So we should take their challenge to play us, right?"

"Wrong."

"But for the championship of St. Louis if we win?"

"*If* we win. There's no guarantee as yet that we would."

"As yet? What is as yet? Whatchu mean, Chollie? You got somehow to guarantee we don't lose?"

"No, but sometimes others will do the trick for you."

"What? Monkeying games? You know I don't like even to think like that."

"Neither do I, but we can't help the way others think. There are always going to be people willing to jimmy a game, you know that."

"I tell you, Chollie, I won't win that way. Winning is no good when it's not fair and square. The American way, Chollie."

"Like when Latham trips a man as he rounds third base with the winning run?"

"That's different. That's trickery. This is cheating I'm talking."

"How is it cheating if you keep your ears open and make your move when you happen to hear something?"

"Yah? Whatchu hear, Chollie, what?"

"Nothing definite, but there's a game tomorrow in Cincinnati that some of my friends in Chicago say a certain individual has a heavy investment in."

"Which game, Chollie, the Maroons?"

"Right, between the Maroons and the Outlaw Reds for the so-called championship of the Union Association."

"This certain poison, Chollie, who is he?"

"Ah, you don't want to know, and I don't know anything for sure anyway. What we don't know can't hurt us, so let's leave it that way. The American way."

They ended the conversation moments later and never had
another like it. Comiskey would go to his grave in 1931 denying that he
had ever had a conversation like it with anyone, but the claim made him
seem either a liar or a fool. Many of the eight players who sold him out
in 1919 later said he'd have had to be blind not to have known what they
were doing and why. And they may have been right. After the very first
game of the 1919 World Series, Comiskey purportedly cornered
National League president John Heydler and glumly laid out his
suspicions. But there is a theory that Heydler, who was still smarting
from his ignominious failure to nail Hal Chase for throwing games
earlier in the year, saw only further humiliation for his office if he
pursued the matter. The ringleaders among the Black Sox may well
have counted on that. Time after time, they had seen Chase and others
of his influence take the easy money and get away with it, so how much
harm could come to them if they stuck it to Comiskey? These eight men
never thought of their owner as stupid or unobservant. They feared and
despised him because they felt he was insensitive to their need to feel
appreciated.

Appreciated in what way exactly is the issue that may never be
resolved. Court records indicate the eight men who betrayed Comiskey
were paid about as well as the many who didn't and the many more who
were at the mercy of other similar owners of that time. They were
famous too, so it couldn't have been that. Were they merely greedy?
Was Comiskey as cheap as his detractors painted him to be? Or was
there yet another reason that drove the eight to throw away everything
for almost nothing?

October 21

It is still my fervent prayer that Sam will never see the letter I
just drafted and I can therefore destroy it as soon as his train arrives,
enabling us to weigh the terrible implications of its contents man to man.

I would have confided my present quandary to you alone, dear
Diary, but for the awful surmise that visited me even as I sat here at the
depot warring with the gravest decision I will ever have to make in my
life.

Can the true reason Sam has never traveled to Cincinnati this
season be that he fears a repetition of his frightful accident? I'd never
before considered that possibility because he came to see me play
several times in Portsmouth. But a while ago, when the 10:32 rolled in
without him aboard, I remembered he'd always trekked from Blue Creek
to Portsmouth by wagon even though it meant an overnight journey.
Previously I'd accepted his explanation that the horses needed the
exercise, but now I'm made to wonder. If Sam is not on the next train, I

must take it as fact that he is simply overcome by his understandable terror of railway travel.

All his decrees that he refuses to see me in an Outlaw Reds uniform because it marks me a traitor cannot be the real story. I know if it were humanly possible he would not leave me in the lurch now.

In my letter to Sam I spread all my cards on the table as if he were here, and no doubt he will be soon. But in the slim unlikelihood he is not and I must post my missive, then he may never know the outcome of my plight, as the next step I take will end my obligation to keep him abreast of my diamond doings. No matter which way I turn, dear Diary, my diamond career will come to an abrupt halt. Either I'll be assassinated by McQuery for having betrayed him or I'll assassinate myself for allowing comradeship to stand above the integrity of the National pastime.

Yet there is a tiny sliver of hope that I'll survive this day if I can pretend to have witnessed no evil and events this afternoon prove that I truly have not.

What set everything into motion, actually, was a chance encounter with Lucas yesterday when we were leaving Union Park after our last practice session prior to today's Championship clash with the Maroons. He was just exiting from Thorner's office under the grandstand as I and some other boys came out of our dressing room. He might have gone off uneventfully but for the fateful timing of his departure. Upon spotting him, Crotty pursued him all the way to his buggy outside the park. The mission seemed fruitless—Crotty could not even obtain the ear of his quarry. But then, as Lucas was about to climb into his buggy, he spied me and appeared to have a thought. In a moment he beckoned to me. After I approached him, he asked me to meet him within the hour at his hotel, the Burnett House. When I inquired as to the nature of his invitation, he gave only the clue that we had a matter of mutual interest to discuss.

Naturally, no sooner had Lucas gone than Crotty wanted to know what that had been all about. I tried to fend him off, but when he guessed correctly on his own and then said that only a moron went alone to meet with a man like Lucas and reminded me that he'd honored me by taking me with him the evening the two of them powwowed in St. Louis, I had to bow to his logic.

The Burnett House is at the corner of Fifth and Walnut Streets, and until yesterday I'd only seen its exterior. Inside, it's resplendent with giant pillars and mile-high ceilings as well as Foucar's Saloon, which occupies fully half of the ground floor and exhibits paintings everywhere your eyes turn, many of them featuring local landmarks like Harris's Mammoth Museum and even one of Union Park! Foucar's was where we repaired after Lucas descended the lift to the lobby in reply to the telephone call from the desk announcing our presence. He did not seem bothered when he saw Crotty with me. Actually it almost seemed that Crotty and not I had been the one invited, for Lucas at first directed all his remarks to him as if I weren't even there. After our drinks arrived, Lucas talked not about base ball, let alone our mutually impending contest on the morrow, but rather directed the conversation into other channels and eventually the upcoming Election when he observed Herrmann and two other of Cox's lickspittles dining at a nearby table. Sam will be glad to hear he gives Blaine little hope of winning but not so pleased to learn he's no champion of Cleveland either. Lucas thinks the choice might as well be between two nincompoops if they're both really as simple-minded as they appear. In any case, he maintained we're all in for tough sledding the next four years.

Crotty inquired why Lucas didn't run for President himself. He was obviously better qualified than most who sought the office, owing his popularity neither to a specious military record nor a false appearance of being a man from rough cloth.

Lucas looked astonished to have heard such ornate language from Crotty. Then he gathered his face and said: "I may yet do that. But right now my full contribution to base ball still is to be made. I won't leave the game until I've achieved complete autonomy not only for its current participants but, more importantly, the thousands who will follow in their footsteps."

"Neatly put," said Crotty, laying down his cigar as if sensing the conversation had at last veered toward the reason we'd assembled. "But it begs me to ask when you will leave behind the first rung on your climb up the ladder to immortality."

When Lucas sat silent, as if to smoke out Crotty's precise meaning before he committed himself, Crotty was made to clarify: "I'm talking about the Union Association. How much longer have we, Saint Henry, before you kill our flame by taking our only receptacle than has sufficient fuel to a camp with a brighter fire?"

Lucas still played mystified. He said: "I'm afraid your lengthy metaphor lost me at an early turn, Crotty."

And Crotty said, matching his tart smile: "Is it only that I too can speak with several tongues that keeps you from offering me a contract for next year? Or is it more that you yourself don't yet know what circuit will house your Maroons?"

"We have our home," Lucas said. "We're at the forefront of the Union Association, and that's where we'll be for years to come unless some other club in our alliance finds a way to rival my mastery at amassing the best team on earth."

And Crotty said: "Then I repeat, sir, I want to join this juggernaut. Because I think you're frank about your goal if not about where you plan to achieve it."

"Crotty," said Lucas narrowly, "I wouldn't have you on my team if you batted 1.000 and had hands of iron. Is that baldly enough said? If not, let me add that I won't have you in my circuit next year if I have my say, and I think I will."

And Crotty said, bridling now too: "Don't be too fucking sure of that."

"My," said Lucas, "how the gutter emerges when you come out from behind that mask of ironical Devil's advocate. Crotty, I'm reminded that you're here without invitation. I've tolerated you this long only so Draves could see for himself what sort of man his teammate really—"

And Crotty cut him off sharply: "Then let's find out what he's seen. And while you're at it, Ducker, tell us what opinion you've formed of our pseudo savior."

I fiercely resented being put on the carpet like that and also that Lucas had turned to stare at me now as if he no less than Crotty was curious how I would squirm off the hook. For the truth is that I thought both of them were equally contemptuous of one another and discourteous toward me whom, until that moment, neither of them had remembered was sharing their table.

So I said bluntly that the pair of them reminded me of two male dogs in the way each was struggling to mount the other to no worthwhile purpose. At that Crotty looked amused. "Cheers for you, Ducker," he said between puffs on his cigar. "But it's not that we're alike. It's that Saint Henry isn't used to men he believes beneath him telling him his shit smells no sweeter than theirs."

And Lucas said tautly: "Mister, that's all from you I care to hear. I'll thank you now to remove your coarse cigar and your coarser mouth."

"Your wish is my command," said Crotty. He rose, bowed facetiously to Lucas and seemed about to go. But then his face darkened and he said: "But one final warning. Maybe I'm too much my own man for you to stomach, but if you try to stop me from earning my living as a ball player anywhere but with your own club, I'll fucking crucify you, you little tin Christ!"

Lucas gave a curt wave of his hand but otherwise suffered the parting shot by sitting stone still until Crotty had stormed from Foucar's. Then he said: "Well, Draves, are you man enough now to converse without your go-between present or shall we again turn the subject to politics and the weather?"

I started to deny Crotty had been there as a go-between even though there might have been some truth in the jibe, but Lucas cut me off to say: "In short, are you prepared tonight to commit yourself to the Maroons for next season?"

Flabbergasted, and yet flattered too as I was, I nonetheless reminded him I could hardly do as he asked when I was still under contract to Thorner and McLean.

To which Lucas said that was no longer a barrier as he'd already gotten Thorner's permission to bargain not only with me but also with several of my teammates.

I must have looked as incredulous at that as I felt, for he pulled a folded paper from his pocket and said if he showed it to me as proof of his sincerity, would I pledge that its contents would never go beyond the two of us?

Still areel, I nodded my assent, and Lucas then unfolded the paper for my inspection. Upon restoring it to his pocket, he said: "Understand, it's not a contract because you're correct. You're all still bound here in Cincinnati for now. All it does is give me the first right to bargain with you when your contract expires and guarantee you in return that I'll top any other offer you receive."

That was the God's truth, dear Diary. Those were almost the exact words on the paper, and it had been signed by John W. Glasscock and Charles F. Briody.

"Now do you see why I don't want Crotty?" Lucas said when he'd permitted me some moments to digest the shock of it all. "Even if he weren't a corrosive element, I already have a first-rank catcher lined up for next season."

What I really saw was why I wanted no part of his offer even above and beyond its dubious timing when we were on the eve of the Championship game between his forces and ours. How could he want me, I said, when he already had Glasscock as his short stop for next season?

And he said because in all candor he didn't feature me a short stop. I had the arm for it but no longer the accuracy. No, my talents were best suited now for the box, which was where I'd be next year: the Maroons change pitcher when Sweeney and Boyle needed rest and probably at first base otherwise to take advantage of my bat.

In time I could become a celebrated hurler, he went on, and the ideal complement to Sweeney, my curves alternating with his inshoots to keep the opposition constantly at bay because they'd never face the same type of pitches two days in a row.

I must admit that what he said made sense except for the part about my throwing no longer being accurate enough for the short field.

There's nothing wrong with me that a winter's rest and maybe surgery to straighten my injured finger won't cure. But when I told Lucas that, he said he doubted surgery would help much at this late juncture. What's more, even if my finger could be mended, at best he might consider me a candidate next season for third base.

"That still can't sell me," I was bound to say, "when my enduring dream will always be to become the new King of Short Stops."

Lucas sat as if unbelieving that I remained unswayed. At last he said: "I respect your ambition, Draves, if never your judgment. Still, I wish you luck tomorrow after reminding you to keep our discussion tonight under your hat for now."

I reckon I've violated that pledge by writing of it to Sam—unless I end up destroying my letter to him when he arrives. Should he not come, nothing he knows could possibly worry Lucas since he's way out in Blue Creek and seems bent on staying there come Hell or high water. And if by some miracle he does get here in time for our game, unlikely as that now seems since it's nearly one p.m., then all he'll hear me tell of is the mortal blow of the two I was dealt last night.

After leaving Foucar's, I wandered over to Vine Street and into Kissel's Concert Hall, thinking it was that my talk with Lucas had left me too agitated to sleep. But then I remembered that Briody frequented Kissel's, and it seemed that I must find him and ask about the paper he and Glasscock signed and in particular whether he knew what baffled me above all else: Why Thorner would have given Lucas permission to bargain with them before their contracts expired?

There was no sign in Kissel's of Briody, but Phil Powers was slumped near the end of the bar and lifted his saturnine countenance when I poked my head in the door. Now I was committed to stay there for a few minutes at least, if only so Powers would not think the mere sight of him was the cause of my leaving.

I made for an empty stool at the other end of the bar, but before I could claim it a voice hailed me by name. Thinking it belonged to Powers, I turned reluctantly to greet him. To my relief, however, what I saw was not Powers but a total stranger motioning for me to join him at his table and a second man who looked familiar, but only vaguely so, patting the back of the vacant chair beside him.

I thought at first that he was a crank who wanted only to introduce a renown ball player to his pal and perhaps buy him a libation, especially when he said cheerily: "Ah, Draves, you're the very man to brighten our conclave." But once I'd seated myself and taken a sharper look at him, I realized my error.

The man was the nefarious Tierney, he who tried last spring to inveigle crooked work from me while I was with the Red Stockings colts.

"We've been pondering something ever since we spotted you," he said.

"Which is," his crony then took up, "whether you will strike more safe blows tomorrow off Sweeney than you make boots behind McCormick. We contend your miscues will so greatly exceed your hits that the Maroons are a cinch to win and certain of our colleagues contend otherwise. What say you? Answer correctly and you'll earn a prize the likes of which will tide you munificently over the long cold winter."

I had only to say excuse me but you have the wrong man and then get up and leave this pair cold. So that was what I said and set out to do.

But when I got to my feet Tierney said: "Before you go off halfcocked, bub, you'd best know we already have one of your mates in our pocket. We need just one more, ideally a stellar batsman like yourself, to secure our investment."

"You're lying," I said. "You've boughten none of our boys. Each and every man on our nine will be playing tomorrow to win—and win we will!"

"Yet I hear a hollow note in your windpipe," Tierney said. "Ain't it because you know we're on the level?"

"You?" I hooted. "You're a mountebank—and everyone knows it!"

"But what about me?" said a voice behind my chair, and when I turned to see the speaker it felt as if a trapdoor had suddenly opened beneath me.

An eerie sense of resignation came over him almost instantly. It was a full day's journey from Chicago to Cincinnati. Only one matter could have brought such a man here to this crossroads in time.

"I see you know who I am," Dick Higham said as he seated himself at the table in a chair that had seemed to materialize from nowhere.

Aware his face made plain he did, Draves still sought to believe that he was being made the dupe of some sinister charade.

"So I'm a mountebank, am I?" Tierney asked him, and a contemptuous echo from the spittoon punctuated his question.

"You can't have boughten any of our boys. You just can't have done it."

"It only takes one bad apple to tip the cart," Higham said.

But there was no pressing desire to inform Draves of the traitor's identity.

"Though to feel secure we'd like two," Tierney volunteered.

"Who do you claim to have already?"

He had hit accidentally upon the right way to ask the question. It seemed to hint he might be coming around to them.

"Only your biggest man," said Higham, and followed it by giving him a look of such penetration that he had to turn away.

Their biggest...? "In size, do you mean?"

No one answered him, but two pairs of eyes glanced toward Higham, expecting some signal on how to reply. Draves misread their intent and presumed his surmise had been right. He addressed himself directly to Higham.

"You don't mean McQuery? You can't mean Mox?"

Higham stared quietly at him as a lap dog might curl his lip away from a rotten slab of meat. Perhaps that was the only way he could finally have captured his prey. A man is never more convinced of something than when he has convinced himself while thinking it was done to him by another, and Draves was unaware that he had been baited in whichever direction his own nose had already inclined him to go.

"A first baseman can do a bushel of damage," Higham said offhandedly, "if he knows how to make it appear his mates' throws to him are off the mark."

"And especially with help from one whose throws ain't too reliable anyway," Tierney put in.

Higham looked warningly at him, but it was too late. Draves had already turned angry wounded eyes on Tierney and then folded his arms and stared toward the door. He was again readying himself to bolt, it appeared.

"But we need you since you're the best hitter on your team at the moment," Higham offered hastily, and then, for the sake of credibility: "Besides Glasscock."

"Well, you can't have me. I'm not for sale—and I'd die before I'd ever let myself be!"

"Fine speech, bucko, but listen up careful now. It means a broken left arm—permanently broken—if you ever breathe a word to anyone of our little confab."

Tierney said it like an actor in a hackneyed melodrama and glared at Draves with all the theatrical venom he could muster. But if his manner was overbaked, Higham's was laden with unaffected calm as he said: "In plainer words, we'll ruin you forever for base ball if you open your trap."

Draves plunged out of the saloon, not waiting to learn how Higham meant to implement his threat, though a hand tried to seize his left sleeve.

But what was a broken arm when his career would be over anyway after tomorrow? A few hours ago he had imagined nothing worse than the possibility that nary a loved one would come to see him play all season. Now even that seemed insignificant when he considered that his closest comrade on the team was a Judas.

"In 1878 I played ball with the Allegheny club in Pittsburgh. After disbanding around July of that year I went over to Cleveland under the management of Hollender, who had started a club there, and we played at Cedar and Kennard Street. The following year we went into the National League, the first club of your city to enter it. I was a third baseman then and played that position that year, and in 1880 they put me at short," wrote Jack Glasscock in a letter to the *Cleveland Plain Dealer* some 46 years after he left the Cleveland Blues in 1884 to cast his lot with the Union Association. He had been the most popular player on the Blues, and his defection left deep resentment. Whenever he returned to Cleveland during the remainder of his career in the garb of another team, he was given a hostile reception. Eventually he won back a measure of public favor, but he was never again anything like the darling of the Forest City he had been before his desertion.

The irony is that until the Outlaw Reds began courting him, Glasscock had been debating whether to quite base ball and pursue his off-season trade as a ship's carpenter on a full-time basis. For he was lost without Fred Dunlap. His lone distinction had been that he was the only one on the Blues Dunlap could never make look too slow to play beside him. Clevelanders loved him for that and for his insouciant good looks. In the picture of the 1879 team, the city's first in the National League, Glasscock, then just turned 20, looks as Jimmy Connors might have with short hair at the same age. There was little expectation back then that he would ever be more than an average batsman, but the Blues counted on continued improvement in the field. And his obsession for keeping the diamond free of anything that could alter the path of a ball hit in his direction might eventually be an added attraction. The way Glasscock was constantly "groundskeeping" the area around his position made him the target of many jokes about his excessive fastidiousness. Some of these were combined with his surname but always with an element of risk. Although Jack Glasscock was not big and had no particular reputation as a fighter, he did exhibit a certain recklessness— or perhaps an unerring accuracy—when throwing a ball around during practice. Several teammates in his first year with the Blues sported lumps on their skulls for weeks after calling him "Transparent Pecker" in a jocular moment, yet he was not above playing the wag himself. It was Glasscock who sent recruit players in search of a can of red and white striped paint to decorate the walls of the Outlaw Reds dressing room with the team colors, and Glasscock also led the taunts that hounded an elder member of the team who admitted to never having seen his wife naked. If a grown man could still be that green, Glasscock reasoned, why should anyone have to resist the amusement he provided?

The Outlaw Reds weren't a team for the long haul anyway, he saw that very soon after his arrival in Cincinnati. So there was no point in trying to build camaraderie and morale. He was in the Union Association to escape the lowly Blues first and the money second, and he just took it for granted that McCormick and Briody had the same motive for jumping to Cincinnati. People in Cleveland had already made up their minds about him, that he would never amount to much as a hitter. But he knew that he wasn't on a fluke tear, he'd be coming into his own now at the plate even if he were not facing lesser pitchers on most days. Men he hardly recognized were often waiting outside Union Park to glad-hand him and talk as if they were long lost friends. This kind of thing had never happened in Cleveland.

"We wish we could afford to have you back next year," Thorner told him.

"I could do with less in salary if you gave me a deal like the one I hear Lucas is going to give Dunlap next year."

"A share of the profits? First you'd have to get on a team where there are likely to be some."

"Why is everyone around here so pessimistic all of a sudden when we're the hottest team going now?" He truly didn't understand.

"Guess," Thorner said, and then a few minutes later: "There's a steep price we're going to have to pay to keep our club afloat, and you're part of it. The biggest part, if it will make you feel better."

"I'm beginning to catch on." The rumor he had been loath to believe appeared to be true after all. In which case, he was compelled to inquire, what of the lifetime ban that faced him and all the other former National Leaguers who had fled to the Union Association?

"You'll be fined by the League, and pretty heavily, but don't worry," Lucas told him the following week. "I'll pay it for you and you'll be reinstated."

"How can you be so certain of all this?"

"You don't think for a minute, do you, that the League and the Americans are going to let us Onions stay in business for another year?"

"I suppose not."

"Believe me, Jack. Commit yourself now to the Maroons for next season and you'll only be glad you did. With you at short stop we'll be nigh unstoppable."

"I still don't like the feeling I get even just talking about this when I'm going to be playing against your team in a few days for the Championship."

"Jack, be serious. Now you must know that game means next to diddle."

"Maybe to you, but to many of our boys their whole season is riding on it."

"Is that true for you too?"

"Well, I definitely want to win," he hedged

"And you well may, but so what if you do? Or so what if you don't? Either way, it won't make a whit of difference."

"Then why are you promoting the game like it's a matter of life or death?"

"Oh, Jack, please." The sneer angered him. His fist came up as part of a reflex action and made Lucas raise a mollifying hand when he saw it.

They parted as friends, even as future business associates, but Glasscock kept that dark sinking sensation. He never did work himself into feeling good about his pledge to join the Maroons while his professional spirit still dictated that he look upon them as the enemy. It had no bearing on how he performed, it was never in question that he knew how to play only one way: his best. And regardless of how little the game might ultimately mean in the scheme of things, the incentive was there for him—if only to have the joy of knocking Dunlap off his high horse.

So Jack Glasscock went to Union Park on that Tuesday afternoon in October determined to treat the game as any other. Winning was important, but the satisfaction of knowing at the end of it that he had played well was uppermost in his thoughts. If the game truly had been for the pennant, these priorities would have been reversed. But it was really little more than Lucas had implied: an exhibition contest, staged for the extra revenue. Glasscock recognized that. He had no reason to look upon it as anything out of the ordinary. He might have done it differently, though, if he had known that he would never again play in a game nearly as important in the 11 years remaining to him in the major leagues.

Cincinnati, O., October 21

Dear Sam:

I pray you got my wire in time to obey its urgent request. They couldn't promise it would reach you within 24 hours, as per their guarantee, because you live so far off the beaten track; but I had to take the gamble.

What it said (in the event you didn't receive it) was: PLEASE DESTROY MY LETTER POSTMARKED OCTOBER 21 WITHOUT OPENING IT. AMENDED LETTER TO FOLLOW AT ONCE.

But before I begin the amended edition, Sam, I'm wondering if I should go to Blue Creek tomorrow to intercept my earlier letter in the event it arrives before my wire or in case you, for some reason, ignored its directive. To do that would be tantamount, however, to saying I don't trust either you or the Western Union company, which is not how I wish to feel after having overcome the terrible distrust of my fellow man that ravaged me until the events of this afternoon demonstrated my near-fatal error.

Hence I will follow my instinct, which at this moment is to write as if you've not heard from me since my letter of yesterday morning and to disclaim responsibility in the event today's earlier letter was inadvertently read by you despite my every effort to prevent that from occurring.

And besides, your absence this afternoon, however excusable it may be, has left me feeling too raw to contemplate visiting you right now.

Plainly and simply, you missed the greatest game in all of history, Sam.

It contained every ingredient of what makes base ball our National pastime. Agility, strength, stamina, speed, courage, quick thinking—all were on majestic display today, along with a cornucopia of sunshine and blue sky. It was an afternoon made especially for base ball, so perfect that I fairly lost myself for the full hour and a half the contest lasted. Just about my sole disappointment was that there weren't a few more people in attendance—one in particular.

Still, we didn't have a bad crowd for a weekday although it ought to have been ten times bigger with the Championship of the Union Association at stake along with the right to challenge for the World's Championship.

I say the right to challenge, Sam, because it can never be more than that now. After the way our Champions played today, whoever wins the World's Series between the Mets and the Providences will surely refuse the challenge.

Radbourn may have won 60 games this year in the League and Keefe and Lynch 74 games in tandem for the Mets, but none of them could ever hope to match the towering feat achieved today by Sweeney and McCormick. Between them, Prince Charlie and Scotch Jim allowed just two runs, and none at all after the first inning—a mere two tallies, Sam, with the Championship on the line (although there ought to have been several more that I'll discuss in due course).

But first I want to squelch any rumors that may have reached you about a member of our side fixing it for us to lose. All nine of our boys played every single pitch on the square, although I will allow that those same rumors must have reached Crane's ears along with doubts about whether certain of us perhaps owed only part of their allegiance to the Outlaw Reds now and part to the team they've already clandestinely committed themselves to join next season.

What other explanation can there be for why Crane abandoned his second-base post and spent the entire game on the bench where he could scrutinize the proceedings with an eagle eye? Let alone for why he put Bradley at short stop today and demoted Glasscock, the world's best short stop, to second base.

It was as if he was sending Glasscock a message. I won't be coy, Sam. The nature of Crane's message was all in that letter you kindly destroyed, and I won't reiterate it here as it's only tomfoolery that may or may not be in the offing.

And anyway, there's never been the slightest suspicion of Glasscock's honesty, only of his fidelity.

As for the one whose honesty has recently come under fire, I'll say only this. It would have been calamitous if I'd acted upon my doubts of him because he is now above suspicion. Were he anything less, he would not have played as he did, which was nothing short of heroically.

I know, Sam, because I watched him like a hawk every second, and I never once saw him do anything even slightly off color either at bat or in the field.

Crane meanwhile said nary a word to him all afternoon, and I have to believe our captain would have made at least one scathing remark or even benched him and played Hawes in his stead if there were any doubt about his sincerity today. But, actually, Crane's only reproach all day was directed at Burns, and even it was tame compared to what wee Dick deserved after his stupid blunder.

In the fifth inning McQuery (no other) led off with a two-bagger and then darted to third base when Bradley sent a squibber to Quinn along the first-base line. Quinn shoveled the ball to Sweeney racing over from the box to cover first, but Umpire Johnson said Sweeney's foot missed the bag and ruled Bradley safe. While Sweeney was jawing with Johnson, Burns, our third base coach, foolishly coaxed McQuery to sneak home. Only Sweeney wheeled around before Mox was halfway to the plate and hung him out to dry with a perfect peg to Baker.

So instead of having runners at the corners with no hands out, we now had one down and a man only on first. Crane was properly fit to be tied because Burns's imprudent coaching had snuffed out what should have been a gorgeous rally.

He'd have been ever more furious, and so would we all have if we'd known at the time that we'd never again come so close to denting the marble.

Well, Sam, I can no longer skirt the bad news. The Maroons were the team that scored the only two runs today and won the Union Championship. Dunlap led off the game with a liner over Glasscock's head at second base that scampered all the way to the fence and enabled him to score a four-bagger before Harbidge could flag down the ball and gun it homeward. Then Shaffer beat out an infield single and Rowe gave one a ride over Harbidge's head for a triple to drive the Orator across the platter, and I could have gone home and kicked the dog right then and there because the game essentially was decided before the crowd had scarcely got settled in their seats.

But no one knew that at the time, and every man played accordingly. Down to the very last pitch we continued to believe the game was ours to win. I can't say enough, Sam, about how valiantly all of us tried to the bitter end to pull the fat out of the fire while the Maroons fought with equal valor to thwart us.

It was base ball played to its uttermost, abrim with so many brilliant fielding, batting and pitching gems that it would be unjust to single out any one of them for citation. But I might say the scorcher I struck in the eighth inning that would have been a sure triple if it hadn't curved foul at the last possible instant must be high on everybody's list.

It would have been a sublime contest merely to have witnessed, and to have played in it is a treasure that I will savor for the rest of my life even if I never play in another.

Of course there will be many more historical games in my column before I'm done, Sam, but none can surpass today's because I knew, even as I saw our hopes for the Championship dimming, that I had at last found my true calling.

Always before it had felt as if I chose to become a base ball player for your sake more than my own. But from today forward the feeling every time I step onto the diamond field will be that I'm where I'm meant to be.

Sam, I learned something wondrous this afternoon. I learned that base ball stands above suspicion and betrayal and, yes, even above winning. Out there on the diamond infield today, with the warming sun above my head and the dirt baked hard beneath my feet, I felt like a king in his castle. I felt like a king, Sam, because I realized that during every game I play I am a king. Win, lose or draw, I'm doing what I love most among men who love it too and in front of people who are there to canonize us as the heroes they can no longer dream of becoming in their own harsh and careworn walks of life.

If I were to die this very moment, I would die content although I might wish not to die after being viewed in the game that marked the recognition of my life's destiny by people who know me only as Ducker.

Sam, if you'd been here today your voice would have sounded like a clarion each time it cried out for me, Earl, to mash that pill. As it is, I like to have forgotten my baptismal name so used I've become to answering to Ducker. Sam, surprise the living daylights out of me, I beg of you. Visit my room tonight while I'm aslumber to whisper to me as if in a dream: "Earl, guess who was secretly at your game today?"

Your nephew, Earl.

"All that ability and he's blessed with clean good looks too," the cranks from every city but Providence said enviously, studying the Grays' team photograph. Even with part of his face hidden under his cap Charlie Sweeney looked so darkly handsome that he dwarfed all of his teammates. There was in addition the appearance of a magnificent body—from a youth put in at hard physical labor in San Francisco—a promontory of wide shoulders and long tautly muscled arms. Not everyone, however, liked Sweeney with a mustache. It lent him a faintly sinister cast, a tinge of the villain. But what in 1884 was merely thought an air of intrigue was transformed into a homicidal mien several years later when he killed a hooligan named Con McManus in a barroom fracas. By then his arm was long gone, some said from overdoing a pitch that curved inward to right-handed batters, a kind of "screwball" pitch that caused his wrist and elbow to twist unnaturally.

As early as the spring of 1885 there were indications that the pain he was feeling in his elbow might be more than normal soreness, but he said nothing of it to anyone. Even if he had not had a reputation as a chronic bellyacher to live down, it was critical that he get off to a flying start. He wanted them to say in St. Louis as was being said in Providence of Hoss Radbourn: "As Sweeney goes, so go the Maroons." For a while there had been a lot of bickering in print over whether he and the other jumpers would be allowed back into the National League, but he knew all along it was only posturing. Although the verdict was not officially announced until a few days before the 1885 season was due to open, really the League owners had decided months earlier to reinstate all the defectors. So he left San Francisco in late March and drifted east to St. Louis. He was working out in a gymnasium at his usual leisurely pace when Lucas informed him to start stoking the coals because the League had just voted to accept his signed contract for the coming season. Sweeney was privately amused by all the mock skullduggery, but he took it as it came, reckoning there would always be a place in base ball for any man with his kind of talent. Lucas said he would bat third and play centre field on days when he didn't pitch—not even Radbourn and Hecker were treated with so much esteem, and he was still just turned 22.

On April 30, 1885, in the Maroons' first game as a member of the National League, Sweeney beat the vaunted Chicago White Stockings, 3-2, before a crowd of nearly 7,000. The Opening Day win put the Maroons into a tie for first place and Henry Lucas into ecstasy. It was only one game, but still he could not help but feel vindicated. Call his Maroons a cardboard powerhouse in a jerrybuilt league, would they? Somehow he got the notion that Chris Von Der Ahe would have led his Browns in a victory celebration on a like occasion and therefore so should he. He bought round after round of drinks at a saloon nearby the ball park and then stood back to watch the revelry. Naturally shy with men in large groups, he would frequently play that he was a fly on the wall. In this role he managed to overhear, without being observed listening, the following conversation between his star pitcher and two crack keystone operatives.

"Cap's boys must have been fiddling today to lose to you with what little you had on the ball."

This, from Glasscock, was met hotly by Sweeney.

"Come again. There wasn't a single thing they did wrong— fielding, batting, throwing—*nothing* that looked intentional."

But he was silent when Glasscock said, "Dropping balls or throwing them away deliberately aren't the only ways to fiddle a game, as we all know."

"Oh, you're not going to start humming that song again," said Dunlap. "You were bushwhacked straight and sweet, face it."

"Well, you'd naturally say that, being on the winning side. I've never yet heard a man say it wasn't all his own work when he came up a winner."

"I'm almost ready to think you knew something was off the books, Jack."

"Somebody knew a deal more that day than he'll ever dare let on. That's obvious, when you consider how much better a team we were by then."

"Give me another laugh."

"And we had more to gain by winning and were playing on our home ground."

"There you could have something. But it took nine men to go scoreless for a full nine innings, and you can't tell me that all of you were in the bag."

"I'd like to have seen, I'll just say, whether you'd have been given more than two runs if we'd happened to score along the way."

"Given? Who gave us anything in that game we didn't earn, Jack?"

"Does your mouth still water remembering that pitch you hit like a bullet over my head? The first one of the game, no less?"

"You can't mean McCormick. If anything, Harbidge was at fault it went for a home run. He was playing me too shallow, and Rowe too when he came up."

"The pitcher is always guilty when something goes wrong," Sweeney muttered, coming back into it. "Don't we know that, though?"

"And what about like today when it goes right?" said Dunlap.

"Anyway," Glasscock said, "all that's done. This season is my concern now, and I just hope it was us that made the Chicagos play like shit today."

The next day the Maroons lost 9-5 to the White Stockings as the team, perhaps hungover, made 15 errors behind Pudge Boyle, but two weeks later the National League standings showed St. Louis with six wins and four losses, not far off the pace. Then it all went rotten. The White Stockings won game after game—they would eventually claim the pennant with a near-record .777 winning percentage—and the Maroons sank like a rock. At the season's close they had the poorest record of any team in either major league, and Sweeney was designated the whipping boy. After his glorious triumph on Opening Day, he won only 10 more games while losing 21.

Over the winter he vowed to get into better shape and return to form the next season, but who could ever again take him seriously when he was fit to pitch only 11 games all year? In one of them he was rocked for a record seven home runs by Detroit. That the Maroons nevertheless escaped the cellar was only because the National League put two new teams in Kansas City and Washington, and both were so execrable they could not win even a quarter of their games. Lucas fought to keep the Maroons in St. Louis even though he was verging on bankruptcy, but the other National League owners voted to transfer the franchise to Indianapolis for the 1887 season, and he left the game a bitter and broken man. Though Lucas was just 29 years old then, he never again even remotely approached the heights to which he had ascended in 1884 when his name eclipsed every other in base ball, and by the time of his death, in 1910, he was already, a mere quarter-century later, regarded by most of the game's authorities as no more than a sidebar in its history.

His prize acquisition fared even worse. Charlie Sweeney last played in the majors with Cleveland in 1887, where he teamed briefly with Hugh Daily. Local wags said the team now had two pitchers who had but one good arm each—only Daily's at least was the one he threw with. After giving up 36 runs in 24 innings, Sweeney was tried at first base for a while and then released. Only 24 when his major league career ended, he returned to San Francisco and continued to play there for local teams, mostly in the California League, until he was sentenced to San Quentin for manslaughter in 1894. In prison, where alcohol could not ignite his temper, he was so well behaved that he was released before the completion of his 10-year term, but it mattered little to him. He had contracted tuberculosis at Quentin, a terminal case, and died in 1902, nine days short of his 39th birthday.

Louisville, Ky., October 22

Dear Sam:

How shall I explain what you will find bitter news no matter how I try to doctor its flavor?

I reckon I can do no better than to begin at the beginning or when I got back home last night from the post office after mailing my amended letter of yesterday to you. I'd venture you could never guess who was awaiting me at my boarding house if the postmark on the envelope hadn't given you all the clue you should need.

The happy note in the tune I'm about to sing is I didn't go through my entire recruit season as a major leaguer after all without having a loved one see me play. But the melancholy note is that Constance (which is again the name she's adopted) posed a conundrum in the course of our reunion, the answer to which I shudder to think may not be as I've always been led to believe by my only other loved one.

Before I get ahead of myself though, let me retreat to the moment I first saw Constance standing on the footpath. It would have made me think I must be dreaming if she hadn't instantly spoken, saying that she'd just chanced to pass my boarding house on her way to the train depot. She'd come to Cincinnati for the day, she explained, to audition for a role in a new revue at Heuck's Opera House. Since that seemed to mean she was resuming her career, my mind swarmed with questions. But before I could think which of them to ask first, she preempted me by professing it had been a wasted trip because they wanted someone younger naturally. Then she said: "Probably I should be going now that I've caught my breath."

Well, it's the same way with her, I thought, but then she did something new. She seized my hand in both of hers and said: "But first let me say how glad I am to see you again, Earl." Whatever I might have felt, the memories evoked by her hands embracing mine compelled me to echo that I was equally glad to see her.

Soon after that she let go of my hand, but she did accept my invitation to sit and rest on the glider on my front porch. For just a minute, she said.

In a while, gazing up at the two or three forlorn flowers left over from the summer that still lingered on the trellises, she said: "Well, how is base ball going for you?"

Thinking she was still just making chitchat, I said only: "Fine until today."

"Spoken as if today was a bad one for you."

"It was. We lost the Championship game to Sweeney and the Maroons."

"Umm," she said. Then in a changed voice she said: "Earl, what would you say if I told you I not only know who these Maroons are but have seen them play?"

You could have knocked me over with a feather, Sam, but a still greater shock lay ahead. For upon my asking her when, she said: "Well, this afternoon actually." Then in a flurry she said: "And now what will you say when I announce I didn't come to Cincinnati to audition for a singing role but to see you?"

"You were at our game today?" I said, still unable to credit my ears.

"Yes," she said, "since it seemed the proper place to start trying to atone for having disappointed you so often before."

To which I had to say with equal forthrightness: "Alma, you've surprised me so much that I'm at nearly a total loss for words."

"Pray," she said, "call me Constance again. Maybe we can never go back to the way we were when we first met, but I, for one, would like to try."

That was music to me, but after the cruel way we had ended I could go no longer without asking the question that was so near to the surface of my brain.

"What about your rich horseman?"

"Can you really imagine I would be here if that were not all over?"

"Well, but you were so sure he was everything you wanted only a few days ago."

She busied herself with a dead flower as she said: "Earl, I know I have a lot to explain, but can it wait till we're aboard the train?"

"Aboard—what train?"

"My day-trip ticket is good only till midnight, so I'm praying that you'll accompany me to Louisville tonight and help me to pack up all my belongings—"

"Whoa," I was bound to interrupt. "What is this now? Where are you going?"

"Why, Earl, I'll go wherever you wish."

"I'm still not clear, Constance, what it is you have in mind."

"It's very simple. I'm yours now, Earl, to do with as you want, though it would be lovely if you still thought enough of me to make me your wife."

Well, Sam, I've already told you more about the circumstances surrounding Constance's reappearance in my life than you care to hear, so I won't recount the turn matters between us took no less than three times last night after we arrived at her hotel in Louisville. Nor will I remark on how she intervened just a few minutes ago while I was in the midst of writing to apprise you that the grief I felt over your not having come to see me play this season has now been surmounted by my seemingly inexhaustible joy that someone else did.

But I must make mention of a conversation Constance and I had last night that was spurred by our being on the train at the time. I'll allow that even that setting would not ordinarily have enticed me to tell her the story of your accident. But then I thought: After all, she's practically one of the family now.

At any event, Sam, Constance was properly sympathetic when she learned how you'd lost your leg. It helped her to understand your present state better, knowing that your own dreams of base ball stardom had been severed on the eve of the very day they seemed about to be realized. I had to explain who the Kekiongas were, that they were a team representing the city of Fort Wayne, since she knew only the Indian tribe by that name. Then I had to backtrack and tell her how you would never have gone to Indiana to launch your professional career if the Red Stockings, the team that had stolen your heart and soul, hadn't disbanded just as you were about to join them as an understudy to George Wright.

Constance of course had never heard of Wright, but she was otherwise able to follow my tale until I got to the actual accident. Then something began to puzzle her, until she interrupted me to ask a question I couldn't answer. How, she wondered, could you have been sucked beneath the wheels of a moving train while being carried from it if it had struck another train only moments earlier?

Do you see the problem, Sam? Her question drives me too now to wonder how the well-meaning efforts of the anonymous Good

Samaritan who tried to help you off a wrecked passenger car could have ended in disaster, when a train that had only just crashed into another ought to have been at a complete standstill.

Sam, I truly loathe to ask you the question Constance asked me: If that train was moving when your leg slipped beneath it, is there perhaps something you've omitted from your account of the incident?

Well, it's not for me to speculate, but Constance hypothesized that a man in your position might have been in a celebratory mood that night, knowing he was only hours away from playing in his first professional game. And while in that lightheaded mood, might he have stepped off his train to Fort Wayne unawares that it hadn't as yet finished pulling into the depot?

Is it really conceivable such a misadventure could have befallen you? Any man so luckless I'd say would have every right now to brood about the hand Fate dealt him. Yet and still, he might (both literally and figuratively) never again have a leg to stand on whenever he started lecturing his nephew about the evils of drink and of failing always to tell the truth,

Be that as it may, Sam, I still pray you'll overcome your fear of train travel in the very near future. Only now you must voyage to Louisville rather than Cincinnati. That is where the simple ceremony will be held in the home of one of Constance's friends a week from Saturday, November 1, with Browning or McQuery as my Best Man. I haven't yet asked either to serve but shall before the week is out, unless someone else has volunteered by then to do me the honor.

Your nephew, Earl.

Redleg was sprawled on the carpet in the puddle of the sunshine that splashed into the office from the window behind his master's desk. The yellow light made the dog look even more sallow and bloated.

Redleg was gravely ill. Thorner knew it. There was no way to deny it any longer, and there was no point in denying it; everyone and everything died eventually. But what disturbed Thorner was that the dog's time had come so soon. Redleg was barely four years old and had been in perfect health until just a few short weeks ago. That none of the doctors Thorner had consulted could find the cause of his deterioration made it all the more depressing. From the outset Thorner had suspected that O'Leary's dog was responsible, but now it seemed certain: The mongrel had infected Redleg with some horrible disease, worse even than rabies. Rabies was an honorable way for a dog to die. But to have to watch helplessly as an animal you loved grew fatter and more slothful every day was thoroughly demoralizing. Moreover, Redleg's illness violated every law of nature. Thorner had tried to cure the dog by feeding him less, but it had the opposite effect. Redleg continued to gain weight and grow ever more lethargic.

Thorner himself somewhat resembled a dog. He was a portly, dark-haired man with dark brown eyes and a touch of perpetual gloom about his expression which was heightened by the folds of limp skin that hung down either side of his jaw like the jowls of a Saint Bernard. But he was not as dour as he looked. Most of his players distrusted him, but none denied that he had a sense of humor about life, even when the laugh was on himself. About the only area where Thorner would tolerate no frivolity was Redleg. The dog was nothing if not pampered to the point of nausea. He had the run of everything, from Thorner's office to the team dressing room. Draves could not imagine the punishment that would be dealt Hawes and Harbidge if Thorner ever found out why Redleg looked so obese and spiritless these days.

Thorner eyed the carpetbag in Draves's lap. "Where are you going?" he asked.

"Actually, I'm returning—from Louisville. I went down there Tuesday night after our game with a special someone."

A cliché—but he meant it even if, paradoxically, he himself did not feel special to Constance so much as necessary. The rent on her hotel room was paid only until Saturday. And after that? "Earl," she had said last night, "shouldn't you strike while the iron is hot and take care of your contract for next season now?" Spoken from the edge of sleep, but it had led to a near argument until he'd conceded that it made a fair amount of sense to solicit Thorner while the memory of his sterling play down the home stretch was still fresh in mind.

"You're not thinking of getting married, I hope?"

"Not at the moment."

That was a bald-faced lie, and Thorner went on as if he had said the opposite. "Marriage is a serious business, and any man undertaking it in this day and age had better be very sure of his ground."

Thorner remained so somber that he held silent for some seconds, taking care in his nervousness not to move his chair for fear of awakening Redleg.

"Well, that's actually what I came here to do," he said at last, "make sure of my ground for next season."

"You've come at the right time then. Mr. McLean and I just finished our annual review of the club's prospects yesterday."

Though Thorner spoke firmly, Draves could not miss that his eyes were evasive.

"To tell the truth, Draves, I was about to send a wire to your boarding house asking you to come in before the month was out. But you've beaten me to it. Sadly, however, your taking the bull by the horns has only hastened the grim tidings I must bring you. We're going to have to let you go, it seems."

"*What*?"

"Cool down," said Thorner with an anxious glance at Redleg, who had opened one glazed eye to the ceiling. "It has nothing to do with your play this season, I assure you. It's just that with the market flooded now with players from so many bankrupt teams, we'll be able to field an all-veteran corps next season."

In his shock, Draves blurted the first thing that came to mind. "How can you fire your top hitter this year save for Glasscock? I batted .322, Mr. Thorner."

"Yes, but you're still a recruit who has yet to establish himself over a full season. The same applies to McQuery," Thorner said upon seeing this has not appeased Draves any, "although I ask you to hold this in confidence until I can speak to him myself. In any case." Thorner rose from his desk and extended his hand. "I regret how the cards have fallen but know you'll understand. We must have a veteran hand at both of the diamond corners if we're to improve next year."

Draves remained seated. "And who'll be your short stop?"

"Why, Glasscock naturally."

"No he won't, Mr. Thorner, and you and I both know that."

Thorner screwed his forehead into a scowl and said, "I'm afraid I have no notion of what you're talking about, Draves."

"Your bargain with Lucas that would have included me if I'd gone for it."

Thorner made no comment.

"Now I'm wishing I had. Loyalty appears to count for naught around here."

And thereupon Thorner laughed, a loud guffaw that he seemed nonetheless to force out of himself. He glanced down at Redleg and addressed his words to him.

"Who gave this man a job when no one else would? And who would have fled our nest at the drop of a hat if he'd been made a better offer?"

"Not I, Mr. Thorner. I want you to know I turned down Lucas, ready to stay with the Outlaw Reds through thick or thin."

There was something about the laughter that now seemed genuine.

"It's dog eat dog, base ball is now, Draves. Being an owner is no picnic, you know. It's become a matter of constantly having to rob Peter to pay Paul."

"You could also try to be honest with your players."

"How honest can an honest man be nowadays?"

"I was never taught to believe there were varying degrees of truth."

"Honest enough to report if someone offered him a bribe to fiddle a game? Would you expect an honest man to do that?"

They were on the brink of a dangerous interchange, Draves felt, yet he could not back away from it. "Unless he was facing a higher priority than honesty."

"What is there more important?"

"Comradeship. The loyalty he felt to a friend and had to keep feeling until proven absolutely that it was no longer deserved."

"Do you mind talking in theory like this, Draves?"

"But we're not talking wholly in theory and I think you well know that."

"Well, this conversation is after the fact in any case. I just want you to know I've heard nothing against you personally. And I have no reason on my own to hold you in suspicion."

"Then why am I really being given the gate?"

Thorner's struggle was now as much a physical as an emotional one. To slow his pulse rate, he sat down again and began stroking Redleg's bulging belly.

"Partly because it's our educated guess that you'll never make a dependable fielder and you won't hit as well next season when the weaker pitchers are pared away. I'm sorry to have to say this, Draves, and I could be wrong. You're a man not easy to categorize. It isn't that you aren't hard working or without talent, yet I wonder if base ball really is for you. The men who succeed at this game often do so because they're too dim to grasp how little their lives will amount to if they don't. You're likely to fail at it because it means too much to you to succeed. It's the way of the world, lad. The more you crave something, the stronger is the probability it will elude you."

He did not proceed when he saw Draves looking at him as if he did not understand. Redleg stirred irritably, and Thorner watched a damp spot slowly form on the carpet. With an inward grimace he got to his feet again. He put his notion of a fatherly hand on Draves's shoulder and used it to steer him toward the door as he said, "I wish I could be half as sure about the Outlaw Reds as I am that you'll survive to play again somewhere next year."

Thorner would have been appalled if he had known how prescient his final words to Draves were. He had only meant to bring a palatable end to what had become an awkward situation. But ever afterward he would wonder if he had jinxed himself. The plan at the time he met with Draves was for both the Maroons and the Outlaw Reds to join the National League in place of Cleveland and Detroit. The official announcement would come from League headquarters over the winter, and at that point Thorner would inform his stockholders that Glasscock and Briody had been the price Lucas extracted for his help in getting the Outlaw Reds into the League. Instead the Detroit franchise at the last moment scraped together enough money to stay afloat, leaving the Outlaw Reds without a home and Thorner without a place in base ball when the Union Association collapsed following the Maroons' desertion.

He trusted it would be only temporary. He stayed in Cincinnati, leading an uneventful life, and he waited for another opportunity. When the wait grew into years he gradually abandoned his dream of returning to base ball. He even allowed himself to be seen now and then at local amateur games, stationed along one of the foul lines in his buggy with Redleg at his side. The dog had made a miraculous recovery after the Outlaw Reds players scattered for the winter. With Harbidge gone home to Philadelphia and Hawes staging roller skating exhibitions at his rink in Lowell, Massachusetts, there was no one to slide a saucer of beer under Redleg's nose any time he strayed out of Thorner's sight. The dog consequently died a natural death, and so probably did his master. But who can be sure anymore of how Thorner met his Maker? If his name were mentioned today in Cincinnati to a hundred people—make it a thousand—perhaps one or two would give a murmur of recognition. Or perhaps none would know of him. It's sad how Justus Thorner came to slip between the cracks. With different luck he might have been famous and his Outlaw Reds a championship team. But they got off to a slow start, and their final game of the season was tinged with a bad aroma. So Thorner lost his gamble on the Union Association, and that ruined him for, when he hitched his wagon to Henry Lucas's, he stopped being viewed as a member in good standing of the base ball fraternity. He already had intimations of that when he met for the last time with Draves, but he still didn't really believe his own dire prediction. That was on October 23, 1884—a sunny but extremely windy day everywhere in the Eastern half of the country but especially in New York, where the opening game of the first World Series in base ball history, between the Mets and the Providence Grays, was getting underway even as Draves left Thorner's office in a state of numbness and confusion.

He set off on foot, but not far, to Vine Street, where he encountered Joe Crotty and John Ewing, brother of Buck, the great catcher, and two or three other players he knew who made their homes in Cincinnati. He had a dissolute few hours, plain and straight, and he got all the advice he needed. Ewing also had been cut loose recently by the Outlaw Reds and Crotty knew his own days were numbered. They

both commiserated ardently with Draves until he muttered that now his
fiancée once again would probably refuse to have him. At that point
they gave him a friendly piece of their minds. Much later, because he
was in no condition to go home alone, they hired a hack and escorted
him to his boarding house. They waited until he was safely inside, and
then they rode off. Draves only dimly heard them departing, horses'
hoofbeats clattering away on the cobblestone street, but he suddenly
turned sober and cold when he saw the letter awaiting him on the
hallway table. Until he picked it up, he did not see the cable beneath it
that had been signed for by his landlord. Standing there in the hallway,
he was unable to make out the words in heavy type; it was not the poor
light but his head again, throbbing and spinning.

                                                       New York, N.Y., October 25

Dear Sam:

    Hooray! High time you started reading the papers again
although I don't appreciate the way you tried to slip the news past me!
It's too much like my old school marm used to do. "Oh, Earl," she'd say
absently as she looked up from her desk, and then she'd drop the lead
weight on me that I had to stay in the classroom during recess and scrub
the blackboard or some such thing.

    So it doesn't come as a total surprise to me, Sam, when someone
pens me a letter that starts out as if it aims to rehash all the ways in
which his nephew has become a traitor and a lusher and then sneaks in a
comment that he's just that morning read in the *Commercial-Gazette* that
the Union Association is about to sink in a sea of red ink. Nor do I
marvel that you claim you could have predicted I'd try to decry the
Maroons' victory in the Championship game by pretending the outcome
had been swayed by gamblers. It hardly is my fault that the second of
the two letters I wrote you on Tuesday reached you before the first,
which allegedly had still not arrived as of your reply to me. Had you
received it in proper order and not obeyed my wire requesting you to
destroy it unopened, you would know you barked up the wrong tree
when you wrote that I simply could not bear that the Outlaw Reds were
outgunned by a superior force, and tried to cloak our defeat in "some
made-up shenanigans." Ha! It just proves a man can have the best
intentions, but if Fate and the U.S. Postal Service are against him
someone looking for an excuse not to apologize for his own deficiencies
will misconstrue everything.

    Sam, how could you answer my plea to bring me a grand
surprise the other night by once again attacking my behavior and my
motives? I can only think my message concerning Constance and her

inquiry into the true manner in which you lost your leg will produce yet another attack when you finally get around to replying to it.

However, do I ever have a string of grand surprises for you! First off, although I journeyed to New York yesterday just to do my civic duty, now, through an incredible turn of the screw, I'm about to participate in one of the most mammoth historical events of our time. Before I get to the present moment though, I ought to regress to the beginning—except I don't rightly know where the beginning is. In one way it all began Thursday night with the cable from Inspector Byrnes that awaited me along with your letter of the 22nd. But in another way the beginning is really back in June when my hotel room in New York was invaded by that thieving woman, and in yet another way there would be no happy ending now to the tale of my first major league season if I hadn't injured my finger in that game against the Mets when I was given my nickname.

Well, actually, I probably should begin by explaining how I came to be at liberty to help make history in just a short while. On Thursday afternoon I formally parted company with the Outlaw Reds and the Union Association. Yes, Sam, you read that aright; but before you cheer, I should mention that I still think Henry Lucas and his mode of operation are the wave of the future. Justus Thorner, however, must be the most wrongly forenamed man on the planet. Can you believe, Sam, that he told me I must still be classified a recruit because I didn't play the full season with his team? Rest assured I did not sit quiet for that when we began to talk turkey for next season. Instead I rightly demanded my release once I saw Thorner's aim was to keep from paying me my true value. There are too many other fish in the sea to sit and dangle my line over water that has only a fat cat like Thorner and his stupid dog beneath it.

Still, I don't wish him and the remnants of his Outlaw Reds any particular ill luck, as his feckless analysis of my worth proved to be a blessing in disguise. Nor do I harbor bad will toward the Mets anymore for causing damage to my finger and christening me Ducker—but I'm getting ahead of myself again. Sam, if Thorner and I had not crossed swords, I would probably be in Louisville now instead of New York since I would have had a berth firmly lined up for next season and reason to refuse Byrnes's invitation to travel to the Gotham at its Police Department's expense. For a man who's just become betrothed must put first things first, but a man somewhat at loose ends will naturally leap at the chance to catch the first train to the East the next morning, especially when the funds for a round-trip ticket were sitting in the Western Union office right around the corner from him.

Sam, I would have written you yesterday on the train ride here while your letter was still fomenting in my stomach like contaminated water, but first I had to rid another of her wrongful assumptions about wither I must go next in my quest to make a lasting name for myself in base ball. So I had to wait until today to turn my thoughts toward Blue Creek. And now I find myself writing to you from a peak of such optimism it is impossible for me to remember the mood into which I was plummeted on Thursday night when I opened your letter and saw you would still give no quarter.

Providences		AB	R	BH	TB	PO	A	E
Hines	c.f.	2	3	1	1	1	0	0
Carroll	l.f.	4	1	1	1	0	0	0
Radbourn	p	4	1	1	1	0	1	0
Start	1b	3	0	0	0	6	0	0
Farrell	2b	3	1	1	1	1	3	0
Irwin	s.s.	3	1	1	1	2	1	2
Gilligan	c	3	1	2	4	4	0	1
Denny	3b	3	2	2	2	1	2	0
Radford	r.f.	2	1	0	0	3	0	0
Totals		27	11	9	11	18	7	3

Metropolitans		AB	R	BH	TB	PO	A	E
Nelson	s.s.	3	0	0	0	0	1	0
Brady	r.f.	3	0	0	0	1	0	1
Esterbrook	3b	3	0	2	3	0	1	2
Roseman	c.f.	3	0	2	2	0	0	0
Orr	1b	3	0	1	1	12	0	0
Draves	2b	3	0	0	0	2	4	1
Reipschlager	c	2	0	0	0	2	2	6
Kennedy	l.f.	2	0	0	0	1	1	0
Becannon	p	2	0	1	1	0	4	0
Totals		24	2	6	7	18	13	10

Innings	1	2	3	4	5	6
Providences	1	2	0	0	4	4—11
Metropolitans	0	0	0	0	1	1—2

Earned runs— Providences, 2. First base on errors— Providences, 3; Metropolitans, 2. First base on balls— Providences, 2. Struck out— Providences, 1; Metropolitans, 2. Left on base— Providences, 1; Metropolitans, 4. Three-base hit— Denny. Two-base hit— Esterbrook. Double plays— Kennedy and Draves, Farrell, Irwin and Start. Wild pitches— Radbourn, 1; Brennan, 1. Passed balls— Reipschlager, 2. Time of game— 1 hour 20 minutes. Umpire— Timothy Keefe.

But why mince any more words? I'm going to play in an hour's time for the Mets in their third and final World's Series game with the Providences, and even if the verdict is no longer in question because the Grays won the first two legs of the match, the occasion still is history in the making. Wounded as I may have been by the recent events leading to my separation from the Outlaw Reds (and hence, in all likelihood, from my intended as well), I now feel only vindicated. In very short time, Sam, I will take the field in the uniform of the New York Metropolitans, the finest team in base ball this season, the past two days notwithstanding.

Whereupon I enclose the box score of yesterday's contest so you can see for yourself that premature darkness brought on by overcast skies hamstrung the Mets more than Radbourn's sore-armed slants. As for today's game, you'll have to glean information of it on your own; although you should have your pick of sources now that you've started reading the papers again, as all will carry a detailed report of the monumental event. I will mention in aside, however, that my name will be found at second base and sixth in the batting order.

How I ascended to so lofty a pinnacle merits a longer story than time allows me to pen at the moment. One day I'll recount it to you in its entirety, but for now you must be content with a thumbnail sketch of my activities for the past 24 hours. Yesterday, when my train arrived in New York, a policeman met it and then convoyed me to the city jail, where waited Inspector Byrnes with a woman who called herself Kate Manning. It needed only a glance, however, for me to peg her as the maiden who besieged my hotel room under the pretense of sleepwalking. My identification, coupled with one made by another man who had been similarly molested by her, removed her mask of being anyone but Little Annie Reilly and helped affix the accuracy of the most recent charge against her. This Reilly woman makes ball players her special prey. Last week she applied to Candy Nelson of the Mets for a position as a nursemaid to his wife and their newborn infant. Within hours of her hiring, she then made off with several Nelson family valuables. Thankfully, she hadn't the opportunity to dispose of her ill-gotten gains before she was apprehended. Now she sits under lock and key, certain to remain there after I and others attest to her long criminal history at her trial two days hence.

Naturally, Nelson felt beholden to me for the service I'd done him and invited me to pitch batting practice to the Mets this morning during their informal workout at the Polo Grounds. In truth, the invitation was only to shag fly balls, but it was expanded when Mutrie learned I could pitch some and the Mets had no one else because Keefe had a sore arm, Lynch was hung over, and Becannon, the only other available hand, is slated to occupy the box this afternoon.

But all of this is neither here nor there, for the pitcher's box is not my meat as I discovered today once and for all when Dave Orr, the first man I faced, clouted several of my tosses so far over the outfield fences that the balls could not be retrieved. To him I feigned I was dishing up deliveries meant to hone his batting eye, but confidentially, Sam, I paraded my best stuff in the hope of impressing Mutrie. Only this Orr is a brute with a bat in his hand. Even when he doesn't meet a pitch on the nose he hits shrieking daisy cutters that have so much pace and spin on them infielders have to play him back on the outfield grass to have any prayer of knocking them down without being maimed.

It finally got so the other Mets began whining for Orr to give up the plate before he killed somebody. I will confess to some apprehension myself, Sam. To protect against being drilled by one of Orr's smashes I finally began feeding him pitches down at his ankles, as it is high ones that he particularly clobbers.

Despite all my care though, Orr still injured someone. The second or third low one I threw him whistled off his bat so wickedly that Troy couldn't pull his leg out of the way quick enough to avoid it. If the Dasher had been a horse, they would have shot him on the spot with the way his thigh looked when they lowered his trousers to inspect where the ball had hammered him. So ended my stint as a batting practice tosser, but it nonetheless worked out to my advantage. Troy was too hobbled to play this afternoon, and the Mets had no substitute for him at second base with both Keefe and Lynch also ailing and Holbert needed in reserve to go behind the bat in the event Reipschlager was injured. So Mutrie said: "Well, Ducker, how'd you like to earn a day's pay?"

Sam, you won't hear me proclaim that I've at last found my true niche in this game. If I've learned nothing else, it's that a man can never in his wildest dreams know what Fate has in store for him. And besides, Troy could still recover the use of his limb by next season; although even if he does, I would think Mutrie might replace him with a younger and faster hand. Hard as that ball Orr hit was, Troy must either have atrocious reflexes not to have dodged it or else he was corned, which is also not likely to earn him Mutrie's sympathy.

Mutrie is the epitome of all a manager should be, Sam. He has the profile of a stage idol and the intelligence and patience of a solon. Too, it took a rare creative streak to light upon a nickname like the one he gave me on the spur of the instant. It is only fitting that I should end my first season in the major leagues under his supervision.

Still, I'm not so bold to forecast how I'll fare today against Radbourn, being that he's the world's greatest pitcher. So I'll close only with this, Sam. You needn't reply to the awful doubts of your story of your fateful accident that I raised in a reckless mood any more than I need to be told that you foresaw Constance would turn up on my doorstep the moment she no longer knew where her next meal was coming from. Each of us has already shown himself man enough to weather the other's occasional unfortunate urges to impugn him, but why push our luck, right, Sam?

Your nephew, Earl.

There he was, his sneering face less than 50 feet from the batter when he released the ball, his arms and legs flailing every which way, all those distractions he had mastered—cap on crooked, back turned to home plate until the last possible instant, the frayed blouse sleeve on his pitching arm. Shoulder throbbing like an aching tooth but never less than supremely confident, it was how he would always see himself whenever he remembered the last two months of the 1884 season.

There he was, this warrior, this prince, in a gray uniform. He was so close the batter could sometimes smell the spicy lacquer on his hair and see brown teeth bared when the ball was propelled homeward. Knowing how he must look, he loved to work quickly. He would take so little time between pitches that batters learned to step out of the box after each delivery. To appear as if they were stalling with a purpose, they would rub dirt on their hands, tug at their belts, swat the air with their bats—but then, there was no more they could do to avoid the confrontation. No sooner were they back beside the plate than the ball was once again launched. It seemed as if his timing was so perfect that he was already into his windup even as the umpire signaled play to resume.

That was Charles Gardner "Hoss" Radbourn, often spelled Radbourne in base ball chronicles until his last surviving sibling corrected the long-standing error in 1942. One of 18 children, he grew up learning to play ball on vacant lots in Bloomington, Illinois, where he was known for his quick temper and fiery disposition. When he was nearly 22, Radbourn left home to work as a brakeman for the Indiana-Bloomington-Western Railroad and stayed at the job for two years before its boredom turned his dreams once again to base ball. Although now viewed to have been a natural for the game, Radbourn was actually a flop in 1880, his first major league season, as an outfielder with Buffalo and was ready to quit base ball to become an apprentice butcher. The following spring he would not even answer telegrams from the Providence Grays, who sought to hire him to play right field and serve as their change pitcher, fit to take a turn in the box on days when Johnny Ward's arm was too tired. Finally a boyhood friend, knowing that Radbourn was prone to give in to a self-destructive streak unless his back was put to the wall, sent a return wire to Providence in his name accepting the Grays' offer and then goaded him to get on the road East and do Bloomington proud.

In 1881 Radbourn won 25 games and then upped the total to 31 the following year. By 1883, Ward's arm was used up and he was no longer with Providence, so Old Hoss became the Grays' ace by default. He proceeded to pitch in 76 of the club's 98 games and notch 49 wins to set a new major league record and thereby make Charlie Sweeney, a highly touted rookie hurler from San Francisco, practically superfluous.

So Radbourn was the most famous pitcher in the land when he reported for duty in the spring of 1884, and he behaved accordingly. He argued with umpires every time a call went against him, he complained when his teammates made errors behind him, and he disdained the effort to keep himself in condition, using his regal stature as license to indulge to the hilt in his appetite for booze and harlots. Sweeney meanwhile annoyed him by ceaselessly demeaning his work habits and his outmoded underhand pitching style. On the evening of July 16, 1884, Radbourn's swift fall from grace was seemingly complete when he was suspended without pay for lackadaisically lobbing the ball up to the plate in the game against Boston that afternoon.

But within six days of Radbourn's suspension, Sweeney left the Providences shorthanded when he walked off the field in the middle of a game and was himself suspended, perhaps according to his plan as he promptly jumped the Grays to latch on with Lucas's Maroons. Left without a reliable pitcher, Grays manager Frank Bancroft cajoled Radbourn into returning, but it had a stiff price. Knowing he had the team over a barrel, Hoss demanded that he be given his release at the end of the season and receive a bonus in the meantime to pitch every remaining game on the schedule.

For the next two and a half months Radbourn truly did pitch almost every championship game the Grays played, and the result was far beyond even his own immodest predictions. At the close of the regular season he had 60 victories and 441 strikeouts, and the Grays had an easy pennant. Then in the World Series against the Mets, Radbourn collected three more wins. The third and last game was called after six innings, ostensibly because of darkness, but really because the Grays led 11-2 and the Polo Grounds crowd of only 300 or so had already seen more than enough. A writer covering the game for the *New York Herald* summed up the home nine's performance in a single sentence: "The Metropolitans played most wretchedly both at bat and in the field, and proved mere children at the hands of the Providence men."

Nothing was said about the individual performances of any of the Mets. Earl Draves therefore was given only a line in the box score crediting him with no hits and no runs in three turns at bat and one error in his seven chances in the field. Although he in no way distinguished himself, since the Mets made ten errors and only six hits he could not be said to have unduly disgraced himself either.

After the game he traipsed with several other Mets to the Home Plate saloon a few blocks down 110th Street from the Polo Grounds. Already there, to his astonishment, were Radbourn and Jerry Denny, the

Grays third baseman. Radbourn looked as if he had been nowhere else all afternoon. He was obviously welcome in the place and appeared to have been there often before. He and Denny were seated at the largest table, surrounded by well-wishers. He had a gracious way in victory that won only all the more admiration. He laughed a lot; he was courteous to everyone and "pallie" with the waiters. Draves stood and watched him in fascination for some minutes.

Here was what it was all about. This Radbourn was the consummate ball player, hugely talented and successful but still human. The way he sat there cradling his right arm and having to use his left hand when he took a drink told you something of the pain he was in. Yet he continued to laugh and to satisfy the fawning, agog questions about his brilliant season. A harlot was trying to sit on his lap, but he slid her aside when he realized Draves was just standing there and staring at him.

"What can I do you for?" he said finally.

"I just wanted to congratulate you. You're the best pitcher I ever faced except maybe Sweeney. Charlie of the Maroons, that is."

"Oh, him." Radbourn's gaze drifted away to the harlot.

"I'm Ducker Draves, the second baseman for the Mets today," Draves supplied since he could not be certain Radbourn recognized him.

"Really?" Disinterest made Radbourn look bored, until he grinned, and his face was friendly again. "Sit down and take a load off. Have one with me and Jerr."

"Actually, I would appreciate a chance to talk with you."

"With me? Why?"

"I'm curious how you could get me out so easily even though it doesn't look as if you throw that hard. With your underhand technique, I mean."

"That's not technique, jack. That's how a smart pitcher saves his wing."

"Still, I was mightily impressed. That curve of yours is a real hummer."

They talked deep into the evening, not always about base ball and not only to one another. Other of the Mets sat down at the table too, and eventually several more of the Grays came into the saloon—Hines, Gilligan, Nava and one whose name Draves never got. By then he was inebriated, or very nearly so. But he would go on drinking as long as it meant more time with Radbourn.

The great pitcher made you feel as if you too must be someone while you were around him, and he seemed to know everything there was to know about life. A few years later Draves would realize that

Radbourn did not know much more than he, but that evening he felt he was in the company of the most worldly man in base ball.

"Here's to your one-eyed trouser snake," Radbourn said, as he took his left hand off his elbow to hoist his glass.

"And yours," Draves said, thinking it was expected of him.

"May neither ever come down with serpent fever."

"Serpent fever," echoed Draves.

"Or ever be more than looked at longingly by a pink coat."

"Amen," Draves hiccoughed.

"What?" Radbourn began laughing, as if Draves's ignorance had only just dawned on him. "Amen!"

"Of course. I always...it's a habit, I reckon."

Radbourn looked at him in silence for some seconds, no longer laughing.

"You're from the middle west somewheres, I'll bet," he said at last.

"Ohio. Right outside of Portsmouth."

"It's the guts of this land. The East, New York now especially...by the end of the century it'll all be mad dogs and pestilence."

"Amen."

"We're living on borrowed time, Draves, in this neck of the woods. Me, I can't get back to Illinois soon enough. The land of Lincoln, that's real living."

No, he wanted to protest. Ohio is—the land of Hayes and Garfield. But he was still just sober enough to stay within bounds.

"Why didn't you ever sign to play with the White Stockings then, in Chicago?"

"Didn't want me. You've got to go where you're wanted."

Silence again, both of them trying to think. This time Draves broke in. "Pink coat...is that something like a red-haired boy?"

Radbourn tilted his chair backward and closed one eye before he answered. "Well, some of them do have red hair."

It probably is amazing that he did not deride Draves then, that he was never anything but tolerant of his ingenuousness. But some men can remember how it went for them when they were young, and Radbourn, for all the knocking about he had done, was still only 29. Besides, he had already been advised that he was one day going to have to pay for the mistakes brought about by his own ignorance. Four or five doctors had warned him that he might have ailed from something other than heat rash a few years back. Radbourn didn't ignore their monitions, but he couldn't see as how there was much he could do about them now either. He had never expected to live to a ripe old age anyway; his every dream depended upon remaining young, and he'd determined early on to live as if he would be young forever. If tonight wasn't perfect, the absolute pinnacle of his life, it was only because pain thundered up his right arm every time he forgot himself and moved it.

Radbourn never again had a sound arm, but he continued to pitch a decent game for several more years and to flip the bird sassily in team photographs.

Then in 1891, beginning to feel the inroads of paresis, he ended his base ball career and returned with his wife and stepson to Bloomington, where he opened a billiard parlor. It was never a thriving concern, but it had his name in the window, and he would have been reasonably content to spend his last days drinking and schmoozing with the men of his town if a hunting accident had not blown off half his face in April of 1894. Minus an eye and the power of speech, unable to bear having others see him as he now was, he retreated to a back room in his billiard parlor, where he sat night after night in dim light listening to anyone who would talk of the games he had pitched for the town team or the time he had posed as a college student so he could play for Illinois Wesleyan.

He died of paresis on February 5, 1897, about eight weeks after he'd passed his 42nd birthday silent and alone in an upper bedroom of his Bloomington home. At his burial a fierce wind blew in from the west carrying flurries of snow. The afternoon, sunless, lacked color. The sky and the earth merged together in a blend of soft grays as if sketched in pencil. Only the wind, sharp and bitter, was alive. The wind was inescapable, bitingly cold on the flesh of all who were gathered at graveside to pay their last respects to the finest pitcher the game had yet known. Bancroft, the Grays manager in 1884, was there, along with Ducker Draves, who had come all the way from Blue Creek where he again made his home, and Bid McPhee, representing the Cincinnati Red Stockings, the last team for which Radbourn played.

When two workmen began to fill in the grave, Draves turned to go. Snow was falling now, heavily, after starting as only a damp mist. He had a train ticket to nearby Decatur, where he planned to stay overnight with a former teammate before heading back to Blue Creek, but something—perhaps the snow—changed his mind. Perhaps it was only the way it clung to his face that made him long for home.

AFTERWORD

Some readers may like help in distinguishing the fact from the fiction in this story. All of the baseball-related events really happened and, with very few exceptions, happened very much as Draves depicts them in his diary and letters. The games, the players, the umpires, the egregious blunders, the dark undercurrents, and the catastrophic occurrences—everything is straight from history, as are Annie Reilly, Inspector Byrnes, Little Faun, Johanna McNamara, and many of the other colorful and exotic characters that Draves encounters in his travels through the 1884 major league season. Of the scattered exceptions, each was made only when pinpoint accuracy interfered with the story and, at that, shouldn't jar any but the most ruthless sticklers for detail. Who else reasonably will quibble with me for changing the two mid-October games in Cincinnati between the Outlaw Reds and Louisville for the Championship of the Ohio River to a home-and-home affair so that Draves could have a showdown with Constance in the Falls City at a psychologically propitious moment?

But while each and every on-field event is real, many of the off-field conversations are invented, as are Draves and his uncle. Yet Draves also has a strong thread of reality. His diamond doings parallel those of four different players during the 1884 season. The first, Earl Ohler, a member of the Cincinnati reserves or "colts" team in 1884, carried him until his release from the Red Stockings; the second, Charlie Barber, carried him through his early days with the Outlaw Reds; the third, Elmer Cleveland, carried him from August 29 throughout the rest of the regular season; and the fourth, Tom Forster, put Draves on a course to serve as a last-minute substitute in the final game of the first World Series in baseball history.

Wither went Earl "Ducker" Draves and what did he do after that raw October afternoon in 1884? Well, that may just be, like the dreams of all who have ever played the game he grew to love, a tale without end.

ABOUT THE AUTHOR

David Nemec grew up in the Cleveland area and is a life-long Indians fan. Like many boys, he had aspirations of becoming a major league player. Admittedly not very good at ball playing at Ohio State University, Nemec soon turned his dreams to becoming a writer. To date, he's written well over a dozen books on baseball, seven books of fiction, and has appeared in numerous magazines. Nemec won the Society for American Baseball Research/Sporting News baseball research award in 1998 for his highly illuminating *The Great Encyclopedia of 19th Century Major League Baseball.* Nemec has served on the Seymour Medal Committee, which selects the finest baseball works of history or biography in a calendar year and he is considered one of the foremost historians on baseball's early years.

OTHER BOOKS BY THE AUTHOR

Novels and fiction
Remember Me to My Father
Stonesifer
The Systems of M.R. Shurnas
Mad Blood
Bright Lights, Dark Rooms
Survival Prose

Baseball
The Encyclopedia of Major League Rookies
The Ultimate Baseball Book
The Great Book of Baseball Knowledge
The Great Encyclopedia of 19th Century Major League Baseball
150 Years of Baseball
The Beer an Whisky League
The Rules of Baseball
1001 Fascinating Baseball Facts
The Great American Baseball Team Book
Players of Cooperstown
The Baseball Challenge Quiz Book
20th Century Baseball Chronicles
The Most Extraordinary Baseball Quiz Book Ever
Great Baseball Feats, Facts & Firsts
A History of Baseball in the San Francisco Bay Area
The Even More Challenging Baseball Quiz Book
The Absolutely Most Challenging Baseball Quiz Book Ever

www.ingramcontent.com/pod-product-compliance
Lightning Source LLC
Chambersburg PA
CBHW051648260626
47170CB00004B/1394